Driver Needed
Immediate Openings
Clear CDL a must
Some experience preferred
(201) 555-0091

Chapter 1

"YOU REMEMBER that old Cougar you had, right?"

He spooned another heap of sugar into his coffee, and stirred. Tried a sip, added another hefty spoonful, then spoke again. "Same thing goes for these trucks. They *always* break down, doesn't matter what time of year, they always, *always* breakdown."

Topher watched as his unexpected early morning visitor tried another sip, grimaced, and then proceeded to scoop up another spoonful of sugar. What did he expect? It was reheated from yesterday. People who work night shifts don't usually brew coffee at six in the morning, but rather six at night.

Topher watched as another spoonful joined the previous four and then the coffee was stirred some more.

"You've only been there six months, Donny," Topher reasoned. "How do you know what they always do? And, lay off my sugar, I don't get paid 'til Friday, and these groceries got to last 'til then."

"That's like three more days."

"And, that's the last of my sugar, so lay the fuck off and leave some for my cereal."

The sun would be up in half an hour, Topher thought, and from experience he knew if he wasn't in bed by then it would be twice as hard to fall asleep. Not only did the sunlight start to mess with your internal clock, tell you it was time to get up no matter how tired you actually are, but the rest of the world starts to move around. Cars drive by and honk their horns as cats cross the road in front of them. Birds chirp. The kid across the street with all the hair starts blasting that type of heavy metal music where the lead singer sounds like he's trying to yodel after drinking liquid nitrogen.

3

"Fine, whatever," Donny shrugged. "Anyways, in six months, I've already had one truck blow a head gasket, on another the alternator gave out, and *another* snapped a belt when I was doing sixty on the turnpike. They only got one full time mechanic there to maintain all the trucks, so there is always a backlog for maintenance. He just ends up going from repair to repair, and never has a chance to do any preventative work. Breakdowns are just a matter of routine."

"All right, I get it," Topher acquiesced. "This happens a lot."

"All the time!" Donny emphasized. "Of course, when I had just started, and had the head gasket blow, I didn't know these things were routine. When I was waiting for the tow, I was all freakin' out 'cause we had already made a couple of pick-ups, but the guy in the back--"

"You try to bring him in on this too?"

"What? No way, I need him for my alibi," Donny rolled his eyes at Topher's supposed ignorance, and then continued. "No, it was then that I got the idea. The other guy was like totally cool about it. No big deal, right? We had to have had at least like eighty thousand sitting in the back at that point, and he just locks up the back, and comes to sit in the cab with me until the tow arrives to haul us back to the lot, right? He told me we just wait until they take us back in, switch the bags to another truck, and then get back on schedule, okay?"

"But, that's not what happened."

"No, see," Donny paused to giggle.

He was getting excited, and to be totally honest, Topher was getting a bit excited too. If Donny was right, this might get him out from under for the rest of his life. This could be his ticket to the Keys, where he would never be freezing his ass off for just above minimum ever again.

Still, the fucking giggle got on his nerves. He sounded like a seventh grade girl, or one of those swishy fags who had to put rainbows and sparkles on everything. Had it ever been cute? Topher couldn't ever remember thinking so.

"See," Donny continued. "Turns out, these trucks are so friggin' armored, they're too heavy for a normal wrecker. You try to haul it with a hook, and --"

Donny slammed his hand down on the bowl of the spoon, and flipped the handle into the air, mimicking what would happen to the tow truck.

"Watch my fucking table, Donny!" Topher warned.

"Jesus, don't be such a fag," Donny nearly earned himself a punch in the chest, but -- maybe from a little guilt because Donny's words had echoed his own thoughts towards Donny just a few moments before -- Topher let it slide.

"Anyway," Donny continued. "It has to be a flatbed, one of the big ones, and we were waiting around for hours for one to get there."

"Why didn't they send another truck to pick up your deposits?"

"They got schedules to keep too," Donny explained, as if talking to a child. "They end up pissing off twice as many clients. So, what they do is call the rest of our pick-ups for the day and tell them the driver will be coming later, re-distribute the rest of our schedule to the other trucks, and everyone makes one or two more stops at the end of the regulars. Everyone gets a little bit of overtime, so everybody is happy."

"So, everybody is happy, you switch out to a new truck, you get back on the road," Topher stated, trying to steer the conversation back on point. "Why are you here talking to me?"

"Because the boss is a cheap fuck is why." Donny nearly spat. "So, last time, the flatbed didn't come for hours. All the trucks were already out, so we would need to get it to the lot, wait for another truck to come back switch the load to a new truck, take it to the bank, drop the shit in the overnight deposit, and then return the truck to the lot. We would have been on the clock for nearly twenty hours."

"So, a long shitty day for you, but-"

"He had us rent a truck."

"You can rent an armored truck?"

"Nope."

"So you rented a-"

"Yep."

Topher sat dumbfounded and disbelieving while his brain attempted to absorb this bit of information.

"Stupidest fucking thing I have ever heard," Topher shook his head in shocked amazement. "Like a box truck?"

"Yep."

"The sides of those things are like quarter inch plywood."

"The idea is what you lose in security, you make up for with stealth."

"Fucking retarded," Topher shook his head again. "Like, glue eating, hand-clap laughing, gotta wear a helmet kind of retarded."

"Yeah, true," Donny agreed. "Bottom line is, they're insured if we're robbed, and robberies rarely happen. They just got to keep us rolling and keep the customers happy."

"Why not take it back to your lot and run it out in the morning?"

"He never keeps a load at the lot," Donny looked comically appalled at the thought. "Too much temptation he says. If we get taken on the road, at least we were trying to get the load to the recipient. If we took it home, and it went missing, well . . ."

"Okay, yeah, that would look worse."

"Also, it would actually be more likely. At our lot, the box guard would know what was in there, he might tell somebody else, and it would be pretty easy to take a spare set of keys from maintenance. Just because we're bonded, doesn't mean we're saints."

"Speaking of 'licensed and bonded,'" Topher asked, partly to buy some time to think and partly because it had been nagging at him. "How the hell are you a security guard?"

"I bargained it down to a few misdemeanors, paid a fine, and I'm still doing my community service. I volunteer on the weekends at the library."

"You were stealing *cars*," Topher marveled. "How did you bargain down to a misdemeanor?"

"Nah," Donny said dismissively. "I wasn't charged with any of that. I got it pinned on the owners. They were douchebags, anyways."

Donny grinned, obviously proud of himself. "No, I got hooked on the cell phones. I took the cell phones and other shit which were left in the cars and sold them. In those recycling kiosks at the mall? You know the ones I mean, looks like a big vending machine, but you deposit the cell phones in it, it scans them, and then buys them for like a fraction of what their worth? But, I wasn't paying for them, so it was all profit to me, right?"

Topher, at a loss for words, simply looked at the guy he had known for close to a third of his life, and was freshly amazed at how paradoxically brilliant and stupid this person could be.

Often at the same time.

Donny had to have been pulling down thousands a week from boosting cars, had worked out a way to steal the cars without taking any of the risk, but then got busted for selling stolen cell phones for pennies on the dollar.

"Anyways," Donny, as he so often did, filled the silence. "When they busted the place, I had like three phones in my car I hadn't unloaded yet, so I copped to three counts of receiving stolen property. Misdemeanor, 'cause the values of the phones were too low to be a felony."

"And, they know about it at your current job?"

"Sure," Donny shrugged. "They know what the court knows, which is I was busted with three stolen cell phones, which I told them I had bought at the swap meet as Christmas presents for my sister's kids."

"And they let you carry a gun," Topher said with queasy amazement.

"I know, right?" Donny laughed.

They sat quietly for a few minutes, Topher thinking things over and Donny apparently adept enough at reading his old friend to know all he had to do was to stay silent while Topher thought, and it would be the strongest argument he could make.

Topher looked around his shitty studio apartment. It had been advertised in the paper as a "loft," which technically he supposed it was: a hay loft. It was the space above an ancient carriage house, the three narrow garage spaces below taken by the tenants of the main house filled the lot in front of him. They got the parking spaces, which meant he had to park on the street and walk up the long driveway, past the big house, and climb the stairs past other people's cars to get to his home. However, he got his own little kitchen, his own bathroom, and never had to do someone else's dishes.

He considered it a pretty fair trade off.

The floor was always cold in the winter, though. He had two pairs of sox on and it still felt as though he were resting them on a block of ice which never melted. There was no insulation between the big open spaces below, and the floor of his "loft" so the floor was always freezing in the winter, and warm in the summer. In the summer, the floor transubstantiated from a plane of inscrutable ice to a field of cryptic coals which never burned but neither did they seem to cool.

The rest of the place was okay; it had been renovated into a fairly conventional apartment: sheetrock walls painted a soft pale yellow and hanging ceiling with inset halogens, rather than the banks of ugly fluorescent lights, fake wood flooring which appeared to be real -- from a distance anyway -- but was actually some kind of rubbery material.

Windows on all four walls to let in plenty of natural light.

It wasn't great, and it wasn't bad. It was certainly a damn sight better than a jail cell, which is where he would most likely end up if he went along with what Donny was planning.

Still, he had to do something.

Spinning his wheels for six years now, ever since he had got out of high school and gotten a job. His football playing had not been good enough to get him into college but his football physique had been able to land him an immediate position as a bouncer, lotta tips and a lotta ass, but as for take home . . . he had $797 in a savings account.

Life had taken everything else.

Every time he managed to add an extra digit into his savings account, something would come up: the car needed brakes, he got his hours cut at work, he'd start dating someone, and soon enough the extra digit had gone away again.

Donny had been a year behind Topher in school, but had been arguably far more successful. They both worked shit jobs for low pay, at least they did now, but Donny had been able to purchase a condo just two years out of high school.

Sure, it had been purchased with money made from stealing cars, but he had his own parking place in the heated garage below his building, rather than living just above someone else's parking place.

More to the point, he had gotten away with it.

"Why does it have to be tonight?" Topher asked, already knowing he would cave.

"Because today is just a one-run," Donny started to giggle again. "We only have one pick up stop, and then we need to run it up to Hobart, New York. It's not going to a bank, so it's probably diamonds or gold."

"You don't know?"

"Asshole, I'm the driver," Donny rolled his eyes again and Topher had to resist the urge to slap them back into place. "I get an itinerary with a point A and a point B. The other guard in the back gets the invoice. All I know is the last time we had a one-run it turned out to be a shitload of gold going to be melted down and made into like circuit boards and airbags."

Topher waited for further explanation, but again Donny had decided to play coy.

"What the fuck are you talking about?" Topher finally spat.

"That's what I said, when the box guard told me about it later," Donny giggled his swish giggle again. "Apparently high end computer stuff uses gold in the circuits because it conducts well and doesn't rust. Some airbags are made with a thin gold mesh for the same reason, and it's, shit, some fancy word for bendable."

"Malleable," Topher said, but couldn't say why he knew it.

"Right," Donny nodded. "So we had just hauled several hundred grand worth of totally untraceable gold. The box guard told me that was nothing, the last summer he had ridden next to three million dollars' worth of uncut diamonds which went straight from the airport to the city, to some little Hasidic hole in the wall in the jewelry district. Raw gold and uncut diamonds have no serial numbers, nothing can be tracked, so it'll be easier to sell it."

"Why don't we just wait for a big load of cash?" Topher asked, but Donny was already shaking his head before he had even finished the question.

"The cash bags are rigged," he explained. "They've got ink bombs, GPS trackers, and are made from some kind of shit that is almost impossible to cut without messing up the cash inside."

"Couldn't they do the same thing to whatever you're picking up?"

"They won't use paint or dye for gold and jewels 'cause it'll wash right off," Donny reasoned. "They may try to use a GPS tracker. If you see one, you can toss it into a trash can outside for them to find, if you don't see one we're still covered because I bought a GPS jammer that plugs into the cigarette lighter."

Topher tried to find fault in Donny's reasoning, but so far it seemed to be fairly free of bullshit. Admittedly, Topher was far to ignorant of the whole process to have much of an opinion one way or the other.

"So?" Topher prompted once again.

"Okay," Donny was off and running again. "So, the truck breaks down right?"

Topher nodded.

"We will have to switch the load out to another truck, but I am going to make sure we break down later in the day-"

"How?"

"Because I'll sabotage it later in the day, dumbass."

This time Topher did pop Donny a quick punch to the chest. A quick, side of the hand chop, directed at the solar plexus, which he pulled at the last second to keep from knocking *all* the air out of Donny's lungs.

The effect, much practiced over the last several years on mouthy drunks, and tweaker freaks, was instantaneous. A quick exhalation, usually sounding like a question, "Huh?", or a kindergarten curse word, "Poo!" Then a sudden inhalation, a shrieking gasp, because the diaphragm behind the solar plexus was now twitching and spasming, and not allowing Donny to pull in as much air as he was used to, so would feel a bit like he was suffocating. Just above that, a bundle of nerves was flaring up in a spreading flash of pain, which would then subside to an ache. It would feel like it was sure to leave a ghastly bruise, but very rarely did.

Topher waited patiently for Donny to get his breath back.

"You fucking. . ." Donny started to say a moment later.

"Call me any more names, and I won't pull the punch next time, D," Topher said with a smile.

Donny paused for a moment to consider his options, shrugged briefly, as if to say "fuck it," and returned to his plan.

"So, anyway," Donny continued, fishing in his pocket for something while keeping his eyes on Topher. "We switch the shit to a new truck, and at that time of day it will have to be a rental. No real security there, so you just follow along until we stop some place."

"Why are you going to stop?"

"Because I am the fucking driver!" Donny pulled a pack of cigarettes from his pocket and flipped one out about an inch with a practiced flick of the wrist. He clamped the filter with edge of his lips and withdrew it the rest of the way. Speaking from the other side of his mouth, he continued. "I will find a reason to stop. Food, coffee, diarrhea, some fucking thing. When we stop, you load the stuff into another truck, the one with the GPS jammer in the cigarette lighter, and come on back here."

"Don't you even think of lighting that fucking thing," Topher snapped.

Donny paused, the cheap gas station lighter which had returned in his hand after re-securing the pack in his pants pocket, seconds away from flicking the flame to life.

"Don't be such a --"

Topher's glare was more than enough to leave the insult unfinished.

"Jesus!" Donny whined, but took the cigarette from his lips and dropped it on the table between them. "I'm not smoking again for real."

Topher glanced significantly at the contrary evidence where it lay on the table.

"I quit," the whine got worse. "You *know* I quit! I need these as part of my cover story to stage the breakdown. It's just window dressing."

Topher let the silence speak for him.

"I need a reason to be out of the truck," Donny insisted. "Otherwise, how am I going to be able to rig it for a breakdown?"

Topher let the silence draw out a little longer, enjoying the view of Donny's squirming under the weight of the, obviously forgotten, promise he had made to Topher. A promise Donny had just been inches from breaking, and from which he was silently pleading for release from keeping.

"At the end of the day, the pack goes in the trash?" Topher asked.

"Absolutely!" Donny actually drew his finger across his breast to cross his heart.

"Where do I get the other truck?"

Donny reached into his other pocket and slapped his palm face down on the table, with a loud and exuberant clack of metal against the wood. It was a pair of keys, one with a round head and one with a square, and no alarm key fob, so the vehicle was very likely at least thirty years old. A homemade leather tag was attached to the keychain, onto which someone had used a soldering iron to burn the words "Shit Heap."

"Can they trace this back to you?"

"Nope," Donny smiled. "Bought it for cash. In Pennsylvania."

"What will happen when you get to where you're going and the back is empty?"

"Oh, the shit will definitely hit the fan," Donny allowed. "There is no avoiding *that*, but whoever is riding in the back today will swear up and down we did everything right, because no one will believe one guard stole something right out from under the nose of the other guard. If one is guilty, then both are guilty. If one is innocent, then . . ."

"What if they come here?"

"First, they have no reason to come here. Second, they can't search the truck without probable cause or a warrant. If you lock everything in the back up securely, and they can't see anything inside, then there is no probable cause. Then, park it on the street and even if they do get a warrant, then, sure, we're screwed out of the money, but they won't be able to pin anything back on us. The truck may be out front, but you never saw it before in your life."

At least, Topher thought, they couldn't pin anything back onto Donny.

Still, it was doable.

Sure, there were risks, but if he took some reasonable precautions, and moved quickly, Donny was right. As long as he wasn't caught in the act of actually stealing the shit, and Donny wasn't caught in the act of sabotaging the breakdown, Topher figured there was very little chance this could be pinned on either of them.

There was one thing he needed to clear up though, one last little detail that had to be put to bed.

"So, why come to me with this?" he asked.

"You're the biggest guy I know," Donny said, and then giggled. Then added, "We're taking a coin truck on this one."

"Meaning?"

"Coin trucks are designed to carry even more weight than normal, because $5000 in quarters weighs around 20,000 pounds."

"So we're risking prison for a few grand in change?"

"No way, not on a one-run. When we do a coin run, we are either picking up a shitload of coins from a shitload of banks, or delivering a shitload of coins to a shitload of banks. This is a one-run."

"Again, meaning?"

"Meaning, it is probably something really fucking heavy, but really fucking valuable, like gold."

Topher nodded. For all his faults, Donny really was pretty good at planning things out. Topher could only think of one more legitimate objection.

"This doesn't mean we're back together, D."

"So, you're in?" Donny nearly squealed.

"Yeah," Topher sighed. "If you can pull off all this other shit you say you can do, then I can do some heavy lifting. Even split, right?"

"Fuck that!" Donny nearly choked on his coffee. "I am doing most of the work."

"And, despite all that work, you are dead in the water without me."

"Fuck you," Donny spat. "I am bringing this to you as a favor, because we have history, and you-"

"Even split, or it is not worth the risk," Topher said quietly. "And, of course, I would know who had done it."

The tacit threat hung between them in the kitchen.

Donny would either storm off in a huff, and Topher would have to plan on finding his tires slashed at some point in the near future, or the police show up from an anonymous tip about a meth lab in a garage, or any number of other petty vindictive acts Donny would dream up until he felt he had been avenged, or Donny would back down and they would move forward as planned.

"You're gonna do me like that, huh?"

"You never used to complain about how I did you," Topher demurred, blatantly playing the ex-card.

"Yeah, well, it never cost me anything before," Donny pouted. "When did you become such a whore?"

"You came to me with this," Topher reminded him. "You need me, not the other way around. You want to find another way to do it, one I don't know anything about, then you go ahead and do it. If you want to do it this way, today, then this is the way it is going to be."

Donny sat quietly for a minute, wanting to make Topher think he might walk out the door, but Topher knew better. Donny wanted this, and he didn't want to wait for another opportunity to present itself. He was great at planning, but terrible at patience. If he was going to leave, it would have been after the first outburst. This was simply posturing.

"Fine," Donny relented.

"Alright," Topher said. "I'll see you this afternoon."

Topher got up and headed over toward his bed, kicking off his shoes as he went.

"You know," Donny said, his giggly tone had returned. "As long as I'm getting fucked metaphorically . . ."

"Good night, Donny," Topher said, raising his middle finger over his shoulder, but not turning around.

"Tease!" Donny accused, but he headed out the door.

The sun was nearly fully up, so Topher pulled the covers over his head in hopes of finding enough darkness to sleep. He listened to Donny's feet skipping gleefully down the stairs to the garage below. At the bottom of the stairs, Topher heard Donny open the door to the driveway, and then pause.

A moment later there came a loud thump, and then the car alarm of one of the three vehicles started to sound just below Topher's head. The noise of the one car set off the alarm of the car next to it, which in turn set off the third. Though he knew it to be impossible for him to hear it over the cacophony below, Topher could hear Donny's bitchy little giggle nonetheless.

He closed his eyes, wrapped the pillow over his ears, and tried to imagine the sound of the surf in Florida.

Chapter 2

LIKE TAKING a money shot from Jack Frost, was how Not's barber liked to describe stepping outside into a New Jersey winter; you knew it was coming, you knew you weren't going to like it, you brace for it, but still it makes you flinch every goddamn time.

Not was reversing his route from the day before, following the footpath which ran alongside Indian Lake which was infested with joggers, bikers, and strollers in the warmer months, but was blessedly empty, except for the occasional diehard fitness fanatic, on this frigid February morning.

It was, ironically, too cold for snow once again.

At least once a year, Not had to sit through a meteorologist's diatribe on the morning news that the phrase "too cold for snow" was an inaccurate statement, and in fact there were myriad factors determining whether or not snow could be produced, but Not knew when it got this goddamn cold, and the air stung this damn much when it touched your skin, that it was too goddamn cold to snow.

It was not too cold for the snow which had already fallen to have been salted, melted, diluted enough to freeze again, and then refrozen into a horribly ultra-slick layer of nearly invisible ice often hidden below layers of powdery snow drifts. On the highway, it was called black ice because it was virtually indistinguishable from the rest of the asphalt.

Here on the cracked concrete of the jogging path, is was most often referred to as "Oh sh-!", "motherfu-!" or Not's personal favorite: "Wuh?!"

These names were regularly accompanied by the wet, stinging slap of hands attempting to break falls, the thicker, slapping thud of asses attempting to do the same, and the

15

occasional snap and screech of a bone shattering when those attempts had failed.

It was just before six in the morning, and it was still too dark to see any kind of ice in the first place, so Not stomped through the snow to the side of the path, rather than risk a limb by heading down its center, as he made his way back to the bus stop.

The 165 was far more crowded when he got on just after six. Most people held cups of coffee and the morning paper, a few were gnawing their way through granola bars and off-brand toaster pastries. Not a single tie adorned a neck. Earbuds and vacant stares was the favored method of passing the time, though a couple slouched forward in the seat, either scrolling through whatever updates were displayed on their phones, or sacked out for a few more minutes of sleep before another day begins in earnest.

Not figured most of his fellow commuters were wearing uniforms and name tags beneath their winter outerwear. With any luck, Not would be sporting similar attire under his own coat at the end of the day. Most businesses which required a uniform no longer provided a changing area, nor a locker to secure personal belongings during the day. People dressed at home, brought nothing more than what they needed for work, and wrapped up warm for the walk between the bus and whatever building they needed to staff for the next eight hours, maybe more if they were lucky enough to warrant some overtime.

Six am buses were the domain of the clock punchers, like himself.

He had packed two slices of leftover pizza and a couple bottles of water into one of the hard-shell lunch-box coolers his dad kept in the closet. Dad had a habit of losing them, leaving them in a work truck, at a job site, only god knows where else they ended up. As a result, when they went on sale every August for the back to school rush, his dad would buy half a dozen and toss them in the hall closet, from which they would slowly disappear throughout the year as he inevitably lost them.

He also had the remaining twenty-five dollars and some change in his pocket from the hospital yesterday, in case everybody went for coffee or something. He offered up a small silent prayer of guilty gratitude that prices for plasma were holding pretty high. Likely thanks to all the black ice.

He would make the cash last for as long as he could, but he didn't want to stand out either. As soon as he walked through the door, Not would make it his mission to not only do his job well, but also to fit in. To make it seem as if he had always been there, so the decision of whether or not to keep him on would seem like something of a no-brainer. If fitting in meant everyone went for a three dollar latte at the beginning of the day, then he would be there too. He would run through the paltry wad of cash pretty quickly, but his dad would spot him, if he needed it, until his first paycheck.

Now that he would be earning one, Not would be willing to ask.

At Main and Mercer, Not had to abandon the warm if overcrowded bus and boarded the 770 at Mercer and Moore, which thankfully was just as warm, if also just as crowded. Same kind of crowd, same coffee, newspapers or smartphones, and portable breakfasts. He rode in moderate comfort back to 1st and Berry, where he had boarded the day before, and then retraced his steps once again back to Railroad Avenue. Halfway up, between Berry and Passaic, was Alto's All Tow, a horrible pun which Not would be happy to live with so long as the paychecks kept coming in.

He had been told 8 by . . .

Holy shit.

He never even asked the man's name who had hired him. Not assumed Alto is the name of the owner, and that the man who did the hiring would be the owner, thus it was very likely he was Mr. Alto, but what if he wasn't?

His gut felt like it was dropping, somehow miraculously drawing in and down into itself like a black-hole which had just been embarrassed into existence inside his lower GI tract, and as such was currently in the process of collapsing itself into a singularity aching to be reborn as a new nebulae of humiliation bursting forth miraculously through either his cock or his butthole. Both unlikely openings to such a manner of inadvertent creationism seemed to be drawing themselves inward in an attempt to prevent such a glorious tragedy.

Goddamn it, he thought, his hand hovering over the door handle for a split second, before he grabbed it and pulled the door open. What if he called the manager -- or was it the owner? -- by the wrong name? Would it be enough to earn him the good-bye speech at the end of his trial week?

Jesus, his heart started to race.

Was this a panic attack? He had heard about them, but had never experienced one. Was he really having a panic attack about not knowing a guy's name on his first day of work? What the fuck was wrong with him? It was his first fucking day! He wasn't supposed to know their names yet.

He would simply stick with "sir" until he was sure. It was hard to go wrong with "sir." Unless the boss was a woman, which, as of yesterday, he most certainly was not. There would be introductions, and plenty of time to get the names and faces right. He felt his heart as it began to slow a little bit.

It wasn't just the name, and he knew it.

It was partly the job, the idea of once again climbing behind the wheel of a tow truck, climbing back into the saddle once again, as it were, after a year of being out of it. After it had cost him everything he had.

Goddamn it, though, he needed to work! He was good at this job.

There was no reason why he shouldn't be here.

Not stepped into the small customer area in the front of the larger garage bays, where a large Plexiglas window allowed customers to view their vehicles being repaired, while maintaining the clear message: stay out. In front of the bay window was a complimentary coffee station. Someone had just recently filled and switched on the pot, because it was just starting to dribble out a stream which smelled to Not like liquid heaven.

To the right of the coffee pot stood a door marked Employees Only, which he knew, from his interview yesterday, lead to a break room with a refrigerator, microwave, television, and a couple of thrift shop tables and mismatched chair sets.

Beyond the break room was the small, office of the manager which dead-ended into the rear of the building, where he had interviewed yesterday. He wasn't sure if he should proceed yet into the back, as it was still before eight o'clock. Unless the coffee pot was on a timer -- and they left the door unlocked overnight -- there was someone already here somewhere. It might be the man who interviewed him yesterday, the man Not assumed to be Mr. Alto, but it might be someone else who may or may not know that a new guy was starting today.

Not decided he would wait here with the coffee until either someone else arrived and he could follow them in, or the coffee was ready and he would bring two cups with him into the back.

As the slow drizzle filled the pot, Not scanned the repair bays through the viewing window. The bays had no vehicles waiting to be repaired because they were currently housing Alto's six trucks of varying sizes.

He wasn't surprised to see the bays were filled with company vehicles rather than customer vehicles. The mechanics bays had roll up doors from the street side of the building, and a second set at the rear side of the building, where the impound lot was located. It got extremely cold at night, and the tow vehicles were expensive equipment to purchase and maintain. At the end of the business day, any vehicle not done, or not picked up, was rolled out into the lot behind the bay, and the trucks were parked inside for the night. The next morning, the trucks got rolling to head out to various calls, and the jobs that needed finishing were rolled back into the vacant bays.

Three were the same cab and frame as a Ford cargo van, but with the cargo area left off and an arm and hoist installed. These were good for general service calls, towing a disabled vehicle, providing a jump start, or bringing a couple of gallons of gas to get someone off of the turnpike.

Two were mid-size International flatbed rollbacks, like grocery truck, but with a large flat tilting bed with a heavy-duty chain hoist to haul larger vans and trucks, or vehicles too damaged to roll.

In the last bay, the one with the two story vaulted ceiling, and the fifteen foot rolling door, was a Peterbilt 337 heavy duty wrecker, a flatbed rollback capable of lifting and hauling a disabled semi cab, or an entire box truck loaded with bowling balls. The chain hoist on the back of the cab looked like it could lift a ship's anchor, and maybe the ship along with it.

He could drive them all no problem, and could probably run the hoists and tilts without missing a step.

"Thank God," Not gave voice to the relief as it edged out the anxiety. "I can do this."

"Hello?" a male voice called from the back. "You the new guy?"

"Um, yeah," Not called back. "Hi."

"Coffee ready yet?"

"Uh, 'bout half-full," Not estimated.

"Pour us a cup, yeah?" the mystery voice enquired. "And, come on back."

Not pulled two thin Styrofoam cups covered with idealized cartoons of coffee beans and wisps of steam, or perhaps they were supposed to indicate aroma, from the stack next to the pot and wondered briefly if the owner of the voice took cream or sugar. He decided against, figuring it could always be added, but couldn't be taken back out.

Not pushed through the door into the break room and found a stocky, Hispanic man who was likely on the far side of forty. Not's first impression of the man was that he was chubby, but almost immediately Not saw, though, such an assessment was not quite right. His initial assessment, the "stocky" label, didn't seem to fit either. The man looked like a five foot six inch Lego mannequin someone had decided to cover in skin tight, toffee-tinted leather. His nearly cylindrical head seemed to merge with his broad torso without even a consideration of a neck. His arms looked nearly as thick as his legs, and his legs looked like pillars in a parking garage.

Squat, Not decided. If ever there was a person to describe as squat, this man was it.

"Josue Viejo," he said, pronouncing his name Ho Sway, but then pointed to the name badge on his shirt. "But, on the job, I go by Josh."

"Four letter rule?" Not asked.

"Yeah, *and* no one around here can pronounce my name on sight anyway. Everyone tries it like Joe Sue or Josh You, so I figured I give them a break."

"Why not Bob?"

"Already taken," Josue smiled. "So, I saw a note on your folder says you go by Not, is that right?"

"Yep," Not said, waiting for the question.

"Nice, easy to remember but hard to use in a complaint call," Josue said with a laugh, and then continued, switching between a snotty falsetto and his own lightly accented voice. "The driver, Not, was very rude and scratched my Bentley. So, the driver was not rude? No, he was rude. So, he did not scratch your Bentley. No, he did! Who did? Not! He did not?"

"Third base," Not finished, laughing.

"Yeah, right!" Josue laughed. "Alright, so the deal is, we're going to roll together for the morning, and if you don't fuck up royally, you'll be rolling solo this afternoon. Don't fuck up royally, because as of right now I am working a split shift from eight to noon to babysit you, then rolling from six to twelve. If you can prove you don't need a babysitter, I can go home, have a nap, maybe get a quickie with the wife, if the kids don't get home from school right away, and then be back tonight."

"But," Not finished for him, "if I screw up, no nap, no quickie, and it will be all my fault."

"You got it," Josue nodded; the smile was friendly, but his eyes said Don't Fuck Up. "So, you saw the trucks on your way in?"

"Yep."

"Which one can you run without help?"

"Any of 'em," Not said with confidence he almost felt.

"Really." A statement and a question at the same time.

"Yeah, even the Peterbilt. I've run wreckers that big before. It was a Kenworth, but the size was the same."

"Goddamn, the boss lucked out on you. I'm the only other one around here, aside from the boss himself, can run the Peter Eater. Shit, you're white too, I'd be worried about my job if I weren't so good looking."

THEY ENDED up in a standard, run-of-the-mill hook and winch tow, the kind with the same cab and frame which anyone could rent for moving a two room apartment. Bench seat, cheap fabric and plastic interior in varying shades of grey and blue-grey, automatic transmission, and factory standard AM/FM radio. The only non-base-model addition was a touchscreen monitor snaked out from beneath the dashboard on an elbow mount wrapped in a bundle of cables. When Not started the engine to let the truck warm before venturing out from the chilly but at least wind free garage, the screen flicked itself into consciousness and offered three possible choices: Dispatch, Maps, and Help.

There were scuffed dents worn into the screen over the first two options, but the screen above Help was pristine. Not wasn't particularly surprised. He had never known anyone who worked on or around cars to give even the slightest acknowledgement he didn't know what he was doing. In the same regard, they were on par with doctors and televangelists in terms of confidently being able to diagnose what was wrong without even the slightest degree of doubt, regardless of the fact they had already misdiagnosed the problem twice or more in previous encounters. Car guys too would simply bluff their way through, never admitting wrong, and, as the screen would give evidence of, never asking for help.

After shivering for five minutes in the cab of the truck with the engine running, and the heat lever cranked all the way to the right, the air being blown from the vents became notably warmer, though not yet what anyone would call hot. Five minutes after that, Not was able to remove his gloves without fear of frostbite. Five minutes after *that*, Josue joined him in the cab with a fresh cup of coffee.

"Jesus, there you are. Next time, let it warm up from the breakroom. You don't need to babysit the truck when it's in the garage. Now, on the street, you never go further than line of sight, and even then no further than a distance you can sprint back before some GTA wannabe can get the bitch into gear."

There had been about a month of wrecked nerves for all tow drivers, a little over a year ago, when a crew of auto thieves had come up with a fairly novel new approach to theft: random opportunity. They simply waited until they found a car or truck running unattended, climbed in and drove away.

They would cruise around for a short period of time, and then cut off another car, being sure to block the road, and then would wait for the driver to get out of his/her own car to confront them. When the angry driver approached the driver's door, the thief would slip out the passenger side and run to the previous car, which was now unoccupied and almost always idling with the key in the ignition.

The thieves would repeat the same process several times in a row, always trading up to a slightly better vehicle each time, until they were satisfied with their score for the night and cruise to their closest fence or chop for their payday. However, the first theft of the night was usually a large commercial vehicle of some kind. Sometimes a delivery truck, once an ambulance, but more often than not it had been a tow truck.

They had eventually been caught, as all thieves eventually are; Not ground his teeth at the thought.

"Here," Josue tossed him a shirt which matched his own, right down to the name tag on the left breast pocket. "I was waiting for you inside to lend you one of my spares. You can hang onto it until yours come in."

"You won't need it?"

"Nah, I graduated from XL to double-X around my birthday last year. I can still fit in that one, but I'm afraid I might blind someone if one of those buttons lets go."

"Well," said Not as he got out of the finally warm cab and back into the cold of the unheated garage so he could more easily change into the borrowed shirt. "At least you've still got triple-X to look forward to."

"Yeah, I hear it comes with a free tube of lube!" Josue called after him.

NOT RETURNED a few minutes later complete with new shirt and his own fresh cup of coffee in a lidded to-go container. Josue had rolled up the chain driven garage door while Not was changing. After pulling the truck out into the driveway apron, while Josue was still reaching toward the door handle, Not leapt from behind the wheel and knocked the chain free from its anchor and watched with a practiced eye as the segmented metal door unspooled in its track toward the ground; when only 18 or so inches separated the bottom of the runaway door from a loud and possibly damaging impact with the concrete, Not closed one gloved fist around the quickly moving loop of chain.

He did not attempt to stop it completely, as such a course of action would A.) not work B.) possibly put a kink in the chain which would then get lodged in the pulley C.) give his shoulder a nasty pull which, if it didn't dislocate his arm from the socket, would make the rest of the work day a living hell, or, D.) all of the above. Instead, he simply applied enough pressure to slow the chains progress quickly, but safely. The door stopped perfectly on the pavement, with no more noise than an empty can of soda being placed on the floor.

Perfect landing, he thought.

Of course, when the door reached the bottom, he had effectively trapped himself in the garage with his truck idling on the opposite side.

He tried the door back to the break room, but it swung inward to the mechanics bays, with a push-bar on the other side to disengage the latch. On the mechanics side, there was a large square brushed metal button mounted about halfway up the door frame which read "OPEN" in grease caked inset letters. Not tried the button, but the power was not yet on.

Sheepishly, he returned to the rolling door. Painfully aware he had left an idling company truck outside of his visibility for nearly two minutes as he stooged his way around the mechanic's bay looking for a way out. He rolled the door up to about thigh high, just high enough for him to duck under without getting on his knees, and then let the door drop behind him as he returned to the truck. He climbed back into the cab of the truck, next to a patiently waiting Josue, who merely stared out the windshield.

"So, ah, there's no power in there right now," said Not, as a way of excusing his absence.

"Nope, the garage is on a timer. Grease-monkeys don't show up until ten or so."

"Ah," said Not. "Is there another way out you were going to use?"

"Nope," said Josue, his voice deadpan, but a smile showing in the corners of his eyes. "I was just gonna do it right the first time."

"Ah," said Not again. "Well, sure, if you're stuck in a rut."

Josue snorted a laugh through his nose, and Not felt his embarrassment fade a little.

"Head on out to Passaic," Josue said. "You know how to get to the Cedar Lane bridge from here?"

"Yeah, I can get us there," Not said and then dropped the transmission into drive.

"Good," said Josue. "We're heading over to a house in Teaneck, pick up a car, and bring it back here. Don't worry about the computer, it's not in the system."

Not had been reaching for the "Dispatch" button on the touch screen, so he could claim the job and be able to log his miles. His apprehension must have shown because Josue answered the first question on Not's mind.

"Don't worry, it's kosher. It's a practice run before I turn you loose on a paying customer."

"So, whose car are we taking back to the shop?"

"Mine."

JOSUE'S HOME was narrow two-story clapboard, very similar to Not's father's house with the exception that

Josue's was not above a raised basement. Parked on the street was a ten to fifteen year old import sedan beneath the layers of road salt, dirt, and refrozen snow. It could have been a Nissan, Kia, Hyundai, or any other number of mid-range, mid-price saloons you see lined up in a baker's dozen in any second-hand car dealership.

"Okay, so Auto Club throws this one up on the dispatch, you're in the area so you take it, and the only info you have is it won't start. Walk me through it. What do you do first?"

"Well, the cold probably just knocked out the battery, so I'd ask if he wants to jump it."

"Could cost you the tow fee . . ." Josue prompted.

"Already got the 8 mile fee just for showing up. If I don't at least offer, he'll know I'm just trying to jack up the price, so he'll have me haul him somewhere close. Be honest, and you're one of the 'good ones' and we'll likely get the work if it's anything more than a dead battery."

"Good answer," Josue affirmed. "Always play it straight is the rule at Alto. Happy customers are return customers."

"Can do," Not felt relieved. One test passed.

"Alright, so do."

"Wait," Not tried to read Josue's face to see if he was serious. "It really won't start?"

"It really won't start," Josue smiled. "Treat me like any other customer."

"A customer who decides if I'm getting fired," Not tried for humor.

"Hey, all joking aside, one bad review this week and *any* customer can decide if you get fired."

"Thanks for the heads up," Not strived for a confident tone. "Very comforting."

"Isn't it?" Josue said, and then laughed. "So, come on newbie, fix my fuckin' car!"

Not flipped on the yellow hazard lights on the roof and backed the tow hitch up to within a few feet of the front end of Josue's car.

"Could you pop the hood for me, sir?" Not called over to Josue, and then proceeded to search the lockers over the rear wheel well of the truck, where he knew he would find the jumper cables as well as the lock down straps, chains, various wrenches, hammers and other tools, a bag of kitty litter for fluid spills, flares, pop up reflective triangles indicating a closed lane, and any other number of useful bits a pieces.

Like with any job, the most used items were placed in the most easily accessed places. Tow drivers use jumper cables like waitresses used serving trays, so Not found them in the first locker he checked, in the small flat locker directly above the driver's side wheel well.

On most modern wreckers, there was a jumper cable outlet on both the front and rear bumper. The cables only had the familiar red and black alligator clamps on one end of the cables, and the other end was a fat, black, square plug. This allowed the tow driver to be able to provide a jump start no matter which end of the truck was facing the vehicle. These cables were also about twenty-five-feet long, so a car could still be started if it were head-in against a wall in a parking garage, or some other equally difficult to reach spot, with a minimum of disruption to the traffic around it.

Not flipped the plastic cap free from the outlet in the bumper, the cap prevented road gunk from dirtying the contact points in the outlet, and plugged in the cables. Then, careful to keep the alligator ends of the cables from touching either each other or himself, Not brought the cables over and clamped the appropriate colors on the appropriate terminals.

Of course, the only one part which mattered was the red cable on the positive terminal, and the black hooked on any route to ground, but most customers wanted to see both cables on the battery. Why would there be two terminals and two cables if you really only needed to use one? The unspoken follow up question: did he just mess up my car by doing it wrong? Then, if the car still didn't start, or if anything else went wrong with the car, in their minds it would be his fault because he didn't hook it up right.

So, Not always used both cables.

When the circuit was completed, the computer in the truck recognized the jumper outlet was now active, followed its programming, and cycled the idle a little faster. The rpm pushed a little higher, cranked the alternator a bit faster, and produced a bit more juice to recharge the dead battery enough to get the cold engine to turn over.

Not waited a full minute count in his head, although thirty seconds would likely have been enough if the battery was still capable of holding a charge, and then signaled for Josue to give it a try.

Josue turned the key, and the engine immediately roared to life. Not smiled and disconnected the cables. Josue smiled and killed the engine.

"Good," Josue said as he climbed out. "Now, let's see you hoist this puppy up."

It had been nearly a year since Not had last had to drop the arm and secure a load, but he found he had not gotten rusty in the least. At the bottom of the tow arm was a cross-bar which ended on each side with the calipers that usually put customers in mind of scorpion pincers, though in truth they were closer to enormous slotted spoons. The front tires of the disabled vehicle sat between the calipers, and then were secured into place with a strap wrench looped under both calipers and above the axle directly behind the towed car's tires.

Not had them ready to roll in less than five minutes, and, after checking Josue's car to make sure the steering column was locked and the transmission was not, Not climbed back behind the wheel and pointed them back towards Hackensack.

THEY HAD not yet returned over the Cedar Lane bridge when Josue's cell phone started ringing. He glanced at the screen, but then dropped the phone into the left breast pocket of his work shirt, just behind the embroidered name badge reading "Josh." Not said nothing, but simply guided the truck with its load toward the mouth of the bridge and listened to the faux-flamenco ringtone, slightly muffled against Josue's generous proportions.

Not counted six rings before either the phone kicked the caller over to a voicemail system to allow the caller to leave a message, or, if no voicemail box had been activated, the caller simply gave up.

Moments later, Not realized both of the previous options were irrelevant as Josue's phone started to ring again almost immediately. Apparently, if a voicemail system was in fact active, the caller chose not to avail him or herself of its services, and was opting instead to tenaciously persevere in their quest to speak to Josue. Which, as Josue did not appear to be making any move to answer his phone, may be a quest of Quixotic proportions and nature.

"So, I gotta ask," Josue started when the phone fell silent for the second time. "Why 'Not'?"

Josue was able to finish the question a fraction of a second before the phone once more sounded the opening strum of a computer idealized flamenco guitar chords. Then the synthesized and somehow autotuned maracas began to rattle and shush.

"I was named after my maternal grandfather, Harris Teague," Not began.

Normally, he would go through a bit of a song and dance, a few false anecdotes before getting to the real reason for his name. The song and dance was not so much for his benefit, but for the benefit of the listener.

With a chosen name as uncommon as Not, people expected an interesting story to accompany it. Of course, there *was* a story, and it was no doubt a humorous anecdote when told with a bit of showmanship, but in the end the anecdote really wasn't long, nor particularly strange. It came as a bit of an anticlimax, and despite the fact that Not had done nothing but truthfully answer the question asked of him, he always felt like he had let the other person down when he finished.

However, Not had the impression that this time the inevitable question had come as a way to distract them both from the ringing phone, so he skipped right to the punchline.

"Harris isn't a bad name," Josue observed.

"No," Not allowed, "but when coupled with my last name, Johnson . . ."

Not allowed his voice to trail off, and took his right hand from the wheel to roll his hand out face up, like one half of a balance scale, a nonverbal cue known the world over as "well, there you have it."

"So, when you introduced yourself . . ." Josue began as the phone began its ring sequence for the fourth time.

"I would say 'Hello, my name is Harris . . .'"

"'Not Harry'"

"Johnson," Not finished. "After a while, people forgot the Harry part, and just went with Not."

"Could be worse," Josue said. "When I was growing up, I knew a kid called Pacquetito."

"Which would be worse because . . . ?"

"Literally translated, it means 'little package.'"

"Okay, I agree," Not said with a smile, " Little Johnson would definitely be worse. Is it okay if I ask about the phone?"

"My wife," Josue shrugged. "She is likely upset because we took her car."

"But. . ."

Before Not could properly form an objection, Josue answered his phone and began speaking in rapid fire Spanish, most of which Not was unable to keep up with in the slightest. However, using his meager supply of words gleaned from his high school language requirement, movies, and pop/hip hop music of the last decade, he was able to catch a couple interesting shots fired, including *anoche, tu sancho*, and pretty much every Spanish curse word Not knew.

"Sure, fucking walk in this weather," Josue said, suddenly switching back to English. "I hope you freeze your tits off!"

Josue angrily tapped the screen of his phone until the default home screen showed once more.

"Man, I miss real fucking phones, sometimes," Josue said, sliding his smartphone back into his breast pocket. "Nothing more cathartic than slamming down one of those big old Ma Bell tabletop models, you know the one I mean? They still make the kids toy phone with the big goofy eyes that looks like it, though I doubt any kid playing with one of those things nowadays has any clue it's supposed to be a phone. Probably thinks it's some kind of Muppet."

"Josue?"

"Yeah?"

"What's a Muppet?"

The look of horror his question earned from Josue was exactly what Not had been hoping for, unfaithful wife forgotten momentarily from the shock of being generation gapped so badly. When he understood Not had only been joking, his knowledge of Jim Henson's legacy was indeed complete and whole, Josue barked out a lung full of stress in an odd, dry-heave of a laugh.

"So-o-o-"

"Nope," Josue cut off Not's attempt to gain more insight into the situation. "We take MY car back to the shop, and I will finish out this half of my shift, and then drive MY car back to MY house, and that's all there is to this goddamn thing.

Remember, I am the client right now. You gonna try to get involved in the personal lives of your clients?"

"As a general rule, I try to avoid it."

"Good rule," Josue agreed, but all the humor had left his voice. "Now get us on back and watch out for black ice. You fuck up my car, man, and . . ."

Josue opted not to finish that particular sentence, and Not decided it was in everyone's best interests, his own in particular, if for the remainder of the trip he kept his focus on the road.

BY THE time they returned to Alto's All Tow, two of the garage doors were open and all bays were free of tows, except for the big Peterbilt 337 at the end. Not glanced at Josue, and questioned with his eyebrows in regards to what he should do next.

"Pull up past the last door, and drop me on the street," Josue pointed to where he wanted Not to go. "However, NEVER do that to a job. Always drop it in front of whichever bay has an open door. Give them the impression they will be the next one in. Which, sometimes they are. If they are not, we'll roll it into the parking lot when the owner is gone. Got it?"

"Always keep 'em happy," Not agreed, and pulled past the two open and four closed doors. He expertly dropped the load at the curb, and went through the motions of filling out the receipt paperwork with Josue. When he was satisfied Not wouldn't, through either ignorance or idiocy, provide someone with towing service free of charge, Josue nodded towards the open bay doors and said simply: "Coffee."

As they walked past, Not looked through the window and saw that although the doors to most of the bays were down, likely to hold in as much heat as possible, all of the bays were also in use. Vehicles of clients receiving the usual maintenance for cold weather: cracked hoses, snapped fan belts, and any other bit of rubber in the engine which shrinks down and gets rigidly fragile when left out on the street overnight, and then snaps when the person, usually already late for work, tries to drive it without letting the engine compartment warm up and the resulting sudden, rather than gradual, temperature shift hits the brittle rubber like a hammer.

Of course, Not saw, there were the constant needs in automotive maintenance as well: brakes, oil changes, starters, water pumps, alternators, batteries and cables, and all the other bits and pieces which just wear down or wear out from use.

Not counted eight mechanics in the five occupied bays, but only six or so were actively working at one time. At least two people, at any given moment, were standing, drinking coffee, fetching a tool, holding or adjusting a spot-light into an engine compartment, or offering unwanted advice. Not wondered why so many when the job could be getting done with five or six at the most.

"They're waiting for me to take out the big Peter Eater at the end, and free up the space," Josue said, as if reading the question from Not's face. "So, one cup of coffee, and then we gotta get back out and rolling. Gotta empty the bays so we can refill 'em. Turnover is money, a truck taking up a spot in the garage is costing us on both ends."

"Why isn't Mr. Alto running the big one?"

"Excellent question," Josue said, his smile from earlier this morning either returning of its own accord, or being forced back into place for the sake of office gossips. "Because, he is supposed to be. He promised to roll it while I trained you this morning, so I assume there is a good reason why he is not. However, since the money it is costing the company is his money, 'because I didn't fucking feel like it' is a good enough reason for me."

"Me too."

Not followed Josue through the last open bay, and nodded greetings to the various mechanics Josue and called out to some of them by name. Not tried to follow names and faces, but the names came so quickly, and the men each looked up or waved when they had a moment to pause in what he was doing, so Not had little chance of matching the right name to the right face. So instead, he tried to collect the names and would try to match up the faces later.

He figured it wouldn't hurt in securing his position at Alto's if he started calling people by name right away. If nothing else, it would help to stave off a recurrence of this morning's anxiety. For now, he knew there was Matt, Chris, and Nicholas. The last had been referred to as Saint Nicholas by Josue, but Not was going to go out on a limb and guess the Canonization had been honorary on Josue's part.

They crossed from the frigid temperature of the garage, only slightly warmer than outside due to less wind chill, to the comparatively Saharan warmth of the break room. The door to the office, which Not had to correct himself once again from referring to the casting room, was closed, and a mutton-chopped man, aged somewhere between fifty-five and God, sat in one of the mismatched break room chairs methodically working his way through a cinnamon bun with a plastic knife and fork.

"And Mary wept," said Josue by way of greeting. "Are you eating a pastry with a knife and fork?"

"Well, I'm sure tortillas and tequila are fairly easy to eat with just your fingers," the old man said after an exaggerated sigh. "But here in America, we tend to prefer a bit of civility at breakfast."

"I was born in Newark, you racist old fuck," Josue said, but with kindness in his voice.

"Well, then, you ought to be used to the local customs by now," mutton-chops replied. "Piss off, and let me finish my breakfast. The forecast is coming up."

The man with the mutton-chops poked another piece of cinnamon pastry into his mouth, and returned his attention to the television mounted in the corner.

"Man, I wonder what it is about age and the weather," Josue said to Not. "Is there a switch somewhere in our genes, like with puberty, that when you hit a certain age you just have to know what the weather will be at all times?"

"My ears still work fine, Jose," mutton-chops said without turning from the television. "And, it comes with your first diagnosis of arthritis. If the weather is going to determine whether sitting in a truck cab for the next eight hours is going to be tolerable, pleasant, or hell on earth, it tends to attract your notice."

The older man poked the last bit of pastry into his mouth, and then held his hand out palm up.

"You bring a truck back for me, or do I get to be paid to sit on my ass today?"

Josue nodded to Not, who remembered he still had the keys in his pocket to the wrecker they had just returned. He pulled them out and lay them into the waiting palm.

"You didn't tinker with my presets on the radio, did you?" He asked, as if this would determine whether Not would be marked down as friend or foe for the remainder of his days at Alto's All Tow.

"Nope," Not answered simply, and hope he made it onto the right list.

The older man said nothing, but simply nodded the answer supplied had been the one for which he had been hoping. Then zipped up his coat and headed out to the truck before all the warmth bled away into the chilled atmosphere.

"Is this where you tell me he is really a nice guy under the gruff exterior?" Not asked.

"No, he *is* a racist old Appalachian hillbilly asshole. Grew up in some mining town in Pennsylvania, and came out this way when the town literally collapsed, like, *into* the mine, like thirty years ago. We get along okay, though." Josue shrugged.

"What's his name?"

"Troy Miller, though, no matter what anybody tells you, don't call him Helen."

"Okay, now that requires an explanation."

"I forget who started it, but it was just an off the cuff remark, you know?" Josue had opened the door to the little front room, the customer room which was still empty, and poured a fresh cup of coffee. "It was one of those throw away jokes, the kind that ends up being funnier than you ever intended? I think Troy had just got a haircut, and the barber had reigned in the sideburns quite a bit, and someone, I think maybe Francis, said he looked so pretty we ought to call him Helen of Troy."

"Okay, I see the connection now," Not poured himself a cup of coffee, silently thankful this shop seemed to prefer to brew their own, rather than making a run to the local coffee franchise a regular part of the day.

"Yeah, well what you don't see was Troy's reaction. He went fucking nuclear. Turns out Troy is one of those old-school hillbillies, the kind who keeps a gun in his boot."

"Holy shit," Not turned to glance at the door through which Troy had disappeared, suddenly concerned about getting a bullet in the back.

"Troy was all casual about it, too," Josue spoke with a little admiration in his voice. "Just bent down, all calm, and came up with a little nickel plated revolver in his hand. Stopped the laughter pretty damn quick."

"God damn," was all Not could think to say.

Not had no plans to call him on it, but he was fairly sure it had been Josue who had originally coined the nickname

Helen, and either did not want to admit he had come away from the experience with if not a measure of fear, than perhaps a small amount of respect for his bewhiskered co-worker, or he did not want to be accused of trying to continue the joke at Troy's expense.

"So, what happened?"

"Well, you remember in grade school how if you found out something about someone they didn't like, Becky hates it when someone pulls on her ponytail, Billy goes apeshit over a wet willy, that sort of thing?"

"You found his button, so you wanted to push it as often as you could, right?"

"Bingo," said Josue. "But in this case, if you pull Becky's pigtail, you might end up gut shot on the floor. I figured I ought to warn you before one of the other guys tries to get you to say it within his earshot."

"Ah, good to know," Not nodded. "Thanks for the heads up."

"Come on," Josue said. "Let's go see the boss. If you can run the big truck, and Troy took the last of the others out, then maybe I don't need to be here right now."

Not followed Josue across the now empty break room and waited as he knocked on the closed office door. There was no answer, and the handle didn't budge when Josue checked.

"He hasn't come in yet, or the door would be unlocked," Josue stated. "The office is always his first stop."

"Can I ask," Not followed after Josue. "If he pulled a gun on somebody, why is Troy still working here?"

Josue, either not hearing or choosing to ignore the question, headed back to the door to the garage, and Not followed along.

"Hey, Matt, did Alto call-in this morning?"

"Nah," said a sandy haired man who stood in front of an economy Asian import whose brand Not didn't recognize. Judging from the quality of the parts he saw from the open hood, Not guessed this was the generic version of what Korea had to offer the car market several years ago. Matt the mechanic was holding a battery cable which looked as thin as speaker wire. No wonder it had needed to be replaced. Of course, the battery from which it had been disconnected looked like it would be more at home in a golf cart. Matt was wearing his winter coat over his coveralls to stay warm while he worked, and his breath puffed out white as he called down to the other mechanics.

"Anybody hear from Alto this morning?" he called.

The assorted negative grunts and half-words were from people who were too focused on what they were doing to respond to something filed under the none-of-my-business category of their minds. They had been on time, had punched in on time, and they had plenty to keep them busy before they punched out again at the end of the day. The boss would get here when he got here.

"Shit, I hope he's not up in Yonkers again," Josue shrugged.

"The racetrack?" Not asked, having been relieved of most of a car payment on his first and only time betting on the ponies, and it was pretty much the only association he had with Yonkers, other than the occasional Neil Simon revival in the city every few years.

"No," Josue said, and then corrected himself. "Well, yeah, but no. Video poker at the casino there. They've got them rigged now so you can't even play with cash. You buy a card, like a gift card, and load it with money. Makes it seem even less like you're losing real money."

"Should I be worried about my check bouncing at the end of the week?" Not asked, only half joking.

"No, believe it or not, he wins more than he loses," Josue assured him. "That's why he only plays video poker. It's all based off of algorithms so there will always be a pattern, and logic to it. Or so he says. The way he explains it, it's like hitting shuffle when you're listening to music. The machine is supposed to pick songs randomly, but sometimes the same songs keep popping up a lot more often than the others."

"Come on, I've heard of that, but it has to be bullshit, right? Don't casinos fix it so it doesn't happen?"

"They make the program more complex, sure," Josue agreed, "but in the end it is still a fixed program and there will be patterns. Alto says the trick is to watch for a machine throwing a lot of one particular digit, wait for whoever is on it to either win and cash out or lose all their money and then take over the machine and try to play toward the heavy number."

They were back inside and getting another refill on coffee when Josue began zipping up his jacket and digging through his pockets for his gloves.

Not followed suit.

"What do you mean play toward the heavy number?" Not asked.

"Like if its giving a lot of two's, then you always keep twos when you discard. If the algorithm of the machine is cycling out a lot of two's, you know, to try to balance out its usage of numbers, then you will be more likely to get a three or four of a kind."

"Does it work?" Not asked as they crossed back into the garage and started down toward the last bay, where the big truck sat waiting.

"Sometimes," Josue shrugged. "Sometimes it doesn't, and to answer your question from before, it's when it doesn't that keeps Troy around here."

"What do you mean?" Not asked.

"A few years back," Josue glanced around to make sure they were alone, "I got a call from Alto, two or three in the morning, asking for a loan. I work for him now, but he and I go way back, and, well, let's just leave it at saying we've got history."

Not just nodded.

"I couldn't help him," Josue shrugged. "He never brought it up again, but two days later, Troy was on the rotation. No interview, no probation period, no explanation or anything."

"So . . ."

"So, nothing," Josue shrugged again. "I don't know why I'm even getting into all this with you. I don't know if the two things connect at all, but I do know that you, new guy, do not want to fuck with Troy, got it?"

"Warning heard, loud and clear," Not assured.

"Actually," Josue continued, "It's not Alto losing money we need to worry about. It's if he's is on another streak."

They climbed into the cab of the big Peterbilt, Not climbing behind the wheel without being told to do so, and Josue pulled the keys from the glove box and handed them to Not.

"Why is a streak a bad thing?" Not asked.

"It isn't really," Josue agreed. "It's just inconvenient for us. If a machine is paying out big time, the casino can't really do anything about it until the player leaves the machine. If they stop a person from playing, just because they are winning, then the Gaming Commission can revoke their license. Worst case scenario, they would most likely have to pay a big fine, but then word would get around they won't let people win if they're winning. You know how it goes."

Not nodded but said nothing.

"So, they won't stop a person from playing, but they will try to coax them away from the machine. Big congratulations, can we treat you to a free meal? Free room? Want to join us in the sky box for the next race? Anything to get you away from the machine, so they can check it to see if you rigged it in some way, and to get it off the floor before it pays out any more."

"But if you don't go?"

"If you don't go, they can't really do shit."

"So, if Alto gets on a really good streak?"

"He doesn't move again until he starts to lose, no matter how much they sweeten the pot to get him away from the machine."

"Gotcha."

Josue glanced at his watch, and then focused his attention back to the truck gently vibrating as it idled beneath them.

"Okay, so this big beautiful beast has its own ups and downs --"

"Ba-dum-chish!" Not made a rimshot sound. Josue gave him a puzzled look, so Not explained: "ups and downs. The back tilts up and down . . ."

"Oh lord, that was bad," Josue said, but smiled. "Anyways, there is more paperwork, but less actual work because we only pick up big loads with this one. Right now, almost all the calls are highway, because it's our turn in the rotation."

The Hackensack Municipal code 202-2 provides that registered and approved towing companies get the exclusive towing rights for the city for a week at a time on an alphabetical rotating basis. The rotation begins every February, and Alto's being near the top of the list gets their turn this week, which explains why every bay is full, and every truck is running. Every accident, every stall, every breakdown on the turnpike, interstate, and surface street to which the police are called would all be handled by Alto's All Tow.

"Yeah, I hope you don't have a problem with cops, 'cause you are going to be chatting with them for the rest of your shift."

"Yay," Not sarcastically enthused. He glanced around the cab as something clicked in his brain, and he realized he was missing something. "Where is the sat nav?"

"Yeah, no," Josue shrugged again. "This one is old school. Get out and cruise the highway and listen for the police scanner."

Josue pointed to an old school Bandit-style CB microphone was plugged into a much more up-to-date looking radio mounted under the dashboard.

"The blue button there will put you on the police channel," Josue pointed to a faded oval blue button on the face of the radio, near the LCD display. "The red one takes you back to the citizen's band. The channel we use is already programmed in, so don't mess with anything. You ever use a CB?"

"Once or twice, but . . ."

"Forget all the cornball trucker shit from the 70's. If anyone ever talked like that, they don't anymore. Got it?"

"Ten-four."

Josue ignored him.

"Anything unattended on the highway is ours. Breakdown calls will relay mostly from police dispatch, but you might hear from one of us here as well. Take the driver wherever they need to go and clock the miles. Otherwise, collect any and all abandoned vehicles and bring 'em back here. Drop them in the back lot if you can, on the street with a tag if you can't. We get an impound fee on each and every one of them, so this is a big nut week for us."

Josue paused and fixed his gaze on Not, scrutinizing Not's expression in order to assure the importance of this bit of information was properly impressed upon him. After a few moments, he seemed satisfied and continued with what sounded like a fairly rehearsed short speech.

"Remember: hoist from the rear, 'cause they're probably in gear. My record is four in one trip, but to be fair it was a motorcycle pile-up. Questions?"

"Nah, I've done all this before," Not half-lied. "I got this."

"Think you can find your way back to my house around five?"

"I should be able to," Not said.

"Well, call if you get lost."

"I don't have your number," Not said. "Actually, I don't currently have a phone."

Josue looked like he was about to ask why not, but apparently decided against it. Instead he reached into his pocket, took out his own phone, and tossed it to Not.

"February thirty-first to unlock, my home line is under 'home.'"

"February thirty-first?"

"0231 is the passcode to unlock it. Call it February thirty-first, and you'll never forget it."

"But, there is no February 31st . . ."

"Which is why it is weird enough for you to remember," Josue said, and hopped down from the cab. He called up before closing the door, "Good luck!"

Chapter 3

WELL SHIT, thought Donny, it wasn't diamonds. They weren't going anywhere near the airport, or little Israel, as Joe, the box guard, liked to refer to the jewelry district in Manhattan. Too bad, a shit load of diamonds would have been easier to hide than a shitload of gold.

Then again, if it were enough diamonds to require a coin truck, maybe not.

Ah, well, thought Donny, smiling to himself, I guess good ol' Tops gets to do a bit of heavy lifting tonight. Not matter what, Donny would make it work.

"Donny always does," he mumbled to the empty truck cab, the thought broadening his smile a little bit more.

He didn't even know yet what he was going to do with the money.

Of course, if Topher were to ask, Donny would give him the good old buy-a-boat-and-sail-the-world speech, but just because the Tophers of the world needed there to be a reason for the action, a plan for what was coming next. They only had two types of vision: either zoomed way in on the day to day trivial bullshit, or zoomed way out to try to view their life as a whole. It was like there was no in between for people like them. Donny got the day to day stuff: you had to pay your phone bill or they cut off your service; you had to put gas in the car or you'd stall out on the freeway. Sure, that sort of shit made sense to be aware of, it had to be somewhere on the radar, but there was no point in worrying about it.

When people tried to zoom out too far everything loses focus. Why the hell should he try to plan what he will be doing twenty years from now, when he has no idea if he is still going to want to do it? Whatever it was might not be what he expected, it could be different than how he had imagined it, whatever it might be. Or, maybe he would be different, you know? Maybe his wants will have changed.

Twenty years? Shit, he might be dead.

Anyone who doubts the simple fact that a person shouldn't really plan more than a few months ahead needs to listen to the top ten songs from five years ago. Not just the songs you still listen to, but all the songs from the top ten-- especially the one you used to bop your head and sing along to in the car but haven't thought about in years.

Listen to it again, five years later, and it's embarrassing.

Shit changes, tastes change, so why work your ass off for something you may end up not wanting by the time you get it?

The thing was, though, people don't trust you if you don't have a long term plan. It makes them nervous. It makes it look like you haven't thought things through, or worse it makes them realize they might not like their own plans a few years from now. Uncertainty and change make people anxious and unsettled.

Donny had actually taken the boat idea from some Michael Douglas movie set in a South American jungle. Pretty stupid movie, the lead actress had screamed way too much, but when he had told the guys at the club they had all thought it was a phenomenal idea.

They apparently hadn't seen the sequel, the one where Michael Douglas's character got the boat, sailed the world, and ended up hating it. Maybe it was because he was still with the chick who screamed too much, and she hadn't let up any on the screaming in the second movie, but Donny was pretty sure it was because he, after like ten years of hustling and busting his ass, he had gotten exactly what he thought he had always wanted, but now he didn't want it anymore.

Donny knew better.

Douglas' character had never really wanted the boat all along. He had told himself he did, had built up in his mind as the end-all-be-all of everything, but he was wrong.

He had wanted the hustle.

Once he had what he thought he had wanted, he was miserable. Once he lost it, in the second movie, and had to start moving again, he was happy.

Simple.

So, Donny had developed a different kind of vision. He didn't bother to look at the day to day to closely, and he could give fuck all about the big picture. Instead, he looked for what's next. The next opportunity. The next score. The fun in life came in the planning, and the doing, but very little came from the having.

So, whatever the fuck they ended up loading up in the back would be fine with him.

Totally Zen.

Still, though, it would be cool if it was gold.

The building, though he had to admit, once he got a good look at it after they cleared the guard gate and both the external and internal fence, didn't really look like it would house gold, or any other precious metals either.

Of course, Donny didn't really know what a gold storage building would look like, so it could still be one. They certainly could use some more security, though, if it was some sort of gold depository. There wasn't even a fence around the place, for Christ's sake. Sure, it could be part of the strategy, he supposed. To *not* look like it was a warehouse that stored gold. Good camouflage was good security, couldn't be denied, but still . . .

It just didn't give off a gold-y vibe.

The had turned onto Hunter avenue off of Maywood, past some little Thai restaurant, and the street had come to a dead-end at a little guard shack with a barrier arm. Although, what good a guard house would do without a fence around the place, Donny had no idea.

The guard had raised the gate and waved him past, didn't even ask to see the pick-up orders, and had let Donny drive right on through.

"Drive an armored truck," Donny muttered. "And the world will welcome you with open arms."

The place looked gross. The buildings were filthy and the paint was peeling. Big storage tanks, like huge upended propane tanks, stood in groups around one building, and some were connected with pipes to the other buildings. It looked like it was a paint factory, or a place where they recycled electronics.

Maybe that was it, Donny thought, getting excited again. Maybe this place pulls the old gold from circuit boards and used airbags and things, and they were coming to pick up the finished product.

It had to be something, he decided. Nobody hired an armored car to haul paint, no matter how good the paint was. It just didn't make sense. It had to be something valuable.

It had to be something worth stealing.

They followed the cracked and gravel-scattered asphalt around to the back of the building, where there was a loading dock with a roll down steel door. The door was still closed and secured, when they pulled in, but as Donny was reversing the truck toward the dock, he could see in the mirror the door was trundling upward.

Donny put the truck in park, and killed the engine. Normally, he would keep it running, particularly on a cold night, but he has required, for security reasons, to shut it off if he was going to be out of the cab, and to take the keys with him.

He heard the rear door open. Joe climbed out of the back, onto the loading dock, and peered up the driver's side to where Donny was climbing down out of the cab.

"Why'd you kill the engine?" Joe called up.

"Taking a quick break while you load up," Donny called down, and waved a pack of cigarettes in the palm of his hand.

"When the hell did you start smoking?" Joe called back.

"I quit for about a year," Donny called, and then added sheepishly, "Broke down and bought a pack yesterday. I'll quit again, when this pack is gone."

"Yeah, sure," Joe said dismissively, and shook his head a little. "Well, hurry up. This won't take long."

Joe disappeared back around the corner of the truck, and Donny moved up to the front of the truck and sat on the large front bumper. For the sake of appearances, he pulled a cigarette from the pack and lit it up. He really had quit over a year ago, but he couldn't think of any other reason why a person would be sitting out in the cold instead of inside the warm cab of the truck, and for the next part he needed to be out of the cab and with the engine off.

He held the cigarette with his left hand, and stuffed the right hand into the deep pocket of the big winter jacket he was wearing. Earlier in the day, just after he had left Topher's sad little apartment, he had cut through the pocket and lining of his jacket and then had sewn it shut once again with one line of very weak thread. Inside the pocket was an aerosol can of industrial cooling spray intended for use in electronics. It promised to chill items down to sixty degrees below zero, be non-flammable, and guaranteed to leave no residue.

The brittle-point of a fan belt, the temperature where the rubber and fabric mesh become rigid enough to break, was thirty degrees below zero, according to a mechanic's bible he had failed to return to the owners of the shop after the termination of his previous employment. A figure which he had also confirmed on several different web forums.

It had better be.

It had cost nearly $180 for the one can of the freezing spray from a computer and electronics superstore. But, Donny reasoned, if you want premium merchandise, you have to be prepared to pay the premium price.

In cash of course, he certainly didn't want a credit card record of this purchase waiting for the police to find, should there be an investigation into this convenient breakdown which was about to occur.

Donny held the can firmly in his gloved hand -- he had taken many pains to ensure he had never touched the can with bare skin -- and pushed down through the bottom of the pocket, bursting the fresh thread. He pushed his arm in as far as it could go, attempting to look like he was hunching over for warmth in case anyone was watching him, either live or on a screen somewhere.

There was a space between the grill of the truck and the bumper on which he was currently resting the most narrow sliver of his ass. He pushed his arm, the can still firmly in his hand, down the back of his coat and through the space between the bumper and the grill. Tilting the can upward then bending his hand toward his wrist as far as he could go, he began to spray a steady stream of supercooled inert gas into the bottom of the engine compartment.

The gas condensed upon contact and coated everything it touched in a quarter inch thick layer of frost which immediately began to sublimate back into an invisible inert gas.

Donny was sitting dead center of the engine block, so directly behind him was the engine's flywheel and the bottom-most section of the long serpentine fan-belt which ran the water pump, alternator, cooling fan, and the power-steering. Without it, even in this cold weather, the engine would overheat within minutes, and the battery, running everything without being recharged by the alternator, would also drain fairly fast. The worst, though, would be the power steering. Without it, he would likely be unable to execute the turning of a corner at anything faster than five miles an hour.

The long thin nozzle of the can was currently coating just a single section of the belt, making it brittle and weak; weak enough, Donny was betting, it would snap within ten miles of getting on the freeway.

Donny had stalled the pick-up as much as he could without causing suspicion. He came in almost two hours late, blaming a flat tire, but had been calling them every fifteen minutes saying he was almost there, just hang on, he would be in.

He had pulled the fire alarm, a stunt he hadn't done since middle school, on his way into the bathroom, and then had made a big show of coming out with his pants still down, to show it couldn't have been him who had done it.

He had taken an unnecessarily long and circuitous route to the destination.

They had been supposed to make the pick up at nine in the morning, but they were hours behind schedule by the time they had pulled in onto West Hunter Avenue.

The rush hour traffic would soon be in its full horn and finger glory, making it even more difficult for the big tow truck which would be required to get through. It would still be several more hours to wait if they were going to switch the load to another truck back from its route. If they had to wait for a truck to come back, Joe would already be into overtime before they even started to head up to Hobart, which was another eight hours away.

A breakdown right now *had* to mean a rental.
Donny emptied the can onto the flywheel and belt. It *had* to.

HE FLICKED his smoldering butt, the fourth smoked all the way down to the filter during his wait for Joe to return, off onto the cracked and potholed lot behind the loading dock. He had pulled his arm and the can back up into the pocket, but had to hold it there, since there was no longer a bottom to the pocket for the can to rest upon.

His arm was starting to get tired.

He considered walking over to the edge of the building, out of the line of sight of the loading dock, and pitching it into the scrub land between this building and the larger warehouse next door, but decided against it.

He might not be able to see anybody watching him, but it didn't mean there weren't cameras on the buildings which he couldn't see. He would switch it to the left pocket when he got into the cab and then ditch it later on. Shit, no, he thought, there was a camera in the cab that ran a wireless feedback to an independent security company. There was another one in the upper corner of the box kept an eye on Joe 24-7 as well.

"Get the thumb out of your ass," Joe called from the back of the truck. "We're loaded, so let's roll, Donny. I want to get home before midnight."

"I gotta take a leak first," Donny said, suddenly inspired.

"Jesus Christ, Donny, can you make us any later today?" Joe moaned.

"Look, it's either now or maybe half an hour down the road," Donny reasoned.

"Just make it quick, okay? I'm locking up back here."

Donny climbed up the stairs on the side of the loading dock, and banged on the rolling door which had been secured once more. The impacts on the door made a loud, stage thunder type of rumble. On the far side of the door from where Donny stood, a normal steel fire door opened up slightly, and a suspicious looking security guard, about sixty years old and skinny except for the pot belly drooped over his belt buckle, looked out and scanned the loading area. His eyes stopped when he saw Donny, but the suspicion didn't leave his face.

"Yes?" the old guard asked.

"Can I use your restroom before we go, sir?" Donny asked in his best I-respect-my-elders voice. "Please?"

"Yeah, okay," the old man nodded, but the suspicion didn't leave. Maybe it had frozen there over the years, Donny thought.

On the left shoulder of his brown and beige security uniform was a gold shield with the word "SECURITY" stenciled in black, and on the right shoulder was a white rectangle with a large red S, split in the middle with a white line to make the S appear to be two pieces fit perfectly together and a small copyright symbol next to it, also in red. Above the left breast pocket was a brass nameplate which read "Smith."

"Second door," Smith nodded to the left side of the fairly empty loading bay. "First door is the Ladies."

Donny nodded his thanks and then hurried toward the door. The loading bay was small, maybe twenty feet by twenty feet, and mostly empty.

What little there was in the room, though, was fairly confusing to Donny.

Against the far wall, was a small forklift, a pallet skiff, and two wooden pallets. One pallet contained four large blue plastic barrels, each stenciled with the same logo on Smith's uniform, and all four secured together with large plastic binding straps. The other pallet was loaded with boxes, each about the size of a box of tea bags, which had been wrapped from a large roll of plastic wrap to secure the smaller boxes for shipping.

Nobody would ship gold in either of those methods, nor leave an old guy like Smith as the only line of defense against its theft.

What the hell did they have in the truck?

Donny pushed the door to the restroom open, and located the trash can. It was almost full he was pleased to see. He grabbed a handful of paper towels and wiped down the can coolant to make sure he hadn't accidentally left any prints on it, and then stuffed it down into the middle of the trash.

Even if the police suspected someone had tampered with the belt, retraced their steps back to here, decided to search the trash of the bathroom, and if no one had taken out the trash by then, even if all those things happened, they still couldn't prove he had put the can in there.

He flushed the toilet and washed his hands for the sake of keeping up appearances, and then headed back out to the truck.

He pounded on the side as he walked up to the cab to let Joe know they were about to get rolling, and then climbed in and started up the engine.

He was a little afraid the belt would snap immediately. That would be a little suspicious given he had just been sitting up there. However, the engine rumbled to life without a hitch, and Donny got them rolling back out the way they came, passing the Thai restaurant on the corner as they turned back onto Maywood Avenue. They made it about a mile down Maywood, and hit a red light at Essex Street, the entrance to the 17 North on the other side.

When the light turned green, out of habit Donny stamped on the gas and revved the engine a little too hard; the truck had horrible acceleration, and the on ramp to the freeway was not a long one. Donny knew if he was going to have any hope of being anywhere near freeway speed by the time he made it to the end of the feeder lane, he had to take the turn on the ramp as fast as he safely could.

He had just cleared the intersection, still accelerating, when he heard the snap and felt the steering wheel lurch in his hand. The engine still rumbled along, but the power steering was gone. He switched his foot from the gas to the brake and applied firm but steady pressure to make sure the truck didn't skid.

He couldn't make the sharp turn without the power steering, and even if he did, they wouldn't have the momentum to make it clear onto the freeway. So, he eased the truck to a stop, trying to keep it as straight as possible to make it easier to load onto the tow, second nature really as a former tow truck driver himself.

Wait.

He didn't want to make it easy.

He wanted this whole run to be a clusterfuck of epic proportions.

This run needed to have so many expensive problems, the bosses would do anything just to stop hemorrhaging money and get the trip over with.

So, he eased his foot off the brake, and let the truck make it down to the tightest point of the turn, and steered it directly into the wall.

"Fuck!" came a muffled cry from the back.

Without a water pump running the coolant through the block and back into the radiator, and without the fan to blow cool air across the radiator fins with the truck was no longer moving, the engine would overheat in a matter of minutes. However, if he shut it down now, he could let the engine cool, and save power to the battery which the lifeless alternator was no longer charging. Donny let his hand hover above the key and watched the needle on the thermostat steadily crawl up toward the red.

"Donny?" Joe called from the back.

Wisps of steam began to slither out from under the edges of the hood, and then were swept away in the wind.

"Donny?" Joe called again, his voice more urgent this time.

The thermostat was now planted firmly in the red, and the wisps had become steady streams. The battery gauge, though, still showed at least a half charge.

Once he shut it down, Donny wanted this truck to be, for all intents and purposes, entirely dead.

"Donny, man, what the fuck!" panic was beginning to creep into Joe's voice.

Good enough.

Donny turned the key and sat and enjoyed the silence for a minute.

It was so nice when everything works out like you planned.

Chapter 4

THERE WERE three patrol cars, red and blue pulsing lights reflecting off of the iced over snow, blocking off access to the far end of the street from where he turned the corner. The officers were milling about, taking statements from those who had gathered around. Through the fogged over windows, he could see one figure sitting in the back of each patrol car, each figure slumped forward as if praying.

Not had to fight the immediate insane anxiety which told him, beyond the shadow of a doubt, the officers were there to once again take him into custody The horrifying worm of irrationality lodged deep into his brain, creeped down the back of his neck, and drew his shoulders up into a cringe at the sight of an unexpected uniform.

Not forced himself to take three deep breaths and released each one slowly.

He pulled the big Peterbilt to the side of the road one house up, where there was enough street parking available for the enormous truck. After going through the shutdown routine, which took quite a few more steps than a typical vehicle, Not made sure both doors were locked, and pocketed the keys along with Josue's cell phone and headed, against every instinct, toward the flashing lights.

The police cars were definitely situated in front of Josue's house, and the large, squat silhouette in the last car was almost certainly Josue. Not approached cautiously, trying to hear what had happened before committing to becoming a part of it.

As he approached the outskirts of the neighbors, most were dressed for work, having just returned home but had decided to check out the circus at the neighbor's before going in to get changed and start some dinner. They were the outer layer of people, the new arrivals, like Not himself, who were trying to figure out what was going on.

Those who knew what was going on, who had been there when whatever had happened had in fact happened, were closer in and speaking to one of the uniformed officers. There appeared to be three elderly couples, all dressed in thick layers in an attempt to hold in the body heat their parchment skin no longer did. Each of the three couples appeared to follow the same fifties-sitcom dynamic: the husband told the story to the police, and the wife corrected what he got wrong.

Unfortunately, from the back of the crowd, Not could hear neither the story the husband was trying to tell, nor the corrections the wife would make from any of the three couples. Perhaps he could have heard better if his heart were not pounding his blood hard enough to make his ears burn. His adrenaline was surging and the desire to turn and flee was nearly overwhelming.

Why not just return to the shop, leave the truck in the last bay with the keys in the glove box, and head home? If he made good time in traffic, he could easily catch the 165, it ran just about every ten minutes between six and seven, and be home and showered before eight. There were cold cuts in the fridge for dinner, and half a two-liter of cherry cola on the counter, if his dad had left him any.

Of course, he knew, to make that choice would mean he was walking away from the job.

It had been a good day. He had kept the tow running the whole time, eating his leftover pizza in the cab while cruising the turnpike for breakdowns and abandoned vehicles, of which there were a surprising amount. He had fielded radio calls from the local PD, which for some reason had not been weird or stressful,, and the calls had all been more of the same: picking up cars left on the side of the side of the turnpike for more than four hours.

A car can be on the highway or interstate for twelve before it is considered abandoned, but on "limited access highways" the limit is four. So, if a person's car breaks down and they have to get to work, they might come back later in the day to find their car is already gone. So, in addition to the repair bill, the owner will also have to pay for the tow, the impound fee, and a fine of up to $500 on the first offense, and up to $1000 on further offenses. Not had collected about eight abandoned vehicles from the turnpike today, so the city of Hackensack had earned at least $4000 in fines alone, and at least eight people are having an even worse day than they had thought.

Still, it had been good to be working again, and the work was pretty easy. It was a good job, and Not certainly didn't want to lose it.

Yet, the temptation to get right back in the rig, return to the garage and head home was strong.

He had taken a car from this address this morning.

It was true, Not thought, he had been assured by Josue that he was the owner of the vehicle and Not had been doing nothing wrong.

It was also true, he had been told the same thing before and ended up in cuffs just the same.

God damn it.

If he had fallen for it again, they would end up arresting him anyway, he reasoned. Only, they would come to his father's house and arrest him there, with his dad watching this time. That alone was reason enough to just face the music here, and find out what was going on.

Not pardoned himself and he politely pushed his way through the crowd and approached one of the police officers. He stopped a few feet away when the office raised a hand, palm out, to indicate Not should approach no further. Not then waited for the officer to complete his interview with one of the three elderly couples, realizing he might be politely waiting for his own arrest, but also understanding it was his best option given the current situation.

After a few moments, Not heard the officer thank the pair for their statement, and someone would be in touch if there were any further questions, or if they would be required to testify. They both nodded their understanding, and then began to carefully walk back toward their own home, keeping a sharp eye out for ice.

No bones shatter easier than old bones.

"I am looking for Josue Viejo," Not said before the officer could speak.

"May I ask what your business is with Mr. Viejo?" the officer asked back.

"He's my supervisor," Not figured this was close enough to the truth, though in reality he had no idea if Josue had a title other than driver. "I was supposed to meet him here to turn in the truck."

Not pointed to the big truck down the street, and the officer followed the line of sight until he spotted the big wrecker.

"Mr. Viejo is currently in police custody," the officer said, staring blank faced at Not in a manner that had to have been taught at the academy.

"Can I ask what for?" Not tried to sound casual.

"I am not at liberty to discuss any details at this time, Mr. . . .?"

"Johnson," Not said, and held out his hand as he had been taught to do since he was young. The officer took it and give it a brief shake.

"Could I at least speak with him for a minute?" Not asked. "I need to find out what he wants me to do with the truck."

The officer looked hesitant.

"It's my first day," Not added, hoping it would be the clincher.

It was.

The officer nodded and led Not over to the rearmost patrol car.

"I will have to remain present for the conversation," the officer warned. "You are not to speak with him about the events leading to his being in our custody, understand?"

"Yes, absolutely," Not agreed. He noticed the officer avoided using the word "arrest."

The officer opened the rear door to the squad car, and Josue brought his head up to look at Not. There was blood caked under both nostrils, and a bib of dried blood on the front of his work shirt. His left eyebrow was beginning to swell, and by tomorrow the soft saggy skin around the eye would be a deep shaded bruise. The knuckle of both of his hands were all scraped and swollen. His hands themselves, however, remained uncuffed.

"Hey, Not," Josue smiled. "How'd everything go today?"

"Well, the seal around the passenger side window is shot, and there is a really annoying whistle from the wind coming in when you drive on the freeway," Not said, deadpan. "Other than *that*, I suppose I can't complain. How about you?"

Before he could answer, the officer jumped in.

"Mr. Viejo, please remember anything you say at this point is admissible as evidence," the officer warned. "I have asked Mr. Johnson here not to discuss the events resulting in your custody here today."

"Thanks, Bill," Josue said and smiled. Turning to Not he said, "Bill here is worried I'm going to say something and get myself into trouble. We've worked quite a few fender benders together, and he's being a stand-up guy. But, I keep telling him: nothing happened."

Not raised his eyebrows questioningly, and Officer Bill just snorted and looked away.

"Really," Josue said. "The top stair is a little loose, and I fell. That's it."

"And the other two?" Officer Bill asked.

"I don't know," Josue said. "I wasn't really paying attention when I fell."

"Right," Officer Bill said, then slowly shook his head to either indicate his disapproval, or at the very least, his non-belief.

"So," Not decided now would be a good time to jump back into the conversation. "Is Alto's number in your phone? Should I call him so see if he's back yet to drive your shift?"

"He's not likely to answer," Josue darkly chuckled.

"He doesn't answer when he's at the casino?"

"Well, no, not usually," Josue allowed. "But he's not at the casino."

From the angry but amused tone of Josue's voice, Not couldn't help but glance at the other two squad cars, and the other two figures in the other two back seats.

"Is he . . .?"

"Yep," Josue nodded.

"And . . . your wife?"

"Yep," Josue nodded again.

"I suppose they tripped on the same stair you did?" Officer Bill asked, without looking at either one of them.

"Well, it would be hard for me to say, as I was too distracted with my own bad fortune at the time," Josue said. He paused a moment, but then added smugly, "But if I had to guess, I'd say yep."

HALF AN hour later, Not was back behind the wheel of the Peterbilt, and trying to decide if the big truck could make it through the overhang of a fast-food chain without ripping off the roof of the truck, the roof of the building, or, worse yet, both. The only other choice would be to park the big truck across five spaces in the lot, like an asshole, and run inside. Of course, destroying the truck and the building would make him and even bigger asshole, so he opted for the lesser degree of assholiness and took up nearly all the spaces in the cramped lot.

It was going to be a long night, and his body needed fuel.

I know I am asking a lot of you on your first day, but I need you to keep on rolling until we wrap up all this nonsense, Josue had said from the back of the squad car. *I know Alto and I know Sophia well enough to know this will end with no arrests. Alto or I will call you on my cell as soon as we're done here. One of us will take over and we'll even drop you at home, okay?*

Not took his place in line and checked to see what he could order the largest quantity of for the least money, and chicken sandwiches off of the value menu appeared to fit the bill. Three of those and a soda, would ring up just under five bucks.

A boy with his hair cut down to a quarter inch, bleached until it was nearly white, and spray tanned pallid skin to a shade reminiscent of pumpkin pie, rang up the sale, $4.28 with the sales tax added in. As he collected his change, Not noticed the kid was also sporting a pukka shell necklace and realized what he was seeing was an east coast dollar store version of surfer-bum chic.

Not had never really followed fashion, he was the first to admit, and still continued to be more of a follower, wearing whatever everybody else was wearing, usually a few months after they had started wearing it, and a generic version of it became available on the clearance rack.

Still, the trends seemed to be getting weirder.

Or, he had, at the tender age of twenty-two, begun his descent into middle-age. Not a pleasant thought, he freely admitted, but if the alternative was to look like mozzarella stick dipped in ranch dressing, then he could live with being an old fart.

Not grabbed his bag of sandwiches and headed back out to the truck, sipping on his cola as he went.

"Great parking, asshole," a lady shouted out the window as she headed for the drive-through.

"Always nice to meet a fan," Not called back, and then smiled and waved. The woman returned his wave with a single finger, before turning her attention to the illuminated menu and speaker box to place her order.

Not got the big diesel running and sat back to let the engine regain whatever heat it had lost during his brief time inside, and while he did he unwrapped a chicken sandwich and tried to decide if he was in trouble again.

On the surface, this appeared to be a run of the mill domestic disturbance which just happened to coincide with his first day of work. He had towed a car from their address earlier today, but with the consent, hell at the request, of the car's owner. It was also under the direct supervision and request of his supervisor, who just happened to also be the car's owner. So, on both counts he should be in the clear.

If it actually was Josue's car.

Alternatively, if it was Alto's car, then Josue had enlisted his unwitting help to steal a car in an apparently successful attempt to strand the boss at Josue's house so Josue could return to inflict bodily harm on Alto. That could definitely be viewed as premeditation. Not didn't know if such a distinction made it something more than assault, if it bumped it up to some worse form of assault or even attempted murder, but premeditation would definitely make the crime worse.

He could be charged as an accomplice.

Again.

An unwitting accomplice, but an accomplice nonetheless.

Again.

Goddammit.

A car honked, and Not realized he was still occupying multiple parking places. He certainly didn't need a parking ticket on top of everything else, so he put his sandwich down on the seat beside him and put the truck into gear.

He eased out onto the street, rush hour traffic in a truck the size of four or five normal cars stacked bumper to bumper is no easy feat, but as long as he moved slowly the size worked to his advantage. He could merge just about anywhere so long as he did it gradually enough. The other cars had no real choice other than to stop and let him in or watch as their front end disintegrated beneath the rear wheels.

It was amazing how distant the angry car horns and shouts of rage sounded when you were sitting high up and on top of a pounding diesel engine.

He pointed the truck in the direction of the turnpike, where he had spent the majority of his day already, but had to turn around almost immediately.

"10-43 on Route 1 North on-ramp from Maywood Avenue . . . repeat, 10-43 on Route 1 North on-ramp from Maywood Avenue. We're gonna need the big one."

Not had discovered, after he heard his first radio call earlier that afternoon, there was a small list of radio codes carefully printed in blue ballpoint pen on a three by five index card, laminated, and then attached with a zip tie to the coiled cord of the microphone. When he pulled the mic from the cradle, preparing to press the red button and call back to the shop to ask which codes he needed to listen for, the card and slapped against his knuckles and saved him the call. 10-43 was police code for "wrecker needed."

"This is Alto's All Tow, I'm just outside of Teaneck in the big rollback. *En route* now."

"Copy Alto."

Not returned the radio mic to the cradle under the dashboard and headed for the Cedar Lane bridge for what felt like the zillionth time today. When Cedar Lane dead-ended into Main, Not took a left and headed south. Ten minutes later, not too bad considering the time of day, Not hooked a right onto Essex, which would lead him directly to the on-ramp at Maywood.

He wondered if doing this would end up getting him fired.

He hadn't had a chance to speak with Mr. Alto, to see if this is what Not should be doing, i.e. doing a favor for the person who had apparently been administering a beat down on Alto, at least until the police had arrived to break it up. In all likelihood, Not was currently doing a favor for someone no longer employed with Alto's All Tow.

Of course, the favor he was doing was also keeping Alto's in good standing with the city, and fulfilling their municipal towing contract, so Not had a hard time entertaining the thought that Alto wouldn't at least be a little grateful.

If he wasn't, then fuck him.

Not needed the job, and was doing the job.

Nobody would fault him for that.

If Alto had been sleeping with the wife of an employee, or with anyone's wife other than his own, if he had one, then he had earned the beating he had received.

Not could see the now familiar flashing red and blue's up ahead. He flipped on his own lights, yellow, mounted on the top of the truck's cab. Road flares had been lined in front of the on ramp, and the patrol officer was currently in the middle of the intersection, directing traffic to the next access point for the freeway.

As he pulled into the intersection, he could see why they had opted to simply close off the entrance. About a hundred feet from the intersection, the on-ramp made a sharp hairpin turn, and t-boned into a k-rail, across the tightest point of the curve, was an enormous armored truck. Some armored cars Not had seen looked like especially well built conversion vans, but this one looked like a SWAT assault vehicle painted white and red, like an ice cream truck from beyond the Apocalypse.

It couldn't have picked a worse place to break down, or a worse time of year.

Normally, the on ramp was open, no walls on either side. In the winter, though, the city lined the on-ramp on either side with concrete barriers to keep snow drifts from blowing across, with the added bonus of keeping drivers from sliding across an icy on-ramp and directly into freeway traffic.

If it had been summer, the armored would have just ended up dead in a patch of grass between the ramp and the freeway. Not would have all sorts of space to loop around in order to position the truck. As it was, the k-rails were blocking almost all access.

However, they might have prevented the armored truck from rolling directly into rush hour traffic, so Not couldn't complain too much.

The curve of the road where the armored truck was stopped would prevent Not from being able to line up with the load properly, so he would need to attach a winch and try to roll it into position with the driver of the armored steering it straight as they went. Hopefully, all the wheels were still in rolling order.

The patrol officer stopped all traffic at the intersection, and Not swung the big truck around so he could reverse into position as best as possible. He made it to within about ten feet of the truck, and then left the rest for maneuvering space. In the mirror, he saw a uniformed guard emerge from the back of the truck, and another from the driver's side.

Not waited until they passed the rear bumper of his truck before climbing down to say hello, and discuss the limited options available to them to get the armored vehicle out of this fairly tight spot.

"Holy shit!" called a voice Not had hoped to never hear again. "Harry, is that you?"

To cap off what had to be a record-holding turn of weird-ass, rat-fuck, who-did-I-wrong-in-a-former-life, just flat out bizarre, events of anyone's first day at work ever, standing within punching distance, but unfortunately well-armed, was the dipshit who had ruined Not's life.

"Hi Donny," was all he could politely manage.

Chapter 5

"I'M CALLING it in!" yelled Joe from the back. "Donny, talk to me. Are we okay?"

Meaning, thought Donny, are we being robbed?

Not the way you're thinking, Joe my friend, thought smugly.

Not the way you're thinking at all.

"I think a belt snapped," Donny called back. "Power steering went out and I couldn't make the turn."

Joe opened a small window, not much bigger than a man's hand laid flat with the fingers close together, and looked through cautiously, making sure Donny didn't currently have a gun to his head.

"Why'd you kill the engine?" Joe asked.

"We were overheating," Donny explained. "If we don't shut it down it could seize up. Cost a hell of a lot more to fix than a belt."

"Yeah, but at least we'd stay warm until it does," Joe groused. "Alright, I'm gonna call it in before we turn into popsicles out here."

"Yeah, you do that," Donny said, and pushed the switch to turn on the hazard lights. "I'm going to go put out some road flares so we don't get rear ended."

"Yeah, right, you addict," Joe laughed from the back, the tension gone from his voice. Breakdowns were a matter of course for him, and they fell firmly into the not-my-problem category. "Smoke one for me while you're doing it."

Not a bad idea, Donny thought, as he climbed down out of the cab. Through the little window, Donny could hear Joe on the radio calling in their location and situation. From under the driver's seat, Donny pulled a half a dozen road flares and strolled down to the back of the truck to survey the situation and place the flares accordingly.

From about ten feet away, Donny could see just how badly he had jammed the truck into position. About twenty feet back, cars had started to stack up, seeing there was no way to pass, no room to turn around, and were blocked in from behind by people who couldn't see the on ramp was blocked.

Then the horns started to flare up from down the line.

"Yeah, good luck with that," Donny muttered, and fired up his first flare. He tucked the other five into the left pocket of his jacket, the one without the hole in the bottom, and held the burning flare in his right hand. When his left hand was clear, he held both hands up, the right to get attention with the flare, the left held flat with the palm out and waving gently but firmly back to front, in what he hoped would be an unmistakable signal for back the fuck up.

He moved to the leftmost part of the road, up against the K rail, and tried to catch the attention of the driver of the car at the rear of the line. He couldn't see the driver from the glare of the sun, already low on the western horizon, reflecting off the windshield, but the driver either saw him and got the idea, or came to the same conclusion on his own and reversed back into the big four lane intersection and headed up Essex to try to find the next northbound on ramp.

Once the rear car backed out, the next in line got the same idea, and then the next, and so on. Within a few minutes, the K rail alleyway was cleared of all vehicle except for the busted truck wedged firmly into the hairpin.

Donny was lighting up the other five flares, creating a line of crimson sparks and a prison bar wall of smoke columns across the entrance to the on ramp, when the local PD arrived on the scene.

"Is everybody okay, any injuries?" the officer called from the window of his vehicle over to Donny.

"No injuries," Donny said, and dropped the final flare into place. He walked quickly over to where the cruiser was idling. "But, the truck is blocking the on ramp completely. I lost the power steering and couldn't make the turn. I think a belt snapped."

"Is is still operational?" The officer asked. Then, without waiting for an answer, "we could probably get it out onto the freeway even without the power assist. It would sure make picking it up a lot easier."

"No," Donny considered lying, saying the truck stalled out, but remembered he had already told Joe the truth. "I was worried about it seizing up, it was already boiling over so I killed the engine."

"Well, better safe than sorry, I suppose," said the officer, in a tone suggested the Donny was in fact a little bitch who should have been able to turn a steering wheel . "I'll call in for a wrecker, but while I do, go see if you can get it started again and try to muscle it out into a better position."

"Will do," Donny nodded in eager agreement, but didn't bother to warn the officer to get a big truck because a regular tow wouldn't do the job.

Fuck him and his tone.

Donny walked quickly, wanting to appear in total compliance with the officer's request, but once in the cab, he put the key in the ignition and turned it to the auxiliary position and then held his hand there for about a ten count. The camera in the upper corner of the cab recorded only video, no sound, so if anyone checked, it would look like he was trying to start the truck. However, as far as the cop needed to know, the truck was as dead as the dodo.

"Not even trying, huh?" Joe spoke up from behind him and Donny let out an effeminate squeak and almost jumped out of his skin.

"Jesus, Joe!" Donny yelped. "Don't do shit like that!"

"Sorry," Joe said with chuckle indicating he was anything but. "So is it?"

"Is it what?" Donny snapped, still mad at being scared, but not sure if the was mad at Joe or mad at himself for overlooking Joe.

"The engine," Joe said, as if stating the obvious. "It's not even trying, is it?"

"No, it's totally dead," Donny confirmed without having any idea if it was true or not. The battery might have enough juice stored in it to get the motor to turn over, but without the alternator they wouldn't be getting very far even if it did start.

Sure, he could probably getting it going if he wanted to, and he was confident he could get it out to the freeway. Donny was tempted to do so just to show up the shit-toned fucking cop.

He came to his senses just before he reached again for the key.

He still didn't want to make it any easier for the tow truck to pick them up, so as far as anyone was concerned, the truck was fucking dead.

He let his hand fall back into his lap.

A tap at the window made Donny yelp again.

The patrol officer was standing on the saddle step beside the driver's door, and looking at Donny with the kind of smile that said he knew Donny was going to scream, and it merely confirmed what he had established before: Donny was in fact a little bitch.

"It's dead!" Donny shouted through the glass.

"Alright," the cop nodded. "The wrecker is on it's way. Keep with the truck, and keep an eye out for it. I'm headed out to the intersection to make sure the on ramp stays clear."

"Thanks Officer!" Joe shouted from the back loud enough to make Donny wince.

The officer merely smiled and nodded, dismounted from the step, and knocked twice on the back of the truck as he walked past.

Be as smug as you like, dipshit, Donny smiled to himself. You're helping me to get rich, so you can be just as smug as you want to be while you freeze your nuts off, waving off traffic to help me get rich.

Dumbass.

IT WAS a thirty minute wait before he saw the big flatbed wrecker starting to reverse its way up the onramp. Donny spent the time watching the clouds from his breath get thicker as the heat seeped out of the truck cab, the relative silence punctuated only by the occasional grumbling kvetch from Joe.

It looked like the cop hadn't needed any help in figuring out a truck as massive as this one would need a big tow. It looked like a flatbed semi-truck.

Donny knocked on the wall behind him with a knuckle, just a quick double tap to get Joe's attention.

"Looks like our ride is here," Donny called back.

"About goddamn time," Joe sounded pleased. "Something finally went right today."

63

"Are we headed back to the lot, switch to a new truck?" Donny asked, trying not to sound too innocent, but instead he bordered on a whine.

"Nah," Joe said from the back. "All the trucks are rolling, and everyone is getting stuck in traffic right about now. You be okay if we rent one again?"

"You serious?" Donny hopped over the border and went into a full-on whine. "Those things are about as secure as a shoebox. We get no protection at all."

"Yeah, I know, but I signed for this load, and I'm on the hook for it until we drop it. I'll wait with you for a truck to come back, if you want, but. . ."

"No," Donny managed to suppress the smile and sound sincere. "I'm not going to do that to you Joe, and you know it. But you're buying donuts on the way."

"Whatever, man," Joe sounded relieved, but only for a moment. "No, you know what? Most of today is your damn fault, so stick the damn donut up your ass. I just want to get this damn job done, and then I want a cold beer and a hot shower, but not necessarily in that order."

"*Porque no los dos*?" Donny inquired, imitating a little girl from a taco commercial.

"Ooh, yeah, and a taco," Joe agreed. "Sounds about right."

"That's not what it means, Joe," Donny laughed. "It means . . . "

Donny looked in the driver's side mirror and saw the tow driver climbing down from the cab.

"It means?" Joe prompted.

"Hey, I think I know that guy!" Donny said.

"I don't think that's right, Don," Joe said, with mock-ignorance. "Doesn't sound like it has anything to do with tacos."

"No," Donny laughed. "No, the tow driver. I think I used to work with him."

"He one of the ones who stole the cars?" Joe asked, suddenly serious again.

"Well, yeah," Donny admitted. "But it wasn't like that. All the driver's took the cars, because they thought it was legal. They were all told the cars were repo's."

"You didn't know what was going on either?" Joe asked, and not for the first time. "No idea at all?"

"Nah, it was my first real job, you know?" Donny lied, and not for the first time. "I was totally clueless. It didn't even cross my mind it was sketchy, because I had never seen it done any other way."

"So, is this guy okay?" Joe asked, his tone all business now. "Because we got a load in here which *I* signed for."

"Yeah, he's okay," Donny was quick to confirm. "He's no rocket scientist, but he's okay."

Donny opened the door and hopped out onto the saddle step and looked back at the little hole in the wall toward Joe.

"Come on, I'll introduce you," Donny said. "You can see for yourself."

Donny jumped the rest of the way to the ground, and slammed the door behind him. He caught up with Joe at the back of the truck, and they walked down together in the quickly fading light of the day. The driver of the truck with Alto's All Tow on the door has started walking towards them.

"Hi Harry!" Donny called jovially, knowing all too well it was one of the only things he had ever seen really get under Not's skin.

He watched as Not's shoulder pulled up a little, either at the sight of Donny or at the use of the name he truly hated.

"Hi Donny," Not returned, his voice even but the look in his eyes was less than kind.

"Harry, this is my partner Joe, Joe meet Harry," Donny said in his best friendly and innocent voice.

"Not," said Not, holding his hand out to Joe.

"Not what?" Joe asked.

"I prefer to be called Not, rather than Harry," Not said. "I guess Donny forgot."

"Or, he's just being a prick," Joe said, shaking Not's hand. "It wouldn't be the first time."

"Well, fuck you too, Joe," Donny laughed, but could feel the heat rising to his face.

"Donny says you two used to work together," Joe said, letting the implied question hang in the air.

"Yeah, Donny was my manager there," Not agreed, looking Joe dead in the eye as he spoke. "Scheduled all my pick-ups, repos included."

The unspoken accusation floated there on the clouds of their breath.

Donny let it the pause in conversation draw out to just a little beyond uncomfortable before he made up his mind, and decided to make the peace.

"Yeah, we all got our orders from a couple of assholes who didn't come in more than once a month, but were apparently hauling in a huge amount of money from having us do the dirty work. We all got fucked, Not."

"Yeah, I guess so," Not nodded. "So, what's the deal with this?"

"Snapped a belt, I think," Donny said for what felt like the millionth time. "Lost steering as we headed into the curve. Sorry, but I think I got it stuck in there pretty good."

"If I jump it, do you think you could back it out into a better position?"

"If it's only a belt, I might be able to," Donny allowed. "But we can't get under the hood. It opens forward, hinge is just above the bumper. The whole thing comes forward, headlights and all, and the battery is right up front, on the driver's side. No way we can get the hood open far enough to get the alligators clamped on."

"Alright," Not shrugged. "I'll winch it into position. Can you steer while I pull it out of the curve?"

"You know I can," Donny said with mock offense.

"Alright, well," Not nodded, "let's get this done, then."

Chapter 6

"I NEVER fucked you, Not," Donny said, his face serious. "I want you to know that."

"You never even bought me a drink, Donny," Not said dryly, keeping his eyes on the road.

Donny went silent, but Joe, situated between them in the cab of the wrecker chuckled a bit.

The truck secured in the back after thirty cold minutes of hooking up the winch line, tugging a few feet, turning the wheels, tugging a few more feet, re-adjusting the wheels, tugging a few more feet, correcting an overcorrection, tugging a few more feet, and then finally rolling it right up the incline and onto the bed.

"I mean it, Not," Donny persisted. "I came in for the day, there was the list of repos in on my clipboard, and I assigned them. That was all there was to it."

"So your conscience is clear?" Not asked, realizing as soon as the words were out of his mouth he had taken the bait.

"Don't give me any of that shit," Donny said hotly. "The *cash* you got, I was told, was a finder's fee. I got a percentage, sure, what I was told was basically a bounty from the finance company, at the end of each week from George."

"I don't think George made the call."

GEORGE WAS one of the two absentee owners of the shop which had previously employed both Not and Donny, in one of the nine tow shops George and his brother in law, John, used to own, and who had denied knowing anything about the use of company trucks for the repossession of cars, either legally and illegally.

As far as he was concerned, they had been a breakdown and collision operation.

67

George had said, if anything illegal had been going on, it must have been John behind it.

John, the least favorite husband of George's most favorite sister, had also denied all knowledge of any wrongdoing, but had been equally ready to throw his partner under the bus at the first opportunity.

George had made John a partner when he had just the one garage and a mere three, second-hand, tow trucks. John's employment had been a wedding present for his sister, Laurie, who, though very much in love with John, had grown increasingly concerned about their financial future together, as John had been unable to hold the same job for an entire year.

George had made no secret that he fully expected to be supporting John and Laurie financially anyway, and so he might as well be able to write the expense off as salary rather than charity every year when he filed his 10-40.

John, not wanting to be outdone at his own wedding, toasted his new brother-in-law and promised he would "make him eat those words."

This was brought up during the trial.

Despite the fact that the two rarely got along socially, they seemed to do exceptionally well professionally. Most people chalked it up to success due to spite; neither wanted to end the day before the other did, so they both ended up working insanely long hours.

Not remembered the older drivers, the ones who had been there from the beginning, saying they thought George had opened a second shop just so he could leave at a normal time again.

Of course, once the second shop opened, John ran one while George ran the other, and as one can fairly easily imagine, and friendly rivalry soon began between the two tow shops. Both owners spent so much time trying to show up the other, they soon ended up very wealthy. George opened a third shop, so John opened a fourth.

The next four worked the exact same way.

The ninth shop ended up being the one to break the tie. George opened up Citywide Collision and Tow #9, and John could not answer to it. His four shops were turning a steady profit, but not enough to be able to support a fifth while it got off the ground.

This was also brought up in court.

John, deciding to be the most gracious loser he could, purchased an 18-inch black latex rubber dildo, wrapped a federal income tax form around it *papier mâché* style, and sent it to George's newest garage with a card attached:

Go Fuck Yourself.

This too was brought up during the trial

The two had demanded separate trials, believing if they held to their own Not Guilty plea, blame everything on the other party, then the jury would acquit.

Each believed he would be the one to go free and would, in fact, have the entire company to himself.

Of course, they soon realized, since all of the accounts were linked to them both, all of the shops were in reality in both of their names as an equal liability partnership, they could both go to jail for what they believed the other man had done.

The case against George, as the District Attorney's office described it, was that in order to open the final shop, George had needed to resort to illegal activity in order to best his business partner once again.

The same office, though through the mouth of a different assistant DA, stated that John had resorted to stealing the cars, using the drivers and trucks of the business his brother-in-law founded in order to try to even the score and one up his partner once again.

In the end, though, the judge on each case had allowed both men to enter a plea of no contest and also avoid prison time, provided that, in each of their separate trials, they paid the maximum penalty, $15,000 per count, for each of the stolen vehicles, 82 in total.

So, the state of New Jersey was able to rake in about $1.2 million from each man, and then was able to avoid paying for his room and board for the next 246 years, if they received the minimum three year sentence for each count of grand theft.

All in all, it was a pretty good day for the state.

Unfortunately, both George and John had been forced to sell all of their shops in order to pay the fine, along with the hefty lawyer's fees. It was unfortunate for Not and Donny, and all the other driver's as well because even if the shops had been able to remain open, they would all likely have been unemployed anyway because they had all been called to testify in court that the towing orders had come directly from the top.

They had all been called, but Not had been the only one to show up.

Not had been the only one to show up, because Not was the only one in custody.

Not was the only one who had been caught hooking up a brand new E class from the parking lot of the hospital, where several months later he would be selling his plasma so he could afford to treat his dad to pizza, with what the public defender later told him was "intent to intentionally, and permanently, deprive the owner of its use."

The PD had also informed him the police had received an anonymous tip that the car was being stolen. The tipster had even provided the time, location, and physical description of both the thief and the tow truck being used.

Donny had denied the tip had come from him.

But, he always had a fuck you smile on his face when he said it.

"YOU DON'T think they knew it was going on?" Joe asked.

"No," Donny said before Not could answer. "Not got arrested because someone called it in. My take on it was George, one of the owners, was trying to set up John, the other owner, or the other way around. Not still thinks, despite the fact it makes absolutely no sense, that I called the cops on him."

"John and George didn't even know my name," Not said. "John's lawyer told my PD that John had no idea I even worked for him, so how did he give the cops a description of me, Donny?"

"So, it was George then," Donny agreed. "Anyways, it doesn't make any sense for it to be me, Not. I mean, what would I gain?"

Not stayed silent, because it was actually a pretty good point.

It only made sense for Donny to be a rat if he were in on the theft, but if he was in on the theft, then why get it busted? It was working, they were apparently getting away with it, and it didn't profit anyone but the state of New Jersey to put a stop to it, and Donny wasn't civic minded.

Donny had also provided a statement on Not's behalf -- well, on behalf of all the drivers he had scheduled -- saying there was no way that Not had any idea of what he was doing was

70

illegal. That Not had been, as far as he knew, simply been doing the job for which he had been hired.

So, when John and George pled no contest, Not had been compelled to appear before the court, swear to the best of his knowledge no one but John and George had any knowledge of the finances and operations of the shops, and then all charges against Not were dropped.

It had taken, in total, just under thirty days.

It had also poisoned Not's name to any possible new employers.

He had dropped application after application on the desk of every shop manager he could find, but the trial had been widely publicized. Not's name, both his preferred and his given, tended to be memorable.

He was never sure if it was his having been labeled a thief, a rat, or a dupe which had worked so hard against him.

Whichever it was, it had been effective.

He had burned through his down payment savings in about three months, then started selling stuff and had been able to stretch it for another two months. Then, seven months ago he had been forced to admit defeat and move back in with his dad.

Now, on his first day of employment once again, albeit a weird day already, here was Donny to make things even stranger.

"So, where am I headed with this?" Not asked, wanting to change the subject from the past.

"Can your shop store it for the night?" Joe directed. "We'll take care of it in the morning."

"I don't think our insurance will cover-" Not started.

"There won't be anything inside," Donny spoke up, and earned a glare from Joe.

"We'll need to make a stop on the way and switch over the load," Joe said, trying to stifle a yawn. "Just start heading for Main down Passaic. I'll tell you where to turn. It's been a long day of shit going wrong, and I would just like to be done with it."

"I second that," said Donny.

Strangely, to Not's ears it sounded like Donny was trying to stifle a giggle when he said it.

"HERE?" NOT asked, unable to keep the incredulity from his voice.

"Donny, you sign off on the paperwork for the ride," Joe said as soon as Not pulled the parking brake. "I'll take care of the rental."

Donny opened the door and hopped out to let Joe climb down and head for the warmth of the office.

"Invoice about the same as ours?" Donny asked.

"Only difference is the name at the top," Not agreed. "The board is under your seat there."

Not climbed down and began to work the lever controls on the side of the truck, first sliding the long bed back several feet, so when the bed tilted up, the very back edge would be resting on the ground. As per Joe's instructions, Not got ready to tilt the truck, but not to drop it off yet.

The phone in his pocket began to ring, the same almost-flamenco tune Josue had tried so hard to avoid this morning. Not pulled his left glove off with his teeth, keeping his right hand on the control lever, and fished the phone from his pocket. He caught his glove in with the inside of his elbow, cradling it like a football, and thumbed the touchscreen on the little green box with an outdated image of a telephone receiver on it.

"Hello?" he answered, hoping it was not Josue's wife.

"Not?" came the voice of the man who had interviewed him just the day before. "Paul Alto here. Did I catch you at a bad time?"

Not, his attention divided between the phone and the truck, had brought the end of the bed down too hard and banged it against the cold concrete. The armored truck, still secured in place on the bed, rocked on its springs adding a bit to the noise.

"No sir, on a pick up now and then headed for our lot. Dropping off, then headed back out," he added to make sure Alto knew Not was still working.

"Appreciate you putting in the extra hours, especially on your first day," Alto said, sounding genuinely thankful. "Have you had dinner yet?"

"Not really, sir," said Not, thinking of his other two chicken sandwiches, which he had given to Joe and Donny. Really, he had offered one to Joe, but there was another sandwich in the bag and there was Donny sitting right there.

Not couldn't bring himself to be that much of a dick.

"Alright, well, after this call, check in with the local PD by radio, tell them the big truck is 10-17 for the next hour or so, but all the others are running, okay?"

"Okay," Not agreed.

"Then come on back to Josue's place, I'm frying up some chicken, should be ready by the time you get here."

"Uh, okay," Not managed. "Um, thanks."

"Thank you!" Alto returned. "See you soon."

Not thumbed the little red "end" button on the touchscreen, and dropped the phone back in his pocket.

"Hey, I used your training as an excuse to bang an employee's wife, then we got in a fight about it and got arrested," Not mumbled to himself. "How about some chicken? Yeah, sure. Why not?"

IT HAD taken all of ten more minutes to finish unloading the armored truck. Joe had backed up a box truck to the tail end of the tow. Rolling up the rear door, Joe unfolded two aluminum cargo ramps, and placed them from the rear bumper of the armored truck to the inside floor of the rental.

After a quick look around, Joe quickly opened the rear lock of the armored truck and popped inside. His head popped out again moments later, again scanning the surroundings, before he quickly ducked back inside and a hand cart with a large blue barrel strapped to it emerged from the open door. Joe muscled it down the edge of the armored truck and onto the ramps. From there, it was more a matter of holding the barrel back from rolling freely down the ramps. Not watched as Joe returned from the back of the rental truck and repeated the whole routine again. When all was secured inside the new truck, Joe re-secured the door of the armored, rolled down the door of the rental, and slammed the latch closed. He didn't even bother to put a lock on it, Not noticed.

He briefly wondered what the hell a person would transport in blue barrels which would require an armored car, but could just as easily be transported in an unlocked rental truck. Maybe they were decoys or something. Maybe it was a training day for Donny, too.

Donny had completed the paperwork and signed where he was supposed to before Not had finished putting the truck bed back into place. He handed the clipboard to Not, and then joined Joe inside.

Whatever it was, he shrugged, it was no longer his problem.

"It was good to see you, Not," Donny had said before disappearing into the little cab of the rented truck.

"Take it easy, Donny," Not returned.

Fifteen minutes later, he left the disabled truck at the shop. Not decided to put it in bay number 1, since the mechanics had already clocked out for the day. He thought it might attract the wrong kind of attention sitting in the open lot in back.

Unattended armored trucks seem like they would be a magnet for a certain kind of person.

After a quick piss, and a cup of coffee to go, Not was heading once more for the Cedar Lane Bridge and back to Teaneck.

This time, at least, there would be chicken.

Chapter 7

TRAFFIC HAD sucked getting through Paramus, but once they had crossed into New York, the cars had thinned out.

At least, they had for a little while.

Just outside of a little town called Sloatsburg, whose name only showed up on the GPS if you zoomed in to the point you could see houses and cars on the satellite imagery, all three lanes came to a standstill.

Donny and the fat, older guard were in the rental truck in the number two lane, but Topher had been in the three lane trying to get around an ancient AMC Eagle, stricken with such a malignant case of road-salt cancer Topher was surprised the highway speeds didn't simply shake the thing to pieces.

He had been signaling to return to the two lane when the car in front of him had flared his brakes, and stopped hard. Topher was able to wrangle the Shit Heap to a stop a foot short of rear-ending the guy.

All three lanes were stopped, but the road ahead curved to the right, around a rest stop, and he couldn't see what was holding up the show.

The engine of the Shit Heap had started to rattle and gasp, a charming idiosyncrasy Donny had failed to mention when he had left in the driveway that morning, pissing off all of the tenants of the front house when they had all tried to leave for the day a mere hour after Topher had at last fallen asleep. It had turned out the old Shit Heap had a tendency to stall whenever its gluttonous intake of fuel was even slightly interrupted.

He had stalled it out twice just trying to get out of his own neighborhood that afternoon.

Topher had learned quickly that if he needed to be stopped, but not stalled, he had to slip the transmission into neutral and keep his foot gently on the gas.

The Shit Heap had turned out to be an early eighties American-made pickup with weather faded camper shell covering the bed. The paint around the wheel wells was beginning to bubble out, but seemed to be caked into place with decades of mud.

It had been someone's weekend truck, Topher had figured, used for heading up into the mountains during deer season, and hauling a bass boat during the summer.

The miles were still in the low hundreds, unless this was its second trip around the clock, but it sure didn't sound like a new engine or even a rebuilt and there was no way a nearly forty year old truck was a daily driver.

Like every old truck Topher had ever been in, it smelled like spilled transmission fluid, gear oil, and layer after layer of dust. The springs of the bench seat sagged, and the heater rattled like the blower fan was coming loose, but at least the heater worked and the engine had some muscle when Topher stomped on the gas.

It just didn't do so well when sitting still.

Topher wasn't doing so well sitting still either.

Blue barrels.

Who the hell transported gold in blue barrels?

Topher had watched from down the block, having followed Donny in the Shit Heap from the moment they drove out of the armored service lot. He had pulled into the parking lot of the Thai food place when they had gone into the chemical plant; the GPS map on his phone had confirmed they would have to come out the same way.

A chemical plant.

Topher had found their homepage while waiting for Donny to come out again.

The company made polymers, and food additives, and something called surfactants. Topher had snooped for a few minutes, tried every tab and menu, and could find nothing about gold or diamonds, or anything else which would be of any value to them.

Maybe if they owned a polyurethane factory, or were in need of industrial amounts of dietary supplements.

Later, after the breakdown, he had parked up the block, and watched as the other guard and looked around, paranoid, while he switched the two barrels to the back of the truck.

Who hires an armored truck to haul two barrels of food additives. Or polymers? Or surfactants, whatever the hell they were?

They wouldn't if it weren't worth it to them, but the question was: would it be worth anything to Donny and Topher?

After a few minutes, his lane began to creep forward.

Topher still couldn't see what the hold-up was, but at least they were moving again.

Then stopped again.

The car in front of the Shit Heap moved forward about a yard and then slammed on the breaks once more. Topher had just put the transmission back into drive, his foot still on the gas, and then surged forward only to immediately slam on the brakes to prevent himself from again nearly rear-ending the car in front of him.

The Shit Heap again gasped and struggled and threatened to stall, so Topher returned the shift indicator over the N, and gently replaced his foot on the gas.

Less than a minute later the whole slapstick routine happened again.

And then again.

And again.

It wasn't until nearly the fifth or sixth cycle of this frustration, and Topher noticed he had pulled up even with the rental truck.

The number two and one lanes had not moved an inch. Whatever was holding up traffic ahead, people were able to edge around it on the left, but it was blocking the middle and right lanes completely.

Fuck me, thought Topher, *I can't get ahead of him. I don't know where the fuck I'm going.*

The Shit Heap had pulled up completely even, cab to cab, with the rental truck now. Topher kept his eyes on the tail lights of the car ahead of him.

Don't look at me.

You cocksucker, don't look at me.

You know you can't keep a straight face.

It's exactly why I stopped taking you to Atlantic City, so don't you look at me.

Goddamnit, you're looking at me, I can feel it.

Topher glanced over at Donny, and sure enough Donny was staring at Topher with an enormous toothy grin just begging to be slapped off of his face.

Topher jerked his eyes back to the tail lights ahead of him.

If Donny had still been driving the armored, it wouldn't have mattered. The other guy would have been in the back with the barrels.

Instead, now, the guy was sitting shotgun right next to Donny, who was grinning like the cat who had somehow managed to bang the canary. The other guard is going to notice and after seeing such a fucked up grin and he'll *have* to ask.

Sure, Donny will cover with some line of bullshit -- he'll cover himself anyway, he's good at covering his own ass -- but the other guard will no doubt see Topher.

He'll see and he'll remember him.

The tail lights moved forward another yard, and Topher very nearly made the mistake to follow suit again before he realized he had a solution to the problem.

He dropped the Shit Heap into gear, and moved his foot to the brake pedal instead. The engine began to choke and rattle, the whole truck seemed to shake a bit, before it very quickly fell silent. All of the idiot lights on the dashboard lit up, and he saw the reflection of his headlights on the bumper in front of him dim a bit.

The car ahead of him moved forward another yard, but the Shit Heap remained inert.

Unfortunately, Donny was not taking the hint yet.

The car ahead moved forward another yard, and still the Shit Heap remained still.

The car behind him, reduced to a pair of overly bright halogen bulbs in the side view mirror from Topher's perspective, began to lay on the horn.

Topher reached under the steering column and pulled the knob to flip on the hazard lights.

The car ahead lurched forward once more, leaving almost a full car length ahead empty behind him, but Donny was still just sitting there.

Topher risked another glance over and saw Donny was no longer looking at him but appeared to be instead arguing with the other guard in the cab. Donny was waving his hands toward the car in front of the box truck, and then held them apart about a foot.

He didn't have enough room.

Topher and the Shit Heap had boxed them in.

God. Damn. It.

Topher dropped the tranny into neutral again, and cranked the engine, and pumped the gas pedal until the big eight cylinder roared to life again. Topher revved the engine high and loud for a few seconds, until he was sure he had gotten Donny's attention.

He raced the engine again, then let it drop down, and a second time, then down, on the third Topher dropped the transmission into drive and heard a worrisome clunk before the old truck threw itself forward. The Shit Heap covered the gap which had grown between it and the car in front alarmingly quickly, and Topher had to slam his foot down on the brake once again to avoid the accident.

Shit Heap stalled again, though this time accidentally.

Topher heard a horn behind him, and glanced at the passenger side mirror. The only thing visible was the side of the rental truck.

Donny had jumped into the gap made by Topher and Shit Heap's great leap forward, much to the dismay of the owner of the overly bright halogen headlamps. Said owner of those headlamps was currently expressing his opinion of Donny's actions through a healthy dose of horn.

If it had been summer, and thus warm enough to comfortably have the window open, the driver of the other car would likely have been seasoning the horn with sprinklings of profanity as well, but things being what they were, the plain old horn would have to do.

It was too cold for cursing.

No doubt now the other guy with Donny would see the truck, and would probably remember it, after all the noise and commotion, but he wouldn't be able to see Topher's face at least.

Hopefully, though, Donny would signal early so Topher could follow from in front.

Topher pushed in the hazard knob, and the steady click/pulse of the blinkers ceased. He dropped the transmission back into neutral and got the Shit Heap running again. There was some resistance this time, though.

The sudden drop into drive had not done the aged transmission any favors.

When it was time to edge forward again, the lever didn't want to move at first. Topher had to wiggle it up and down a little before the indicator slid back onto the D. Topher decided he would just keep it in drive, and use both feet.

Not recommended for an automatic, but it seemed like a safer bet than chancing the transmission locking up on him. He had probably sheared some teeth off of a gear. Not good, but maybe if he could keep the truck running for a while, the broken bits would work their way down to the bottom of the pan.

Topher had driven his share of run down cars, and more than one had a worn out tranny. The bits of metal in there would circulate through, wearing down the other gears, and eventually tear the whole thing apart from the inside, but it could still drive for hundreds, maybe thousands of miles before it happened.

He hoped they weren't going to go much further tonight.

Chapter 8

SWEET FUCKING Christ it was awkward.

At least the kids had already eaten and been excused to their rooms by the time Not had arrived.

He was thankful for that.

If there was anything which would have made the dinner with his new boss, his new boss' lover, and her husband, who also happened to be his new supervisor, who had all been in the backs of separate squad cars as a result of some sort of domestic disturbance mere hours before, if *anything* could make it more awkward, it would have been to also have their kids at the table.

They were situated around a small square wooden table, tucked in the rear of the rear of the kitchen, which looked out on a snow covered backyard.

Josue and Sophia's children were apparently more of the indoor type, as the snow in the back appeared to be pristine. No evidence of a snowman, sleds, or other wintertime amusements.

At the moment, though, the great outdoors looked like a far warmer atmosphere than the small, cozy kitchen.

Josue and Sophia sat opposite each other and Not sat opposite of Mr. Alto. Each had a plate heaped with roasted red potatoes, some kind of green bean casserole, and an enormous fried chicken breast still on the ribs.

All but Not had a large glass of wine, each filled to nearly spilling, and two other empty bottles stood on the counter near the sink.

The chicken smelled good though.

"I suppose we owe you an explanation," Alto began after only a couple of bites of his dinner.

"No," Not nearly shouted. "Honestly, sir, it is not necessary."

"Well, be that as it may," Alto continued. "I am going to offer one anyway, if only because I don't want to lose you over this. You came through today above and beyond expectations, and I don't want to . . . "

Alto seemed to falter for words, his previous outward confidence slightly diminished.

"He doesn't want our personal shit to fuck up his business shit," Josue finished for him, and then took a gulp of his wine.

"Not quite the way I would put it," Alto nodded, "but the sentiment is about right. I made a mistake today, Not."

"*We* made a mistake," Sophia Viejo said, speaking up for the first time since saying hello to Not when he arrived. The volume and timbre of her voice gave a good indication where most of the other two bottles of wine had gone.

Josue said nothing, but took another sip of his wine.

He stared at his wife from over the rim, but Not did not think it was with anger or contempt. Josue looked at his wife the way a child looks at an ice cream fallen off the cone.

There was obvious desire there, but it was a calculating desire.

Like, it was obvious the scoop had fallen, and there was no way to get it *all* back on the cone, but you could, like, scrape most of it back onto the cone and just leave the dirty part on the ground.

Like, if you moved fast enough, you still might be able to salvage some of sweetness before it melted away.

Not did not think though, in a situation such as this, the five-second-rule would apply.

He didn't think Josue did either, for desire was not the only emotion in his gaze. There was sadness and disappointment, too, but also a kind of reluctant acceptance; a look of inevitable loss.

"I know this doesn't make it any better, but maybe it might make things a little easier to understand if you knew Sophia and I used to be married."

"Twelve years, Paul," Josue nearly spat. "It's been--"

"Not an excuse," Alto said, holding up his fork and knife in a gesture of surrender. "Just a bit of history."

"Whatever," Josue said, and took another swig of wine.

Sophia said nothing and avoided eye contact with everyone by simply staring at her plate.

"She left me," Alto continued, then added quickly, "and yes, she did leave me for Josue."

Josue and Sophia both appeared ready to refute this claim as well, with fists again if necessary.

"They were not having an affair," Alto said, before they could object. "Let there be no doubt about who the better man is at this table, Not, it is Josue."

He paused to allow them to raise any further objections, but none came.

"I was gone a lot, Sophia was around the office a lot more back then, and, well, they got close," Alto continued, though it was unclear if it was more for Not's benefit, or his own. "She left because, well, I'm the first to admit I have no end of shortcomings."

Alto paused there for a beat. Not thought he was maybe hoping Sophia might correct him, maybe say she was also at fault for their split, or maybe just tell him he had some good qualities too.

The silence dragged on into uncomfortable.

"I, uh, didn't know any of that," Not said lamely, breaking the silence.

"No reason why you should," Alto said with a kind smile. "Anyway, I tried to catch Josue this morning before he left, to talk some business, not important now, but when Sophia opened the door, well, it, what I mean to say is, I, um--"

"It brought up a lot of old feelings," Sophia spoke up. "For us both."

"What happened today should not have happened," Alto said, casting a grateful glance at Sophia. "And, I think Josue acted as any husband would act in such circumstances, regardless of the motivations."

"Okay," Not said, unsure of what he should be saying now, but aware that Alto was addressing him, but really speaking to the rest of the table.

"What I need to know from you Not is did I just lose a good employee, or can you still work for me?"

Before he answered, Not looked to Josue.

True, they hadn't known each other long, and there was no reason at all so seek his approval before answering, but regardless Not felt to accept without at least an acknowledgement would somehow be a betrayal.

Josue offered the most slight of shrugs, conveyed through a miniscule elevation of his shoulders, but it was enough to make it clear whatever answer Not gave would not be held against him by Josue.

"Uh, yeah, I can do it," Not said.

"Good," Mr. Alto said, and offered Not a kind but guilty smile. He reached into his pants pocket, and pulled out a thick money clip. He flipped five bills off the stack, paused and seemed to run a few calculations in his head, and then flipped off five more bills.

They were all hundreds.

"I don't like to do this to you, Not," Mr. Alto said, still with kind but guilty smile. "But, we still have some personal business to sort out here tonight."

"But, the big truck needs to keep rolling," Josue jumped in. "Any other week, it wouldn't be a big deal, but if we leave the city hanging, then we get bumped from the rotation for the rest of the year."

Alto slid a thousand dollars across the table to Not.

"This is a bonus," he said. "You stay on the clock, and I will cover every hour of overtime you put in tonight."

Not pushed the money back across the table, but cut off Alto's stricken expression, "You don't owe me a bonus. I can keep rolling until you or Josue can sub me out."

"What did I tell you?" Josue said to Alto. "You hit the jackpot on this kid."

Alto nodded to Josue, and then turned his kindly, but slightly embarrassed smile back to Not.

"Take the money, Not," Alto said, sliding the cash back across the table. "It will let Josue and I take our time and talk without a nagging conscience."

Not looked over at Josue, who smiled and gave him a slight nod. Not shrugged, and folded the bills and tucked them into his front pocket.

"You still got my phone?" Josue asked.

"Yeah, in my jacket," Not assured him.

"Good," Josue said. "I'll call when we're done here, and take over for you. Alto will take the morning shift tomorrow, so you can sleep in and take the four to midnight.

Tomorrow, take some of Alto's cash and buy yourself your own phone, okay?"

"Will do," Not said, and stood from the table.

Alto, who had been looking sadly at Sophia, quickly turned his gaze down at his hands when he caught Not looking at him. Sophia seemed focused on the plate before her, and did not bother to say goodbye to Not.

Josue had seen Not taking all this in, and offered another small shrug, as if to say, yeah it sucks, but what can you do?

Not returned to the big truck, and started the big diesel up to warm. He pulled the card with the police codes out and scanned to see what would come after a 10-17, "meal stop." He couldn't find one for "meal finished." Finally, he opted for 10-8 "In Service," and keyed the button on the mike, identified as Alto's All Tow Big Truck, and called in the code.

"10-4 Alto, we have no 10-43 calls at this time," the radio blurted back, then returned to the quiet static hiss. The truck was warm enough now to warrant removing his gloves, which Not did, and then headed back to cruise the turnpike for breakdowns and abandoned vehicles.

Not fantasized about a one car collision. Maybe a patch of black ice, or swerved to avoid a dog in the road. The car would be totaled, of course, but a good kind of totaled. The kind when the driver had been wearing her seatbelt and the airbags deployed just right, so although her heart racing a mile a minute, she would be able to walk away unharmed, and perhaps simply thrilled to be alive.

The heater in her car would no longer be functioning, not with a totaled engine, so she would be shivering when Not arrived. He would help her into the warm cab of the truck, and crank the heater up high so she could warm up, while he loaded her totaled car onto his flatbed.

By the time he came back, the cab would be so hot she had removed her heavy coat to reveal a slender but shapely form, a thin snug red cashmere sweater hiding none of her curves. The cross-chest strap of the seat belt pressing the soft material of the sweater down into the valley of her breasts. She would look over at Not, her bright blue eyes contrasting against her black hair, making them appear larger than they were, almost startled, but not quite. Excited, was more accurate, and her smile. . .

"10-43 on the Southbound 17, just north of Rochelle, Alto please respond. Repeat, 10-43 on Southbound 17, just north of Rochelle, Alto please respond."

"This is Alto's, uh," Not fumbled for the code card and scanned it quickly. Near the top of the list he found "go ahead with message." "Again, uh, this is Alto, uh, 10-3."

"There is a disabled vehicle on the shoulder. May have a broken axle, so flatbed is advised."

"10-4," said Not. "Alto is rolling."

Chapter 9

IN THE end, Donny was a little disappointed in how easy it had been.

After the back-up near the rest area -- caused, he had found out when they finally passed the accident, by a semi-truck which had attempted to cut across all three lanes as it came directly off the rest-stop on-ramp and back onto the road -- where two cars, in the middle and right hand lanes, had plowed right into the truck, stopping it before it had been able to block off all three lanes, thank god.

They had left the last of the city behind for a while, and were now surrounded on all sides by white light reflected off the snow and pure darkness where the light would not reach.

Topher had gone to the far right lane as soon as he had been able, which had allowed Donny to take the lead once again. He kept the pace right around the speed limit, and pretty much lived in the center lane.

On the rare occasion he did need to pass someone, it was always on the left side, and he always signaled first.

He even kept his hands at ten and two.

At Harriman, he merged onto the 17 West, and considered pulling into the outlet mall, but then decided against it. There were a lot more people there, and the chances were high that Topher would not be able to find a parking place near enough to the truck.

"I see restaurants up ahead," Joe pointed out from the passenger seat toward several large signs beaconing drivers to a variety of chain restaurants. "Buy you a burger and a beer?"

"You serious?" Donny asked.

"We're still a couple hours away, you said, right?" Joe persuaded. "We'll get some mints at the counter. Come on, one beer won't kill us."

"I figured you would want to hit a drive-through," Donny wondered if he was pushing his luck.

"Just park it where we can see it," Joe shrugged. "To be honest, I actually feel like we have less of a target on our backs in this thing. It looks like we're just moving some furniture or something. Even if someone did open the back, what we got doesn't look worth stealing."

Unfortunately, Donny had to agree with the last statement. He had been watching in the sideview mirrors like a hawk while filling out the insurance forms, hoping for a glimpse of something glittery.

Though he didn't know it, his thoughts had echoed Topher's almost word for word.

Who the hell transported gold in blue barrels? The answer, as far as he could tell was fairly obvious: no one did.

So, what exactly were they trying to steal?

Was it still worth it?

It had to be worth it. No one hired an armored car to transport something not valuable.

It just didn't make sense.

It was like having UPS deliver your dirty laundry to the laundromat.

It was worth something to someone.

"Burger and a beer sounds good," was all Donny said out loud.

He put his indicator on plenty early, to make sure Topher had ample notice to follow.

In the parking lot, he circled once to see which windows would be facing the parking lot. Then he chose a space dead center of visibility. He pulled the truck straight through the space, so it ended up nose out of the parking spot, and facing the building. Ostensibly, this gave them full vantage of their truck while inside, but in reality created a perfect blind spot at the rear of the truck.

If they sat at a table directly in front of the truck, they would be able to see the front of the truck completely, but very little of what was directly behind it. If Topher was smart, he would be able to take the old camper truck, bought from the front lawn of a foothill trailer dwelling just across the border in the Keystone State, back it right up to the rear of the rental truck and be nearly invisible from the restaurant.

So long as he didn't bounce around too much while moving the stuff out, Joe might never even see he was there.

"Nice spot," Joe approved. "Why don't you stay here while I get us a table at the window. I'll wave you in when I'm seated."

"Mind if I wait outside?" Donny asked, with just the right amount of embarrassed sheepishness.

"Why, oh," Joe nodded. "Yeah, fine, you fucking junkie. Have another smoke."

The door hinge creaked and squalled when Joe swung it open, and Donny felt the truck shift a bit from side to side as Joe's weight shifted out of it.

"Keep your jacket on inside, okay?" Donny cautioned. "If people see the uniform, they start to look for the truck."

"Not a bad idea, Don," Joe nodded. "Have your smoke if you're gonna. I'll get the beers."

Donny pulled the pack, now more than half-empty, from his jacket pocket. He pinched the edge of the filter with his teeth, and pulled into his lips in a manner which always reminded him of a horse eating a carrot. He pulled the glove free from his left hand and retrieved the cheap gas station lighter from his pocket, sparked the wheel, and lit up in one fluid upward motion of the arm. A trick he had perfected in high school, and one which was apparently ingrained into his muscle memory even after a long year of being tobacco free.

Donny tucked the lighter into the empty space of the pack, and stuffed both back into his pocket. Jetting the smoke from both nostrils, he tugged his glove back onto his hand, which was already stinging from the cold, and scanned the parking lot for Topher and the Shit Heap truck with the Pennsylvania plates.

He heard Topher's approach before he was able to see him. The rough gargle of the old eight cylinder, likely with a hole or two in the exhaust somewhere to give it such a hot, wet, chili-fart sound, approached from the row behind him, almost in sync with Joe walking through the door.

Topher had been watching from a safe distance, apparently.

Donny watched as Topher pulled the old truck to a stop with his rear bumper just beyond the line of the vacant parking space behind the box truck. The truck stayed motionless for a few seconds, long enough for Donny to take in and exhale another drag on the cigarette.

A worrisome muffled grinding sound came from underneath the old truck, like an eggbeater on high hitting against the edge of a heavy plastic bowl. Then the reverse lights flashed on, and Topher swung the truck back into the space, perfectly between the parallel lines on the first try.

Donny heard the telltale squeal of the driver's door swinging open.

"Not yet," Donny called quietly, with the cigarette up and covering his mouth. "Wait until I'm inside. You'll be able to see me through the window. The center table. Try not to bounce the truck around."

"No shit," Topher called back, and then Donny heard the door slam shut.

Joe appeared in the window and waved at Donny to come in. Joe forked the first two fingers on his right hand, and pointed them at his eyes and then at the truck.

The message was clear enough.

Donny gave a short wave back, and flicked his cigarette across the parking lot, where it fizzled out in a dirty bank of plowed snow near the concrete base of a lamp pole. Donny trotted carefully across the lot, keeping his eyes peeled for any slippery looking patches.

Inside the restaurant was hot, and Donny nearly peeled his jacket right off, although he had just warned Joe against doing exactly that. The hostess, a high school girl who was not yet old enough to serve booze and thus not old enough to be a waitress, began to gather some menus, and looked behind him to see if more would be coming.

"My friend is already at a table," Donny said, and walked past the girl without breaking his stride.

He wanted to see if the old truck was visible from the window.

More importantly, he wanted to see if Topher was visible from the window.

Donny let out a short sigh of relief as he approached Joe at the table, who was scanning the menu in front of him, rather than keeping his eyes on the truck. Even better, the old Shit Heap could not be seen at all from this vantage point.

"Do they make tacos here?" Joe inquired as Donny sat down.

"Why would you get tacos at a burger place?" Donny asked.

"It's not a burger place," Joe said, and displayed the front of the menu to Donny. "It's a casual dining bar and grill."

"And why does that mean they serve tacos?"

"Because this is America and everybody serves tacos," Joe declared, and returned to searching his menu.

"Well, I don't see tacos anywhere," Donny said, looking through his own menu. "But, I do see a whole page dedicated to burgers, you know, at this non-burger joint."

"Eat a dick, Don," Joe said, though his tone was as casual as the atmosphere of the restaurant.

"Hmm," Donny said, flipped through the menu with exaggerated effort. "Does not appear to be on the menu either."

"Uh-huh, fuck you, Don," Joe said, as if he were asking for Donny to pass the salt.

"Not even with a borrowed dick, my friend," Donny replied. He risked a glance out at the truck, and saw the box shift, just slightly, from side to side. "Maybe they've got nachos. Did you check the appetizers?"

Joe flipped back to the front of the menu again and scanned the Starters column.

"No, but they do have buffalo wings," Joe said thoughtfully. "Might be good too."

Donny chanced another glance out the window and saw the Shit Heap creeping down the aisle of the mostly empty parking lot, the bed of the old truck sagging noticeably over the rear wheels.

They hadn't even ordered yet and the job was done.

"Why don't we skip the appetizers so we can get back on the road," Donny said, as the waiter approached with two tall glass mugs of beer. "Okay with you, Joe?"

"Yeah," Joe nodded. "I suppose you're right. We still have a long way to go tonight, don't we?"

"Good evening, gentlemen," the waiter said as he set the drinks down in front of them. "My name is Ethan, and I will be your server this evening. Can I get you started with something from our Starters menu? Maybe some wings or mozzarella sticks?"

"I think we'll skip the wings tonight, thanks," Donny said.

"Great!" Ethan said, as if he would have secretly been disappointed in them if the answer had been anything else. "We do have a couple of specials tonight not on the menu, one is the grilled steak tacos with black beans and roasted corn, and the other is a blackened tuna steak with your choice of two sides."

"Great!" Donny said, mocking the waiters tone. "Joe it looks like you get your tacos after all."

Things were working out for everybody tonight, Donny thought.

He followed Joe's lead and also ordered the steak tacos.

Turning his attention back to the window, he was just in time to see the camper shell of the old truck as it made its way back up the aisle and exit the lot.

Chapter 10

THE SHIT Heap was dying.

The barrel, full to the top of fuck knows what, had to weigh around 1000 pounds, so Topher had at least half of a ton of weight pushing down on the worn out springs, and across the long transaxle connecting the transmission to the rear wheel drive differential. It would have put a strain on even a new truck.

The Shit Heap was old.

Topher had tried to take the stop-and-go traffic slow and easy, but having to keep his foot on the gas meant he was putting a constant strain on the transmission.

It had started to slip out of gear when he was thirty minutes south of the New Jersey state line, not long after the 87 South had split into the 287. He had considered taking the 17 all the way through, but it would lead through towns, which meant stop lights and additional traffic.

Not to mention all the local cops who might notice the Pennsylvania plates and see it as an easy no contest ticket.

However, the 17 also would have had a lot of anonymous parking lots, restaurants and bars, where he could stash the old truck and come back with something better. Maybe rent a box truck like Donny and the other guard had done.

Instead, had ended up riding the 87 back for most of the trip, and he knew now it had been the right call. The road had been clear and quiet, and once he nursed the ailing Shit Heap up to a manageable speed, he had been able to cruise the longest part of the trip back without issue.

Just outside of Paramus, the population picked up and traffic had slowed to a crawl. Once again, Topher was constantly riding the gas and the brake to keep from stalling out. The sheet metal floor beneath the sagging bench seat was beginning to grow increasingly hot. It surely had been carpeted at one time, but the carpet and heat absorbing padding had long ago been worn through and then ripped out.

The heat was coming mainly from the curved hump which sloped down from the engine compartment wall below the dashboard. His leg had brushed against it and he had recoiled as if he had leaning against a furnace going full blast. Even with his pants between him and the metal, Topher was pretty sure he'd see a bright red, shiny patch of burned skin when he eventually shucked himself free of his trousers.

The transmission wouldn't last long at this temperature.

As he crept through Paramus, he heard the rpms rise and felt the truck paradoxically begin to slow.

The transmission had slipped out of gear.

He immediately grabbed the shift stalk on the side of the steering column and jammed it to neutral and back into the drive. The truck lurched and groaned as it slammed back into gear.

The Shit Heap shuddered again and again as it tried to shrug off the transmissions yoke and let the engine's horses run free as Topher crept closer to the Garden State Parkway. Each time, he reined in hard with the shifter, and kept the old beast moving.

He remembered there being a truck rental place on the near side of the parkway, just past the car dealerships. He could ditch the Shit Heap and switch the load to a new truck, and be home in time to see if he and Donny had made the ten o'clock news.

He could also take a few minutes to investigate just what the hell they had stolen as well.

The barrel was too big to stand upright in the bed of the truck, so he had been forced to lay it down and try to angle it into the bed beneath the camper top.

No matter which way he tried, Topher had only been able to fit one barrel in the bed of the truck.

Donny would be pissed, he was sure, but the fact was the barrels were too heavy to move without the handcarts, and on the handcarts only one would fit in the bed of the truck.

One would have to be enough.

Whatever was in there was liquid. Topher had been able to feel and hear it sloshing around as he moved it into the bed. There was a small cap on the top of the barrel, but if he pried it open when it was lying flat, then whatever was inside would start to pour out, so the investigation would need to wait until later. Given where it came from, maybe with gloves, goggles, and a facemask as well.

Topher had put on his signal to exit where the truck rental was, when he noticed the sign was not illuminated. He checked and the lights were off in the building as well.

The rental place was closed.

He switched off the blinker, and decided to press on. He dropped his speed to fifty as he passed under the parkway and kept a close eye on both the gauges and the side-view mirrors, the rearview having been rendered useless by the camper cab.

The transmission was concerning, but he also worried about overtaxing the engine. It might just overheat and boil over, or crack a hose.

It might also just catch fire.

God knew how many years of spilled or leaked oil was caked in around the engine compartment, just waiting to combust. True, it was winter time and the frigid winter air whipping past at 50 miles per hour was helping to keep the engine cool, but the way the transmission was heating up would make the weather moot pretty soon.

Heat, he knew, was caused by friction, and the greater the heat meant the greater the friction, which meant the engine was having to work harder to keep the transmission moving. Add the extra half-ton of weight riding in the back and this was likely harder than this poor old truck had had to work in twenty years.

Maybe ever.

Topher kept an eye on the temperature gauge, which was already running hot but not yet into the red. He wished he knew how the oil pressure was doing, but the needle for the gauge had fallen off and lay like a dead fly at the bottom of the glass.

Very hot and very cold was as much a recipe for metal fatigue, as was a sudden heavy strain after who knows how long of minimal use. Piston rings, head gaskets, belts, hoses, fuel lines, water pumps, all things Topher had been forced to replace in his own junkers over the years, were all possible killing blows to which the Shit Heap was prone in its current condition.

Hell, a breakdown right now wasn't just possible, it was extremely likely.

As was the possibility Donny and the other guard had finished their dinner, gotten to where they were going, and discovered they were one barrel short.

Had the other guard looked out the window of the restaurant and seen an old truck with a camper top parked behind their rental? Perhaps, he had looked up and seen the old truck pulling away. Or even was able to see the distinctive vintage blue and yellow Pennsylvania license plate as Topher slowly drove away up the nearly empty aisle of parking spaces.

He had, maybe, been too far away to be able to read the letters and numbers, but to be able to identify the state? Sure, it would have been no problem. The plate was easily visible on the bumper of the bed which was visibly sagging under a heavy load.

The other guard would know how heavy the barrels were; he had loaded them into the truck in the first place. Maybe he hadn't put it together at the time, but when they see they are missing a barrel, wouldn't the old truck with sagging bed, camper top, and Pennsylvania plate be the first vehicle to come to mind? With a description like that, you don't need to see the actual plate numbers.

So, Topher alternated from watching for red and yellow trouble lights on his dashboard, and red and blue trouble lights in his side-views.

He passed donut shops and coffee shops, and considered going inside to grab a sugary snack and a cup of caffeine. It would also give the engine a much needed chance to cool off.

He decided against it, though, because all of their lots faced the road.

Also, he was not confident if the shut off the Shit Heap's engine it would ever start up again.

Donny and the other guard might not have made it to their drop point yet, but maybe they had. The other guard might not have seen the old Shit Heap, but maybe he had. A BOLO alert, a term he had picked up from the countless cop shows of his youth, may not have gone out for an old truck with a sagging bed, camper top, and Pennsylvania plates.

Or, maybe it had.

In any case, he would rather be on the move and feeling like he was doing something, rather than sitting in a plastic booth, with a Boston Cream in his mouth and his thumb up his ass, when he saw the red and blue lights signaling he would very likely be a well-over-the-hill convicted felon before he ever felt his toes in the Florida sand again.

Such was his thinking as he passed the entrance for the enormous Plaza parking lot, a parking lot so huge and full he could probably lose the truck there until Spring, when the ancient struts, which had made a Herculean effort to keep the weight of the truck bed suspended above the rear wheels and axle, collapsed from the strain and brought the entire half ton plus of cargo and truck bed down onto the rear wheels, locking them in place.

If he had been parked, the noise and shock of the collapse would have been frightening.

At fifty miles an hour, it was fucking terrifying.

The rear wheels, no longer turning but instead wedged against the wheel -well by the weight of the truck and its cargo, screamed and smoked against the pavement. The transmission ripped itself out of gear with a shriek of metal being torn, and the engine roared toward the redline, no longer having to expend its energy to make all those other parts keep turning.

Topher was thrown forward, his chest smacking painfully onto the steering column, by the sudden deceleration. The barrel and handcart in the back slid forward, and slammed into the back of the truck cab, and despite the focus of his mind toward the task of attempting to steer the sudden skid toward the shoulder of the road, Topher briefly wondered if the barrel had cracked open and was currently spilling its mysterious but somehow valuable contents all over the dirty, rusty bed of the crippled Shit Heap.

The last five feet came in little hops, as the forward shift in weight made straight up the path of least resistance for the nearly exhausted forward momentum.

Either through skilled muscle memory resulting from years of winter driving in aging, beaten down cars, or through sheer blessed luck, Topher found he had steered the skid to the side of the road, rather than screaming to a stop in the center lane.

A cloud of thick white smoke enveloped the truck, and for a moment Topher wondered if the engine had caught fire after all. Then he caught a whiff of the stench which came with it, and realized it was from the burned rubber of the tires during the skid.

Topher could feel his heart pounding against his bruised chest, his arms and legs trembled from the insane amounts of adrenaline now flooding through his system. He was certain if he tried to stand, he would collapse on the side of the road, possibly in front of one of the other cars currently rocking the Shit Heap in their wake as they swept passed at seventy miles an hour.

So, he sat, and breathed, and waited for the moment to pass. Waited for the queasiness in his stomach to pass, and for his shoulders and neck to unclench. Waited for it to no longer feel like a possibility he would die of a heart attack, in his twenties, while in the midst of committing a felony.

Man, what a pussy way to go.

That thought, more than anything else, was the galvanizing force Topher needed. He felt the trembling, liquid feeling of his legs begin to fade away, and his heart, while still pounding hard, no longer hurt in his chest.

Okay, good deal, he thought. He would not die of fright, which was definitely a step in the right direction. However, the follow up question would now have to be considered: what should he do next?

Topher slid across the bench seat to the passenger side and looked out the window. The disabled Shit Heap was separated from the Plaza parking lot by a small greenbelt covered by at least two feet of road-dirty snow. Even if he could push the truck across the snowy belt, and try to hide it among the parked cars, he would leave tracks through the snow would lead right to where he parked it. A moot point, however, as he would not be able to push the truck in its current state even an inch.

Further back in the lot, separated from the mall itself, was a chain restaurant of some kind. Topher couldn't see the sign from where he was, so he wasn't sure which chain it was. However, he was sure it was warmer and safer than sitting in the cab of a disabled truck on the edge of a busy road, with stolen goods in the truck bed waiting for the first cop to blunder along and arrest him.

Hell, the restaurant probably had a bar, too.

The last point cinched it for Topher, and he climbed out of the passenger side, and began to trudge through the plow piled bank of filthy, crunchy snow toward the welcoming light of the restaurant.

He would order a drink, and call a tow company. If the tow company showed up before the cops, he would head back out to the truck.

If the cops came first, he would order another drink and call a cab instead.

He wondered if Donny had left anything in the glove box or anyplace else in the truck which could tie it back to him. Topher paused and looked back at the sad looking truck, its tail end down like a scolded dog, and considered going back to make sure it was clear.

He was certain *he* had not left anything in the truck, hadn't even touched the steering wheel or keys, which were still in the ignition, without his gloves on.

Donny had definitely touched the keys with his bare hands.

Topher had seen it himself this morning. Topher might have rubbed the prints off inadvertently with his gloves throughout the course of the day, but he had no idea what else Donny had touched with his bare hands in the truck.

Donny's prints were definitely on file too.

"Better hope the tow comes first, D," Topher mumbled to himself, and turned to resume plodding toward the restaurant and the bar inside.

He hoped it was a Mexican place.

He wanted a margarita.

Chapter 11

NOT HAD known a guy in school, Clint McCormick, who had tried to put an air cushion suspension in a 1949 Mercury.

Clint hadn't bothered with the math, though.

Like a kid, which he was, Clint had purchased the cheapest kit he could find; it happened to be out of the back of some Dominican guy's truck at a car show and swap meet near Newark, and then Clint had simply gone home, called his buddies, and gotten to work.

In one fairly busy afternoon, Clint and a few guys from the auto program, Not included, had removed all of the coil springs and struts from the rusted old Merc and swapped in what amounted to little more than four big tough balloons which, when filled completely, would keep the car riding at about the same height it had been before. The airbags were connected to an air compressor, four separate lines and regulators, courtesy of the same Dominican gentleman, which was mounted in the trunk and wired into a control panel under the dashboard.

Essentially, if the compressor was on it would fill the bags to maximum capacity, and the car would ride high. However, if some of the air was let out, which Clint could control via the three basic presets of high, mid, and low, on the control panel tethered under the dash, then the car would raise or lower to the appropriate pre-set height. If enough air was let out, the rusty old Merc would be throwing sparks from its underbelly as it scraped its exhaust system clean on the street below.

At least, that had been Clint's vision.

In reality, the system Clint had purchased had been intended for a much smaller vehicle, like a Civic or maybe a Mini Cooper. Something made of mostly plastic and fiberglass, rather than a ton and a half of Detroit rolling iron which was the 1949 Mercury.

To give manufacturer of the airbags their due, they had been able to last for nearly a quarter mile at more than triple their intended maximum load, if you also added the weight of the four teenage boys who had been inside, Not included.

Not had looked it up the following day, when it was already becoming a funny anecdote rather than a close brush with death.

They had made it out of Clint's driveway without incident, and once on the street, Clint had punched the mid-level button, and they had all howled like lunatics as they felt the slow drop elevator sensation when the bags lost some of their inflation. Thinking about it the next day, Not figured it was the probably the reduction in pressure which had allowed them to make as much distance as they had.

They made it over a couple of potholes, and giggled at the bobbing sensation of the car bouncing on the softened bags. The old Merc was ugly, the upholstery was threadbare and tattered. In fact, the front passenger seat was just exposed rusty springs covered with a pillow from Clint's bed. The last time the car had been painted was anyone's guess, along with what color the paint had been, as it had all flaked off long ago. The Merc was a motley urban camouflage of rust and primer.

It didn't matter to Clint, or, if he was going to be honest, to the rest of them either.

They had made a lowrider, and it worked.

Not still recalled it as one of the proudest moments of his life.

Of course, he also could testify why pride is counted among the seven deadly sins.

After much debate, they had decided it wasn't *only* the train tracks. It wasn't *only* doing nearly double the speed limit. It wasn't *only* Clint re-inflating the suspension to full to make sure they didn't bottom out going over the tracks.

But, put the three together . . .

They probably would have been okay if one, or even both, of the rear bags had burst. Hell, they probably would have just come to a screeching halt if all four bags had gone, but, as they learned very well, physics is all about action and reaction, cause and effect. The majority of the weight was in the front of the car, and it was the front which first went over the tracks.

The speed could be blamed for the front tires, just momentarily, leaving the pavements, and of course the camber of the road allowed the left tire to touch down just slightly before the right. For a split second, the left front tire, the driver's side tire, was holding up all the force the big car was pushing down toward the road.

The rest was just physics.

The strain was too much for the overtaxed suspension bag to take, so it had burst, dropping the frame of the Merc down onto the front left tire and locking it into place. The now stationary wheel squealed against the blacktop, and the friction pulled the car to the left, which of course was directly into oncoming traffic. Clint was powerless to steer, since the front tire was wedged tight against the wheel well, and the rear tires were still trying to push them forward.

If they had been in a smaller, lighter car, they might have flipped. The Mercury though was like an enormous clawfoot bathtub flipped onto its rim. It was large, wide, stable, and most of all heavy. It dragged its mass into the oncoming lane, leaving a thick back skid mark for about eight feet and then an inch deep gash, from when the tire gave up and ripped free of the rim, which ran for another five.

It could have been a bus. A bus definitely would have killed them. It could have been a delivery truck, a firetruck or ambulance, and they would have been dead. As it happened, they barely even felt it when the pizza guy hit them.

It was a compact, some French company Not had never heard of, and the driver had seen them coming, so he was able to decelerate significantly before the impact. Still, if it hadn't been for the airbag, the pizza guy would probably have died. Clint was able to shrug it off, saying it would have been the driver's fault, after all the guy hadn't been wearing his seatbelt.

The Mercury had ended up looking like something from an old cartoon. It's nose was burrowed into the pavement, when its engine stalled out a few minutes after the accident, they listened to the sphincter-tight, squeaky-fart sound of air escaping from the bags, and the rusted hulk had settled, sadly, to the pavement.

It was one of the few times Not was unable to avoid assigning human emotions to an inanimate object.

He had watched the old Merc sink down to the pavement with the cautious motions of a terminally ill patient who knew he would not be rising again.

It was the most pathetic thing he had ever seen on a road.

The truck in front of him was a very close second.

Not flipped on the yellow caution lights mounted to the top of the cab and brought the big truck to a stop on the shoulder in front of the old camper. He reversed into position, and then locked the parking brake in place and waggled the stick shift to make sure the truck was in neutral.

He pulled a large flashlight from beneath the driver's seat, and climbed out of the cab to see if the old thing would hold together if he tried to winch it up the bed. Not was also curious to shine the light through the window on the camper shell to see just what the hell the driver had put back there to totally destroy the rear suspension. Not doubted he would find an air compressor with hoses running into the floor of the bed, but who knew.

People did weird things with their cars.

The "window," he discovered upon closer inspection, was actually a thin sheet of particle board which had been covered in a layer of cheap plastic tint to give it the illusion of being glass.

He gave the handle a quick tug and confirmed it was locked.

Not checked the cab of the truck and found the keys were still in the ignition, and the interior was still warm, though it was cooling quickly. There was no sign of the driver anywhere, but the mall across the parking lot was the most likely destination for a stranded driver.

If he could find him -- Not assumed it was a him as it was difficult to imagine any woman who would choose to drive a vehicle like this -- then Not could save the guy and impound fee as well as an abandoned vehicle citation.

It seemed like the right thing to do, especially since the guy and probably just gone in to call for a tow.

Of course, Not didn't want to lose the fee, or mess up a call from the city either. The most prudent course of action, he concluded, would be to get the old pile of junk secure on the bed, and then wait a bit to see if the driver returned.

Thirty minutes, he decided.

If the driver hadn't come back in half-an-hour, then he probably wasn't coming back at all.

Not grabbed the winch chains and got to work.

Chapter 12

THE RESTAURANT turned out to be a Bubba
O'Riley's, a strange mix of traditional Irish and Appalachian
Redneck which on any other given night would have caused
Topher to turn right around and head back to his car to try again.

The bar, however, was fully stocked, mostly empty, and
it was the first thing he saw when he opened the front door.

Also, he reasoned to himself, say what you will for the
social drawbacks of either one of those particular cultures, those
motherfuckers knew how to *drink.*

Topher hurried over to the bar, and paced slowly
around it, letting his left hand graze the tops of the barstools like
his own private game of duck-duck-goose, until he found a stool
which allowed a view of the roof of the disabled Shit Heap
beyond the snowbank.

Behind the bar appeared to be unattended, and Topher
considered reaching across and helping himself. However, no
more than second after his ass touched seat, a middle aged man,
looking a bit out of place in the plain white t-shirt with rolled
sleeves and blue jeans with pegged cuffs -- the trademark
uniform of every Bubba O'Riley's nationwide -- emerged from
the kitchen with a tray of frosty beer mugs from the walk-in.

"Could be worse," the bartender said, likely reading
Topher's thoughts about the uniform from his face. "Could be a
kilt and a wife-beater, what can I get you?"

"Whatcha got that's big and strong?" Topher asked.

"I'm off at midnight," the bartender smiled. "I guess I
should have clarified, what do you want to drink?"

Normally, Topher would have flirted back, but tonight
he was just too exhausted. "How are your margaritas?"

"Shitty and bitter," the bartender grimaced. "The sour
mix they order sucks. You like sweet or spicy?"

"Sweet," said Topher without hesitation.

"Big, strong, and sweet," the bartender winked. "Can do."

Topher watched as the bartender went to work, pouring three different kinds of rum, curacao, vanilla vodka, ice, and heavy cream into a blender. The blender made short work of the ice, and within a minute, the bartender poured the frothy concoction into a frosty mug.

"It's called a 'banana sling,'" the bartender smiled. "You look like you'd be an island kind of guy if you ever got a vacation."

If his mouth were able to orgasm, Topher decided after his first sip, the drink would bring an instant climax.

"Good, right?" The bartender inquired.

"I think you just earned your biggest tip of the night," Topher affirmed.

"Just the tip?" The bartender pouted. "Tease."

The pout did it. Recognition washed over him and Topher was suddenly, just for a moment, eighteen again.

His first job out of high school was bouncing at a trendy gay bar in SoHo, campily titled The Closet. As the name implied, it catered to gay men who had not yet openly announced they were gay, and thus security and anonymity were the trademarks of the establishment. They even went so far as to provide Masques for those who were worried about a surreptitious snapshot -- although cameras were strictly forbidden once inside -- outing them in the office, at the dinner table, or, god-forbid, on the internet.

Topher had still possessed the chiseled, rock-hard Jersey shore V that a lot of football and very little studying had provided. There had been no shortage of guys hitting on him, and he had never gone to bed alone except for when he had wanted to.

However, not one of them had ever bought him a drink.

Not for lack of trying, of course, but for the simple fact the bartender knew exactly how old Topher was and refused to let him be served.

"Jim told me," the bartender had said, referring to the general manager of The Closet, "if he ever sees a drink in your hand he would fire us both, so please don't hate me."

Then, he had pouted.

It was an ain't-I-cute pout the bartender had given all the clients when he had to tell them their credit card had been declined, or he had to cut them off, or he was going to hang onto their keys for them but he would be happy to call them a cab.

It was the same well-rehearsed pout every time, and it was the same pout Topher had just seen for the first time in about five years.

"Goddamn, Sam," Topher cursed his bad luck. Now, he was sure to be remembered here. "How long have you been out of The Closet?"

"Ahhhhh!" Sam squealed with mock-delight. His voice rose in pitch and took on a movie-stereotyped swish "I have *never* heard that before, not *once* in all my years, not *one single person* ever thought up that horrendously obvious joke! You are so *original*! Are you a *comedian*? Are you going to be the new *Joe P--*"

"Okay, I got it, I'm sorry,"

"Just fuckin' with ya!" Sam smiled again, and his voice returned to normal. "It took you long enough to remember me. Am I really so forgettable? Anyway, it's nice to be able to finally serve you."

"I think this drink makes up for all the well-drinks--"

"And roofies!"

"And roofies, I missed out on years ago."

"My god, you were just a babe in the woods playing tough-guy so well I think even you believed it. You look like you've grown up some."

"I'd like to think so."

"What are we doing for work now?"

"We are still working security."

"Ah," said Sam with obvious disappointment.

"Oh, I'm sorry, does my vocation not meet up to the standards of the Bubba O'Riley's bartender?"

"Point taken," Sam conceded. "But I will admit I was hoping for more. You were a good kid, not stupid, hard worker. I guess I figured something better would have come along by now."

"Yeah," Topher shrugged, suddenly feeling very tired. "I guess I kinda did too."

He took another big gulp from his drink, and hoped it wasn't a large enough swallow to give him a brain freeze. It was eerie how closely Sam's assumption had echoed his own.

He *wasn't* stupid, and he *was* a hard worker.

It wasn't that he hadn't been looking for other jobs, but . . . well, looking for work was too much like work but for no paycheck. He worked hard for the job he had, but he never looked hard for the job he wanted. He had just sort of been waiting for something to come.

So, he had just kept waiting.

Of course, now, something had come and was currently sitting abandoned on the side of the turnpike, and here he was getting drunk, and maudlin, less than a hundred yards from his fortune and he hadn't even called a tow truck yet. He started to pull his phone from his pocket, and then thought better of it.

"Hey Sam, can I use the bar phone? I think my battery died when I was at the mall, and I need to call for a jump."

"I can give you a jump," Sam said coyly, then more seriously. "No foolin', though, I've got a set of cables in my trunk."

"Thanks, but the battery is only one possibility, to be honest," Topher gave a sheepish shrug. "I may need a tow."

"Sure thing," Sam said, laying a cordless receiver on the bar. "Of course, if you need a *ride* . . ."

"Yeah, thanks Romeo, I get it," Topher smiled in spite of himself. He pulled his phone out of his pocket, below the bar where he hoped Sam wouldn't see it, and opened his browser to search for local tow companies. He picked the number at the top of the list, and started to key it in on the bar phone

He slipped his phone back into his pocket and glanced out the window toward the immobile Shit Heap.

Flashing lights.

Shit, fuck, motherfuck, GodcocklickdamnshitshitshitshitSHITSHITSHIT . . . FUCK!

Yellow.

The flashing lights are yellow.

Not cops.

Tow truck.

There is a tow truck at the Shit Heap.

Awesome!

No . . .wait . . . not awesome.

They're gonna tow it.

"SHIT!" Topher jumped up and slammed the phone on the bar. Sam stared at him, startled by the outburst. "I . . . aw shit, Sam, I left my wallet in my car. Can I run out and get it? I'm not skipping out on you, man, really. I just . . ."

"Give me a goddamn heart attack, why dontcha?" Sam wheezed out a laugh. "Calm the fuck down, kid. Yeah, sure, go get your wallet. I'll save your drink for you."

"Thanks Sam," Topher said walking quickly for the door. He had to stop himself from saying it was good to see him again, but it would have given away he didn't intend to come back. He actually was doing what he had just stated he was not, which was skipping out on the bill. He had money of course, and he didn't feel good about stiffing Sam, but he couldn't very well have pulled out his wallet and pay for the drink if he had left his wallet in his car.

Topher practically ran out the front door, but then turned away from the turnpike, toward the mall, in case Sam was still watching him from the bar, which he likely was after the way Topher had been acting.

As soon as he was out of sight from the door, he started to run and circled the building so he would be approaching the turnpike from the opposite side from where Sam had seen him go. He might still be spotted, but it was the best he was going to do right now.

How long had the tow truck been there?

Had the driver already loaded it up?

He tried to judge how long he had been in the bar with Sam, but couldn't really do it. They had talked a bit, maybe a few minutes, it had taken a few minutes to make the drink, it hadn't seemed long.

But, he was really cold now, so he had been inside long enough to acclimate to the indoor temperature, and it usually took him about twenty minutes or so. A half-hour maybe? Could he really have been there thirty minutes? Long enough for a tow truck to arrive and load up the Shit Heap?

No.

So, how had he gotten here so fast.

The answer, of course, was obvious: one of the drivers who passed him had called it in to the cops. Which would mean there was now a police record with the vehicle description. Probably it was just local, maybe on a clipboard somewhere, but it was still closer than Topher wanted to be to anyone with a badge.

From across the parking lot, Topher heard the horrible rending screech of sheet metal being dragged across pavement; a sound which could only be the Shit Heap's overloaded rear end dragging as it is being pulled.

Topher made it to the snow bank, and nearly fell as his leg sank in up to his knee from the force of his running steps. He caught a quick glance over the hill, before the snow gave way and he was forced to stop and take slower more cautious steps.

"Sonofabitch," was his initial reaction. "What are the odds?"

At a glance, it looked like the same truck and driver who had responded to the armored car breakdown.

The breakdown Donny had arranged. Now the truck which Donny had arranged was broken down and the same guy was picking it up.

Maybe no one had called in the breakdown after all.

Maybe, Topher was just getting fucked.

Was it a coincidence, this truck and this driver, or had Donny manufactured this breakdown too? Was he about to get cut out? Or worse yet, set up to get caught? Were the cops on the way?

Stay or go?

It was what it came down to, really. Stay put and watch, or approach and claim the truck. Claim it and the cops show up, then go directly to jail. Fail to act, and it might be the last he will ever see of the truck. *How would I know where the truck went?* Donny would say. YOU *drove off in the fucking thing!*

Topher watched as the Shit Heap thumped and dragged its way up the inclined flatbed. Stay or go? Stay or go?

The nose of the disabled camper reached the top of the bed, and the driver from earlier, Topher was almost certain now it was him, pulled another lever and the flatbed began to lower itself to its horizontal position.

Stay or go?

Topher watched as the driver hopped up onto the bed, and tried to secure the rear axle with a ratcheting tie-down. After a couple of attempts, though, he was unable to get to the strap past the collapsed body, so he loosened the tie down and just tossed the thing over the whole back end and cinched it tight on the other side.

Topher watched as the driver walked back around to the traffic side, and then jumped down from the flatbed.

Go.

Topher topped the snow bank and ran down the other side, trying to keep the truck between himself and the view of the driver. He quickly climbed up onto the flatbed and moved quietly up the passenger side to the passenger door. He waited and listened.

He heard the creak and felt the slight bump in his feet as the driver opened the door of the tow, and Topher swung the passenger door open as well. Climbing in quickly, he swung the door most of the way shut, and then pulled it slowly but firmly until he heard a muted *chunk* as the door latch popped into position.

Laying back on the bench seat, Topher waited to hear the driver's door open once more, coming to see who the hell had climbed in. Instead, he heard the big diesel thrum louder and felt the front springs of the Shit Heap rock gently as they started rolling.

Topher hoped he figured out what to do next by the time they got to wherever the hell they were going.

Chapter 13

ONE BARREL.

What the fuck did *that* mean?

Donny had been relieved of his sidearm. He was sitting in a police interrogation room, and Joe was undoubtedly in the next one right down the hall. Donny had plenty of time to ponder the possible implications of only *half* the load going missing, as he was currently waiting for the next round of questioning. He had already gone through the patrol questioning from the first unit to arrive when they had reached their destination and found part of their load was missing. Then, Donny had gone through the same questions again when they had reached the station house, and then again when the lawyer from his employer had arrived.

They had crossed state lines, so he was likely still sitting here waiting for the FBI to come and ask him the same questions yet again.

His answers had not varied, not that his answers had much room to vary.

I don't know . . .yeah, the truck broke down and we got it towed . . .yeah, I did know the driver, from my previous job . . .no, well, yeah, *we were involved, but we didn't know we were involved, you know? . . .Renting the truck, well, Joe said it was dispatch's idea . . .yes, we* did *stop for dinner, but we had eyes on the vehicle the entire time . . .No, we saw no one approach it . . .I just can't figure what happened.*

Then, they would change the phrasing on the questions, and go through the whole thing again. The lawyer did it four times, with four different phrasings of the same fucking questions. Must be what the extra years of college were for.

He was, of course, on camera right now, and he was sure they were analyzing his body movement, looking for signs he was guilty. He just looked straight forward, and trying to look nervous and confused.

It was actually pretty easy. He *was* nervous and confused.

One barrel.

Why had Topher only taken one barrel?

If both barrels had been there, then Donny would have assumed either Topher got interrupted and had to bail, or he had chickened out and chosen to bail. Didn't really matter either way, if there had been two barrels in the back of the truck, it would have meant a lot of work for no reward.

There should have been no barrels in the back of the truck. Why take all this risk for only half of the load?

Why the hell were they hauling barrels in the first place? Who shipped anything which came in barrels by armored car? Did they ship diamonds in barrels? Had they ever hauled barrels before? Donny had no clue how to answer the first two questions, but he was fairly sure the answer to the last two was no. He didn't always see what Joe was loading into the back, but a huge blue plastic barrel would have caught his notice. The only reason he didn't see it before the changeover tonight was because he had been busy sabotaging the fan belt. Normally, he just sat behind the wheel and watched Joe in the side mirrors.

He would have seen a barrel if they had hauled any before tonight.

Of course, he had never had to drive a load this far before either. A lot of bridge and tunnel runs to Manhattan, mostly to the jewelry district, a few cash pick-ups from the racetrack in Yonkers, but mostly it was restaurants and grocery stores. As far as he could remember, this was the longest work day of his life. If he hadn't arranged the whole thing, he would be really pissed off.

Oh shit, he should be getting pissed off by now.

As far as his story went, he hadn't done anything wrong. He had, in fact, only been following the lead of the ranking guard, Joe, and he wasn't the one who had signed for or secured the load. He only drove the truck, and as far as he could tell no one was questioning how well that had been accomplished tonight. He should be asking when he would be allowed to go home, and starting to get a little pissy if they said things like, it would only be a few more questions.

113

He got up, and stretched theatrically, and then went over to the only door in the room, the one through which he had been herded what felt like a dozen hours before, but was likely closer to two. He knocked politely before speaking.

"Hello?" He called, staring at the door and frame, getting ready to step back if it started to open. "Is it going to be much longer? I'm going to need the bathroom pretty soon. Hello? Is there anyone out there?"

"Please take two steps back from the door," a voice politely, but firmly commanded from the hallway.

Donny complied, and the door swung open a few inches. The cop outside made no attempt to enter the room.

"What do you need, sir?" The cop was on the far side of forty, but still in uniform. Donny saw stripes on his shoulder, but did not really know what they signified. He had heard the term desk sergeant in enough police dramas to associate the term with the man in the doorway.

"Do you know when I am going to be able to go home? It has been a really long day for me, and I'd like to. . ."

"I don't have any information on your release, sir."

"Is my lawyer still here? Would he have any updates for me?"

"The lawyer for your company is in with your partner."

"Could you ask him. . ."

"I will let him know you would like to see him," the desk sergeant nodded as he spoke. He paused, then gave a small shrug. "I wouldn't hold my breath, though, kid. He'll want to be in there when the feds are ready to question your partner, and they'll be heading in as soon as they're done with their pissing match. Speaking of which, did you say you needed the bathroom?"

"Yes, please," said Donny. He didn't really have to go, but he wanted to be out of the room for a little bit.

"So, I'm still waiting here 'cause of the FBI?" Donny tried to get just the right amount of whininess and indignation into his voice.

"Are you really surprised?" the desk sergeant asked.

"No, not really," Donny feigned tired resignation. "We crossed state lines, so I guess it puts this snafu into their domain."

"Yeah, pretty much their take on it."

"What, you guys disagree?"

The desk sergeant just smiled and shook his head, "I'm sure your lawyer will brief you. The head's on the left, you got two minutes, and I will be right outside."

Donny entered the bathroom more confused than before. The cop had the same look Joe would get when there was a colossal fuck up somewhere, but it wasn't his problem; a situation with which he sympathized but for which he had absolutely no empathy. It was a sucks-for-you sort of look, reserved for those who had been in the middle of such issues before, knew exactly how awful they could be, and are relieved to be just an onlooker this time around.

So, with whom then were the feds in a pissing contest?

Donny, unzipped and squeezed out a weak, dribbling stream, whatever remained from the beer with dinner, just in case the cop outside was listening.

This whole thing was beginning to feel like it was starting to slip sideways, but he really didn't know how or why.

Had they caught Topher? Maybe the shitty old truck had popped a tail light or something, and they had seen the big blue barrel in the back? Were they questioning Joe first to get the whole story straight before they came in to lean on him? Get enough info to question him into a corner?

If the locals had nabbed Topher before he left their jurisdiction, then it would make sense the PD would fight the feebs for jurisdiction to get credit for the bust. If they had Topher, and Topher had talked, cut some sort of deal, or maybe not, maybe he just cracked when he got nabbed, if he got nabbed, then it would be a pretty easy case to build. He and Topher had history, Joe and Topher didn't. Not too hard to fill in the blanks.

Maybe he could flip it on Topher? Claim coercion? Topher was a hell of a lot bigger than him, so he could easily claim physical intimidation.

The cop knocked on the door.

"Zip it up, kid," he called from the hall.

He just didn't have enough information.

All he could do was wait, hope he could get more info from them than they got from him, and then lawyer up if things started to look grim.

Donny washed his hands, mostly out of habit, but also he was still aware of the cop outside listening. He swung open the door, and the desk sergeant had taken two steps back, blocking the hallway and physically indicating which direction Donny should turn.

"Any chance I can get a smoke?" Donny asked.

"Sorry, no smoking in the building," the cop said.

"It's okay," Donny offered his most charming smile, "I can go outside."

"No," the cop offered his own sinisterly charming smile, "that is pretty much at the top of the list of things you cannot do."

The cop stuck him back into the interrogation room without saying another word, and Donny was able to stew in silence for a few more minutes before the lawyer from the company made his third appearance and actually came in the room for the second time.

The first time he hadn't actually come in the room, a bald head with glasses poked through the door and had barked three short sentences before slamming the door shut and, Donny assumed, hurrying down the hall to offer similar commands to Joe. The sentences had been:

"I'm a lawyer for the company. The police have been advised you have retained counsel. Shut up until I get back."

When he returned, Donny was amused to see how much the man truly looked like a lawyer, like he had been genetically bred to appear like a cartoon representation of a lawyer from a one-panel comic in the editorial section of the paper. He was short, bald, fat, with glasses and a conservative pinstripe suit with a maroon paisley tie. Hanging up on a coat rack somewhere nearby had to be a thick winter overcoat, with maybe a pipe or cigar in the inside breast pocket.

"Green," he said, as he slid a business card across the table to Donny. The card read: "Neuman, Roth, and Green" across the top, and then "David Green" below and several phone numbers and email addresses.

The card said several things to Donny.

First, it didn't even hint it was a law office, and the only ones he knew that didn't were the ones that didn't need to advertise. The name spoke for itself. Second, very successful law offices had a lot of lawyers, but very few partners, and as a rule, the partners did not come out of the office unless it was something big. The third thing it told him was that he was going to be okay.

The lawyer was there to represent the best interest of the company. Green had come, reviewed the facts, reviewed the statements they had made before his arrival, and had decided that Donny and Joe not to be guilty was in the best interest of the company. If his assessment had told him throwing them to the wolves would have been the best course of action, Green would have advised Donny to retain counsel, shaken his hand, and wished him luck.

However, in this case, they had merely suffered from an unfortunately timed equipment failure, followed an arguably questionable course of action from a supervisor when they rented the truck, and then, and most of all to their credit, they had made the delivery. Albeit, it was only half of the delivery, but in this case it only strengthened the case they were not guilty of any criminal conspiracy. If they had the whole shipment to steal, why would they only take half? And, then why would they have delivered themselves along with the reduced shipment? They could have easily been in Canada, with the entire shipment, by the time anyone knew they were gone.

No, the lawyer must have figured a criminal case wouldn't stick at this point, but a civil case might. Negligence could easily be argued, after all they did arrive with only half the shipment. A civil case would include the armored car company as well, so all the more reason to bring in the legal big guns from the very beginning. Donny and Joe being neither criminals nor negligent employees was therefore in the best interest of the company.

Whether they were or not was inconsequential.

"The good news, Mr. Allen," Green began as a form of greeting, "is you appear to be in the least amount of trouble here. Your partner, Mr. Teoli, made clear in his statement you were against renting the truck, you were against going into the restaurant, favoring a drive-through instead, and it was your idea to remain with the vehicle while Mr. Teoli secured a table and maintained a visual on the shipment. All of which, of course, was corroborated by your independent statement."

"Sounds like there's a but coming," Donny said.

"Oh, well, we're certainly not done here yet, if that is what you mean," Green waved a chubby hand to dismiss the idea as being utterly ridiculous. "The FBI and the DEA will need to come to a decision of who will take jurisdiction, then we'll need to see--"

"I'm sorry, the DEA?" Donny asked.

"Cocaine, Mr. Allen, is what was in the missing barrel." Green paused a moment, to read Donny's face. When he seemed satisfied the stunned look was genuine and not merely a performance, Green continued. "The DEA contends, given the nature of what was taken, this should be their investigation, whereas the FBI maintains interstate theft is their domain regardless of the goods which are stolen. My assumption is they both feel fairly confident they will recover the cocaine without too much trouble, which is why they both want the investigation so badly."

"Again, sorry, but why were we hauling cocaine?"

"As I understand it, the chemical plant in Maywood is licensed by the Federal government to decocainize coca leaves for use in soda, tea, and other food products. The natural byproduct of this process is cocaine. You were transporting this byproduct to a pharmaceutical manufacturer for its use in topical anesthetic most often used in dentistry."

"So, let me get this right," Donny said, trying to wrap his head around the concept. "There is a company in New Jersey who just *makes* cocaine?"

"No, there is a company in New Jersey who makes a food additive. The by-product, the toxic waste of the process, if you will, is cocaine."

"I have lived my entire life within spitting distance of Maywood," Donny pressed. "How have I never heard of this before?"

"I imagine it is not something they like to advertise, and for the exact circumstances in which we currently find ourselves," Mr. Green observed dryly.

"Holy shit," Donny muttered.

"Yes, that is pretty much what Mr. Teoli said," Mr. Green nodded.

"Hold on," Donny sat up straight. "Joe, signed for the shipment. How could he have been okay with putting it in a rental truck, and . . ."

"And then leaving it unguarded?" Mr. Green finished for him.

"Well, we kept eyes on it, but . . ."

"Benzoylmethylecgonine," Mr. Green explained.

"Ben-so-meth . . . can you say it again?"

"Benzoylmethylecgonine is the scientific name for cocaine, and it was listed as such on the shipping invoice. Mr. Teoli did not know the two of you were shipping cocaine. Which, of course, if we had known, if our client had been completely forthright with us about the nature of the cargo, then we would have been better able to protect it during shipment."

Donny understood.

Green was feeding him their defense. They hadn't known what they had, so they hadn't understood the risk inherent to the nature of the cargo. Two big drums full of coke, jesus-mary-and -joseph, who wouldn't have killed them for it?

"We are, of course, currently considering a lawsuit for reckless endangerment of both you and Mr. Teoli due to the intentional withholding of information critical to the safety of those transporting such a hazardous material."

Donny, his hands already under the table, started squeezing his own nuts until they throbbed and he nearly started crying.

It was the only way he could keep from laughing.

Chapter 14

NOT HAD never walked in on his parents having sex.
Now, he almost wished he had.

He had not developed any sudden strange, or prurient
fetishes, nor was he typically Oedipal in nature.

It was really breakfast he was thinking of, truth be
told.

He was of course aware his parents, when his mother
had still been alive, had had sex. He was walking, talking,
physical proof. However, that was knowledge in an academic,
almost theoretical sense. The way you knew A squared plus B
squared was equal to C squared. You knew it was true, you
accepted it, but you didn't really think too deeply about it, or
ponder it. You just took it as a given and then you let if fall
away from your conscious mind.

Of course, it was much harder to let it fall away from
your conscious mind when you just had to share a meal with A,
B, and C, not long after C had discovered A banging B, and then
had to share a silent ride in the cab of a truck, firmly wedged
between A and C.

Maybe, if he had walked in on his parents when he was
a kid, then he would at least have a point of reference from the
breakfast the following day. What was appropriate behavior in
terms of expected social etiquette? Should he talk about it?
Avoid talking about it? Was silence considered rude or polite in
a situation such as this?

Not had received the call on Josue's cell phone a few
hours after securing the old camper truck in front of bay number
one, effectively blocking in the disabled armored truck. There
had been no street parking available, and the mechanics had all
gone home. There was space still available in the back lot, but
not much. Maneuvering the big truck into the limited space was

just not possible. With any other vehicle, he would have just dropped it on the street and rolled it into the lot, but the old truck's rolling days were well beyond it now.

So, Not just dumped it in front of the bay, and would let whoever opened figure out how to get it in the back. He stuck a bright red impound sticker on the windshield, indicating when and from where it had been taken, and had gone back to cruising the turnpike. After several uneventful hours, the borrowed phone in his pocket began its melodic demands for attention once more.

Less than a minute later, he was on his way back to Teaneck.

Josue and Alto had come out the front door together, nearly simultaneously, so much so they came close to getting stuck like an old silent movie schtick, then briskly stomped through the snow to the truck. Alto climbed in the passenger side, and Josue came up the driver's. Not was effectively boxed into the center of the bench seat.

"Where are we dropping you, Not?" Alto asked, his tone was pleasant, but he stared straight out through the windshield.

"Uh, Brandt Street, in Little Ferry," Not said, and then added, "please."

"Teaneck to-" Alto started.

"Winant, yeah, I got it," Josue grumbled, but without any real rancor. Not had the feeling he would respond in the same tone to anyone who offered him directions. It was like telling a professional chef when to flip a burger at a backyard barbeque.

Both fell silent. The only sound was the steady rumble of the diesel, and the hum of the tires on the roadway. The heat was on full blast, and Not caught himself nodding a couple of times.

It had to be after midnight by now, and he had been on the clock for over sixteen hours. He knew he should feel tired, and the fact he kept nodding off verified he was actually tired, but he felt more awkward than exhausted.

"Hey, let me get my phone back, before I forget," Josue said suddenly. Not pulled the slim object from his pocket and was only a little shocked to see it was actually closer to two in the morning, than midnight.

"What time am I back on the clock?" Not asked, slipping the phone into Josue's outstretched hand.

"I'm going to drop the boss at the office after I drop you, and then I'll keep rolling until eight. Alto will take the day shift, eight to four, and you be ready to hop back in the seat at four until midnight. If it works for both of you, I say we keep those shifts through the rest of the week, Not and I will bleed you dry from overtime, and then American Eagle Towing gets their payday and we can go back to more regular hours."

"Does this mean my probation period is over?" Not asked, his tone indicating he was joking, but his eyes betrayed the desperate hope behind the question.

"Without a doubt," Alto said, dismissively, as if it should be obvious. "Probably the shortest probation in the history of Alto's All-Tow, but you have certainly demonstrated your dependability and capability today. Now, can we also count on your discretion, particularly amongst the other drivers?"

"Absolutely," Not said to Alto, but he met Josue's eyes in the rearview as he said it. Alto signed the checks, but the secret belonged to both men and they both deserved an answer.

Josue nodded his head, just once, in thanks.

NOT WAS completely unsurprised to see the porchlight was on, and the ghostly-blue light of the television was still on in the living room. Not couldn't remember if he had called his dad to tell him he was working late, but he thought he had. Maybe not. Maybe, when your child was living under your roof, you just had to make sure he came home safe, no matter what his age.

Or, maybe Dad just fell asleep on the couch with the T.V. on again.

Alto popped open the door and slid out to let Not get by.

"Four pm, okay?" Alto asked.

"Can do, Mr. Alto," Not agreed.

"Good man," Alto nodded. "Go get some sleep, Not."

Not simply nodded, and headed inside without looking back. He heard the truck door squeak as it closed, presumably with Alto back inside, and the big diesel revved up as they pulled away. The cold air made everything silent, which paradoxically made every small sound much louder. His shoes creaked and crunched through the dry snow which had drifted over the sidewalk leading to his steps. His own breath sounded loud in his ears. He heard the front door latch click from the bottom of the steps, and guessed Dad hadn't fallen asleep after all.

The front door whooshed when it was pulled open, as either all the cold air rushed inside or all the hot air rushed outside, Not couldn't remember. All he knew was in the winter, Dad had yelled at him to close the door because he was letting all the hot air out. In the summer, it was the same admonition, but with an interrogatory bent asking if Not had wanted to air condition the whole neighborhood. Either way, the central message of don't stand there with the door open had not been lost on Not, and now here his father was ignoring his own sage wisdom.

"Good to see you, son," his father said, and it immediately woke Not back up and put him on guard. The only time his father ever called him son was when he was in trouble. His dad looked more sad than angry. He was in his old sweatpants and yesterday's undershirt, his hair was matted in funny directions, so he had in fact been to bed. Something had gotten him up.

"Uh oh, you called me 'son,' what'd I do?" Not asked.

His father stepped back from the doorway, and revealed a uniformed police officer standing in the living room.

Adrenaline spiked in his bloodstream, and his heart began pounding in a fashion which would have been frightening if he had been capable of rational thought. The fight or flight response had been very aptly named, because every nerve, every muscle, every pulse of dumb, blind fear was telling him to just go. Like earlier, up the street from Josue's, the urge to turn and run was nearly overwhelming, although he had done nothing wrong. This time was even worse. There weren't just police in nearby, there was a policeman in his living room. A policeman who was here for him.

What the hell had he done this time?

"This officer was just telling me the FBI would like to have a word with you.

Chapter 15

A FEW years back, Topher had worked as a bouncer for the Tri-State Quarter-life Crisis Club Oktoberfest at Bear Mountain State Park. It was mostly ex-frat boys and sorority girls caught somewhere between extended adolescence and adulthood, and filling the time the way they had been trained to do in college: drinking enormous amounts of alcohol and dancing badly to stupid music.

On the whole it had been easy money. They drank, they danced, they puked, they laughed, they screamed, and then drank and puked some more. Nobody started a fight, or even tried to mouth off. The biggest hassle of the entire day had been trying to keep the local teens away from the unguarded kegs.

At the end of the day, he had walked away with $200 bucks of tax free cash in his pocket and a wicked sunburn. All in all, he had thought at the time, it had been a pretty good day.

However, now several years later in the freezing winter, his face as red as it had been that sunny day, though this time from the bitter wind blowing over the river and picking up sharp little ice crystals as it crossed and stabbing them into any soft stretch of skin which had been foolishly left exposed, Topher discovered he had walked away from a long forgotten sunny October day with something else as well.

"There's a garden, what a garden," he mumbled quietly to himself, his breath creating billowy clouds which were quickly ripped away by the wind, "Only happy faces bloom there."

AFTER THE tow driver dropped the old Shit Heap on the street in front of the shop, Topher had hopped on his phone to call Donny, and was very nearly busted by the driver.

Still crouched in the footwell under the dashboard of the old truck, Topher had heard the footsteps approaching just in time to slap the glowing face of his phone against his chest. He figured the glow had still given him away though, as the driver proceeded to slap his own hand against the windshield. Topher was trying to decide if he should play drunk, stupid, or both, in order to explain why he was hiding in the cab of the truck, but as he was trying to get his best mix of dopey grin and sleepy eyes with which to greet the driver, he heard the footsteps receding back toward the truck.

Topher had risked a glance up and saw the driver had simply slapped an impound sticker on the windshield and was getting ready to head back out.

He waited until the big tow truck had rounded the corner, and was therefore well beyond being able to see him in the mirrors, before he started in on the phone again.

He pulled up Donny's number, and then paused.

It was well after midnight now, so Donny must have made the delivery. They would have discovered the load was incomplete, so in all likelihood, Donny was currently in a room with a lot of police in it. They probably had his phone as well, so calling him would just be inviting the police to come find him. When he was able to, when it was safe, then Donny would call. If only to make sure Topher had not run off with their payday.

He had to admit, it was a tempting thought.

This whole deal had turned out to be a lot more difficult than Donny had led him to believe it would be, and the payoff was still uncertain. He was part way tempted to dump the dolly with their stolen booty on the side of the road and walk away clean, but he knew Donny would turn him in without a second thought, if for nothing more than spite. Such knowledge of course tempted him to just cut Donny out of the equation altogether, but it would end with the same result, and Topher was still clueless as to how to turn this big blue barrel into money.

Of course, first thing's first, he would have to get the barrel somewhere safe so he could figure out just what he had.

He looked out the window of the Shit Heap and found the name of the company who had towed him: Alto's All-Tow. Cute. He pulled up the browser on his phone and located the address he was currently huddled in front of. He then selected the "nearby" option on the map and looked for motels.

The closest was nearly a mile away, but it was a converted 19th century Victorian home reborn as a bed and breakfast. No way could he sneak a barrel past the desk clerk there. The next closest hotel was nearly five miles away.

Topher was pretty sure he could make the walk, even while pushing a half-ton of weight, so long as the dolly was still functional after the accident. However, he was very doubtful he could make the journey unnoticed. Even if he was able to avoid the police, someone would be awake and would be likely to remember a man taking his gigantic blue barrel for a walk in the middle of the night.

So, hotels were out.

Another search revealed there were no rental places open at this hour, other than at the airport, and it would require a cab ride to get there, a rental agreement, and then drive back by which time the shop could be open and someone could have already found what had made the suspension collapse.

So, no rentals.

He was not opposed to stealing a car, but he really had no idea how to hotwire a vehicle, and he was not going to attempt a carjacking.

Self-storage was too far away and didn't open for six more hours.

He would have to hide it somewhere close by and come back for it later.

Topher hopped out of the truck and stretched his stiff legs and back, putting on a good show for anyone who might be watching, but also because he had been crouched in an awkward position for nearly an hour. Twisting slowly at the hips, he took in an almost full 360 of the surrounding neighborhoods. The tow shop and it's lot took up most of the block he was on, but he could see houses at both ends of the block.

In front of him was Railroad Avenue, which ran mostly north/south, though leaning a little to the west as it went north, and a little to the east as it went south. Topher was on the northbound side, which was separated from the southbound side by the railroad tracks for which the avenue was named. On the opposite side from where he stood the neighborhood went entirely residential. There were several blocks of tightly packed two-story row houses, separated in most cases by the width of a sidewalk, charmingly referred to by realtors as a "breezeway." Many of his friends growing up had lived in similar homes, and they all joked if you sneezed in your bedroom at night, you would likely hear "God Bless You," from next door.

It was not, Topher judged, the best place to try to hide something without being noticed. However, he did spy something which gave him a bit of hope. From where he stood, he could see into the backyards of the houses up the north side of a little street called Stanley Place. All the windows on the second house in had been boarded up with plywood, and although it was dark, he was pretty sure he could see smoke damage at the top of the window frames.

An empty house.

And, it was only about a hundred feet away.

"EVERY TIME they hear that oom-pah-pah, everybody feels so trah-lah-lah," Topher sang quietly, and danced the dolly around to his right so he could pull it, rather than push it over the first railroad track. Piles of asphalt had been dumped and then rolled flat on either side of the track, just wide enough for a maintenance vehicle to cross the tracks without shaking all the fillings from the teeth of the driver.

"They want to throw their cares away, they want to go lah-de-ah-de-ay."

After pulling the heavy cart from the back of the Shit Heap, and checking for traffic on both the road and the tracks, Topher had discovered the other thing he had kept from the mostly forgotten Oktoberfest were all the lyrics to the Beer Barrel Polka, which must have been played at least two dozen times in the five hours he was there.

"Roll out the Barrel, we'll have a barrel of fun," he chuffed as he muscled the dolly, with his own blue barrel of fun strapped to it, over the second of the train track rails. Wishing nothing but blowjobs and back rubs for whatever person who had had the forethought to lay down the piles of asphalt, he ran the barrel down on the far side of the tracks.

Topher prided himself on maintaining his playing weight and muscle tone from his high school days. Not the glamour muscles which so many at the gym tried to attain -- all bulk, and shaped for aesthetics -- but actual knock you down and make you bleed kind of muscle.

Still, a half-a-ton was a half-a-fucking-ton.

127

Even with the assistance of the handcart, his lower back and thighs were starting to burn.

"Roll out the barrel, we've got the blues on the run. Zing boom tararrel, ring out a song of good cheer. Roll out the barrel, 'cause the gang's all here!"

The lights in the homes on either side of the boarded up house were all dark, which likely meant, given the hour, their occupants were all asleep. Many of the windows had the shades drawn as well, so it was unlikely he could be seen from those. Others were dark, but not covered. Since there were no lights on, there could be some insomniac at any one of a number of windows and Topher would have no way to tell. Each blank dark glass looked like an angry accusing eye, watching his every move, recording his progress to be able to direct the police to his exact location as soon as he stopped moving.

Unfortunately, he didn't have any better options than this one, so his best bet was to just keep moving and hope everyone on this block had taken a double dose of cough syrup before climbing into bed tonight.

He reached the driveway of the boarded house and saw the front door had been covered in plywood as well, likely to keep out criminals and vagrants like himself. Topher turned the dolly up the driveway and hoped the back door had been left uncovered and unlocked for access by the inevitable insurance adjusters, contractors, and fire inspectors who would be coming eventually to decide whether to clean up and repair or to tear down and start over again.

He hoped they wouldn't be coming by tomorrow.

At the end of the house, facing the driveway, was a small white door which had in fact been left unlocked. Topher tried to drag the cart and barrel up the first step, and found it was beyond his ability. He checked around the corner of the house for a garage, but instead found a stack of plywood scraps, left over from the four-by-eight sheets cut down to cover the windows and the front door.

Gathering up three leftovers, both wide enough to accommodate the wheel span of the dolly, and also long enough to bridge the rise of the steps, Topher cobbled together a makeshift ramp. Backing the barrel up to the far side of the driveway, Topher pushed as hard as he was able, and ran the barrel up the ramp with enough force to hop it over the threshold as well.

He stood in a laundry room which led into a kitchen.

Topher was surprised to see the house was still furnished. Pushed against the back wall were a washer and dryer, and in the kitchen sat a table and four chairs. Beyond, a doorway led into a living room, and even in the dim light Topher could make out the shape of a sofa.

Topher rolled the barrel into the corner of the laundry room, and tucked it in beside the washing machine. The muscles in his lower back twinged and threatened to knot up. Pausing a moment to stretch, and to gently knead the tightened tissues to relieve some of the pressure before he returned the plywood to the rest of the pile, and made sure to close the door to the driveway.

He pulled the little lace curtain aside to survey his view. From the window in the laundry room door, he could see across the neighbor's backyard on the corner lot, and had a clear view of Alto's All-Tow the sad looking Shit Heap collapsed in front of it.

The rest of the windows were covered in plywood, so Topher pulled his phone from his pocket and opened a flashlight app, secure in the knowledge that as long as he stayed away from the door to the driveway, the light could not be seen from the outside.

He paused on his way through the kitchen to open a couple of cupboards, which were still stocked with canned goods, boxes of cereal and crackers chewed open by mice, while other cupboards held dingy looking plates and cups.

The refrigerator was still stocked, through it smelled strongly of spoiled milk, as the power had been shut off. However, since the heat had been shut off too, most of the items in the refrigerator were still cold, including bottles of beer on the bottom shelf to which Topher decided to help himself.

He continued on into the living room, and it began to become clear to him why the furniture had been left behind. Despite the cold, the smell of smoke was still strong throughout the house. There had been a large fire, but it had been kept, from what he had seen so far, entirely on the second floor. The fire department had shown up and had done what they did best, which was to put out the fire by putting lots and lots of water onto it. The water had then done what it did best, which was to flow back down to the ground.

Everything on the first floor had been soaked. When springtime eventually came around, all of the furniture, the carpet, the drywall, the subfloor, everything would thaw out become a breeding ground for mold.

However, in the meantime, everything was frozen solid.

He noted the darker squares and rectangles of paint on the walls, not faded by the sun, where the frames of family photos had previously hung. He hoped everyone who had lived here was able to get out safely. At least he could be sure someone had; he doubted very much the firefighters had taken down the photos.

He swung the light around the room and saw end tables and shelves also had obvious blank spaces where items had been removed. Not everything had been cleared, though. There were some old magazines on the coffee table, and junk mail piled on the floor near a key stand by the front door. They had only taken the items of sentimental importance or, he assumed, monetary value.

The carpet crunched like dry snow under his feet. Topher laid a hand on the sofa cushion, and it didn't give at all. If felt like a dish sponge filled to saturation and then put in the freezer, which in a way was exactly what had happened.

Topher played the light across the ceiling, and saw places where the drywall had sagged under the weight of the water, and others where it had collapsed entirely, leaving a hole to view into the room above. He couldn't see much given the strength of his light source, but Topher could see enough to know he didn't want to try to venture upstairs. It looked pretty well destroyed, and he didn't want to press his luck by putting his weight on what might end up collapsing beneath him.

He turned back to the relative warmth and safety of the kitchen. There was no carpeting or padded furniture there, so the water had flowed down to lower points without soaking in. He didn't know if the house had a basement or not, but he was cautious of soft spots in the floor as he walked. He didn't want to get dropped down onto a solid sheet of ice on top of concrete. If he broke his legs or his back, he would likely die of exposure before anyone found him.

He finished his beer, and set it next to the sink, where he also paused to take a quick piss, rather than adventure off to try to find the bathroom. He was cautious not to let his dick touch the cold porcelain, thinking of the wintertime horror stories about tongues and flagpoles.

Finally, he ended up back in the laundry room to see if he could learn a little more about just what in the ever loving fuck he had stolen.

The top of the barrel had no markings on it, and Topher could not remember seeing any labels on the outward facing side of the barrel. So, if there was any label on it at all, it must be on the side facing the dolly when the barrel was strapped in place.

Topher had wedged the dolly pretty tightly between the washer and the corner wall of the laundry room, so now he had very little space to maneuver the dolly back out again. Not trusting his back to support the weight, and having some real concern now of having done some permanent damage, like having slipped a disc or something, Topher did not tilt the dolly back toward himself to roll it from the corner.

Instead, he opted to tilt the dolly about an inch to the side, rocking the barrel to the right and then yanked on the left handle. The left side moved back about an inch before the front corner of the dolly struck the wall. So, he tilted left as far as he could go, again about an inch, and then yanked the right handle. The dolly pivoted this time on its left side, and the right side came about two inches forward before the front corner of the dolly struck the washing machine and stopped. He repeated the process several times, alternating sides each time, and was able to duck walk the dolly, with barrel attached, back out of the corner.

By the time he was finished, he had worked up a bit of a sweat again, and knew he should try to avoid overheating as much as possible. The sweat would cool his body further, which was its job after all, and he was already beginning to shiver. He had been protected from the cold by the more than adequate heater in the Shit Heap, and had even been roasted a little as the transmission started to overheat before it gave up entirely. Even after it had died, the lingering heat of the engine and the transmission had kept the cab of the truck warm during the tow ride back.

However, he had been out of the truck for a while and he was starting to feel the cold. With the wind chill, outside the temperature had to be near or below zero. Inside, it was a little better, but the frozen couch proved the temperature was still somewhere below thirty-two degrees Fahrenheit. If the power was off, then the gas was likely off as well, so there would be no turning on the heat in his borrowed home. He couldn't light a fire either, because the smoke would alert the neighbors to his presence, and given the previous fire and how close these homes are to each other, they would be on the phone to 911 immediately.

Sooner rather than later, Topher would either have to sneak back out, hopefully before any early rising neighbors, and seek better shelter, or he would need to search the house for any blankets or sleeping bags left behind, and hopefully spared a soaking from the fire hose.

First though, he needed to satisfy his curiosity, and, if he was being completely honest, to feed his greed.

The straps were held in place by two quick-release clamps on the right rear side of the dolly. Topher lifted the release bar on each one, and then tilted the dolly slightly to let the weight of the barrel pull the slack of the straps through the clamps. The barrel tilted forward about two inches, pulling away from the dolly, and pulling the slack of the straps along with it. Topher tried to shine the light from his phone into the gap between the barrel and the dolly, and was rewarded with a glimpse of a plastic shipping envelope affixed to the side of the barrel, and a folded piece of paper inside.

Topher set the phone on the washer, maintaining the tilt of the dolly and the gap it created with his left hand, and tucked his newly freed right hand into the space between to retrieve the document. It slid free from the plastic case fairly easily, and after pulling his hand back out, Topher gently released the dolly and then regained his phone.

Most of what the paper said was absolute gibberish to him. There were long numbers preceded by short lettered codes. There were chemical formulas and symbols which he recognized from high school, but could no longer remember the meaning of. He recognized the big C with the number down and to the right as Carbon, and the big H was hydrogen, but he knew the little numbers made them something different than just Carbon and Hydrogen. There was also NO in the formula, and he knew NO_2 was nitrous oxide - he had done enough whippets in high school to remember that one - but this was NO_4. Finally there was a chemical name: Benzoylmethylecgonine.

Topher opened the browser on his phone once again, and then decided to open a new anonymous proxy to run the search. A little extra caution couldn't hurt.

He had no idea how to type in a subscript number on his phone's virtual keyboard, and he didn't want to search for it, so he just typed in the numbers and letters in all caps, and then painstakingly copied the long and confusing name as well and hit enter.

The result came up almost immediately, with 34,600 results.

It couldn't be right, though.

Topher cleared the search bar and typed everything in again. This time he did take the time to find the subscript in the special characters screen of the phone.

The result came up almost immediately: 46,000 results, which all said the same thing.

$N_{17}H_{21}NO_4$ Benzoylmethylecgonine was cocaine.

He had stolen a barrel full of cocaine.

Chapter 16

SPECIAL AGENT Gregory Morris, FBI, and Special
Agent Erin Saunders, DEA, looked and acted very much like a
happily married, middle-aged couple. It would be easy to
picture the two of them at a PTA meeting or speaking to their
children's teachers at back-to-school night. They looked like
they should be making small talk at a neighborhood potluck, or
Christmas party. If this had happened in July, they likely would
look like they were headed to a barbecue or perhaps to play a
couple of rounds of tennis when they finished for the day.

Special Agent Morris, who almost certainly would ask
you to please call him Greg, looked to be in his late thirties or
early forties. A sprinkling of grey hair at the temples, and a
couple of wrinkles around the eyes, but just enough to make him
look mature but not old. He was average height, did not appear
to be skinny or fat, and appeared to be dressed entirely in items
from the J. Crew catalogue. His hair was an unremarkable shade
of brown, conservatively cut, and he had the eyes to match. He
looked like an advertisement for a Christian dating website.

Special Agent Erin Saunders, who probably had a
sorority nickname like Rinny, from her first name, or Sandy,
from her last, was the female version of Special Agent Morris,
right down to the J. Crew wardrobe, though her hair would best
be described as sandy, isn't *that* just perfect, rather than brown.

They lived in the suburbs.

They drove hybrids.

This year they avoided gluten, and next year they
would probably be on the paleo diet again.

They made Donny's skin crawl.

"Mr. Allen," said Special Agent Morris started after the
introductions had been made. "I would like to confirm the

police read you your Miranda Rights earlier in the presence of your previous attorney."

"Um, yeah," Donny nodded, "but what do you mean previous?"

"We have been informed Mr. Green has recused himself as your counsel, but your Miranda rights are still in effect, are we clear?" Morris sounded like he was going down a checklist.

"Um, yeah, I guess so," Donny found his mouth was starting to get dry. His lawyer, correction, his *company's* lawyer had bailed on him, which couldn't be good. They were distancing themselves from him now. Something had changed, but if he re-lawyered up now he wouldn't be able to find out what it was.

"I have only a couple of questions for you, Special Agent Saunders may have some more when I am finished, but I don't think this will take too long."

"Okay, sounds like the FBI won, huh?" Donny smiled.

"Won what?" Morris asked, appearing only mildly interested, asking merely to be polite.

"The piss-, uh, question of jurisdiction," Donny attempted to avoid appearing rude to the DEA agent. "The officer who took me to the bathroom said there was a question of jurisdiction which was holding up my release."

"Oh, I see," Special Agent Morris nodded pleasantly. "No, actually what is holding up your release is you were driving a truck which is now missing a rather large amount of a controlled substance, and not too very long ago you were involved in a criminal conspiracy to steal a shockingly large number of cars."

Morris pulled a large manila file folder from where he had set it on the floor when they came in. He opened it to display the top sheet, upon with Donny was able to read "The State of New Jersey v" before Morris started flipping through the pages. From the photos and shop diagrams in the folder, it was fairly easy to see it was either the state's case against John or the state's case against George.

Didn't really matter either way; it was pretty much the same case.

He was, Donny recalled, named as a person of interest several times in the police reports, but wasn't sure how he was portrayed in the trial.

He had not been called to testify.

"In addition to your prior involvement with auto theft, and your current involvement in the theft of a class three controlled substance, you were in contact with another member of the previously mentioned criminal conspiracy just prior to the theft of, to reiterate, what is a rather significant amount of cocaine."

Morris paused for a moment, and glanced up from the file folder to make sure Donny was following him so far.

"So, what took a little while was getting ahold of the case file, and then of course reading and noting the names of all those involved, you know, just in case they were involved tonight as well. There was quite a lot to read, and we didn't want to miss any important details. Anything to add, Sandy?"

"Not really," said Special Agent Saunders, who then went on to add something anyway. "I think perhaps Mr. Allen here has been a little jaded by television and movies. Contrary to popular belief, Mr. Allen, the various federal law enforcement agencies actually cooperate all the time. The same holds true with local law enforcement, we help them when asked and they help us when asked."

"Such is the case right now," Morris jumped back in. "When we asked for the local PD in . . ."

Morris glanced back down at the paper in his hand.

" . . .Little Ferry, New Jersey, to bring Harris Johnson in for questioning."

"They were happy to lend a hand," Special Agent Saunders added.

"You think Not stole the coke?" Donny asked.

"I'm sorry, was that a complete sentence?" Morris asked, sounding both paternal and patronizing.

"Not is Harry, or rather Harris," Donny couldn't believe how stupid he was sounding. "Let me try it again. His name is Harris, but everyone called him Harry, as in Harry Johnson, so he started introducing himself as 'Not Harry,' and I guess the name Not just stuck."

"Fascinating," Morris deadpanned.

"So, you think he took the coke?" Donny asked again.

"Oh, no, not at all," Saunders said. She smiled pleasantly, and Donny again thought she looked like a PTA mom.

He wondered if she drove here in a minivan.

"I think you, and Mr. Teoli, *and* Mr. Johnson conspired to steal the cocaine," Saunders continued. "I think Mr. Johnson has it in his possession, or has hidden in somewhere, and as soon as we arrest him he will confirm your involvement."

"But, I'm not involved, and Joe's not involved . . ."

"And, Mr. Johnson?"

"I have no idea, to tell you the truth," Donny lied. "I hadn't seen him since just before the trial for John, our former boss and the one who was actually guilty of stealing the cars, along with his brother in law George. I mean, sure, Not actually *took* the cars, but he thought they were repos. He didn't know he was stealing cars, and neither did I. Besides, seeing him again tonight was just a coincidence."

"And, it was just a coincidence you happened to have two enormous barrels of cocaine in the truck you were driving when you saw him again. A truck which, coincidentally, broke down, and then, coincidentally, was towed away by someone you, coincidentally, used to steal cars with," Morris said, and raised a finger for every repetition of the word. "Oh, and then you were, coincidentally, robbed of several million dollars of cocaine from a truck which you, coincidentally, neglected to lock."

Coincidentally, Donny decided, Agent Morris was a dick.

"Did I miss any?" Morris asked, glancing over to the other agent.

"Don't forget the GPS," Saunders added.

"Oh, yes, I nearly forgot. The barrel containing the GPS tracker inside just happened to be left in the truck, which is a heck of a coincidence since the only way to know which barrel had the tracking unit was coded on the shipping invoice in Mr. Teoli's possession," Morris raised the second finger on his left hand and added it to the five held high on his right.

"So, the way I see it," Morris continued after a moment's pause to let the weight of all the implications sink in. His expression and tone were still pleasant, almost cordial, but with just a hint of disappointment. He was a 1950's television father explaining to his comically wayward offspring how he wasn't really angry at the child's transgressions, but he had expected better.

Everybody watching at home knew, as soon as the camera cut away for a word from the sponsor, the belt was coming off.

"One of you is going to fill in the details first, in return for my recommendation for leniency to the US Attorney's office. Such a recommendation is likely to knock at least five years off of the sentencing."

It sounded so calm and reasonable, Donny actually found himself wanting to explain where Morris had gotten it wrong. Some of the things he had listed, as hard as it was to believe, actually *were* coincidences, or maybe dumb luck would be a better way to view it. He was just as shocked as Not was when they ran into each other again tonight. Topher hadn't even known he had a fifty/fifty shot of getting a barrel with no GPS tracker; hell, he hadn't even known he would be taking a barrel. Sure, the breakdown had been arranged, and the timing of it had practically forced the need of a rental truck.

He hadn't told Joe to leave it unlocked, though.

Donny really had to side with the feds on there.

That really was just plain old negligence.

The good news, though, was the two people who they thought were his accomplices were actually not involved at all, so they could offer them leniency, or event total immunity, and neither one would have any information to give them.

Of course, it didn't mean Donny couldn't muddy the waters further by pointing them in the wrong direction.

"When you put it all that way, I can see how you guys think I'm involved," Donny conceded. "And, I am sure I'm not the first person to tell you he didn't do it, but I don't know what else to say, because I really didn't do it."

"Well, now that is another coincidence," said Morris holding up an eighth finger. "Mr. Teoli said almost the exact same thing."

"Really," said Saunders. "Almost word for word."

"I get it," Donny snapped. "It looks bad, but it really *was* just a coincidence. Joe never even met Not before tonight, I just introduced them a few hours ago, for God's sake, so there is no way they could have planned this whole thing. I know Joe and I made some dumb choices, but it was only because we had no idea what we were hauling."

Morris and Saunders shared a knowing look, the way old friends and married couples do. There were no eye rolls, or exasperated sighs, or even a shoulder shrug, but the message came across loud and clear: bullshit.

"Really!" Donny insisted. "I'm not crazy, and I don't want to get shot. Do you think if Joe and I knew what we had in there, we would have used a *box truck*? Or *stopped* for dinner? I would have just had Not tow us back to the place in Maywood where we picked the stuff up."

"But you didn't," Morris replied. "You and Mr. Teoli had Mr. Johnson take you to rent a truck intended to secure boxes of dishes and clothes, couches, lamps, and instead you loaded nearly a full ton of cocaine."

"And, you didn't even lock it," Saunders added.

"And where," Morris asked, almost as an afterthought, "was Mr. Johnson when you took the cocaine from the secure armored vehicle and placed it in an unsecured, non-armored vehicle?"

"He, uh," Donny pretended to think hard about it, "he was standing next to the tow truck. He had to tilt the bed and lower the armored truck just a little so the two trucks would line up."

"So, then he was able to see the load as it was transferred?" Morris asked.

"Um, yeah, I guess he could," Donny said, sounding a lot more grudging about giving up the information than he felt.

"And, where was Mr. Johnson when you failed to secure the back door of the rental truck?" Saunders asked.

"He, uh, he was putting the tow bed flat again, and making sure the truck on the bed was secured."

"Could he see the back of the rental truck from where he was?" Morris asked.

"Maybe," Donny shrugged.

Special Agents Morris and Saunders shared another knowing look, and Morris flipped the manila folder closed once more.

"You and Mr. Teoli will remain in custody of the Hobart Police department on our behalf until we have completed our investigation," Agent Morris stated.

"Am I under arrest?"

"As of this moment, you are once again a person of interest," Agent Saunders said.

"So, is this one of those 72 hour hold things?" Donny asked hopefully.

"Actually, the way the law is phrased it does not set a definite limit; it allows for a 'reasonable time to conduct an investigation'," Morris stated. "So, let's see how the investigation goes."

Morris and Saunders stood to leave.

"I think I am ready for my lawyer now," Donny sighed.

Chapter 17

THE LAST time he had been arrested, Not had been in Hackensack. He had been picked up outside of the hospital in the act of stealing a doctor's brand new German import. It had been the middle of the night then too, so he had been taken directly to the Bergen County Jail. The cell had been everything he had been taught to expect from television and movies. A narrow bed had been bolted to the wall. At the back of the cell, a stainless steel sink was mounted just above a stainless steel toilet. Opposite from the bed was a small table surface, about the size of a medium pizza box, also stainless steel and also mounted to the wall. About a foot and a half lower, and just to the left of the table was another table, the exact same as the first one, just lower and to the left. At first, Not had thought it had been put in to accommodate prisoners in wheelchairs, but then he realized it was intended to be a seat for the table. The wall had been painted a sickly pale mint green until about shoulder height, and then plain white above it. The bars which enclosed the entire cell had been battleship grey.

It had looked exactly like a prison cell was supposed to look.

The holding cell in the Little Ferry Municipal Building looked like someone's basement which had been converted, poorly, into a bomb shelter.

It was about fifteen by twenty feet of floor to ceiling cinder blocks. As he entered the cell, he saw immediately to his right was a stainless steel sink and stainless steel toilet, but this time they had been combined to comprise a single column, with the sink at the top and the toilet bowl protruding from about halfway down. A short cinder block wall came directly out from the wall to the right of the toilet, marching straight out toward the middle of the room, Not supposed to afford a little privacy for anyone needing to use the toilet, but he wasn't quite sure from whom, as the wall only came up to about waist height, and there was no door on the front.

Not figured this was to prevent anyone from attempting to hide and ambush an officer, which he had to admit it certainly did, but it also rendered the wall absolutely useless, as it offered none of the privacy it was intended to do.

The longer wall, which made up the rear of the holding cell, had a wooden bench which ran the entire length. "Bench" was really a fairly generous term though, as it was just a plank of 2x12 bolted to two 4x4 fence posts, which had in turn been bolted to mounts in the floor. Similar, but shorter, benches bookended either side to form a lopsided U-shape. Lastly, the entire room, floor and ceiling included but with the exception of the toilet, had been painted in multiple coats of thick high gloss paint, the color of French vanilla ice cream.

A large drain, covered with a heavy iron grate, had been positioned in the exact center of the floor.

Not was fairly sure he had been put in what was referred to on television police dramas and countless sitcoms as "the drunk tank."

At least, he had the place all to himself.

At the end of the day, all those who had been arrested throughout the day were taken to the Bergen County Jail holding facility. The Little Ferry PD was not equipped to hold overnight guests. Those who were arrested during the night were only there long enough for the Bergen County Sheriff to pick them up and take them to the jail for processing.

Not, however, wouldn't be going to the jail.

The officer who had brought him in had explained, very carefully and thoroughly, he was not under arrest. The officer had spoken quietly and calmly, and had done everything he could to be reassuring, short of giving Not a hug. The FBI, he had explained, had contacted the Little Ferry Police Department and asked for Not be secured at the station until they could arrive.

He had then proceeded, in the same quiet and calm voice, to read Not his rights.

Not had questioned the officer, if he was not under arrest, then why was he being read his rights?

Just a formality, the officer had tried to assure him.

Not had never felt less assured.

When they had arrived at the station, his rights were read to him again, but this time accompanied by a document which affirmed his rights had been read to him and he did in fact understand said rights.

It was then stated, again, he was not under arrest.

Then, they locked him in the holding cell.

NOT WAS doing everything he could to prevent himself from falling asleep.

He remembered an old adage about how to catch a criminal. You arrested everyone you thought might have done the crime, and then put them all in a cell and wait. Most of them will be nervous, or angry at being accused of a crime they didn't commit, but one of them would go to sleep.

The one who went to sleep was the guilty one.

The logic which followed was the person who was guilty had been scared of getting caught, but now that he was caught he couldn't do anything about it so he might as well get some sleep.

Not had no idea if the police actually thought that way, but he sure as hell knew he didn't want to fall asleep.

So, he paced.

He stretched.

He splashed water on his face from the toilet-sink.

He looked around the room for the cameras which he knew had to be watching him.

He hoped he looked nervous.

He hoped he looked scared.

He hoped he looked angry.

He hoped he looked as far from guilty as he could get.

God, though, he was tired.

He didn't know how long he had been in the holding cell, but he figured it had to be close to dawn by now, and he would have been awake for a full twenty-four hours, while working a sixteen hour double shift in between. In about another twelve hours, he would need to be back at work again for another eight hour shift, making it twenty four hours worked out of less than a full forty-eight.

Back at work.

It was nice to be able to use the phrase again, even if it was only to himself. He hoped it was a phrase he would still be able to use after today.

He wondered if there was another holding cell in this building.

Were Josue and Alto sitting on plank-and-post benches like the one lining the wall of his own cell?

Or, was he still sitting here because the FBI wanted to question them first?

Bottom line: did he still have a job after tonight?

His fight to stay awake was forced to continue for another thirty minutes before the door to the cell finally swung open once more.

The man wore a navy sweater vest over a light blue button down, and a tweed blazer, complete with suede patches on the elbows, and dark toned khakis. The lady carried a designer shoulder bag and wore a red cardigan over a white blouse, and dark wool slacks. They looked like moderately wealthy accountants or bankers, but Not figured if they were here at this hour then they were more likely to be the FBI agents who had asked for him to be brought in.

"Good morning, Mr. Johnson," The male agent began. "Or, may I call you Not?"

"Sure," Not agreed, wanting this to be over as soon as possible, and completely missing the importance of the use of his preferred handle.

"You have not requested an attorney to be present," the female agent now spoke. "And, I have a form here for you to sign in a moment, two actually, one which states at this time you have requested a lawyer, at which point we will leave and you will need to remain here until the lawyer arrives. It could take a while."

She let the implication sit in the air for a moment before continuing.

"The other says you have declined your right to counsel, at this time anyway, and are volunteering to speak with us."

"Now, before you say anything," the man jumped back in before Not could even take a breath to speak. "I would like to inform you of a few things we already know. We know you have an alibi for all of last night when the crime we are investigating took place. We have checked the police call log and verified you could not possibly have been anywhere nearby when and where the crime was discovered."

"So, at this point I would like to ask you if you would be willing to talk with us at this time, or if you would like to exercise your right to counsel?" the lady asked, pulling two forms from her bag.

"Yeah, sure," Not agreed, relieved to hear he didn't need to convince them of his innocence. "I'll be happy to talk to you."

Not initialed the spaces which indicated he had been read his rights, he understood his rights, and he was waiving his right to an attorney at this time. He signed and dated the form at the bottom, and handed it to the lady who swiftly deposited both forms back into her bag.

"Excellent," said the male agent. Both stood casually in front of the exit to the holding cell, appeared almost anxious to be going. Not imagined he was not the only one who was enduring a very long night.

He had been so wound up, nervous, and wondering what had happened and why he was in jail once again, that he could actually feel his muscles begin to loosen and relax. Anyone who has ever suffered through a terrible head cold, and then wakes up one morning to discover it is again possible to breath, can attest to what a relief normal can be.

The lady pulled a small notebook from her bag, and then followed it out with a pen. She flipped open the cover, and poised the pen in a ready-to-write position.

"Just a couple of questions," the man began, "and then I think we'll be all done here."

"Okay," Not agreed, almost eagerly. He could be home for breakfast, and then he could catch a few hours of sleep before heading back into work.

"Can you confirm you were the driver who picked up an armored car last night?"

"Yes," Not said immediately. "Yeah, around five o'clock."

"Do you know the current location of the truck?"

The truck. Not almost allowed himself a smile in his relief. They were looking for the truck. Donny and Joe must not have reported the truck was being stored in the garage, and now they think it has been stolen.

A person could certainly get up to a lot of trouble with their own armored car.

"Oh, sure," Not was happy to confirm and put the matter to rest. "They asked me to store it in the garage for the night and for it to go back to the armored car company in the morning. I secured it in the mechanic's bay, rather than in our lot."

"Very good, Mr. Johnson," the male agent said, and glanced over to review his partner's notes. "You are being extremely helpful. If you can provide an answer for the next question, then we will be all through here today, sound good?"

"Absolutely!" Not agreed, thrilled this was almost over.

"Is the cocaine still in the back of the armored car, or did you move it to another location?"

"Did I . . .wait . . .what?"

"Still in the truck, yes or no?" The male agent pressed.

"What cocaine?" Not nearly whimpered. "I don't know what you are talking about, but I have had nothing to do with any cocaine."

"Okay," the male agent sighed, and then shrugged to his partner. "Looks like we won't be done by breakfast after all."

"I'll ask for a couple of chairs," the lady agent said, and turned towards the door. "Coffee?"

"Yes, please," the male agent replied.

"Can I also have a coffee?" Not asked, miserably. "And, is it too late to ask for a lawyer?"

Chapter 18

AT ELEVEN years old, Topher discovered the addictive thrill of gambling. His initiation came, from all of the possible sources, in his Christmas stocking. From his grandmother.

Every year up until then, his grandmother had sent a Christmas card to all of her fourteen grandchildren, dispersed among her own four children and their spouses. Included in all of the cards was a crisp, new five dollar bill. That year, whether trying to be more adventurous, or perhaps just a little more cost efficient, she substituted a scratch-off lottery ticket for the fiver.

It was both disappointing and intriguing. He had been expecting cash, in the innocently unappreciative and entitled manner only children seem to possess, he had felt like Grandma had cheated him. Like she had promised something, which of course she hadn't, and then had given him nothing, which of course she had.

What was intriguing though was the concept that instead of five dollars, this fancy little piece of cardboard promised at least a chance for a thousand dollars.

The title proclaimed, in bright red and gold lettering which was both friendly, and somehow also a little aggressive, the ticket was a Tik-Tak-Toe instant winner. Inside the traditional tic-tac-toe crosshatch, numbers had been covered with the fake silver gummy paint which never seemed to rub away from being in a pocket or wallet, but yielded easily to the edge of a penny. At the spaces above and to the right side of the crosshatch were various levels of prizes, ranging from $1 to $1000. The spaces of the crosshatch were already filled in with numbers, digits one through nine, and if you got three of the same numbers in a row, then you would receive the prize at the

147

end of the row. If you got three of the same numbers, but they were not in a row, you at least got a free ticket.

Topher had carefully scratched away each of the spaces, one at a time, happier for some reason when he uncovered a nine or a one, and less thrilled with the lame middle numbers like a five or a six.

When all was finally revealed, he found a trail of two's leading from the bottom right to the top left, where it ended at the $50 prize.

Grandma's card had, in a matter of seconds, become his favorite Christmas gift.

He had begged his parents to take him to the store immediately so he could cash it in. They had laughed indulgently, but had made him wait until after all the presents were opened, the paper cleaned up, breakfast was eaten, the dishes were cleaned up, and everyone had showered and dressed festively so they could go to Uncle Phil and Aunt Stacy's house, like they did every year, where all the parents and cousins would exchange gifts, have a mid-afternoon holiday dinner, and then the parents would drink beer and wine and play cards, while the kids drank soda and ate candy and played video games.

He had been proudly displaying it to his cousins all day, and Harvey, the oldest, had tried to trick him into throwing it away. Harvey explained to him about the joke lottery tickets he had seen in a store at the mall, the one with the coffee mugs with boobs on them and the room in the back with all actual porn in it.

"All of us won fifty bucks, but then we saw it was fake, so we tossed them in the fire."

Topher had felt both skeptical and crushed at the same time. He suspected Harvey was full of shit, but at the same time felt absolutely certain he was not.

"Christopher," piped up his cousin Becca, she was Harvey's younger sister and therefore ready to sell him out simply for the joy of doing so. "Harvey is a mega-liar. He got one too, but it didn't win anything. I won a free ticket, and Dad picked it up for me on the way over. I won another free ticket, but Dad was already back on the road, and didn't want to stop again. Look, see?"

Becca produced the Tik-Tak-Toe scratcher from her pocket. On it were three 3's, but they did not form a row.

Topher had given Harvey the finger, and then wouldn't speak to him for the rest of Christmas.

The day went on, like it did every year, until around seven or eight o'clock when one of the eight parents, usually the one whose spouse should have stopped one glass previously, announced they should really be getting the kids home to bed. As soon as the seal was broken, then other parents started saying the same, and within twenty minutes or so, all the kids were back in the family car or minivan and headed back home.

On this particular year, however, on the way home his parents paused briefly at the Stop and Shop so they could cash in the ticket for him. Topher had been disappointed he was not permitted to hand the ticket in for the cash, but Mom had pointed to the back where it read in bold lettering "Must be 18 to play."

When his Mother got back in the car, she had with her a twenty and three tens. She handed the tens to him, and told him the twenty was going into his savings account.

"I asked for tens in case you wanted to share your good fortune with your brothers," Mom hinted.

Topher absolutely did not want to share his money with his brothers, but he knew if he didn't then his mom would snatch back the money, do it anyway, and call it a lesson. He also knew if he did, he basically had a free pass the next time his little brothers tried to take something of his, and they would get yelled at for being greedy.

So, Topher shared out the cash like a good boy.

The next day, he was back at the Stop and Shop, which conveniently had the automated ticket vending machine located near the front door, and the view of it was blocked by a display case. He fed the ten dollar bill into the machine and punched the $1 ticket option, Pot-O-Gold, ten times. The machine spewed out a giant paper tongue of tickets, which reminded Topher of Skee Ball. Topher grabbed the tickets and was out the door before the clerk could investigate the noise.

He walked around the corner of the store, and felt the same thrill as the day before as he scratched away the fuzzy-paint coverings from the nine pots of gold. Seven of the tickets were losers, not even a free ticket, but the other three scored a ten dollar win, a two dollar win, and a five dollar win.

He had talked a customer heading in to cash them in for him, explaining his grandmother had sent them to his brothers and him, but his evangelical mom considered it gambling, and had thrown them away. He said he had fished them out of the trash, and he promised he would give his brother's their money too.

The customer offered a knowing smile, like he knew at least some of the story had to be bullshit, but he shrugged and took the tickets inside and cashed them out.

Topher waited nervously, wondering if the man would just pocket the cash and walk away, but when he came back out he handed Topher a ten, a five, and two singles and walked away.

The man never even said a word.

Topher didn't buy any more that day, but he revisited the Stop and Shop often. Sometimes he won, but of course more often he lost. The times he won, he would give a variation of the same story to whichever customer looked like he or she might be kind. If it was around Christmas time, he would use the original story. Any other time of the year, and any winning ticket became his, and they were all from a birthday card from his grandma. He got turned down sometimes, but he never got turned in.

He never got ripped off until he won big.

On a Super 7's, five dollar scratcher, which offered prizes up to $77,777, Topher won an even grand. This was the second summer after he had discovered the lottery, and he considered asking his Mom to cash it in for him. He knew he would be in for a lecture, and she would likely put the whole thing into his savings account for college, but she might also make him share it with his brothers again.

He had decided to go with what had worked so far.

He rode his bike to the Stop and Shop and waited for a likely target. Almost immediately, a man who looked to be in his thirties came riding up on a bike, a toddler sat behind him in a child's seat. The man parked his bike right next to Topher's, and Topher immediately launched into the spiel. This time, he added he was going to put the money into his college fund.

The man had smiled, and asked him where he was planning to go. Princeton, Topher had answered automatically, like any good kid from Jersey who was looking to brown-nose a little. The man had nodded approvingly, and then taken the ticket from Topher's hand.

After about fifteen minutes in the store, much longer than normal, but then it was a much bigger prize than normal as well, the man returned and strapped the baby into the child seat on the back of his bike. He looked around, as if to make sure no one was watching him to help a child gamble, and then produced a one hundred dollar bill from his pocket and handed it to Topher.

"Where's the rest?" Topher had asked, knowing full well he was about to be screwed and there was nothing he would be able to do about it.

"That's the prize, kid," the man shrugged. "You won a hundred bucks. You should be happy."

"The ticket was for a thousand!" insisted Topher.

"Nope, sorry," the man said, as he started to peddle the child away. "You must have read it wrong."

The man had looked like a nice guy, and the worst part was he probably was.

Money and opportunity can make just about anyone into a complete bastard.

After all, Topher considered himself to be a pretty decent human being, and look where he was now.

Topher stared at the blue barrel, his jackpot, and knew he would have to depend on someone else once again to help him cash it in.

The problem was, though, and he never thought he would have regretted it: he had never done cocaine. True, he was not now nor had he ever been a straightedge kind of guy. He had smoked his share of pot, tried mushrooms once or twice, acid once, ecstasy at a few different club scenes, and of course there was alcohol everywhere he worked.

But, he had never done coke. He had, of course, known there was coke going around inside the clubs he bounced for, but nobody wasted blow on a bouncer. He never had friends who did coke, and he certainly didn't know any coke dealers, so he had absolutely no idea how he would turn this barrel full of thick liquid, which was somehow cocaine, into cash.

He didn't even know how much it was worth.

He pulled up a new proxy window on his phone and started searching for current cocaine pricing in New Jersey, and fervently hoped when the proxy service promised "complete internet anonymity," they were not just full of shit.

He was shocked by the amount of sources of information available. There were discussion forums, which included open offers to sell and requests to purchase, and then just a lot of threads of discussion about the "responsible cocaine lifestyle" as posted by "educated cocaine enthusiasts." He found one thread which started with someone asking if $10,000 was a good price for a kilogram of "pure Colombian." The next dozen or so posts informed the original poster, in so many words, he was either a poser, a moron, or an incompetent narc if he thought he could get a full kilo of pure cocaine for "a third of what it would be worth." The next dozen posts suggested if the price was correct, then the product was not, and stated it had likely been cut with something.

Topher reasoned, if ten grand was one third of what should be expected for a kilo, then the simple math involved would equate to thirty grand for a kilo of pure cocaine. Topher was certain he had to have at least a dozen kilos in the barrel, even though it sounded like it had been dissolved in water, and the water must account for some of the weight.

Wondering what the concentration of the cocaine was in the barrel, Topher scanned further on the label until he found 2.5g/mL and then the same formula for cocaine again as the numerator and H_2O as the denominator. So, two and a half grams per milliliter would equal two and a half kilograms per liter. He wondered briefly why they didn't just write it that way instead, but then decided he didn't care.

He ran another quick search for a conversion table and found there were .254172 gallons per liter, and this size barrel was commonly referred to as a 55 gallon drum. He punched in 55 on the gallon side of the converter, and it instantly switched the liter side to 208.198. So, if there were two and a half kilograms per liter . . .

It meant there was over five hundred and twenty kilograms of cocaine.

At thirty grand each, it totaled over fifteen and a half million dollars.

Jesus.

Topher came to the conclusion he must have fucked up.

Math had never been his best class in high school, but he had been a C or better student, and he knew he could handle basic multiplication, especially with the aid of a calculator and conversion tables. Still, if he had punched in decimal wrong, or transposed some numbers, he could easily have messed up.

He ran the whole sequence of conversions again.

Fifteen million dollars.

Not that he thought he would get top dollar. The coke was stolen and hotter than brimstone, and a motivated seller had to expect to sell at a discount. At twenty thousand a kilo, they would still make over ten million dollars. Hell, at ten thousand each, they would still make over five million dollars, and two point five million would certainly take care of Topher just fine.

Not Donny though.

Donny would want the most he could get, even if it meant shopping the stuff around and increasing the risk. Topher knew from experience there was no such thing as reasoning with Donny, or convincing Donny of anything he didn't already secretly agree with.

Donny would simply nod and agree to your face, and then go and do whatever the hell he had been planning to do all along.

Of course, Donny probably still had no idea what it was they had stolen. Or, if he did, he didn't know how much there was in the barrel.

If Topher could move the stuff quickly, line up a buyer and unload the whole thing, even at a steep discount, before Donny tracked him down, then he could just present Donny with a couple of million dollars and go on his merry way. If Donny was sore, or felt like they could have done better, then fuck him. He could go rob another armored truck if he thought he could do better.

Next time, Topher thought bitchily as his back twinged again, Donny could do the heavy lifting.

Chapter 19

DONNY'S LAWYER was pretty much as far from David Green as one could get and still be a lawyer.

If one were to look for a symbol of their differences, one need look no further than their business cards. Green's was plain but elegant, printed with high quality ink on thick stock paper which felt like cotton.

Jennifer's was a refrigerator magnet.

Where Green had been bald, tastefully dressed, and seemed to exude authority, Jennifer Jones had hair like a show poodle, wore clothing which could be seen from orbit, and seemed to feel it was necessary to remind whomever she happened to be addressing at least once per conversation she was, in fact, a lawyer.

Donny wasn't sure if she did so because she felt the need to remind others or to remind herself. He had once told her she seemed more like a game show host than a lawyer. It was only half-true, though. He thought she seemed more like a game show contestant.

Donny could not imagine her ever winning the confidence of a jury; their sympathy, perhaps, but not their confidence. Fortunately, Jennifer Jones rarely, if ever, saw the inside of a courtroom. Like many lawyers, her practice consisted almost entirely of creative interpretation of vague legal language and the filing of enormous amounts of paperwork.

During his last legal go-round, he had seen a brown accordion folder, at least three inches thick, which had borne his name on the label. When he had asked, with a bit of appreciative awe in his voice, if those were all of the motions she had made for him in the case so far, Jennifer had smiled mischievously and informed him those were just the motions she would be filing today.

"All of them will be denied though," she had warned him.

"Then," Donny had asked, puzzled, "why?"

"If you can't beat 'em with brilliance, Don," Jennifer had confided, "then you bury 'em in bullshit."

It was a strategy she had perfected well. She had numerous, several hundred page motions, set up as a boilerplate document in which she merely needed to type in a find-and-replace command with her current client's name, and hit print. Her opposition must then investigate the merits of each motion, under the due diligence requirements of all state and federal mandates, in order to determine the veracity of each claim. It consumed huge amounts of her opponent's time, and often allowed her to sneak in an occasional meritable claim, which would go overlooked and thus under opposed, or it would earn her a sanction from the court, sometimes a fine or sometimes even a formal reprimand to file no further frivolous motions. As the definition of frivolous is subjective, and all she needed to do was to demonstrate "good faith" she felt she was filing motions in her client's best legal interests, a formal request to stop filing motions on behalf of her client was a near automatic appeal if they lost, or a counter-suit for bias if it was a civil matter, which would inevitably waste even more of the court's time and resources. It was a strategy which nearly always led to a plea-bargain or deal of some kind.

It had even earned Jennifer a nickname: The Paper Princess.

Despite her penchant for legal shenanigans, and her loose definition of justice, Donny had discovered Jennifer was also horrifyingly faithful to the letter of the law. If she had any knowledge a crime had actually been committed by her client, then she would enter no plea other than guilty. She would then do all she could to plea-bargain or try to get the sentence reduced as best as she could, but she would not represent a person whom she knew to be guilty with a not-guilty plea.

So, Donny was very selective with what information he shared.

"Now, Donny, I'm your lawyer," Jennifer reminded him. "And I will do everything within my ability to get you out as quickly as I can, but I need to know everything if I am going to be able to get out in front of this thing."

Donny had given her, word for word, the same version of events he had told the police. Her reaction had been disappointingly similar; she too seemed to think he was full of shit. It was really rather infuriating. He had set everything up so the evidence would not point to him, and everything had gone exactly as he had planned, better than he had planned, actually, and still everyone just took it as a given he was involved.

The fact they were right just made it all the more frustrating.

"Get out in front of what?" Donny asked, with just a hint of righteous indignation. "I did my job as I was directed to do by my supervisors, and part of the load got stolen. I did what I was told to do."

"Yeah, no, sorry, but the Nazi defense doesn't really ever work," Jennifer said wryly. "In this case, all they need to do to prove criminal negligence is to demonstrate 'gross deviation from the standard of care that a reasonable person would observe in the situation.' It's the 'reasonable person' part which kills your 'I was just following orders' defense."

"A reasonable person would ignore what the boss tells them to do?"

"A reasonable person would *never* consider a rental truck to be a proper substitute for an armored car."

"We didn't know we were hauling coke!"

"It doesn't matter, moron!" Jennifer yelled back. "Anything transported by armored car is valuable, which is why they hire you in the first place instead of renting a goddamn truck themselves!"

Donny really wanted to be able to say something back, but she was absolutely right. Topher had said pretty much the same thing, and Donny had agreed. It was completely and utterly stupid. Unfortunately, he had been counting on the fact it was someone else's stupidity being his defense. He had no idea his own actions were going to be held to a reasonable person's standards. What reasonable person would willingly make a target of himself by driving an armored car for only slightly more than minimum wage?

"So, what, does criminal negligence carry jail time or is it like a fine?" Donny asked.

"It depends," Jennifer continued as if they had not just been shouting. "Usually, criminal negligence is attached to another crime, kind of secondary charge to show how bad the first charge is, you know?"

"Is that what is happening here?"

"Not yet," Jennifer attempted, but utterly failed to achieve, a soothing tone. "As of this moment, you have not been charged with anything. But . . ."

She let Donny finish the thought himself.

"But, they can use it to lean on me," Donny finished.

"Only if they feel they need to lean on you," Jennifer amended. "If they think you are holding back on them."

"So, how do I avoid that?"

"Cooperate," Jennifer advised, and then added "without self-incrimination. Give them everything you can to help point the finger anywhere but at you."

"So, you think I should tell them Not did it?"

"No!" Jennifer nearly shouted again, looking horrified. "At this point, it would be admitting both prior knowledge and withholding evidence. Maintain your innocence at every opportunity, but answer their questions, with me present, and don't go out of your way to defend your partner or your old buddy."

Donny had already been trying to think of ways to point the investigation toward Not, so he figured Jennifer's plan was very doable.

"Do you need anything?" Jennifer asked. "Do you need me to call anybody for you?"

"Yes," Donny nodded. He reached across the table and scribbled a phone number on the margin of Jennifer's notepad. "Can you call my friend, Topher, and ask him to look in on my cat, Mr. Creepy?"

"Your cat's name is Mr. Creepy?" Jennifer smirked.

"Yes, and he is an absolute diva," Donny said with an exaggerated swish. "Tell Topher Mr. Creepy needs to be handled with a velvet glove."

"A velvet glove?" Jennifer repeated. "Tell me you don't mean literally."

"Just an expression, sweetie," Donny said, laying it on.

"Not one I've ever heard," Jennifer said, as she gathered her things to go. "And, don't go trying to play the gay card on the feds. Just play it straight."

"Ha ha," Donny pouted.

157

"I didn't mean it like that and you know it," Jennifer sighed. "Are you serious about the goddamn cat?"

"Absolutely," Donny said, and then grinned. "Topher will know exactly what to do."

Chapter 20

NOT HATED *deja vu.*

Is that what this was? He knew if you felt something had happened before when you were sure it *hadn't* actually happened before, it was *deja vu,* but what was the feeling for when something had happened before when it actually has happened before? Was there a French phrase for that one too?

Experience, he guessed best fit the bill.

The cell was different, and it was plain clothes feds, rather than uniformed cops, but the feeling was the same. The feeling he was in deep shit, mixed with indignation from the certainty he had done nothing wrong, and layered with the anxious voice constantly whining in the back of his mind which wondered if he actually had.

"So, who's your horse?" the male agent asked.

Not glanced up towards where they sat, in folding chairs on either side of the one door in the room. Not himself was sitting on the bench, his back in the corner and his legs up on the bench in front of him to keep from tapping his foot nervously.

The male agent was not looking at him, but instead was addressing his partner.

After Not had requested his lawyer, the female agent had sighed, taken the document out which he had signed, and marked the time he made the request below his signature and initialed it, then pulled out the second document, and asked him to sign it and mark the time.

She had then gone out to collect two chairs, two cups of coffee, and presumably to request a Public Defender. When she returned, she had handed a chair and a coffee to her partner, unfolded her own chair, sat, and began scrolling on her phone and sipping her coffee.

The male agent had done the same.

They both completely ignored Not.

"Well, it depends on how many horses you think are in the race," she replied without looking up from her phone.

"How many do you think there are?" he asked.

"I think three," she replied.

"Not just the two?"

"Three," she confirmed. "I don't think the second barrel ever left the truck."

"Well, of course you would say it didn't because then it wouldn't have crossed the state line, right?"

"Why would they take both barrels all the way north, just to bring one of them back?" She reasoned. "It makes no sense."

"They could have taken both and already sold the one along the way."

"Where's the cash?"

"They stashed it."

"Would you let that much money out of your sight?" she snorted.

"Joe took both barrels out of the truck," Not said, and then immediately wished he had kept his mouth shut.

Apparently, the agents felt the same.

"We're not talking to you," the male agent snapped. "So, don't say a word until your lawyer gets here."

"The guards could easily have moved both barrels out for our young friend over there to see, but then moved the one back in when he wasn't looking," she offered. "But, whether he cops to it or not, it would still mean three. Anyway, we'll find out soon enough. Barrel in the truck means it never left New Jersey, and I've already got my three horses ready to run."

They sat silently for a few minutes, both agents still scrolling on their phones. The male agent retrieved his Styrofoam cup of coffee from where he had placed it on the floor right after receiving it, having declared it too hot to drink.

"Ugh," he mumbled. "Cold."

He set the cup back on the floor, still nearly full.

Not would have gulped the whole steaming cup down the moment it was placed in his hands, if they had brought him one. Of course, maybe it was for the best they had not. Coffee went right through a person, and he did not relish the thought of having to have an audience while he added his own small percentage to the water cycle.

"Okay," the male agent started in again on the female agent. "Devil's advocate: say they don't find a barrel?"

"Then it would still be three," the female agent maintained, "Unless, you think they stashed the barrel somewhere along the way, and even if they did my money is they stashed it in New Jersey. But, if you think about it, stashing is only an option if it is somewhere safe. Like maybe in an armored car, stuck in a locked garage."

They both looked again at Not.

"Three, huh?" the male agent said, considering.

"Three," she confirmed.

The male agent stared coldly and consideringly at Not for a few more moments, and then shrugged, nodded slightly to himself, and then returned to his phone. His thumbs tapped quickly over the touchscreen. He scrolled up and then down briefly, re-reading whatever it was he wrote, and then tapped the screen once more and set the phone gently on his thigh.

Text message.

About a minute later, the phone buzzed briefly one time.

Return text.

The male agent scanned through the message, and nodded again to himself, as if it was exactly what he was expecting.

"Okay, direct from Executive Assistant Director, as there is no evidence the cocaine ever left the state, and the DEA has a working theory and boots on the ground, the investigation is no longer shared."

"Thanks Greg," she said, sounding like she actually meant it.

"I can stick around if you want, but overtime is coming out of your budget, so . . ."

"No, I can call in some back up, if I need it, from the local office," the DEA agent demurred. "Go home and get some rest. We've already got everyone, it's just a matter of time."

"You picked your horse?" Greg asked.

"Yeah," the DEA agent turned her gaze again at Not. "I got him."

The male agent, Greg, nodded again, and then knocked on the door to be allowed to leave. A moment later, the door was opened by an unseen guard and Agent Greg from the FBI was gone.

Lady DEA took another sip of her coffee, looked consideringly again at Not, and then returned to her phone.

Not knew he was being played. He wondered how much of the whole back and forth was just stage dressing to soften him up and get him to talk. Some of it? All of it? Maybe, none of it?

Still, he hadn't done anything wrong, to his knowledge, but maybe he did have some information which would help them find the cocaine they were looking for.

He had been able to glean from the conversation that the coke had been hidden in the barrels, and from the conversation about money, it was apparently quite a bit of coke. Probably a couple of kilos or more, and if television crime shows could be believed, then it was a couple of big paper and plastic wrapped bricks likely stuffed in the middle of the barrel surrounded by something far less valuable. In the eighties cop movies, it had been coffee, supposedly to confuse the drug sniffing dogs, but Not didn't figure anyone would ship coffee in a drum. Or, transport it by armored truck, for that matter.

Whatever it had been, it was heavy. Joe had been straining to keep the barrel on the tracks, and it had been on a downward slope thanks to the tilt of the flatbed.

Shit.

"Um, ma'am?" Not began.

"Do not talk until your lawyer gets here," the agent reminded him again. "Unless, do you want to sign a third statement? Maybe a fourth one a few minutes later? Waste some more of your tax dollars, and my time?"

"I just thought you should know the other guy was right," Not shrugged. "About the barrels, I mean. They didn't go back in the armored truck."

"Not that you saw," she corrected. "At least, according to your story."

"No, really," Not felt absurdly compelled to correct her, simply because what she was proposing was not possible. "I had the armored secured on the flatbed and I tilted it to help Joe get the load transferred. They looked heavy, but even if they weren't, he would have been hauling them up a ramp, which went up an inclined bed to an inclined truck. It just didn't happen. He put both the barrels, strapped onto moving dollies, into the rental truck, and then pulled the collapsible ramps down while I tilted the bed flat again."

"Again, says you," the DEA agent still gazed at her phone.

"Why would I lie now?" Not asked. "I already told you where the truck is, and admitted to putting it there. If a barrel were still in there, why would I have told you where the truck is?"

"So, the second barrel is for sure not in the truck?" She asked, her tone once more conversational, which should have put him back on guard. "Is that what you are saying?"

"Yes," Not agreed.

"You are certain?"

"Yes," Not again agreed.

"Okay," the agent pulled a third set of forms from her bag, identical to the first set he had signed. "Let's go through this once more. . ."

The cell door swung open once again, and a young man, about the same age as Not, entered the cell. He wore skinny jeans with an untucked Oxford shirt and paisley tie. A messenger bag hung over his shoulder, and he held up a post-it with his right hand.

"Harris Johnson?"

"Yes," Not affirmed.

"I am from the public defender's office and . . ." he then noticed the form in the agent's hand. "Have you been talking to her?"

"Well . . ." Not left it to hang in the air.

"I am going to have to insist I speak to Mr. Johnson alone," the young PD stated in a tone which was as close to scolding as it could be without actually shaking a finger at the two of them.

"Of course," the female agent smiled, and then stepped over to the door and knocked to be let out.

Not and his attorney waited in silence until the door closed behind her.

"Okay," the attorney said as soon as the door was secure. "Exactly how badly have you fucked yourself over? Tell me precisely everything which has been said, every word, since you were taken into custody."

"Okay, let me think," Not said.

"Oh boy," the lawyer shook his head sadly. "not a good start."

Chapter 21

"HOW . . .TO . . .sell . . .shit, not 'sail' . . .sell . . .shit. Stop fucking autocorrecting you useless piece of shit," Topher mumbled to himself as he typed into his phone.

He acknowledged, at least to a certain extent, he was in over his head. He was literally attempting to type in "How to Sell a lot of Cocaine without getting caught" into a search engine, on a mobile phone which was registered to an account in his own name. True, he was using a proxy service website, but it likely would not offer much protection. He didn't know, really.

There was so much about this he didn't know:

He didn't know if Donny was in custody.

If he was, had Donny kept Topher out of it?

If he had, then what to do with the barrel full of cocaine?

Was it safe to leave it here?

For how long?

How did he start to go about selling it?

Or, who to sell it to?

Or, how about how to get it there and not be ripped off, arrested, or killed?

He was pretty sure there were things he didn't even know he didn't know. He finished typing and pressed enter. Thirteen million, seven hundred thousand results.

Number one result: How Drug Dealers get Caught.

Topher scanned through the article, thinking maybe he could just do the opposite of whatever they had done, and it seemed to boil down to a central core concept: if one wanted to avoid getting caught for dealing drugs, then one should avoid dealing drugs.

The main problem seemed to stem not from the drug dealers, but the drug users, who had a tendency to become complete and utter dumbasses when stoned, or tweaked, or coked, or whatever else and they would get arrested. The drug users didn't want to go to jail, and the only thing they had to trade which the police wanted was the name of the drug dealer, which more often than not they were all too happy to supply.

The next few articles were of the memoir sort, explaining from a drug dealer's point of view how he -- in all cases it was a he not a she -- got started, built his business, and then retired without ever seeing the inside of a jail cell. All of them started by buying some weed for himself, and then selling it to his friends. Like any other small business, he would start building up a reputation and discovered return business was the key. Then, in order to broaden the sales base, the pot-dealer began to offer a larger assortment of goods. Some, depending on the socio-economic level of his clientele discovered cocaine, if they were selling to the middle or upper middle class tax bracket, offered more profit for less product. Others discovered the same thing about methamphetamines, but at the other end of the income spectrum.

Nearly all the memoirs ended with, "when things started going bad, I got out. Out of the business, and out of the country."

The shortest time anyone of the memoirs stated for going from rags to riches was about two years, and it was because he became the resident dealer for his fraternity and the other frats on campus. He had a built in network.

What Topher needed was someone who already had a thriving business and just wanted a good deal on some coke to sell.

He couldn't believe he was wishing he knew more drug addicts.

When the phone in his hand began to buzz, he nearly dropped it from surprise.

He had been so absorbed in his web searching, he had nearly forgotten the device he was holding was actually a phone. Of course, it could also be because his hand had gone slightly numb. Unable to type with thick padding around his fingers, he had removed his gloves a while ago. Now his fingers were red and getting harder to flex. He could still feel the phone vibrate though, so he checked the screen.

The caller ID was blocked.

"Hello?" he answered, trying to sound casual.

"Good morning, am I speaking with Mr. Topher Mason?" a lady's voice asked.

"Um, who is calling, please?" Topher returned, being cautious.

"My name is Jennifer Jones, and I am a lawyer," she stated, with emphasis on the word lawyer. "I am calling on behalf of my client, Donovan Allen, who has asked me to contact you in regards to some personal requests."

"Did Donny get arrested?" Topher again tried to sound casual, but heard the urgency in his own voice.

"I'm sorry, but I cannot discuss the personal details of a client with you without express permission from said client," she stated firmly. "However, I have been given instructions to contact you on behalf of Mr. Allen to request for you provide care for his cat. Can I confirm for Mr. Allen you will accept the responsibility of the care and custody of this animal until Mr. Allen, or myself on behalf of Mr. Allen, contact you to make further arrangements?"

"I'm sorry," Topher couldn't believe what he was hearing. "Donny wants me to look after his *cat*?"

"It is at his request, yes," the lady lawyer confirmed. "Can you confirm you will accept the responsibility of the care and. . ."

"Yes," Topher interrupted. Man, this lady liked the sound of her own voice. "Yeah, sure, I can take care of his cat."

Donny hated cats, all pets really, but especially cats. He couldn't stand them. Topher had even seen Donny swerve toward cats in the road, rather than try to avoid them. He had never actually hit any, at least not when Topher had been in the car with him, but he certainly came close on several occasions. One evening, Donny had slammed on the brakes to avoid a raccoon, but two blocks later had nearly sideswiped a parked car in an effort to squish a tabby.

Topher suddenly registered the lady lawyer had been speaking again, for a while.

"I'm sorry, ma'am," Topher interrupted again. "It's very early for me, and I kind of spaced out there. Could you say that again?"

"First, I informed you I was beginning a recording to get your verbal assurance you would be responsible for the care and custody of the cat belonging to Mr. Donovan Allen. Second, I stated I am under the impression you know where Mr. Allen lives, and you would have access to said residence and requested that if you do not would you please say so at this time. You did not speak, so I continued. Third, I stated the care of this animal is considered a personal favor, and no monetary consideration is being offered, nor will one be requested by you at a later date. And fourth, I read the special care instructions left by Mr. Allen, which are verbatim: 'Mr. Creepy is a bit of a diva and needs to be handled with a velvet glove.'

"Do you confirm you have heard, understand, and agree with all parts stated?"

"Um, yeah, sure."

Topher suddenly understood Donny didn't have a cat, and was impressed, once again, by just how smooth Donny was when he wanted to be.

"Okay, I have terminated the recording, so feel free to speak openly," the lawyer's tone was much more friendly now. "Without going into detail or breaking confidence, I don't think you will need to be cat-sitting long. Likely, just for the next day or two. However, on the off-chance the situation changes, you may be stuck with the cat for a while. Are you okay with all this?"

So, without saying so, she was telling him Donny was in custody but not arrested. If they couldn't find enough evidence in the next couple of days then they would have to let him walk. If they did find something they could use, then Donny would be fucked. What she was also telling him, likely without even knowing so herself, was if Donny got arrested he would undoubtedly sell out Topher in an effort to reduce his own sentence.

If Donny went to jail and Topher still had the coke, then the only thing Topher could do would be to cut and run. The coke would hold no leverage over Donny, but it would be plenty damning for Topher. However, if he could unload the whole thing quickly, then the money might be enough to keep Donny quiet. He could put Donny's half in an escrow account, or a safe deposit box and leave the key with the lawyer, something to show Donny the money was safe and waiting for him, but only if he kept Topher out of it.

It could work.

Mr. Creepy.

That could work too.

FOR A while, not too many years ago, there was a national obsession with the various sub-cultures of the Garden State, in particular the Guidos and Goombahs, both the fictitious and the reality television varieties, and for quite a few years there was a boom in entertainment industry jobs in many parts of what one television producer called both "the most American state" and "the armpit of America" in the same interview. Topher could agree with both evaluations.

What is never seen on the screen is all the grunt work which goes on behind the cameras. One scene from a cable crime drama was filmed in a club at which he had worked. A total of two pages of dialogue, maybe twenty lines in all and it had taken nearly six hours to film. The parking lot had been filled with twelve large vehicles, including three tour buses converted into rolling luxury waiting rooms for the actors, eight semi-trucks filled with equipment, and one gourmet food truck.

The scene was to take place at the bar, so a ten foot by ten foot area around the bar was cleared, and then people went to work.

Topher had watched as dozens of men and women scurried around the club for over an hour running and taping down cables, setting up lights and screens to deflect and diffuse the lights which had just been set up, standing where the actors would be while one of the directors checked the light, made adjustments, stood again, added more light, stood again, added a blue colored plastic sheet over some of the lights, stood again, and finally confirmed with the director that the light was okay.

Then the whole process began again for the sound equipment. Boom mics, which looked like enormous fur covered pills, were attached to long arm assemblies, and lowered until they were just out of the space which would appear on camera. Some other microphones looked like clear plastic radar dishes, which one of the guys setting them up later told him were called parabolic mics, were set up around the periphery of the scene. Like with the lighting, two of the people setting up stood where the actors would be and read from the script. After a couple of lines, someone would yell "stop!", make a couple of adjustments, and then yell "again!" The testers would then say the same lines again until told to stop, further adjustments were made, and so on until the sound was right.

Finally, the cameras and eventually the actors were brought in. A man and a woman who looked vaguely familiar stood at the bar each holding a drink. Camera people were at their equipment, three older guys whom everyone seemed to fear, directors or producers Topher had guessed, huddled around a bank of screens and computers which displayed all the input from the cameras and sound equipment, and the dozens of other people who had set everything up sat or stood a few paces behind them and watched.

For the next two hours, the actors said the same lines several times in a row, with long periods of waiting in between as the men behind the monitors replayed what was just recorded, adjustments were requested, errors were corrected, until they had the line recorded the way they wanted it.

When all the lines were recorded to satisfaction, the directors and the actors headed back out to the luxury buses, and the men and women went back to work spending almost another two hours taking down all the equipment they had spent two hours putting up. The take down went faster in one respect because no adjustments had to be made, but carefully packing equipment takes longer than unpacking.

Topher listened to the conversation as they packed up. Three of the guys wore headset microphones and carried clipboards and appeared to be overseeing the labor rather than actually doing any. From what they said, Topher was able to discern this crew was only one of three working simultaneously on the same show but at various locations, and most of the people and equipment would be moving on to the next stop to do it all again to film a few more lines. This crew needed to have one camera and one boom mic remain behind to film what they called b-roll of the club when it was full.

The guys with the clipboards couldn't seem to decide if the stay-behind job should be a bonus or a punishment.

Topher realized they were the only ones in the room who weren't local. The men and women rolling up the cables and packing away the lights in their molded foam crates didn't speak much, but when they did the familiar tone, cadence, and slang of New York and New Jersey were obvious. The three in the headsets were from out of town, from the accent Topher would guess somewhere southern. He wouldn't know the difference between Alabama, Georgia, or either of the Carolinas in terms of accents. However, he did know one aspect about the club which might help to clarify if it were to be considered a favorable stay-behind assignment.

"It's a salsa club, if it helps," Topher offered. "Mostly Latino, or Hispanic, whichever, and it is very, very loud."

The tidbit of information seemed to turn the trick for the deadlocked three, and two of them quickly cleared out. The third sat down heavily into a booth, and was immediately on his phone.

"Xanax, Klonopin, Valium, I don't fucking care, Steve . . .what?" the stay behind man asked, a hint of annoyance in his voice. "Fine, Stephen, but I am serious, I cannot handle . . . what?"

The unlucky production assistant listened a bit longer this time, but his anxiety at the prospect of an evening of salsa music unaided by some form of chemical assistance seemed to fade with every second that passed.

"Half an hour, really?" said the man from the south. "Alright, see you then."

Nearly an hour later, the man Donny would later title Mr. Creepy walked in the front door.

The name came in part from the affectations of his chosen profession; he was a pimp and liked to dress and act the part, but mostly the name stuck because of the way he spoke. His quiet, almost effeminate, slightly breathy manner of speech combined with a constant dead-eyed stare and a tendency towards extremely prolonged eye-contact also earned him several other, albeit short-lived, nicknames: Hannibal Bates, Psycho Killer (always followed by *qu'est-ce que c'est*), and Super Die, drawing inspiration from a 1970's exploitation movie about a pimp. However, the one to stick for some reason was Mr. Creepy.

Mr. Creepy was not directly associated with the film company, but was more like the larger group of local muscle hired on for the duration of the shoot.

As Topher had witnessed earlier, it took an army to make a television show or movie, and like every army in the history of the world, it had enormous appetites. His high school world history teacher had shared a quote from either Napoleon or Frederick the Great who had opined an army marches on its stomach, meaning that the armies required a lot of food to keep them going. The same history teacher also said, with a mischievous smirk, the same quote could be taken another way when it is noted that cases of STDs always spike when an army is deployed.

Topher figured it would be just as true to say an army marches on it bottles, ounces, and grams as well. And, of course, wherever appetites exist in sufficient quantity, a supplier will be found to satisfy those appetites.

Mr. Creepy had been found to care for this particular army.

Topher had still been working the door when the man arrived, though it was still an hour before the club would officially open, and several before any real numbers would start to arrive. In the interim, the southern production assistant had slipped him a hundred bucks and a stack of consent and release forms everyone coming in would need to fill out, as they might appear in the b-roll between scenes on the show.

Mr. Creepy did not arrive so much as appear.

Topher had not heard the door to the club open or close, but it must have done both for the man to enter. Neither, had Topher noticed the sudden brightness which accompanied the opening of the door to the still sunny late afternoon light of the parking lot. So, either he had been able to open the door so slightly it went unnoticed, or he himself had slipped in unnoticed nearly twenty minutes prior, the last time someone had come in, and had been sitting somewhere in the darkened entry, calling no attention to himself but simply watching.

Topher couldn't control the involuntary jump when the unexpected voice came from just beyond his peripheral vision, but he was able to stifle the girlish scream.

"What's the cover?" the voice asked, his tone was quiet and cordial.

"$10, but we're not really open yet," Topher said, after recovering to the point where he trusted his voice not to crack.

"Oh, my apologies," the man seemed actually embarrassed. "A friend asked me to meet him here, works for a film company shooting here today. Is it okay if I come in early?"

"Yeah, sure," Topher waved away the ten dollars the man held out. "What I meant was we aren't collecting the cover yet. Your friend is at the booth in the corner."

"Yes, thank you, I have already located him," there was just the slightest hint of humor in his voice. His eyes never wavered from Topher's and not once did he blink. Neither did he move to lower the proffered bill. There was no humor, no anger, no emotion at all which Topher would classify as human behind those eyes. "Please, take the money. I don't know how long I will be, and I would hate for there to be any . . . unpleasantness later."

Topher wasn't sure how there would unpleasantness later if the cover charge was being waved now, but he took the ten bucks, stamped the back of his hand, and handed him a release form, though he doubted any camera man in his right mind would focus in on him.

Mr. Creepy headed over to the booth in the corner.

Then stayed there for about three months.

Of course, he would leave at closing time, but the following day, as soon as the open sign went on, there was Mr. Creepy. It wasn't long before the fact he was a pimp of all things pleasurable became glaringly obvious. Most nights, he would arrive with two young women and two young men, rarely the same two faces for very long, and once they went away they very rarely came back. Topher didn't know if they had moved on, died, been arrested, or were in frozen chunks in one of the many freezers Topher assumed Mr. Creepy kept in his basement.

Not at all subtle about his business, he openly handed out bags of pills and powder for cash across the table of the booth in the back. His two employees would often service customers in the bathroom, or parking lot, again for openly traded cash across the table. He never tried to conceal anything, including when he would smack one of his boys or girls across the face if they dawdled too long on any one customer. If it drew the attention of anyone in the club, Mr. Creepy would simply stare at customers until they looked away.

Topher had never seen anything like it.

He couldn't stop talking about it to all of his friends, and as human nature demands, they all came in soon after to see the man for themselves. The nicknames soon followed.

Topher discovered his real name from the release form from the film company. Topher's manager had insisted they make copies of all the release forms, so no one there that night could complain later they didn't know they would be on television.

Before he had known what Mr. Creepy was, he was well aware Mr. Creepy had been, well, creepy. Which, as a

173

bouncer, had made him a person of interest for Topher. Topher was fairly certain at some point in the future, he would need to call the police to deal with the man, so he had taken a photo of the man's name, address, phone number, and so on in order to be able to provide it to an officer at a later date.

Topher was planning to remove the man himself after the first slap across the face of a young man who had to still be in his teens, which went against the albeit very relaxed morals of the nightclub scene. Consensual drinking, drugging, and humping were all well and good, but as soon as force becomes involved for any of those listed activities, then it was time to step in.

However, as he left his stool to approach the booth, he was waved away by the manager. The same thing happened the second and third time. After the third time being waved off, Topher didn't bother getting up any more. If it had gone any farther, or if one of the boys or girls were ever prevented from leaving or called for help, Topher had intended to step in and the manager be damned, or so he assured himself, but it never happened.

Topher and Donny had been dating, again, kind of, again, at the time. Donny had insisted Topher kept getting waved off by the boss because Mr. Creepy was a member of the Gay Mafia. The manager, Donny had assured him, knew better than to mess with the Velvet Hand if he wanted to stay alive in any part of the entertainment industry.

It was ignorant shit like that which led to the last of their break ups.

Topher assumed the manager let it slide because they were working boys and girls, and they chose to be there, arguably, by their own free will. Or, perhaps, Mr. Creepy was paying him off somehow. He certainly seemed to be in possession of many things people wanted.

Whatever the reason, it went how it went. Every couple of days, Mr. Creepy would slap one of his employees, likely to maintain his dominance, and he or she would shrug it off, all a part of doing business, and everything would be back to normal a few minutes later.

This went on for the better part of the summer, until Topher got a job at another club. When he left, Mr. Creepy was still doing business from the back booth, and Topher never saw him again.

The club closed down later the same year, so Mr. Creepy would have had to find a new place to haunt, but Topher still had the photo of his contact info from the form.

It was a start, at any rate.

Unfortunately, dead-eyed, abusive, low-life pimps were exactly the kind of person who would be most likely to leave Topher's lifeless body in some little travelled part of New Jersey so his animal ravaged remains would be found there years later, while Mr. Creepy was long since retired on the windfall Topher would ultimately provide for him.

Also unfortunately, for Topher at least, he could think of no better alternative, so he tapped his phone to life once more and began to scroll through the hundreds of photos he had.

Chapter 22

DONNY WAS beginning to wonder if there was something wrong with him. Like, something in his head.

He was happy.

He had thought he was happy before, but it could barely be called tolerable contentment compared to how wonderful he felt right now, going into what had to be the thirteenth or fourteenth hour of being detained for questioning.

His pulse was quickened, but not racing. He heard every approaching footstep as soon as they entered the hall.

Topher was out there, holding a fortune of incriminating evidence, and enough information about Donny to be sure a guilty plea would be the only thing which might shave some years from his sentence. A sentence no doubt be long enough to insure Donny would not be eligible for parole until he was well into his middle age.

To make things worse, Donny had no idea if his message had gotten through via Jennifer, a Hail Mary if there ever was one, which could just as easily end with a dead Topher as a pay day for Donny. The bitch of it was, he really didn't care either way.

Both ends would be helpful, given his current position.

True, they could make a connection from Topher to Donny because of their past, but Donny could spin it. He had bumped into Topher the other day, and they had caught up over a cup of coffee, and Donny had told Topher about his new job. Sure, Topher had been unexpectedly interested in Donny's job, but he had said he was tired of being a bouncer, and was looking for a new line of work. Donny had thought ol' Tops would have been a perfect fit for the company, so he had told him all about the job. Of course, he had no idea what Topher had really been planning . . . blah, blah, blah.

It sounded like bullshit of course, but Jennifer could work with it. Reasonable Doubt was all he needed, and if Topher wasn't there to contradict him, then the doubt sounded all the more reasonable.

If Topher managed to actually sell the coke to the psycho pimp with the dead eyes, then all the better. They didn't have enough evidence to charge him, he didn't think, but even if he did, Jennifer would get them to set bail. If Topher got the cash, then bail was all Donny needed. He'd be out of the country before the sun set.

Maybe with Topher.

Maybe just with Topher's share.

Maybe with a call to the DEA telling them where they could find Topher.

Hell, maybe he'd even throw Not under the bus for old time's sake.

God damn, this was fun.

The light slap of leather soles came from up the hall. It must be a Fed, or possibly a detective. Everyone in uniform in this station seemed to prefer rubber soles which squeaked on the hallway tile.

As the footsteps came closer, he could hear the follow-up clop of a flat heel, rather than the peck of a pointed heel. So, either a man, or a woman with large feet and more care for comfort than fashion.

The footsteps stopped outside his door.

A quick, perfunctory knock, and the door swung open.

A pale white man, he looked to be about Donny's age or maybe a little younger, stood in the open doorway. He wore a cheap grey suit and sported a blond young Republican haircut, a film noir tan raincoat, and shiny black and white wingtips.

"Good morning, Mr. Allen," the pale man said. "I am Special Agent Sokolov with the DEA, and I have been asked to give you a ride home this morning."

"Really?" Donny was unable to conceal his surprise. "I mean, great, and thank you, but I kind of figured . . ."

He didn't know how to finish the sentence.

" . . . we were going to charge you with something?" Sokolov finished for him, and then smiled.

"Does this mean you caught the guy?" Donny asked, ignoring the question.

"Sorry, but I can't discuss the investigation," Sokolov held up his hands to mime a half-hearted surrender. "And, I do mean that literally. I have not been given any details of the investigation. All I know is I am to pick you up and drive you down to New Jersey. We need to make one stop at the police station in Hackensack, and then I will drop you off wherever you need."

"New Orleans? Did we miss Mardi Gras?"

"Wherever you need, within reason," the agent amended, but did offer a small smile to show he appreciated the joke.

"What do we need to do at the police station?" Donny asked, attempting to sound casual.

"Likely just paperwork," said Agent Sokolov with a shrug. "Be able to show your release was local to your address, so you don't sue us later for travel expenses. Once you're released at the station you can call someone else for a ride if you want. Heck, you could walk, if you can stand the cold."

Agent Sokolov stepped back from the doorway to allow Donny to exit into the hall. Though he was relatively sure he was being lied to, Donny figured one agent alone in a car offered a lot more possibilities than being locked in an interrogation room in upstate New York.

DONNY FOLLOWED Sokolov into the hallway, through the reception area at the front of the building, and out the front door to where a standard government pool car -- an American made four-door with good tires, cheap rims, powerful engine, and crap interior -- was waiting. Like most of what Donny saw during his various interactions with the law, the car was the perfect visual metaphor for why there would never be an end to crime. It was all function and no style, ordered in bulk, and completely interchangeable with all the other cop cars in the motor pool.

Anyone who looked at it knew right away it had to be a cop car. Maybe police, or maybe FBI, or CIA, or NSA, or DEA, or DOD, or any number of other acronyms which were all just cops with different jurisdictions. The cops knew it looked like a cop car, and they didn't care. They knew everyone who saw it knew it was a cop car, and they didn't care. It was all part of the intimidation game.

We know what it looks like, it said, and we know you know too.

We want you to know we don't care if you know.

The car itself was a kind of uniform, a sign of solidarity. A notice to all the bad guys, no matter how many they may have, the cops had more.

They were everywhere.

They were legion.

Donny suddenly realized he needed some sleep. He was starting to sound a little paranoid in his own head.

"Did you get breakfast yet?" Sokolov asked as they walked toward the generic sedan.

"No," Donny admitted as he debated whether he was supposed to sit in the front or the back. Sokolov seemed to read his hesitation, and opened the front passenger door for him.

"Drive-through coffee and donuts okay?" Sokolov asked. "I'd like to get you there and get back as quick as I can."

"Hot date tonight?" Donny asked, not really caring.

"I wish," Sokolov laughed politely. "No, I've just got some time off coming, supposed to start today, actually, but they asked me to postpone for our little road trip. Just looking forward to doing nothing for a little while, you know?"

"Yeah, I know what you mean," Donny lied. He couldn't stand doing nothing. Doing nothing was, for him, a layover in his own personal hell.

Near the freeway onramp there was a gas station with a Dunkin' Donuts and opposite was another gas station with the Canadian version of the same chain. The second one had a drive-thru, so they opted for the great frozen North's version of America's iconic breakfast pastry, though Donny got an apple fritter to go with his large black coffee and Sokolov stuck with a standard glazed and his own large cup of caffeine.

Sokolov paid, which Donny was expecting, figuring this was a work expense and he would be reimbursed, but when Sokolov extended his arm toward the drive-through window, Donny caught sight of something he was not expecting. About an inch up from the wrist, a little further than where the cuff of a dress shirt normally stops, the agents wrist was ringed with the fringes of a tattoo. Not just the tail end of a tattoo, but all the way around the arm.

Donny had seen similar tattoo work before, in fact several of the buyers for the stolen cars had been sporting tats of a similar style. The kind which went all the way up the arm.

A sleeve.

The thing about people with tattoo sleeves, though, was they rarely stopped with just one arm. In fact, most of the guys, and a few of the girls, Donny had seen with tattoo sleeves had both arms covered in ink, and those who only had the one were already laying plans to get the other done. Along with their backs, their chests, and likely their legs as well.

Now, Donny felt sure there were plenty of DEA agents with ink, just like there were likely a few with hidden piercings, and all sorts of other body modifications, but a sleeve is not the result of a wild night in Cabo, or a fraternity dare. A sleeve took months of return trips, and hundreds if not thousands of dollars to complete, if they were done by any sort of professional, and the ink on Sokolov's wrist looked dark, and clean. A professional job, in Donny's not completely untutored opinion.

It just didn't mesh with the rest of his outward appearance. The plain vanilla suit, and boring tie didn't look like the kind of thing a person with the kind of commitment to personal style would choose. It was like someone saving up to buy a Ferrari, and then getting it painted beige.

At any rate, it made Donny take a second look at Agent Sokolov.

If he hadn't, Donny might never have noticed the young republican haircut the man was sporting wasn't real hair.

Agent Sokolov was wearing a wig.

Suddenly, Donny didn't feel tired any more.

He was intrigued.

Chapter 23

NOT RECOUNTED the whole evening, starting back with the tow job which coincidentally brought Donny once more into his life. That, of course, required a backtrack to explain why Donny was significant in the first place.

It took a little while.

Once they were caught back up to recent history, including his first run in with the police earlier in the evening, due to his bosses' infidelity, the second tangential run in with the police, next to the highway when he picked up the armored truck, and then finishing the first day from hell with the police waiting for him in his father's living room.

He then recounted everything he could remember from the conversation, both with and without his participation, between the two agents who had been here, and finished with the conversation he had been having with the lady from the DEA at the time of his lawyers arrival.

It took nearly an hour and a half, and his lawyer said nothing for the entire time.

"Okay," he began, looking up from his notes when Not had finished. "What is relevant for you right now. One: a significant amount of cocaine is missing, and you are, willing or not, to some degree involved. Two: you have a prior criminal history with one of the other people involved. Three: You were found to be in possession of a large sum of money, in cash, despite having been unemployed for several months. Four: You just stated to a Federal Agent you have knowledge of where the missing cocaine is located."

"All I said was that it was *not* in the armored truck," protested Not.

"If you know for sure it is not somewhere, it implies you know it is for sure somewhere else."

181

Not tried to wrap his head around the circuitous logic for a minute, but couldn't quite swallow it. He was willing to concede the first three points his lawyer, who had accidentally introduced himself about ten minutes into Not's monologue recounting of the past twenty-four-give-or-take hours by answering his ringing cell phone with "Steven Karkus" as his greeting, but Karkus was wrong about the fourth.

"No, the last bit is wrong," Not argued. "The coke is not in this cell, and I can state I have knowledge it is not in this cell, you could state you have knowledge it is not in this cell, but neither one of us could say for sure where it is, just it isn't here."

"Well, one of us can certainly make such a claim," Karkus snipped. "However, I do understand your point. Unfortunately, you are not thinking like a cop. They don't see coincidence. It isn't they don't believe in it, but it's just never where their minds go unless it is proven to them. Most of the time, Occam's razor is absolutely true. Most of the time, if a woman comes into the ER with a black eye and a few loose teeth, then the husband or boyfriend is the cause. Two guys arguing in a bar about a football bet, and one later ends up dead in the parking lot, most of the time the other guy did it. Sure, she could have gotten into a fight in a bar, and the other guy could have been killed by a mugger, but the fact is most of the time those coincidences just don't happen."

"So, what you're saying is I have to prove my innocence, rather than the other way around?" Not asked.

"No," the young lawyer actually looked aghast at the idea. "No, they have to prove beyond a reasonable doubt that you a.) stole the cocaine, b.) participated aforethought in a conspiracy to steal the cocaine, c.) participated after the fact in a conspiracy to steal the cocaine, or d.) became an accessory after the fact by having knowledge of the theft of the cocaine but failed to act upon said knowledge."

"Do any of those seem likely?" Not asked.

"I'd say the wad of cash in your pocket makes C or D the most likely due to physical evidence, but if your boss corroborates the money came from him, and all the rest of your statement here checks out, then no I don't really think they will be able to hold you as an after-the-fact participant."

"Oh, thank God," Not gushed out in a sigh of relief. Alto and Josue, hell even Josue's wife, could vouch for where the money had come from.

"No, I'd say they're going to see your prior involvement with," Karkus paused to review his notes, "Donny, and assume you were involved in the planning and theft of the cocaine, and they will pressure the both of you until one of you points a finger at the other and says, 'It was all his idea.'"

"But I wasn't involved!" Not insisted. "I just happened to answer the call for the breakdown."

"Because you just happened to be one of the only driver's qualified to handle the kind of truck it would take to tow an armored car, at a job you just happened to get the day before, and the guy driving the armored car just happens to be someone you used to steal cars with, oh and by the way, a barrel of cocaine just happens to go missing from the same armored car on the same night.

Karkus locked eyes with Not and watched to see if his words were having the desired impact before he continued.

"Like I said, cops don't see coincidence, Mr. Johnson, what they see are two car thieves who worked out a way to move up in the world. Doesn't it sound a lot more likely?"

"So, you think I was involved too?" Not asked, already knowing the answer.

"I will defend you to the best of my ability," Karkus stated, evading the question. "I will take your statement and verify everything I can. If I can corroborate enough, and I think I can get them to cut you loose, I will do so."

Karkus got up and gathered his notes and phone into his messenger bag.

"However, I will take no other action without consulting you first," Karkus paused for effect. "If, on the other hand, I find out your statement has, well, inconsistencies, then we will need to discuss other strategies when we meet again."

Karkus knocked on the door, which opened almost immediately, and without another word he was gone.

FOR THE first ten minutes after Karkus' departure, Not felt sure he was going to cry. His eyes welled up and blurred his vision, his face felt hot but the rest of his body felt clammy, and he grew aware of a mounting urge to pee. As if the impotent frustration he felt could only be purged from his body in liquid form.

The real bitch of it was, Not could completely understand what Karkus was saying. If he were in Karkus' position, or the DEA's even, Not would assume he was involved too. There were just too many coincidences for it to be, well, coincidental.

But, goddamnit, coincidences happened.

Conspiracy books and social media posts were filled with them, and they always attributed more importance to them than what they were.

Not had watched a dozen shows about it over the years, and followed the clickbait to countless websites on the subject. They all listed off some of the more famous ones each time.

Kennedy and Lincoln were both elected in '60, were concerned with matters of Civil Rights, lost a child while in the White House, and were shot in the head on a Friday, both while seated next to their wives who both survived. Lincoln was shot in Ford's theater, Kennedy in a Lincoln made by Ford. Kennedy and Lincoln both had seven letters in their last names, and Lee Harvey Oswald and John Wilkes Booth both add up to fifteen letters. Both of their Vice Presidents were southern Democrats named Johnson, both were born in '08.

Jefferson, Adams, and Monroe all died on the Fourth of July. Adams and Jefferson on the very same day.

In the 1600s, a ship sank and had only one survivor, a man named Hugh Williams. In the 1700s, a ship sank and had only one survivor, a man named Hugh Williams. In the 1800s, a ship capsized and had only one survivor, a man named Hugh Williams. During World War II, a ship was sunk by a German mine, but it had two survivors.

They were both named Hugh Williams.

Napoleon and Hitler were born 129 years apart, came to power 129 years apart, declared war on Russia 129 apart, and were defeated 129 years apart.

Tsutomu Yamaguchi was in Hiroshima for business on the day the first atomic bomb was dropped on Japan. He survived and returned to his home in Nagasaki just in time for the second atomic bomb to be dropped on Japan.

Yamaguchi survived and lived to be 93 years old.

Coincidences *did* happen. They happen all the time, but most of the time they were fairly benign. A friend you were thinking of calling calls you instead. A movie you haven't seen in a long time happens to be on T.V. You pull into a crowded parking lot and a spot opens up immediately.

Jesus, the odds of the lottery are hundreds of millions to one against, and some motherfucker wins it often enough. Everybody laughs and cheers, or is twisted sick with poorly hidden envy, but at least one honest asshole says loud enough for everyone to hear, "lucky dipshit doesn't deserve it. It should have been me."

We all feel we are owed good luck, because we all view ourselves as fundamentally good people. Everyone who is different from us is strange, or crazy, or bad, or lame, or stuck-up, or prudish, or slutty, or any other number of derogatory, dismissive appraisals. Ourselves, though, at our core we all think *we* are the good ones.

Good people are supposed to get rewarded and bad people are supposed to be punished.

So, we have a tendency to alter our perception of the facts to make them fit into our comfort zone.

Good shit isn't supposed to happen to bad people, and bad shit isn't supposed to happen to good people. God, we so desperately want it to be true. When it doesn't appear to happen, when the bad shit happens to us good people - because in our heart of hearts, deep down, we all know we are the *good* people - or good shit happens to a true and completely righteous fuckwad of a human being, we assume it's because we don't have all the facts.

What we truly fear is the possibility of no causality. We hate to think sometimes good things just happen to bad people. It just isn't fair. It doesn't jibe with our belief the universe is actually an ordered and logical place.

When confronted with it, we'll try to figure out why they actually had it coming.

The sweet old lady who was carjacked and beaten, well, she probably kicked puppies when no one was looking. She probably deserved it.

The non-smoker health nut who is stricken with double-lung cancer, shit, he should have known better than to live so close to the big powerline towers. He deserved it.

The dude who was shot by the police, because the jacket he was wearing was similar to someone for whom they were looking, well he was practically asking for it. Dress like a criminal, someone would say, and you get what you get.

People were quicker to dismiss a happy coincidence, providing the person was somehow an idiot, and of course we are quick to think of anyone other than ourselves as an idiot. Dumb people for some reason get a pass on being lucky. Probably because we already feel superior to them. We're so comfortable with it we even created a term for it: dumb luck.

The converse, of course, was not the same. We might *say* someone was the victim of bad luck, but most of the time the victim had to earn it. Someone finds a hundred bucks on the street: dumb luck. Someone loses a hundred bucks: are you sure you didn't misplace it? Did you put it in your wallet? It was just in your pocket? Well, there you go: should've put it in your wallet. Sure was some bad luck, though.

At best, a victim of bad luck could earn the distinction of being in the wrong place at the wrong time.

When Not was not long out of high school himself, he had seen a story on the news about a girl in California who had been shot coming out of a Friday night football game.

The game had been the homecoming game for her school, where she was a senior, on-track for graduation the following June, and her boyfriend was on the football team. When the game ended, she and several of her friends had walked out of the stadium, planning on walking to where one of the girls had parked her parent's car and joining up with the football team for some celebratory pizza. They were standing at the corner waiting for the crosswalk indicator to change from the angry red palm to the happy white walking stick-man.

While they waited, up the block an inconsiderate driver in a hurry cut off someone who could at best be described, as the television news anchor had put it, as an "unstable individual." The man who had been cut off, rather than laying on the horn, retrieved a .38 revolver from wherever he had kept it stashed within easy reach in his car and pulled alongside the "offending automobile." The "unstable individual" fired all six shots into the "offending automobile."

He missed the driver with all six shots.

Four of the shots were deflected into the interior of the car, where they spent their fury bouncing off the frame and shredding upholstery and pressed vinyl.

Two of the shots, however, did make their way through the "offending automobile" and into the crowd of football fans, and both of them ended up in the head and shoulder of the young lady who had just cheered from the stands for her boyfriend and her team.

She was dead when she hit the ground.

The news anchor opined the girl had just been "in the wrong place at the wrong time."

The expression had never sat well with Not.

She was a high school student attending a high school football game. How could it possibly be considered the wrong place for her to be? What about the guy with the gun? Why did he get a free pass on the place and time? How was outside of a high school football game shooting a pistol into another car, and inadvertently into the crowd behind it, the right place and time to do so?

But no, something bad had happened to someone, and everyone deep down knows bad things don't happen to good people. So, maybe she didn't "deserve it," but it was still kind of her fault because she was "in the wrong place at the wrong time."

Not was a tow truck driver, and he had been doing his job. He had had the bad luck to run into someone who had been bad luck for him before.

Sure, it was unlikely, but not unheard of.

In 1895, there were only two cars in the entire state of Ohio, and they had managed to crash into each other.

It could be said the fact Donny was up to something on the day Not ran into him again was also a coincidence too great to be believed, but not if you knew Donny. The guy was always running some kind of scam. After the trial, Nor recalled the many occasions when Donny had tried to sell him a cell phone or an iPod, supposedly a good find from the swap meet, but as it turned out they were sourced from a more dubious origin.

It would have been a bigger stretch of the imagination to run into Donny when he was not up to something. Not couldn't even imagine Donny doing laundry or stocking up on canned soups during a double coupon sale at the grocery.

Karkus' words surfaced again in connection with Donny: they will pressure you until one of you points to the other and says it was all his idea.

It certainly wasn't Not's idea, and he would have been more than happy to point the finger at Donny, had, in fact, done his best to point the finger at Donny, with what limited knowledge he did have, but could go no further because he knew no more about it.

187

Donny, on the other hand, was not shackled in the same manner.

Donny actually *was* involved in the theft; of that, Not had no doubt, but neither did he have any evidence to back it up. Donny would have plenty of information to trade, and would not hesitate to deal if he could do so in a way which would benefit Donny.

Could Donny or Joe have moved one of the barrels back into the truck?

Not had told the agent earlier there was no way it could have been done, but was he sure?

What if they had?

What if there was a barrel of cocaine in the back of the armored car, the one Not had secured in first bay of his new boss' business?

Could he really have driven off with a shitload of cocaine?

Not got up from the bench and sucked a cold mouthful of water from the sink at the top of the stainless steel toilet column, but his mouth still felt dry.

Goddamnit, he had no way of knowing.

He had just been doing his job.

The very thought of it made his stomach flutter and his testicles feel like they were trying to climb back up inside of him.

He had been doing his job last time as well. He had been sent out on what he had thought was a legitimate run, a repo sure but cars were repossessed all the time, and when he had been lit up by the blue and red flashers, then pinned in the spotlight mounted outside the driver's side door of the patrol car, he had been sure it must have been a misunderstanding.

He was just doing his job, he had thought, and everything would be fine because he hadn't done anything wrong.

Well, he hadn't gone to jail, but everything had worked out pretty far from fine.

He could still see the puncture in his arm from where he had been stabbed with a needle in order to sell his plasma so he could spring for a goddamn pizza to share with his dad.

There was not a thing about this that was fine.

"He's going to do it again," Not mumbled to the empty cell.

The son of a bitch is going to throw me under the bus again, Not thought.

And, he couldn't think of a single thing he could do to stop it from happening.

Chapter 24

HE HAD been here too long.

Topher had intended to just stash the barrel and get to somewhere warm, but had ended up sitting in an abandoned laundry room which could double for a meat locker, staring at his phone for hours.

The first hour had been mostly research into the unexpected nature of the prize he had smuggled back from upstate New York.

After a quick conversation with Donny's lawyer, he had moved away from the more academic nature of his web activities and onto the practical.

Topher had searched through all of the photos currently on his phone, and could not find the information page for Stephen Presley, aka Mr. Creepy. For a panicked moment, he convinced himself he never actually had taken the photo of the release form, that he had intended to do so but hadn't actually done it. Beginning to panic, he had just kept swiping the photos in an unending train of disappointment and frustration until he realized some of the photos he was sure he had taken were no longer there.

The guy in the grocery store who might have been Sean Connery.

The cute kitten in the snow which would make a killer meme once he figured out a good tagline for it.

The selfie he took after his last haircut to show the next time he went, since the stylist got it just right.

He wouldn't have deleted any of those.

Honestly, he couldn't remember deleting any photos ever since . . .

Ever since he had set his phone to auto-archive anything older than 30 days to his cloud memory, so it wouldn't eat up all the space on his phone.

Opening the browser once more, he accessed his account and brought up the photos folder.

He had 9,342 photos.

Sweet fucking Jesus.

How, he thought, awe-struck by the enormity of the idea, does one person, who is not a professional photographer, who, if he were truly being honest with himself, took mostly selfies, accrue 9,342 photos?

He never even looked at them after the initial glance to see how they turned out.

It was fucking embarrassing.

He selected the tiled arrangement, and sorted the photos from newest to oldest, and began to scroll. Slowly at first, and then faster with growing impatience, and increased embarrassment.

Almost every photo was of himself, all from an arm's length away, and each featured one of three looks: badass face, flirty face, and happy face. Each face looked practiced -- which they were -- and none of which looked sincere.

He scrolled faster to avoid looking at his own douchebaggery, and also because he was pretty sure a white sheet of paper would pop up like a road flare among these mostly nightclub interior shots.

He finally found it, after a few false positives when an atypical outdoor selfie worked its way into the mix. Topher zoomed in on the form and found the phone number listed. He copied it over, scrawling the numbers into the dust on the floor, which he scuffed away moments later after tapping the digits into his phone.

He hesitated before tapping the green "send" icon.

What exactly did he plan to say to a man who was, if not an actual clinical psychopath, was working his way towards an honorary status? Hi, you don't really know me, but would you like to buy about fifteen million dollars' worth of cocaine? No? Do you happen to know anyone who might be interested in buying about fifteen million dollars' worth of cocaine? No? Okay, well thank you for your time.

He pressed send, hoping something better would come to him, but also knowing if he kept hesitating he would end up putting off the call forever.

"*Doo-DOO-Do-Do* . . .We're sorry, but the number you are trying to reach is no longer in service. Please check the number that you have dialed and try again . . . *Doo-DOO-Do-Do* . . .We're sorry, but the number. . ."

Of course he had given a fake number. Why would a pimp provide his actual number on a release form?

Just to be safe, Topher pulled up the photo of the form once more and scrawled the number a second time in the dust, and this time copied over the address as well.

The phone number was just as useless the second time, but at least he knew for sure he had not copied it incorrectly. When he searched for the address on the internet, it couldn't be located as the zip code provided did not match the city. If he tried the correct zip code for the city with the address provided, he was directed to a laundromat. If he tried the address without the city but with the zip code provided, it displayed a field in Vermont. He hadn't even tried to get the state right.

Topher spent a few fruitless minutes searching for different variations of his name, but for all he knew it must be fake as well. It had taken much longer than he had planned, and provided very little in results. He wasn't much better off than he had been hours ago.

At least he knew what was in the barrel now.

And, he knew what it was worth.

He was about to run another search when he realized he could no longer feel his toes.

Okay, time to call it.

It was time to get to somewhere warm. He would have to hope the barrel would still be here when he got back, but it was no good guarding an unspendable fortune at the cost of his toes.

He scuffed out the fake phone number and address a second time, for no real reason other than frustration, and then headed for the back door through which he had entered what felt like ages ago. He paused at the door to make sure the barrel was well concealed behind the washer and an errant thought brought him to a dead stop.

How long would it take for the liquid inside the barrel to freeze?

If it did freeze, would the plastic barrel expand to accommodate the growth, or would it split open?

If it did split open, would the temperature stay below freezing all day, or would he come back to find a fortune spilled out on the floor?

Topher rushed over to the barrel as fast as his numb toes would allow without falling, and tapped the side. It still gave a resonating boom, rather than the flat slap of a solid, but was it quieter this time? Was the liquid inside beginning to thicken? Was it turning slushy?

He couldn't remember if the barrel had made a different sound before, but he was certain the people who had filled it in the first place had never intended for the barrel to be left out in the cold. It was supposed to have been in the back of a heated armored truck, not sitting in the laundry room of a frozen teardown.

The very act of thinking was becoming increasingly difficult, and realized he was shivering so hard it was really as if his whole body was shaking. When had he started shivering? He had no idea, but now that he was aware of it, he couldn't ignore it. Even the muscles in his jaw were beginning to tremble, creating a disquieting sensation of trembling in his teeth.

My teeth are actually chattering. He had lived his entire life in the harsh winter weather which affected all the northern Atlantic states, and he had heard the expression on numerous occasions, but it had never truly occurred to him it was anything more than just a colorful expression for being really, really cold.

Holy shit, he realized, *this could actually kill me.*

It was a such an alien concept it stopped him, quite literally, cold.

If he stayed here much longer, in a house in a suburban neighborhood, one not much different from where he had grown up, he could actually die of exposure as if he were in the Klondike.

Topher decided to walk to the nearest open restaurant and keep ordering cups of coffee until he could feel every one of his toes again.

Then, he would go rent a truck and come back to . . .

To do what? To park a rented moving van in the driveway of a burned out house, where everyone on the street could see it, and load up one bright blue barrel, and then drive away?

Maybe if he took a bunch of furniture too, it would look more normal? He could say he was . . .what? With the insurance company? Working for the family who lived here?

If it came to the point where he had to speak to someone and explain what he was doing, then the game was already over. There was no story he could come up with which would stand up to any sort of scrutiny. If he tried taking the furniture too, it would take him even longer, certainly long enough for neighbors to notice, for the police to be called and to come by to check in on him and ask, "by the way, what you got in the barrel?"

If the only thing he took was the barrel, then it would look extremely suspicious. Certainly suspicious enough for someone on the block to copy down the license plate from the truck. Even if he was fast enough to get away, the plate would still lead the police to the rental company, which would lead directly back to him, and they would soon come to the correct conclusion: he had no legitimate business in the house.

Did it matter? If he could hide or unload the barrel well enough, the worst they could charge him with would be trespassing. Was that a felony or a misdemeanor?

He tried to search for the information on his phone, but could not manage to type the words. His body started to tremble with a bit more power and he could no longer classify it as a mere shiver. Topher was beginning to actually shake.

He had to move and he would have to make a choice.

If he left here without the barrel, he knew he would be taking the chance he would not be able to get back to retrieve it until the following night. By that time, the liquid in the barrel would have had ample time to freeze solid. Topher had no idea if freezing would have a negative effect on the value of the cocaine, damage it, destroy its potency or something, but the expansion of the liquid as it turned solid could be enough to split the plastic barrel. He could, of course, bring another barrel to transfer the contents into, but he would then need to melt it if he expected to pour it into the new container, or containers.

He had no means of melting anything in this house without alerting people to his presence here, and even if he could, it wasn't like he could lift the barrel to pour it into another barrel. Maybe he could tip it or something, but still he was sure to spill some of it, even if he remembered to bring a funnel, or a funnel and a tube, like a beer bong, or maybe just a tube like a syphon, like when he was convinced someone was stealing gas from his car at night, so he siphoned off most of it into gas cans and carried it in with him, at least until the other renters worried he was going to burn the garage down with their cars inside, so he had just put the gas cans in his trunk overnight, but eventually it had just got to be too much work, so he had just stopped filling his car all the way, would only put like ten bucks in at a time, so whoever was stealing his gas wouldn't be able to rip him off too bad . . .

What had he been thinking about?

Why was he sitting now, next to the dryer?

He couldn't feel himself shaking anymore. Was that good? It probably wasn't good.

He needed to move.

Christ, he was cold.

He needed to move the barrel too, so it wouldn't freeze. Where?

Why did he feel so tired? He worked nights, for Christ's sake!

Wait, he had had an idea a minute ago. What was it? Gas cans? Was that it? Syphoning the coke into gas cans and sticking it in the trunk of his car?

Would it work?

He didn't have his car, so he didn't think it would work.

He didn't have enough gas cans either.

Damn it. It was hard to think of anything except the cold.

Topher realized he needed to warm up fast and was about to try one more web search for the closest open restaurant when he remembered that although the Shit Heap was not drivable, it's engine still ran. The transmission had been heating up like a motherfucker on the turnpike too, so the cab should warm him up in no time.

And, it was only about a hundred feet away.

The door presented a small challenge, as his hands no longer wanted to grip anything tightly, but between the two of them, Topher was able to apply enough torque to disengage the latch and stumble down the steps into the driveway.

He shuffled like a drunk, not lifting either foot entirely from the ground for fear of leaning too far to one side and going over all the way. The wind had blown small drifts across the sidewalk, salted the day before, so every few feet he sent a cloud of hard frozen snow skittering over the rough concrete of the sidewalk.

It sounded like the beginning of a Caribbean song, maybe something by Harry Belafonte, but slower.

Shoof-Shoofa-Tschisch! Crunch-Crunch.

Shoof-Shoofa-Tschisch! Crunch-Crunch.

And then the bongos would come in, or maybe a steel drum, thought Topher, with a brief follow up wondering if he perhaps was beginning to get a bit delirious.

He made it over the tracks once more, swinging his legs out to either side in order to get them over, rather than risk trying to bend his increasingly stiff knees more than they could currently go, and toppling down onto the tracks.

If he fell, Topher was not sure he would be able to get back up.

The Shit Heap remained where it had been dropped, a crippled mass in front of the auto shop, and Topher was grateful to his earlier self for leaving the door both unlocked, and slightly ajar. He nudged the door open with his elbow and practically collapsed across the bench seat of the old truck. Rocking and bouncing like fish on a dock attempting to hurl itself back into the water, Topher was able to turn himself without striking the steering wheel with his back, head, hips, or shoulders, and turned the key with a hand which felt more like a lobster claw.

The ancient and tired engine struggled to turn over, issuing the warning growl of an old and lazy dog who refuses to move from its position of comfort to confront whomever is at the front door.

Topher released the ignition key and rolled a bit onto his side, then once more turned the key with this left hand, while pumping the gas pedal with his right.

The slow dog's growl erupted into a fury of coughing barks, before settling into the steady farting grumble of the old engine Topher had listened to for most of the evening.

He slid his legs inside, and pulled himself up, using the steering wheel which he had so cautiously avoided moments before, just long enough to swing the driver's side door most of the way shut. It bounced open slightly, something, likely the seat belt, was preventing the door from closing enough to engage the latch, but Topher didn't care. He could hear the blowers running, and soon he would feel the warm air filling the small truck cab and then sinking blessedly into his frozen flesh.

He dimly registered the sweep of headlights as they filled the cab of the Shit Heap, the heard the deep throaty rumble of a diesel rolling past. Probably the tow company bringing another drop off. He considered killing the engine, but could not bring himself to kill the heat just before he began to feel it.

If they decided to investigate, he could pretend to be homeless. He certainly looked the part right now.

Topher listened to the low steady hum of the blower fan and waited for someone to ask him what the hell he thought he was doing. Within moments he was asleep.

TOO HOT.

He dreamt of Florida.

In his dream, he lay in the cool wet sand, while the sun warmed his face and arms. He listened to the rolling shush of waves and he felt content. A passing thought warned him he should have put on sunblock, but the sun felt so good he wouldn't have put a barrier between him and the loving caress of those rays, even if it was just a thin layer of SPF 15.

Too hot.

He felt the skin on his face and arms begin to tighten from the exposure, but he didn't care. He continued to soak it all in. The tightness became a sting, and still he refused to move or seek the shelter of a little shade or a cooling dip in the ocean. The pain began to increase and spread, and he could smell the thin, silky stench of burning hair.

Too fucking hot!

Topher awoke to find the transmission had become dangerously overheated once more. He still smelled the burning hair of his dream, but the pain swelled out from a point in his lower back which had been centered on the bench seat of the truck, and therefore centered over the transmission as well.

He sat up quickly, and placed a hand over the seat. It was far too warm, but was not yet actually burning. The stench of burnt hair filled the cab of the old truck, the stuffing of the seat might actually be old enough to include horse hair in the mix, and now it was being roasted.

Topher gagged, and stumbled from the truck, trying not to be sick.

A deep lung full of bitterly cold air seemed to sear his lungs in a fresh new wave of pain which knocked both the burned skin on his back and the queasy upset of his stomach to the furthest peripheral of his awareness.

It was as if his entire chest cavity had an ice cream headache.

It was so utterly shocking he forgot to breathe again until he had to let the breath go in a burst and suck in another huge, gasping gob of glacial inhalation which stung exactly as much as the first one.

At least, the thought came with a touch of optimism, he no longer felt like he might puke.

Continuing in the power of positive thinking, he realized how a warm body and a cold breath of air had done wonders for clearing his head. He knew, or at least he had an idea of what to do, in the short term anyway, with the barrel full of cocaine.

He would let it freeze.

He would go home, sleep for a few hours, and then head to the local home improvement center for a battery powered drill, a long boring bit, a log splitting wedge, a sledge hammer, and a shit load of gallon freezer bags.

If he could sneak back in without being seen, he could spend the day reducing the enormous coke-sicle into several dozen bags of premium coke-colada. Toss them all into a duffle bag, or maybe two, and then stick them all in the trunk of his car for however long it took him to find a self-storage place which would let him rent a locker without providing a picture id.

After he got the shit stored somewhere safe, he had no idea what to do, but at least he had figured out what to do next.

Topher reached back into the Shit Heap and killed the engine, this time remembering to take the keys with him. He didn't bother to wipe the interior for prints this time, and, because the incriminating evidence was no longer in the back, he didn't think they would bother running the prints from a vehicle for what would amount to a parking ticket.

"Hey man!" A short, broad-shouldered Hispanic man shouted at him from the door of the auto shop. "You can't sleep in the cars!"

Without answering, but doing his best to look drunk, Topher crossed back over the tracks, away from the man who continued to yell at him, and headed to find some sweet fried dough and hot strong coffee. He risked a look over his shoulder to where he had clumsily hidden a fortune.

He had left the back door open.

He could see it from where he stood, an empty black rectangle where there should have been a door.

Damn it.

It would be the first thing the next door neighbor would see in the morning. It would warrant a call to the police for sure. It was bad enough to have a burnt out house sitting next to you, reminding you daily of how close you came to losing your home and possessions as well, but it would be even worse if some crackhead decided to start squatting there.

He had to close the door.

Topher made his way back around the corner, crunching again through the snow drifts, but this time lifting his feet to avoid the shoof-shoofa before the crunch-crunch. He treaded carefully up the driveway, again scanning the neighborhood windows for any sign he was being observed, and again so far he felt he was still alone.

He reached the door, and on impulse, once more pulled out his phone to use as a flashlight, to give one more quick scan of the laundry room to make sure he hadn't left anything which would lead to him if the barrel was discovered before he could return.

He swept the light quickly through the room.

Footsteps crunched on the gravel outside, and Topher turned for a brief glance into a bright flashlight.

Then, all was darkness.

Chapter 25

THE TRIP back down was just about as long and dull as the trip up had been, only a lot more blinding. Now, the snow covered fields and trees they had passed the night before, which had appeared bland and ghostly in the moonlight, were reflecting the glare of the sun shining from a cloudless sky.

Donny wished he had brought his sunglasses.

The conversation had been even less stimulating.

"Why isn't Joe coming with us?" he asked.

"Who?" Sokolov had responded.

"Joe, my partner from the armored car?"

"No idea," Sokolov had shrugged. "Yours is the only name I was given."

The attempts at conversation had gone pretty much the same every time. Polite, but utterly useless. What happened to the agents he had talked to earlier? Couldn't say. Was my lawyer notified I'm being released? Must have been, it's standard procedure.

So, Donny had given up any forays into conversation, and instead had entertained himself by trying to puzzle out Agent Sokolov.

It was the wig which bugged him the most. Tattoo sleeves were fairly distinctive, and he supposed were likely not very common in law enforcement, but uncommon did not mean unheard of.

The wig on the other hand was intriguing.

Sokolov was young, seemingly too young to have naturally gone bald, but again it was not unheard of.

Donny tried to sneak glances at Sokolov as often as possible, without being too obvious about it.

He had seen some people wearing wigs which only covered the top of the head, and was colored to blend into any natural hair still remaining. The bad ones made it look like the person was wearing a hair hat.

Was that a toupee? What was the difference between a wig and a toupee? Donny had only heard women's wigs referred to as wigs, but men wore wigs or toupees. Was that the difference? Was a toupee just a hair hat?

Whatever the case, this one was definitely a wig. Unless all men's wigs were called toupees, in which case it was an all over toupee. It was all one piece, and it covered the whole head. There was no natural hair showing to blend with, perhaps no natural hair at all.

Chemo? Radiation? Perhaps Agent Sokolov is a cancer survivor and the treatment made all his hair fall out. It seemed unlikely, though, as Sokolov appeared to be in good health, and cancer patients always looked like wrinkled sheets of skin draped over skeletons whenever there was a charity drive for the children's cancer center, or a news story about the most recent discovery of how something we all use every day will end up killing us and everyone we love.

The most obvious answer was Sokolov shaved his head, but if he was bald by choice, why then would he cover it up with a wig?

Donny realized the question also had an obvious answer: a white man with lots of tattoos and a shaved head did tend to attract the wrong kind of attention. People associated those things with Swastika's, white-hoods, and burning crosses. Not generally the type of image, Donny assumed, the DEA was eager to promote.

At least, not when he had to interact with the general public.

Having someone on the payroll who looked like that, though, would probably come in handy in certain circles.

"I don't know about you," Sokolov said after nearly an hour of silence, "but I am about ready to get rid of the cup of coffee from earlier. Pit stop?"

"Sure," Donny agreed, though he didn't really need to pee.

Sokolov pulled off from the southbound side of the 87 just short of crossing back into New Jersey and followed a sign toward a town called Suffern.

They cruised past a gas station, but Sokolov did not even glance towards it.

Nor did he stop at the second gas station, or the third. He did not stop at any of the chain restaurants clustered near the highway off-ramps.

"Do we have to stop at a police station or something, so they can babysit me while you take a leak?"

"Something like that," Sokolov said, and chuckled. "And, yes, I do shave my head, and yes this is a wig, so now it's in the open. Feel free to stare."

"Sorry," Donny mumbled, genuinely embarrassed, a feeling he rarely experienced. "I didn't mean to be rude, but I didn't notice until after we had gotten in the car, and then I was, ah, well . . ."

"Curious?"

"Yeah, pretty much," Donny agreed.

"And, now you want to hear the story which goes along with it?"

"Well, I mean, again, I don't want to be rude," Donny waffled.

"Hey, I was the one to bring it up, so don't sweat it," Sokolov soothed, and then offered a friendly yet sardonic smile. As if to say, *everybody* wants to hear the story, but it's cool, I'll tell it again.

"Well first of all, it helps to know that despite this baby face, I'm much closer to my forties than my twenties, but a receding hairline was not why I first shaved my head."

Donny could sense this was just the preamble of a story, no response was needed, so he didn't bother to give one.

"Have you ever heard of *Pamyat*?" Sokolov asked, and then continued, again without waiting for a response. "It means 'memory,' and it's the name of an organization in Russia whose stated purpose is to preserve Russian culture, but who in reality strives to promote white supremacy. My parents were members prior to defecting to the United States back in '85, following a splintering of the group due to what they called 'ideological differences.' I was six at the time, but really don't have any memory of Russia other than it was colder and more snowy than here. By the time I reached middle school, I couldn't even speak Russian any more.

"Anyhow, my parents, and myself of course, were eventually granted citizenship here in the US by being able to provide information, letters of introduction, and, in general, grant access to a network of people in the Soviet Union who, by the nature of its beliefs, were at odds with the Soviet System. Just in time too, really. The Soviet Union was already starting its death spiral. If they had waited until I had hit double digits, their information would have been worthless, and we would have been shit out of luck."

"Timing is everything," Donny agreed.

"I know, I know," Sokolov shrugged slightly. "This is a bit of a roundabout way to explain the wig, of course, but without the background the answer doesn't make too much sense.

"So, anyway, when I was a kid, there were always agents of some kind or another dropping by and bringing photographs for identification, or letters for translation, and to be honest I became a bit enamored with the lifestyle of an agent. So, mysterious and all, cool sunglasses."

He paused to flash another smile, accompanied by a self-depreciating eye roll at the foolishness of youth.

"Unfortunately, by the time I finished high school, the CIA was a lot less interested in Russia and much more interested in Iraq. We still had agents coming to the house on a regular basis, though, but now they were from the DEA. After the fall, the Russian criminals were the first to recover, and they found, like so many in crumbled chaotic countries before them, guns and drugs were the quickest way to make a fortune. They traded old Soviet AK-47's, of which they had absolutely no shortage, to Afghanistan for heroin, of which they had absolutely no shortage, and sold the heroin to the United States for cash, of which *they* had absolutely no shortage.

"So, long story short, I had to learn my native tongue again in order to become an agent."

Donny waited for the story to continue, but Sokolov appeared to be finished. It couldn't be the end of the story though, Donny thought, because the point of telling the story had been to explain why he shaved his head, but he had never even touched on the subject again after bringing it up.

Sokolov pulled into a narrow driveway which ran between two brick buildings, a sign on the left-hand wall read "Parking in the Rear."

"So, what about the hair?" Donny asked.

"Oh! Right!" Sokolov chuckled again. "So, while my parents were feeding information about some of their former comrades to the US Government, they were also passing along useful information to some of their other friends within the movement. Sort of a scratch-my-back-I-scratch-yours, *quid pro quo* kind of situation. Which I have found to be an incredibly useful approach. Sometimes you take, but sometimes . . ."

The car stopped facing a loading dock of a building which was obviously not a police station.

"Sometimes," Sokolov sounding almost apologetic, "you have to give."

After putting the car into park, Sokolov slipped the wig from his head and then pushed up the sleeve on his right forearm to show nightmare gestalt of eagles, crosses, and other occult symbols for which Donny didn't know the names.

"I work almost exclusively in an undercover capacity, and am in fact overdue for some vacation time after a prolonged placement inside of an Aryan biker gang up near the Canadian border. But, I happened to be in the office finishing some paperwork when word came through about you and your friends, and I decided this was something which might interest some of my friends."

There was a tap at Donny's window, but he didn't want to turn to look.

"I have to say, I really couldn't believe my luck when Saunders called for someone to drive you down to New Jersey. Getting you alone for several hours, and having a reason to drive you right past where some of my contacts live, this really, well, what can I say? Sometimes the stars just align, you know?"

The tap at Donny's window sounded again.

"Come on, Donovan," Sokolov's voice, though still kind, offered little space for argument. "Let me buy you a drink."

The tap came again, but much more urgently.

Donny had been expecting the person tapping on the window would be a monster of some sort -- an outlaw-biker sasquatch with a meth-lit short fuse -- who would cripple him just for the fun of it.

Instead, he found a very pudgy finger, attached to a man who could not have been any taller than 5'7" nor weighed any less than 300 lbs. Blue-suede eyes peered merrily out from above flushed pudgy cheeks and beneath a short-cropped bristle of what had once been straw-colored hair being overtaken by silvery-grey.

"Can we please go inside now? I have got icicles hanging from my ball sack!"

What else could he do? Donny was technically in custody, so if he tried to run he would definitely be charged with *something* relation to the theft from the armored car, and there was no amount of motions in the world Jenny could file which would get him bail if was seen as a flight risk.

Besides, other than the Hitler Youth hobby kit of tats on his arm, Sokolov did not give off a threatening vibe, and neither did the ham hock outside.

Famous last words, Donny thought as he grabbed the door handle. Right up there with: Hey, I can do that! Here, hold my beer!

Donny stepped out into a cold gust of wind, and followed the quickly jiggling mass toward a non-descript steel door set in the center of the brick building. He didn't turn to check, but he was certain Agent Sokolov was no more than a pace or two behind him.

The fat man threw open the door and rushed inside, and Donny followed before the door had even started its back swing. Sokolov made it through just before the heavy steel door slammed back into its frame.

The first thing which met Donny's eyes was a bed.

A thick pillow-topped mattress, uncovered by sheets or blankets, in a blond-wood four-post frame. There was an inset spotlight over it, drawing the eye to the mattress, and by contrast, dimming the rest of the room.

I'm going to be raped, he thought calmly, and was then disturbed by how little it disturbed him.

Then his eyes adjusted, and he saw behind the bed was another bed. Behind that one, another bed. All in rather elegant four-post bed frames, and all tastefully lit from above.

"Let me get the rest of the lights," the fat man muttered and walked quickly to the left hand wall to flip up a short bank of light switches.

The room was painted in a subdued forest green, accented by white chair-rail trim, baseboards, and crown molding. Potted plants stood in two of the corners, and small circular tables, each bearing a carnival-glass lamp, a brass bowl filled with what appeared to be some sort of potpourri, and each table matched with a gold-leaf chair padded with maroon velvet cushions. Tasteful reproductions of old-masters hung on the wall in gilded frames. Directly ahead, centered in the far wall was another door, polished mahogany with an aged brass knob.

The whole room gave off an air of European sophistication and aristocratic snobbery.

"The rest of the display models are on the main sales floor up front, but we would be visible from the street, the bay windows you understand," the fat man shrugged. "Not much good having a display room, if you can't display it."

"Sure," Donny said, as if he had the slightest clue what was going on.

"It would be far more prudent for the three of us to never be seen together," Sokolov explained.

"Okay," Donny agreed.

"These are my three top of the line," the fat man stated with obvious pride. "So, I cleared out this old storage room, we don't keep any merchandise on site anymore. Nobody comes in expecting to take a mattress with them, strap it to the top of the old station wagon, and drag it upstairs themselves. Not anymore, anyway. They expect it to be done for them, free of charge you understand, and then for the old shit-, piss-, and cum-stained abomination they had been sleeping on to be hauled out of their bedroom and disposed of to boot. Next, they'll be expecting us to put the sheets on for them too. Fucking internet."

Donny had absolutely no idea how to respond.

Not a one.

It was an uncomfortable feeling.

"I promised Donovan here a drink," Sokolov said pleasantly. "Still got a bottle or two in your office?"

"Sure, sure," the fat man nodded as he spoke. "You know where I keep it."

Sokolov tugged his sleeve back down into place, and took a moment to replace his wig on his head before he walked casually but quickly to the far door and out into the larger display room behind.

"Why don't we have a seat?" The fat man offered.

Donny glanced nervously at the bed.

"Sure, if you want, be my guest," the fat man shrugged. "The frames on these things are too high for me to get in and out of, at least not with my dignity intact, so I'm just going to pull over one of these chairs."

The fat man, swaying a bit as he walked though not quite an outright waddle, stepped over to the table and drew one of the gilt and velvet chairs closer to the bed.

"That model is the Regal Imperial, which I realize sounds like a bit of a redundancy, but Imperial is the name of the line, and Regal is the actual model name. It is the best of the Imperial line, in my honest opinion, but the lowest of the Imperial price points. Individually wrapped springs surround columns of memory foam, and then those are topped with a goose-down pillow finish. Soft and supportive at the same time."

Donny really did not want to get on the bed.

The fat man settled himself into the chair, the joints creaking and groaning with every shift until he made himself comfortable. He rested his elbows on the arms of the chair, and laced his fingers across his now far more visible belly, and looked expectantly up at Donny.

The door at the far end swung back open, and Sokolov returned with a bottle of dark rum, and three coffee mugs gripped by their handles with his middle finger. He spotted the fat man in the chair, nodded, and grabbed the other chair from the opposing corner, on his way over.

Shit, Donny thought.

He turned and hopped up on the bed.

It *was* both soft and supportive.

"I hope rum is okay with you, Donovan, because it was all I could find in the office." Sokolov apologized.

"No, there is scotch in the other drawer," the fat man offered.

"Oh, really?" Sokolov asked. "Would you prefer scotch, Donovan? We can't take too much time here, but it would only take a minute to run back."

"No," Donny held up both hands in objection. "No, I actually do prefer rum to scotch, thank you."

Sokolov set the mugs on the seat of the chair he had hauled over, and then poured a healthy dose of rum into each one. He passed out a mug to each man, and then placed the bottle on the floor near his foot and settled himself into the now vacant chair.

"You," Sokolov began and then paused for a quick nip from the mug in his hand, "are probably a bit confused, am I right?"

"You could say that," Donny agreed.

"Well, let me start by assuring you we are not here to do you any harm, okay?"

Donny nodded.

"Actually," Sokolov took another sip. "We are here because we can all help one another. At least, I hope we will be able to. Allow me, though, to make a proper introduction: Donovan Allen please meet Gregori Fedin."

"A pleasure," said Fedin from his chair.

Donny nodded back.

"Now, my part of the conversation is completed. For all intents and purposes, please consider me no longer in the room."

Sokolov took another sip from his mug, but made no move to actually leave the room.

"What my friend Alexi here means to say," Fedin jumped in. "Is we may speak freely. You can speak honestly with me, and nothing you say can come back against you later, be used against you by the DEA, because he would need to explain how he came by this information, which would put him in as difficult a position as the one in which you recently have found yourself."

"Meaning?" Donny asked, not wanting to say anything more than he needed to.

"Meaning you stole, or perhaps allowed to be stolen, a very large quantity of cocaine, thought you would be able to get away clean, but are now in custody."

"I didn't. . ."

"Please," Fedin held up one hand to put a stop to the objections. "You do not need to convince me, as I have no power to free you. In fact, if you are innocent of this crime, then we really have nothing to say to one another, as I don't have anything to offer you, other than nice drink of rum on a cold day. However, if you did have a part in taking the cocaine, and you or your partners have not yet sold it, then I do have something I can offer which might interest you."

"And, what is that?" Donny asked.

"Before I answer," Fedin demurred, "I need to have a few questions of my own answered. But, answered honestly."

Donny glanced at Sokolov and wondered if this was a set up. This would have to be entrapment, or something, right? Sure, there was the old good cop, bad cop routine in an interrogation room, but they weren't allowed to play crooked white supremacist cop absconding with a prisoner to make a shady backroom deal. No *way* could it be legal in court.

"How about," Donny decided to err on the side of caution. "If you ask your questions, and I will provide whatever information I can?"

"It is a start," Fedin allowed a short smile. "First, did you know what it was you were stealing?"

"For the record, I did not steal anything," Donny began. "However, whoever did take the cocaine, I don't think, had any idea it would be cocaine."

"What did 'they,'" Fedin made finger quotes, "think they were stealing?"

"Well, the last time . . ." Donny paused for a sip. "The last time we did a one-run, when we only have one pick-up and drop-off scheduled for the day, we picked up a whole shitload of gold scraps to be melted down. If someone knew we were doing a one-run, they may have assumed it would be something similar."

"Ah, yes, something which could easily be converted to cash through any number of legal channels, right?"

"I guess so, yeah," Donny agreed.

"Not the same situation with cocaine, is it?"

"No, I don't guess it is," Donny again agreed.

"Not illegal to be in possession of gold, either, so there is not as much pressure to get rid of it right away, right?"

"I guess it stands to reason."

Fedin finished the rum in his cup and held it out toward Sokolov. Sokolov poured another healthy dollop of liquor into the mug, and then tilted the bottle toward Donny and raised his eyebrows inquiringly. Donny shook his head, so Sokolov replaced the cap on the bottle and returned it to its place on the floor.

"So, someone who was expecting to steal a lot of scraps of gold, but ended up with a whole lot of cocaine, might not really know what to do with it. He wouldn't want to give it up, because he knows how much it is worth, but he doesn't know how to cash in on the value of it without going to jail. Does that sound about right?"

"Yeah," Donny cautiously agreed. "I guess it sounds right."

"Well, I would be in a position to help such a man, or

209

men as the case may be," Fedin took another sip. "You see, I make a comfortable living from my business here, but I also support several political organizations, groups who work hard to protect people like me, and Alexi here, and even you Donovan, whether you are aware of it or not, from being muscled under in the name of political correctness. I regret to say, although my business is successful, it does not make the amount of money I would need to offer the support which I feel these organizations deserve. So, I also run an alternative business, pharmaceuticals mostly, things anyone could have prescribed by a doctor, but who do not want to pay the criminal pricing of the big pharmaceutical companies, you understand."

"Sure," Donny nodded. "It cost me over a hundred bucks just to see a doctor the last time I was sick."

"*Exactly* what I mean," Fedin nodded. "They charge ridiculous prices to hardworking men like you and me, so they can afford to also treat all of the welfare *negry* for free. Now, if you ask me *that* is truly criminal."

Sokolov nodded sagely, and Donny said nothing, but tried to keep the distaste from registering on his face, unsure the word meant the same in Russian as it did in English, but figuring, given the context, it likely did.

"So, this other business puts me in contact with lots of people who supply a demand which, for one reason or another, cannot be obtained through normal channels. Many of these people, like myself, are honest, tax-paying decent Americans. Others, however . . .others are trash. Scum. True criminals."

"Okay," Donny said, not sure in which category he was going to be placed.

"That is when I make a call to Alexi, the son of two of my oldest friends from Russia. Like a son to me as well, if I am to speak honestly. It is an arrangement which has worked out very well for both of us. I look out for him, make sure he stays safe when working undercover, provide the right verifications and introductions, and in return . . ."

"He lets you know when an opportunity presents itself," Donny finished.

"I could not have said it better myself," Fedin agreed. "He watches out to make sure my name never comes up, and I make sure he knows who the true criminals are. We both make sure they are brought to justice, and it is really for such a reason we are having this conversation right now."

"You think I am a criminal?" Donny asked.

"No!" Fedin seemed genuinely shocked at the idea. "I think you are a capitalist, and entrepreneur, a man who saw an opportunity to take some gold from some crooked Jews and ended up taking some cocaine from the crooked pharmaceutical companies instead. In my eyes, you are a hero. You should be given a parade, rather than a jail sentence."

"Can I get that in writing?" Donny laughed.

"Unfortunately, as I said before, your situation with the government is something over which I have no power," Fedin took another sip. "Though, I do think we can all help one another out."

"How?" Donny asked.

"I would like to offer you three million dollars for the barrel of cocaine, provided it is still in your possession. Which we agreed is very likely, as you were not expecting cocaine and likely do not have a buyer already lined up for the barrel. Now, before you object," Fedin raised his hands to stop a protest which Donny had not made. "I know three million is mere cents on the dollar for the value of the barrel, if it is in fact full, but please bear in mind two things: one, it is all I can afford, and two, I do not plan to sell the cocaine to the general public.

"I will sell the cocaine, for only slightly more than I am paying to you, to a group of *negry* who have been moving from a nuisance to a real problem. They deal mostly in heroin, but a quantity this large for this cheap, will definitely get their attention. As soon as they are in possession, Alexi will provide intelligence, from one of his undercover contacts, you understand, of a certain group who has come into possession of a barrel full of cocaine. The DEA will get the drugs back, you will have three million dollars to do with what you like, Alexi will likely get another commendation, and I will have helped to have rid my community of some of its true criminals."

"Win, win, win," Sokolov said and smiled.

Donny sat and pretended to consider for a few moments, and then downed the rest of the rum in his mug.

"Before I can give you an answer," Donny said, "I will need to make a few phone calls."

211

Chapter 26

NOT WAS giving serious consideration to breaking his own nose.

About an hour after Karcus left, Not was able to confirm he was in fact being held in the fabled drunk tank when the door to the holding cell swung open, and two uniformed officers half walked and half carried a seriously inebriated man to be held into the room.

The man, a heavy-bellied individual in dirty jeans and stained Devil's jersey, seemed to be exhaling pure beer fumes and sweating pork grease. Both officers seemed unhappy about the need to touch him, and appeared to be trying to keep contact to a minimum. As a result, the drunken man would wobble toward whichever one put up the least resistance, and the officer would end up having to touch him even more, usually through a well-placed shove to maintain forward momentum. To Not, it had the feel of two kids playing 'don't let it touch the floor' with a balloon, but with a balloon filled with beer and sweat.

A balloon which might burst at any time.

The whole operation only took about ten seconds from the door to the rear of the cell, where the longest of the benches stood waiting to take delivery of the barely conscious man, but Not guessed each second felt much longer to both of the cops.

As for the man between them, Not could see no sign the Devil's fan had even a notion of where he was.

The cops heaved the man onto the bench, attempting to leave him in a sitting position, but of course he quickly slopped over onto his side.

They were halfway back to the door when he spewed out what appeared to be a gallon of warm beer and semi-digested pork rinds. Not guessed they were barbeque flavored, based upon the red dye #5 tinting to the entire deluge.

"Sonofabitch," muttered one of the cops, but Not did not notice which one.

As a second heave came bursting forth, one of the two officers quickly left the room, only to return seconds later carrying a coiled garden hose. Not guessed they stored it close by for just such an occasion.

On the wall near the toilet-sink, a small steel door roughly the size of a paper napkin was set flush in the wall. The cop with the hose used a small key, which had been secured to the hose with rubber band, to gain access to the small door, which apparently guarded the spigot for the hose.

"Stand by the door," the hose cop said, presumably to his partner, but Not chose to include himself in that general address.

It took just a few short minutes to wash all the goo down the drain in the center of the room, but only because the cop was doing a half-assed job of it.

Slops and splashes the size and general shape of a child's hand went unnoticed on the wall below the bench, driven there by the pressure of the hose, rather than by any bizarre barf ballistics.

Soggy globs of pork rind caught in the grate above the drain.

"Good enough," said the cop waiting by the door.

The cop with the hose seemed to agree, because he killed the water, re-secured the hidden spigot behind its steel door, and then quickly coiled the hose as he walked out of the door held open for him by his partner.

The odor, though, remained.

The majority of the sputum had been sent down the drain, but it apparently had not gone far. The rancid yeasty, greasy stench of old beer and pork, mixed with the acrid bitter tinge of bile, wafted both from the drain, as well as from the original source.

Over several minutes, it seemed to fill the room.

Not remembered from either a cop movie or tv show that after a few minutes, a person's brain is supposed to become accustomed to a bad smell, and to filter it out of his perceptions.

Not waited for this mythical barrier to be crossed, and for the stench to fade.

After five minutes, it seemed to get stronger.

Not tried getting closer to the source, standing between the drain and the drunk, hoping a stronger dosage would more quickly build a tolerance, but was forced to retreat after only about a minute.

After ten more minutes, his own stomach began to clench, and his temples began to throb.

It wasn't fading.

It was then Not wondered if he would still be able to smell if he broke his nose.

Before going to that extreme, Not decided to try stuffing his nose with twisted wads of toilet paper first. If it blocked the smell, then all's well and good. If it didn't, then at least it would absorb some of the blood if he decided to take more extreme measures.

Jesus, he was tired.

Stress burns up energy like crazy, and he had already been up for over thirty-six hours, and worked a double shift during sixteen of those.

He needed a nap.

Not sought refuge behind the half wall which sheltered the metal throne, and sat cautiously on the press-formed seat after giving it a cursory once-over for any golden residue, which was thankfully, almost improbably, absent.

Not abruptly felt his eyes squeeze tight in an attempt to hold in the sudden flow of tears, but instead scissored free two droplets, clearing the way for more to spill out and blur his vision.

They were tears of frustration, he told himself.

This was not self-pity, this was not fear, and it was definitely not surrender, he assured himself, although those would be exact terms he would use to describe how he was feeling.

Defeated.

No, that was not quite right. He couldn't have been defeated, because he had not even put up a fight. How could he have? He hadn't even known it had been a fight.

It wasn't supposed to be a fight, goddammit!

He had gone to work, done a good job, and ended up in jail.

He couldn't even claim he didn't know any better, because all of this had happened before. Sure, not exactly the same thing, but enough to know as soon as he had seen Donny's smug little weaselly face, Not should have just climbed right back into the cab and hit the gas.

Except he couldn't have, at least not done so and kept his job.

The cops were there, though, for fuck's sake! They were the ones who had called him in. He did what the cops asked, picked up the armored truck, cleared the on-ramp for them, and then they show up a few hours later and put him in cuffs for doing what they asked him to do.

Except that wasn't quite right.

The cops never told him to help Donny and his partner off-load their cargo into a rental truck. They hadn't told him to take the armored back to the garage and store it for them. That had all been Donny, and Not knew full well Donny was a lying, scheming sack of shit.

But . . .shit.

He had almost let the words be said, if only to himself: this time it was different. The same damn thing which always preceded nearly every story someone told and made everyone else shake their heads in wonder at the gullible stupidity of others.

It was humiliating.

That was the word.

It was how he was actually feeling. He was humiliated because he had let it happen again. He had known the dog could and would bite, but just because his tail was wagging he tried again to pet it . . . and got bit again.

He leaned his head against the cool concrete wall and closed his eyes.

From across the room, Not heard what his mind recognized as a party balloon being slowly deflated, and almost opened his eyes to ascertain exactly how a balloon had gotten in here in the first place before realizing it was, in reality, the drunk man's ass.

The laughter which burst from Not's mouth was as surprising as it was loud, and sincere. True, the pitch was a little higher than normal, bordering a bit toward the manic, but it was actual honest to goodness laughter that shook the final remaining tears from his eyes.

It was stupid and pointless to be laughing at this moment, but fuck it felt good.

215

Not enjoyed it for a few moments before slipping into a blessedly dreamless sleep.

"GONNA SHIT or get off the pot?"

Not had no idea how long he had been asleep, but it certainly did not feel like long enough.

"Hey," a voice came from slightly up and directly in front of him. "You gonna shit off the pot, asshole?"

Not opened his eyes and found the catatonic drunk had sobered up enough to regain both his balance and his vocabulary. Either the fat Devil's fan had a truly astounding liver, or Not had been asleep for longer than he felt.

"Listen, pal, I'm pissin' in about ten seconds, whether you're still there or not, so . . ."

"I'm moving," Not assured him, and rolled groggily to his feet.

Not was about to resume his previous place on the long bench, before remembering it had most recently held the greasy and pukey Devil's fan who was currently -- and quite prodigiously -- orgasming into the toilet, if Not were to judge by the satisfied moans accompanying the deep stream splashing into the toilet bowl behind him.

Not turned to occupy the bench to his right, and found a third occupant had arrived during his lapse from consciousness. The man was built like a football player, the kind who specializes in running into others very hard rather than possessing any particular skill with the ball, and did not appear to be in a very open or friendly mood. His head hung down, arms crossed over his chest, legs extended and crossed, and appeared to be focused on one particular square inch area of space about an inch above his right toe.

Not chose to turn to the left and occupy the bench which lined the wall there, though it did mean his view of the Devil's fan at the toilet was, unfortunately, completely unobstructed.

"Oh shit," the Devil's fan said, as if he had been privy to Not's thoughts. "Sorry 'bout this guys."

Then, in a feat of coordination Not would have guessed to be impossible for this man, even in this far more sober state, the Devil's fan, in one fluid motion, freed the buttons on his trousers and simultaneously was able to push the pants and underpants downward with the hand holding the zipper, whilst sealing his pasty white ass to the seat at *precisely* the same moment that what Not could only assume was hot, liquid shit began to spray into the bowl below.

It was actually rather impressive.

"Nothing rolls outta ya like the Rock, 'm I right?" The Devil's fan asked, locking eyes with Not.

Having no idea what that meant, Not felt it best to simply nod in agreement, and then turned his gaze away.

He turned back to find the other man in the room was now staring at him, rather than the space above his big toe. The look did not appear to be one of aggression, but rather curiosity and perhaps, disbelief.

Now it was Not's turn to examine the space around his shoes. He didn't know why the guy across the way was staring at him, and he didn't really care. Sudden flashes of prison stories kept trying to pry their way into his conscious thought, but Not dismissed them as soon as they appeared. That sort of thing happened in the big state prisons, not in holding cells. In the showers, or so he and the rest of the television viewing audience had been trained to believe.

Stop it, he told himself.

He felt his breathing stop, when the man stood and started the short journey across the cell.

Stop it, he repeated. Breathe, damn it, nothing is going to happen. There are cops right outside.

The man sat on the bench beside him.

He leaned in, his mouth just inches from Not's ear.

"Do you," he whispered, "drive a tow truck?"

Not struggled to try to decode whatever the hell he might mean, momentarily relieved the man asked him to "drive" and not to "ride," but then shuddered as he wondered just what in the fuck a tow truck might be, and hoping "drive" didn't mean "suck" and "tow truck" wasn't code for. . .

Then, an epiphany: this was just a straightforward question about his actual occupation.

"Um, yeah," Not affirmed. "Yes, I do."

The man studied him for a few moments, as if trying to make a decision without enough information.

"Do you," the man started, and then stopped. He struggled a moment longer, then took the plunge. "Do you know a guy named Donny?"

217

Chapter 27

WHY THE fuck would someone steal a random blue barrel?

Topher realized the obvious irony of the question only moments after it popped into his head.

He wasn't sure, but he didn't think he had been out too long. Of course, any time you're knocked unconscious it was too long, and likely to have a concussion as well.

He was cold again too.

Why the hell had he left the handcart with it? He had just made it that much easier to rip it off.

The barrel was not in the kitchen, nor was it in the living room.

Of course, taking the handcart with him at the time had not been a realistic option. He had been nearly frozen, with neither the motor control nor the strength to move the barrel off of the cart, and he certainly wasn't going to wander the streets with an empty handcart at night. It might not be at the top of the obvious signs that someone is up to no good, but it would definitely be on the list.

Topher heard a footstep from the driveway.

He had just stepped back into the kitchen from the living room when he heard the muffled knuckle-cracking rattle of heavy-tread boots on concrete. He had worn enough winter boots throughout his life to recognize the sound for what it was, and realized that if it had been daytime, with all of the ambient noise of people going about their daily lives, he likely never would have heard it. But, winter nights are especially quiet, and sound tends to carry. So, it was just as likely that whoever was out there had heard him in here as well, and he was blocking Topher's only immediately available exit.

"Yeah, it's open," a voice came from the driveway.

It was a cop voice. No fear or worry in his voice, which a neighbor or homeowner might have, just the tired resignation of someone who had to yet again clean up someone else's mess. Like a waitress in a dive-bar saying, "yeah, they pissed on the toilet paper again," knowing full well she would be the one to take the old urine soaked roll from the holder, spray everything down with cleaners, wipe it all up, and replace the roll only to have someone do the same damn thing again as soon as she's done.

Should he try to hide? There might be some places upstairs he could get to, and the fire damage might discourage the cops from wanting to check upstairs. Of course, if they did search for him, the harder he made it for them, the harder they were likely to be on him.

Besides, it wasn't like he had a barrel full of cocaine with him. Never in his life had Topher been so grateful to have been ripped off. They might try to get him on breaking and entering, but he wasn't trying to steal anything, and the house was arguably abandoned, so it was more likely they were coming to roust a vagrant.

Topher quickly grabbed another bottle of beer from the fridge, and trudged back into the living room. He settled into the frozen sofa and popped open the bottle. He had made it to his second swig when the flashlight beam fell on him.

"Police!" said a voice from behind the light. "Don't move, and please keep your hands where I can see them."

"'Kay," Topher held up one empty hand, and raised the bottle back to his mouth once more.

"Please put the bottle on the table in front of you, sir."

"'Kay," Topher nodded, chugged the rest of the bottle, and then placed it carefully on the coffee table.

"You look like you had a rough night," the cop said from behind the flashlight. "But, I gotta say, you don't look homeless."

"No, I'm not," Topher nodded his agreement to the negative.

"So, what the hell are you doing in here," the cop asked, with what sounded like genuine concern. "You trying to freeze to death?"

"No, I . . ." Topher heard the truth start to tumble from his lips before he could complete a good lie. "I was doing a favor for a . . .an old friend, and things got kind of messed up,

219

and I ran into someone I used to work with, and he bought me a drink, but then . . . well, then things just got weird."

"Uh-huh," the cop said. Topher still couldn't see his face from behind the flashlight, but his voice sounded like he was smiling.

"Well, yeah, it was years ago, but we used to date . . . and . . ."

"And so you decided a few drinks might help, huh?"

"Well, yeah," Topher admitted, trying to look sheepish.

"Alright, I'm going to do you a favor, if you will do me one in return," the cop lowered the flashlight beam just a little, but now Topher could see the man's face. He was a middle-aged black man, with deep laugh lines framing kind brown eyes. "We received two or three calls about a homeless man who was breaking into this house, then into a vehicle on the street, and then back into this house. Now, if the vehicle in question is the broken down old truck a block away, and from the information I received, I believe that to be the case, I don't think the owner is going to raise much of a fuss."

Topher nodded in agreement.

"As for this place, again, I don't think you were trying to damage anything, and if this had been a public park, or something like that, I would simply tell you to move on and stay out of trouble, you get me?"

"Yeah," Topher nodded again.

"See, the trouble here is this is a private home, and if whoever called you in sees me just letting you walk away, I am going to get chewed out but good."

"Yeah, I get that."

"So, here is what we're going to do," the cop lowered the flashlight and placed it under his left arm, and then retrieved his handcuffs with his freed right hand. "I am going to walk you out of here in cuffs, and put you in the back of my car. Then, while whoever made those calls has a few minutes to get a good look at you in the back of the car, service and protection in action, you get me?"

Again, Topher nodded.

"While they get a good look, I'm going to make a couple of calls and find out which station around here has got an empty treatment center, where we put drunks who need to sober up, you get me?"

"Yeah," Topher agreed cautiously.

"I'll find you a warm place to sleep tonight, and tomorrow you go and get your shit sorted out. I'm going to do you this favor, because you are going to turn around and get these cuffs put on your wrists without a struggle. You're going to sit in the back of the car and look chastised for the nice homeowners of this neighborhood, and everybody wins."

"I get you," Topher agreed.

"Alright then," the cop said and waggled the cuffs, "let go get out of the cold."

Topher was a good boy, and looked both guilty and ashamed of his horrible actions as he sat in the back of the car. The porch light of the house next door flipped on and shone brightly for a minute, and then turned off once more. No one came outside, but Topher was certain he had been thoroughly examined. It would have made coming back for the cocaine much more difficult, if that had still been his problem.

Now, though, he had a whole new issue: telling Donny he had somehow lost the barrel.

There was, of course, no actual way of convincing Donny someone had taken it. Donny just simply would never believe him. He might say he did, he might even let the topic go and never bring it up again, at least not until he found a way to get Topher's balls in a vice, and then he would calmly, and sweetly ask, "What *really* happened to all that cocaine?"

Jesus, Topher thought, Donny really is kind of a psychopath. It was revealed to me so slowly over the years it just sort of added on. Oh, that's just Donny, I guess, and then shrug and forget about it. It was just a way he had which made him seem so harmless. Like an angry toddler. Loud? Sure. Annoying sometimes? Absolutely. Still somehow adorable? Astonishingly, yes.

I just robbed an armored car with the guy, on one day's notice, with only a minimum of convincing. Christ, I'm like one of those women in a Lifetime movie.

Topher continued along this line of thinking, as the officer brought the patrol car to a stop in front of the Little Fairy Municipal Building. He brooded through the processing, where they took possession of his phone, car keys, and wallet.

The patrol officer gave him a friendly wave, and then disappeared back through the front doors. Topher was lead down several hallways and then deposited with little ceremony into a large room with three wooden benches lining the walls.

221

The bench facing the door was mostly occupied by a large pile of drunken Devil's fan, and Topher almost missed the room's other occupant, who was, for some reason, asleep on the toilet.

Topher moved to the bench on the right and sat down, stretched his legs out in front of himself, and tried to get comfy.

HE AWOKE a little while later, to the mushy sounding movements of the fat drunk on the other bench. When the man moved, it gave the wet meaty sound of someone slapping raw hamburger into patties for the grill. Topher wondered momentarily if the fat man were actually masturbating, but was relieved and somehow even more repulsed to discover these were simply the sounds he created while trying to move his sweating bulk to an upright position.

Topher refused to look at the man as he shuffled towards the toilet. Instead, he simply stared at the tip of his own shoe, so he could keep the room in his peripheral vision, without having to look directly at the man himself. A trick he had used for years when dealing with drunks of unknown temperament, as you could never tell when a simple glance would equate to a challenge of their masculinity to their less than rational brains.

"Listen, pal," Topher heard the man say, apparently mumbling to his dick as he unzipped. Then, he remembered there had been a third person in the room, and he had been sleeping on the toilet when Topher had come in. "I'm pissin' in about ten seconds, whether you're still there or not, so . . ."

"I'm moving," another voice answered.

The other man, only a couple years out from being a kid really, took a step toward the bench the fat man had been sleeping on and then wisely, in Topher's opinion, opted for the bench opposite from his own. He was dressed in heavy-weave work pants, and the kind of work shirt you see on guys at tire shops and oil change places: button up short sleeves, worn over long sleeve thermals, with an embroidered name badge over the heart. The badge read "Josh."

For some reason, the guy looked a little familiar.

The obscene moans of relief from the fat, greasy drunk echoed off the bare walls of the room. Topher tried to tune it out, and chose to focus instead on how he knew the grease monkey.

Topher changed his oil himself, and hadn't had to buy new tires for over a year, so it wasn't likely one of those options. The shirt wasn't the same color as those at his usual mechanic shop, but mechanics were not the only ones who-oh-my-fucking-god . . .no way.

It could not possibly be the same guy.

Tow truck drivers also wore that kind of shirt, and the cuffs of this guy's pants were caked with road salt and dirt, just like someone who had spent the day hauling breakdowns off of the turnpike.

Topher had only seen the guy from a distance, but the age and approximate build were about right from what he could remember. He hadn't spent too much time wondering about the tow truck driver. He had been focused on the goddamn blue barrels, and wondering what could possibly be inside worth all this trouble.

No, he decided. It could not be the same guy.

Topher got up and walked across the room anyway, and sat down beside the young man, who was now looking considerably more nervous.

"Do you," Topher took a breath and pushed ahead, "drive a tow truck?"

"Um, yeah" the guy said, after an unusually long pause. "Yes, I do."

"Do you," Topher could not help but feel ridiculous, but felt compelled to ask anyway. "Do you know a guy named Donny?"

The series of reactions on the guy's face was so fast as to almost call it instantaneous. Surprise gave way to confusion, which gave way to understanding and then anger.

"Talk to my lawyer," he answered with quiet, well-mannered suburban venom.

"What?" Topher asked, genuinely confused. "Why?"

"Isn't this some kind of entrapment?"

"What the fuck are you talking about?" Topher nearly wailed in exasperation. "Why are you in here? Is it because of Donny?"

"On the advice of my lawyer, I am not saying another word," the guy said, crossed his arms, and then immediately countered his statement with, "except to say this is exactly why people don't trust cops. You guys are supposed to be on our side. You're supposed to play fair."

"I'm not a cop," Topher stated.

The guy mimicked drawing a zipper closed across his lips.

It was such a faggy thing to do that Topher wondered if he had read him wrong. Walking over, Topher could have sworn he had heard the creak of the kid's asshole tightening up. The body language had been unmistakable. Topher associated it with the straight boys he had hit on over the years, but maybe it was because of this: the kid thought Topher was a cop. If the kid was gay, which if he knew Donny certainly raised the probability of being true, then Topher was going about this all wrong.

It was time to be charming.

"Listen, Josh," Topher let his voice drop and soften to somewhere between a purr and a growl. "I am not a cop. I just got brought in for drinking beer in a burned out house, which I realize now as I say it out loud doesn't make me sound very trustworthy, but I actually had a very good reason for being there."

Josh crossed his arms, and attempted to look cool and aloof, though his eyes could not seem to help but to dart back towards Topher every few seconds, likely to make sure Topher was noticing just how cool and aloof Josh was being.

Topher rolled his head back and then side to side, and listened to the tension crackle from his neck and shoulders, while flexing and displaying at the same time.

He knew better than to check and see if Josh was checking him out. It would spoil the spell if he got caught looking. Just stretch, look around, and let the kid enjoy the view.

The fat man, Topher saw, was slumped, his pants still down below his knees, his chin to his chest, and face hidden by a sewer clog of hair. For a moment, Topher had wondered if the Devil's fan had left the building Elvis style, but then noticed his considerable belly still moved rhythmically with breath.

Topher rolled his head back toward his new friend and tried again.

"Listen, Josh," Topher's first word was greeted with flip of the head towards the opposite wall, and the second brought a brief flush to Josh's face.

Caught him anyway, even when he wasn't trying to.

Oh, well. Sometimes sexy was just a burden you had to bear. Christ, Topher wanted to kick his own ass for every letting such a cringey thought enter his mind.

"I don't know why you're in here, but if you think the cop's would go so far as to stick an undercover guy in here to get information out of you, then I'm pretty sure you're not in here for drunk driving."

Topher got no response, but neither did Josh move further away.

"I have a feeling we're both getting royally fucked here," Topher thought back to the porch light, and his assumption that it had been a neighbor who had called the cops. It could just as easily have been Donny, or Donny's lawyer.

It might also explain where the barrel had gone, and why Topher was now sporting a lump on the back of his head the size of his left nut.

God damn, everything was sexual for him all of a sudden. Maybe he did have a concussion.

Rather than dwell on it, Topher tried to remember if the GPS had been active on his phone. He usually kept it turned off, but he had several apps which kept turning it back on for him. His navigation app was one of them. Had he used it tonight? He couldn't remember. He couldn't check it either, because it was now secured in its own holding cell. If it had been on, then Donny's lawyer could have tracked him, maybe, when she called him. Could people do that? Topher knew photos and other files could have GPS data attached to them, but could phone calls? Shit, he just had no idea. The only thing he could assume was that it probably could if the GPS was switched on, and he didn't know if it was, so he would just have to assume it was.

The fact he was in a holding cell, and the barrel mysteriously disappeared from a house he had never intended on going to, and of which Donny could have no possible foreknowledge, tended to point to the conclusion that he had been tracked, he had been ripped off, and he had then been set up for the cops. Maybe not to take the fall for the coke, but he certainly was going to be out of the way for long enough to allow whoever had taken the stuff to make a good getaway.

Fuck.

"How?"

Topher had fallen into his own internal conversation, and it took him a moment to realize that Josh who had asked the last question.

"What?" Topher asked.

"How?" Josh repeated. "How are 'we' getting fucked?"

Topher weighed his options on how much information he could provide, without putting himself into hot water. If he said the wrong thing, all he was doing was giving more evidence to his involvement. Of course, it could be argued his walking over to a complete stranger and asking if he knew Donny would be a pretty strong indication of his own involvement.

Topher decided to try to keep it general and test the waters.

"What do the words "blue barrel" mean to you?"

"Fuck you, Cop."

"Goddamn it!" Topher shouted. "I am not a cop!"

Without thinking about it, Topher exploded up from the bench, crossed toward the toilet in three bounding steps, and punched the drunk Devil's fan in the side of the head.

"Owwwww!" the fat man whined pitifully, then released a muffled trumpet into the toilet. "What the fuck, you motherfucking fuck!"

"There, see?" Topher shouted at Josh. "A cop couldn't hit a man in custody, right?"

"Maybe he's a cop too," Josh sounded unsure, but stubborn. "Maybe you guys are a team?"

"So, if I hit you, where it will show, you could say any information I got out of you was taken under, um, shit," Topher struggled for the right word. "That I beat it out of you, right?"

"Wait a minute," Josh started to protest, but Topher was able to cross the distance back just as quickly as before.

The time for flirting was over.

Topher grabbed Josh by the front of his work shirt, and raised him from the bench, but not completely all the way to standing. Unable to get his feet under him, Josh was unable to turn away or properly defend against Topher's other hand, which slapped him hard, three times, across the face.

Topher dropped him back onto the bench and surveyed his work. Josh's bottom lip was split and blood was beginning to well up but had not yet started to drip. His cheek would swell, and then bruise, which would squint up one eye a bit for a day or two.

A little too late, Topher wondered if there were cameras in the cell. He tilted his head back and scanned the ceiling for the likely locations. Wouldn't that be perfect, he thought, get away with an armored car theft, only to lose all the money from it, and to top it off, an assault charge on film from inside a jail cell.

"Donny and the other guard took the barrels," Topher heard from the bench below him. "You already know that, and it's really is all I know. I understand you must be desperate to get the shit back, but I really wasn't involved."

Topher stopped scanning the ceiling, and looked down at Josh. Tears had welled up in his eyes, a reaction Topher had seen enough times at the clubs to know it had nothing to do with fear or anger. A slap hurt like hell, and it made your eyes water.

"Listen, Josh, I. . ."

"Why are you calling me Josh?"

Topher pointed to the name badge on the other man's shirt. A look of confusion crossed his face as he followed the direction of the finger, and then he uttered a short chuckle.

"Oh, right," he said quietly. "I forgot that was there."

"So anyway, Josh. . ."

"It's not my shirt, I borrowed it from a guy at work," he shrugged, and then laughed quietly again. "His name's not Josh either."

"So what is your name?" Topher asked.

"Everyone calls me 'Not,'" said the man on the bench, looking him in the eye for the first time.

"Okay, so Not, I want you to tell me everything you know, don't shake your head," Topher said, letting a little gravel into his voice to overpower the non-verbal protest which had started at the suggestion. "No, you are going to tell me everything you know. If I can, I will share with you what I know, and we'll see if we can help each other out of this clusterfuck."

"Doesn't sound like a very good deal for me," Not opined.

"Sure it does," Topher reasoned. "Because this way, I don't have to keep beating the information out of you."

"I can only tell you the truth," Not warned. "I cannot give you information I don't know, and I don't know where the damn barrel is."

"The truth is all I want," Topher stated. "Tell me what you told the cops."

With a sigh, Not shrugged his shoulders and rolled his neck, much like Topher had just a few minutes ago. It was surely more so to loosen the tired muscles than to indicate resignation, but it worked for both.

He started from the beginning.

Chapter 28

NOT, AT his age, had never had the opportunity to ponder the nature of impotence.

It really and truly sucked.

He had always assumed, based on the commercials and internet banner ads for the medications intended to counter the unfortunate affliction, that the primary emotion involved would be a feeling of embarrassment or humiliation.

It wasn't.

At least not in this case, perhaps because it was not sexual impotence from which he was suffering but rather a more comprehensive and pure meaning of the word, the complete inability to take any effective action. The knowledge you could do absolutely nothing to affect the outcome of your own life in any positive manner. No, the emotion which seemed to fill his every pore right now was anger.

Rage.

Not had heard the phrase "impotent rage" before, but had never experienced it until now. Even when accused the first time of stealing the cars, Not had at least been foolishly confident in the fact that he was innocent and his innocence would see him through the legal system unscathed. No longer so confident, nor so naive, Not knew he could be punished unjustly, and if it came down to who could lie better, Donny was at a great advantage. Knowing this, and being able to do nothing to prevent it, Not experienced the strange sensation of feeling his body try to curl into a protective ball, as every heartbeat brought more useless, unfocusable adrenaline into his body.

Topher had been able to fill in the answers for many on Not's questions, but not a single one of them helped Not to get himself out of this situation. There was no information Not could now provide which would not also serve to implicate himself further for simply having provided the knowledge.

Not knew now what had happened, he could provide the names of those who had actually committed the crime, but if he provided the information to the police, it would also mean telling them he had, for a second time in the same evening, been involved in the picking up of a stolen barrel of cocaine from the interstate and returning it, once again, to his own shop. From which, of course, the barrel had promptly been stolen, and, of course, Not had no knowledge of its current whereabouts.

As Karkus had repeatedly pointed out, the police did not believe in coincidence.

The new information only served to make him look even more guilty, and worse, it would look like he was holding out on this information earlier, so someone would have time to come and move the coke to a new location.

And, of course, he had absolutely no evidence to prove any of this.

Topher, likewise, seemed to be stewing in a similar fashion on the bench beside him. When Not had told him about his previous experience with Donny, and how he had been left holding the bag, it didn't seem to surprise Topher, but it did certainly darken his mood. Not imagined this is the expression a person would have when the doctor confirmed that the funny lump in your armpit was in fact a tumor, and what's more it was likely malignant.

They had tossed a few "what if we . . ." scenarios around, but each one seemed to end with one of them being in deeper trouble and the other one still in trouble, with Donny still getting away with everything.

Eventually, they ran out of ideas and lapsed into a brooding silence, interrupted only occasionally by wet snore or rattling fart from the Devil's fan who had elected to go back to sleep with his ass still firmly pressured sealed to the toilet.

After a short while, the door opened and Not's lawyer, complete in fresh skinny jeans, though this time in a pale khaki color to match the khaki-plaid tie, marched in with his messenger bag swinging.

One look at Not's face brought him up short.

Not's eye had swollen a bit, as had his cheek. The bleeding had stopped from the split on his lip, but it had scabbed over instead and was also noticeably swollen. Lastly, he was sitting, in fairly close proximity, to a very large man in a jail cell with many empty areas to sit.

"You fell," Karkus stated in a tone which made it clear he did not want to hear any argument or other explanation. "Right?"

"Um, yeah, let's just go with that," Not agreed.

"Good, because any new charges or allegations would derail all the work I have just completed to secure your release," Karkus said proudly.

"Really?" Not had never felt such a rush of relief with his pants on before.

"Yes," Karkus nearly beamed in such a way as to make Not wonder how many cases the young lawyer had had before this one, and how many of them he had won. "I was able to get confirmation from both Mr. Alto and Mr. Viejo as to the origin of the money, and they both stressed to the DEA you were not even supposed to be driving last night, which you neglected to tell me, by the way, and the only reason you were behind the wheel was due to a, well, an unusual family dynamic."

"Yeah, I think that is safe to say," Not agreed, suddenly smelling chicken.

"This was also corroborated by the local police report, so the argument of collusion gets a big hole poked into it," Karkus was beaming.

"Thank you, Mr. Karkus," Not said with genuine emotion.

"You are welcome, Mr. Johnson," Karkus offered his hand. "Now, we may not be out of the woods yet, but barring any new evidence coming to light which implicates you . . ."

Karkus left the implied question hanging in the air, and studied Not's face for a few seconds, very obviously searching for any tells or ticks of guilt.

" . . . then I think I had better keep my promise to Mr. Alto," Karkus continued, "and 'get you to work by the beginning of your shift, if I can.'"

"Do I have time to stop home for a shower?" Not asked.

Karkus pulled his cell phone from his pocket and checked the time.

"If you're quick, we've even got time for you to buy me a late lunch."

231

TOPHER SAT impassively while Not and his lawyer spoke, trying to will them into not noticing him so he could hear all of their conversation. There was little said that applied to himself, but Topher was waiting for Not to spin on his heels, drop an accusing finger toward him and scream, "HIM! Right there! That is the man who took the cocaine!"

Of course, Not had no evidence to prove it, other than the truck log to show he had picked up a wreck of a truck from the southbound lane of the 17, which was not linked to Topher in any way and which no longer held any incriminating evidence

He hoped.

And, to do so would also offer new evidence against Not and his involvement in the crime, so Topher thought it unlikely for Not say anything. It turned out his assessment was correct.

At least, so far.

There was nothing to prevent Not from spilling to his lawyer as soon as they passed through the door and into the hallway, but Topher didn't think it was likely to happen.

It just didn't do Not any good to say anything.

On top of that, in the short time they had talked, Topher had been able to gain a few insights about Mr. Harris "Not Harry" Johnson: he was endearingly honest and naive, he had no idea how puppy dog cute he was, and he was tragically straight.

Topher watched as Not's lawyer pounded on the cell door, which opened nearly immediately, and they stepped past the still unconscious Devil's fan toward the far better smelling air of the hallway.

Not turned back towards Topher briefly as he walked to the hall, and offered a small nod of goodbye. Topher returned the nod, and then called to the officer holding open the door as Not and his lawyer disappeared up the hallway.

"Hey," Topher kept his tone civil. "The cop who brought me in said I was only here to sober up, and I have. What happens now, do I need to do a breathalyzer or something to go home?"

"If you want to do the paperwork yourself, I can take you to the front desk right now," the cop said with a shrug. "As I understand it, your lawyer is on her way, so you may as well let her do it when she gets here. It's what you're paying for, right?"

"Yeah, right,' Topher agreed, though he had no idea what the cop was talking about.

The officer shut the door and left Topher to ponder why Donny's lawyer was coming to get him out. It had to be her, since Topher didn't even know any lawyers, and the only female lawyer he had ever spoken to had called him on Donny's behalf just a few hours ago.

The question was, how did she know he was here? Why was she coming to get him out when he could just fill out some paperwork and get himself out? Did Donny send her to find him? Did he want to be found by her?

Actually it was several questions. The answers to which he decided were: he didn't know, he didn't know, he didn't know, and very likely an emphatic no.

If she was coming to get him, it was for Donny's benefit, not his own. Topher no longer had anything Donny wanted, and after his conversation with Not, Topher was reminded just how quickly Donny would turn on someone to save his own skin.

Topher pushed himself up, though his ass still felt the ghost of the cold wooden bench pressed against it for about ten seconds as the blood rushed back in to warm the flesh. He crossed to the door, pausing for a moment at the seated, sleeping drunk, wondered briefly if he should wake him to apologize for hitting him, but then decided the man was not likely to remember the punch anyway. Instead, he pounded on the door to the hallway.

It took a minute, but the same officer as before opened the door.

"Listen, my lawyer can take forever sometimes," Topher explained. "Could I just go ahead and sign whatever needs signing, and get on out of here."

"Sure," the officer agreed easily enough.

He led Topher down the hall to a room filled with desks and workstations. About half the desks were occupied, and the others appeared to be rarely used. The officer paused at one of the desks, behind which a uniformed police woman of about fifty sat entering data from a file to a form on a screen.

"Checking out," the delivering officer said with a smile.

"Just a sec," the woman said without looking up from the screen. She typed a few more times, tabbed through the remaining fields to a save button, and then hit enter.

The other officer nodded to Topher, and then returned to his station outside the holding cell.

"Name, please?"

"Mason," Topher stated.

"First or last?"

"Last."

"First?"

"Christopher."

"There you are," the policewoman nodded toward the screen, and selected his name from a list.

She tapped out a few more commands, and a form popped open on the screen. She clicked another selection from a drop down menu, and several of the fields highlighted in yellow. She turned the monitor towards him, and slid the keyboard and mouse across the desk.

"I'll go get your stuff while you fill this out," she said in a friendly but businesslike tone. "Now, you can't change any of the information in the other fields, and you cannot leave this page without a password, so please don't try, or we have to do it all again."

"Understood," Topher nodded.

She left him to fill in his date of birth, his address, the time of his release, and other such mundanities. He had just reached the bottom of the form when she returned. His personal belongings, he noted, were in a normal gallon-sized freezer bag with his name and the date written in permanent marker on the side, rather than an official evidence bag. She set it on the desk in front of him. He noticed his phone indicated he had missed several calls and texts.

"Okay," the policewoman said, turning the screen back toward herself and pulling the keyboard to her side of the desk. "We have a few more hoops to jump through, and then you can get along with your day, sound good?"

"Yep," Topher agreed.

"How often do you drink?" She asked.

"Not often, really, I just. . ."

"Once a week or less, two to three times a week, four to five times a week, more than five times a week?" She asked, cutting him off.

"Once a week or less," Topher stated, realizing she just wanted to get the form filled out, and had absolutely no care at all if the answers were accurate. She nodded but her eyes held absolutely no belief. She was likely used to being lied to by drunks.

"When you drink," she continued. "How many drinks do you usually consume?"

"Two to three," he stated, and the woman clicked the correct corresponding box.

"Are you interested in getting counselling for your drinking?" she asked.

"No, thank you."

"Is your reason for declining counselling a financial concern?"

"No."

"And that is all she wrote," the policewoman clicked the submit button. "Would you like a copy of the form or of the receipt for the return of your personal belongings?"

"Not really," Topher said with complete honesty.

"Then you have a nice day, now," the policewoman offered him a friendly smile which didn't quite reach her eyes, and opened a new document on her computer and pulled another file from a drawer in her desk and began to input data once more.

"Thank you," Topher said, for lack of anything better to say.

He stood and looked around the room for the exit, and spotted daylight coming from a set of glass doors up a short hallway on the far side of the room. Moments later, he was being slapped in the face by freezing wind, and pulling his phone from his pocket to call whichever rideshare app had the quickest pick-up time available.

He requested a ride from someone listed as only three minutes away, and spent the first ten seconds of his wait transferring his keys and wallet from the freezer bag to his pockets, and then another minute trying to find a trashcan in which to dispose of the freezer bag. He considered just letting the wind take it, but decided he didn't want to litter directly in front of a police station, particularly not when the litter had his name written on it in permanent marker.

After locating a trash can, and stuffing it down inside so the wind wouldn't pull it back out and counteract all of his efforts at good citizenship, Topher stood in the cold and felt his ears begin to sting, before eventually going numb.

He was, he decided at that moment, done.

He would get a lift back to his loft above the garage, pack up his clothes and whatever might be worth keeping, there wouldn't be much, and then he would drive directly to his bank and empty his paltry savings.

It would be enough to get him to Florida.

There were lots of bars in Florida, and someone would need an experienced bouncer.

It wasn't retirement, but it wasn't prison either.

If he had to go on grinding out a living, then he might as well do it where the air didn't hurt his face.

"Stick a fork in me," he muttered to himself as a ten year old sedan pulled up with the rideshare sticker in its rear window. "I am fucking done."

KARKUS HAD been serious about Not buying him lunch, Not was a little surprised to discover. Fortunately, when Karkus had affected his release, he had also liberated the stack of money Alto had given him, so Not was happy enough to comply.

From the holding cell, Karkus had driven, with Not's guidance, to Little Ferry so Not could have a quick shower, and change of clothes. While he showered, Not tumbled his borrowed work shirt in the dryer with three scented fabric softener sheets to get another day's wear out of it. Not stuffed the majority of the grand Alto had given him into an old coffee can in the kitchen, but kept a hundred in his pocket so he could buy lunch for himself and his public defender, as well as a cheap cell phone, and some take out later for dinner.

Keeping a close eye on the clock, Not left a note for his dad on the kitchen table. It read simply: Out of jail and off to work. Love you, Not.

After a quick stop for a cheap prepaid cell phone from a rack at the corner market, they chose a coffee shop not far from Alto's, one likely built in the mid-seventies, but had been re-done in the nineties to have a retro-fifties style, which twenty years later now was faded and shabby enough to almost look authentic.

"I need to be at the shop and rolling by four," Not said, as they picked up the menus secured in scratch faded plastic and vinyl covers made to look like record covers.

"So we'll get something quick, like a sandwich," Karkus allowed, and then scanned the menu. "You know you're likely not out of hot water yet."

The sudden change in direction in the conversation, coupled with the fact that Karkus did not alter his conversational tone even the slightest bit, made Not stare vacantly for a moment, as if trying to decipher a cryptic message, rather than a fairly straightforward observation. If he had been on the witness stand, he would have almost certainly been looking like he was trying to come up with a good lie, so no matter what he had answered afterward, he would have looked like a liar to both the judge and jury, which of course was what such a technique was intended to do.

Not was suddenly very glad Karkus was on his side.

"Why?" he asked, knowing Karkus had been hoping for him to either agree or protest, so Not would stay on the defensive and therefore have to carry the weight of the conversation.

"A very large amount of a very controlled substance has gone missing," Karkus stated plainly, his tone suggesting he was speaking with a child, or perhaps someone rather feeble minded. "Until it is accounted for, they will keep going after those who they know came into contact with it until they get a new trail to follow."

"So, what do I do?"

"If you have any more information which could help them find the cocaine. . ."

"If I knew where it was, I would tell them!" Not tried to keep his voice calm, but it was a strain.

"No!" Karkus snapped. "You're still thinking like a kid who got grounded once. In the eyes of the system, you're a criminal. If you have knowledge of the crime, then you will be considered a part of the crime thanks to your prior. If you have information, you give it to me. I will make sure it gets to the police from a channel which does not lead back to you. If they find the coke, then they will likely let the rest go. If they find the coke and the person who took it, then they will forget about you altogether."

He turned his attention to one of the waitresses behind the counter and waved to indicate they were ready to order. Not, who hadn't even considered yet what he wanted to eat, flipped open the large square menu.

"*Do* you have any useful information, Mr. Johnson?"

Not pretended to study the menu for a moment while he struggled with an answer. The fact was he did have new information, but it just wasn't any good. He knew who had taken the barrel from the back of the rental truck, and then driven most of the way back to where it had started. Not now knew that he himself had unknowingly hauled the stolen barrel all the way back to Hackensack and left it in a disabled pick up camper on the street in front of his new place of employment. He knew it had been removed from the truck, and stashed in a burned out house about a block away, and it had then been stolen from there by persons unknown.

Unfortunately, none of this knowledge helped in any way. All it did was bring the focus back on himself, and even worse on his new job. It didn't help them find the coke, and it certainly didn't help them catch the person who took it, because the person who actually did the taking was currently in jail for, of all things, drunk and disorderly, which apparently wasn't even a crime. He just had to sit there until he sobered up, which as far as Not could tell he already had.

Hell, he had probably already gone home.

There was no evidence whatsoever, now that the coke was gone, Topher was even involved. If Not told them the guy he met in the drunk tank also happened to be the guy who stole a barrel full of cocaine from the back of a truck in New York, which I also accidentally helped him to haul back to New Jersey, he would just look guilty and desperate. Also, incredibly stupid, if not crazy.

None of which would help them to get back the missing barrel of cocaine, so Not decided he did not in fact have any "useful" information to contribute at this time.

"No, I don't. I wish I did, because I would really like for this to just be over," Not said with a shrug. "But, I don't have any useful information."

"BLT," Karkus responded confidently, if somewhat enigmatically.

Not tried once again to decipher the Sphynxian nature of this statement. Running through the list of internet and texting lingo he knew, like LOL and FML, but could not remember ever running across BLT on a meme page before.

It was only when he saw Karkus was looking at him expectantly that he realized the waitress had come up behind him while he was thinking, and was waiting patiently to take his order.

"I'll have the same," he said bit sheepishly. "With a coke."

"Make it two," Karkus said, and handed both menus to the waitress.

Chapter 29

"HE'S NOT here."

"What do you mean he's not there," Donny strained to keep his voice calm. "You told me he had been arrested."

Donny tried to avoid looking either Sokolov or Fedin in the eye, and wished he was not sitting like a child on his bed, being lectured to by his parents. He wanted to pace and shout into the phone. Or, better yet, he wanted to put Jennifer on speaker so he could put the phone down and yell at her from all parts of the room while throwing pillows at the wall to vent his frustration. Unfortunately, neither was an option which allowed him any appearance of control in front of an audience, not that his half of the conversation was helping his case either.

"First of all, Donny, I want to remind you that I am *your* lawyer, not your friend's lawyer," Jennifer said, as always, ready to remind him and anyone else she was in fact a lawyer. "Secondly, before you decide you want to use *that* tone, I would like to remind you that after one phone call, I dropped everything I was doing, hauled ass to a police station to represent someone whom I have never met, but did so on your behalf, and now you call me back, to bitch at me for things beyond my control?"

"Counselor Jones, I do sincerely appreciate your superior legal counsel, as always," Donny said, trying not to gag on the honey dripping from his own voice. "Now, how the hell is he out already when you said he had been arrested?"

After several unanswered calls to Topher's cell phone, Donny had tried another Hail Mary pass to Jennifer to see if she could track him down, which she had been able to do in about thirty seconds on her computer. The answer being he was in a jail cell, which of course explained why he hadn't been answering his phone.

"No," the voice of Jennifer Jones buzzed into his ear, "I said he had been taken into custody. There *is* a difference. According to public records, he was taken into protective custody."

"*What?*"

"For public intoxication, in Hackensack, only a couple of hours after I called him, so your cat is probably dead, by the way," Jennifer finished. "Dead cat notwithstanding, being drunk is not a crime in our great state, so he was simply held in a treatment facility, which in this case was a holding cell, until he was sober enough to sign himself out, which he did apparently just before I got there."

"The motherfucker went out and got *drunk?*" Donny hissed as quietly as he could into the phone.

"Maybe he was celebrating you getting busted. He certainly didn't sound very surprised by my call. Anyway, no blood alcohol level was included in the report, and I did a web search for the address from which he was taken into custody and it looks to be an abandoned house, so who knows. Maybe your friend is just a homeless drunk you brought home one night, none of my business." Jennifer's signature hair flip and shrug was nearly audible. "Anyway, even if being drunk was an actual charge, which again it is not, this would never stand up in court. It looks like more of a make-peace deal."

"Meaning?" Donny demanded.

"Meaning, asshole," Jennifer snapped back, "that your buddy was annoying someone, surprise-sur-fucking-prise given who he's friends with, but wasn't full on disorderly or a public nuisance to the point they could get a charge to stick in court, so the cop just took him away to keep the peace. Which is probably, like, ninety percent of all the public intoxication filings. Someone is being annoying."

"So, everything is cool, then?" Donny confirmed, more for his audience than for himself. He smiled confidently and gave Sokolov and Fedin a thumbs up.

"No, you fucking retard, everything is not cool," Jennifer nearly screamed. "You are currently in federal custody for questioning in the disappearance of a shit-ton of cocaine!"

"Well, sure," Donny acknowledged, "there is still that."

"That? *That*? How the fuck is *that* just a *that* to you?" Jennifer sounded both infuriated and amazed. Donny was pretty sure he could have her in his bed by midnight, if he had the desire to see how the other half lives. "By the way, how are you on the phone with me at all? According to the DEA, you are still in custody and on route to Hudson County Correctional."

"We, uh, stopped for gas. I'm at a payphone," Donny tossed off the first lie which came to mind.

"They still have those?" Jennifer sounded amazed. "You must still be in the boonies. How long until you get here?"

"Um," Donny mouthed the words "how long" to Sokolov, and then tapped at an imaginary wristwatch. Sokolov shrugged and held up one finger, then shrugged again and waggled his flat hand in the air. The meaning was clear: one hour, give or take.

"Donovan," Jennifer switched to her counselor voice in order to remind him, "I am your lawyer, and I need to be there to meet you. They will want to get you directly into questioning, so . . ."

"We should be there in an hour or so," Donny assured her.

Sokolov, as if realizing he should also be confirming their arrival time with his own people, pulled a phone out of his pocket and quietly stepped out of the room.

"You sound like you're up to something, Don," Jennifer opined. "Whatever it is, sit on it until we get a chance to talk face to face. I cannot help you if I don't have all the information."

"I know, Jen," Donny soothed.

"I'm serious, here, Donny," Jennifer insisted. "Sometimes the right move is to do nothing at all, and I think this is one of those times."

"I hear you," Donny assured her.

"Yeah, but you sure aren't listening," said Jennifer getting in her final shot. "See you in an hour."

She disconnected before Donny could say anything back, which she knew from experience annoyed the hell out of him, which is of course why she did it now.

"Do we have a problem, mister, ah, I'm sorry may I also call you Donovan?"

"Donny in fine."

"Wonderful, and I am Gregori," the fat man smiled expansively. "Do we have a problem, Donny?"

"No," Donny said after a thoughtful pause. "I don't think we do."

"The man you needed to speak to was arrested," Gregori reminded him, as if he needed reminding. "Sounds like it should be a problem."

"No, not arrested," Donny corrected. "Taken into custody for drinking, probably just to keep the peace, my lawyer assured me."

"This still sounds like a problem," Gregori said, not appearing or sounding at all convinced.

"Not at all," Donny assured him. "He is already out, in fact. But, we may not even need him."

"Why? Does your lawyer know where the barrel is now?" Gregori asked, and then continued in a tone of greater concern. "Did the police find it?"

"Yes, I mean, no," Donny fumbled for the words as he figured out the possibilities of all Jenny had just told him. "Let me try again. No, the police did not find the cocaine, but yes I do think my lawyer did know where the stuff is stashed. I just think she didn't know it herself."

"I think I will need a bit more of an explanation," Gregori confessed.

"If you don't mind, I would like to check one more thing before I can say for sure," Donny stalled. "Do you have a computer around here?"

"Of course," Gregori said, and began the efforts to raise his considerable frame from a seated position. "It, *huh*, would probably be best, *unf*, to, *ungh*, use the desktop in my office. *Ha!*"

With the final exclamation, Gregori attained full standing, and gestured for Donny to accompany him to the doorway through which Sokolov had disappeared not long before.

"Just to be abundantly cautious," Gregori explained, "we shall use my dark web browser, so as to leave absolutely no trace of forehand knowledge, just in case things do not work out as we would like them to later."

"Um, sure, yeah," Donny agreed, though he had no real idea why. "Sounds good."

Fedin led him quickly through the back corner of a large display room, lined as Fedin had promised with large display windows which left them exposed to any curious party who just happened to be in the neighborhood. However, no one strolled past and looked in for the few short seconds they were visible as they crossed to a short hallway lined with several plain and windowless doors. From the distances between them, the rooms they concealed must be little larger than closets.

"A good salesman should rarely be in his office," Fedin explained, as if reading Donny's thoughts. "But rather, he should be out here on the sales floor with the customers."

Fedin, opened the first door on the right, and revealed a ten foot by ten foot cube. A small particleboard and laminate desk was wedged into one corner, with a fairly recent computer tower stuffed into the foot space beneath it and what had to be the last functioning CRT monitor in the northern hemisphere sitting on top of it.

"Please, be my guest," Fedin invited.

"Is there a password?" Donny asked before sitting at the desk, knowing he would just have to get back up in a few seconds if there was.

"Not to get to the internet," Fedin allowed. "However, I will caution you not to open any of the files on the desktop. They are password protected, and the password must be entered within ten seconds or my security system will go off."

"Slag your hard-drive?" Donny guessed.

"Well, yes, of course," Fedin nodded. "Also, though, a small charge of explosive will detonate behind the monitor tube, and send blast of shrapnel glass toward whomever is sitting in front of it. Maybe not lethal, you understand, but certainly disfiguring and very likely permanently blinding."

"Goddamn, man," Donny muttered, both in terror and in awe.

"It certainly dissuades me from trying to do any business after I have been drinking," Fedin laughed.

Donny could muster no more than a polite chuckle, partly due to the fact he found the idea of having his eyeballs shredded by shattered glass projectiles a little less amusing than did his new comrade, but mostly because he was eager to see if he could find the information he was hoping for.

Opening up the browser, the icon of which appeared to be either an onion or a turnip, which he found to be the most Russian thing he could imagine, other than perhaps a hammer and sickle, and entered the search phrase "police blotter Hackensack NJ." He got over thirty-four thousand hits, and at the top of the list was the city of Hackensack homepage. Donny clicked on it and found several ways he could provide information to the police, but little information which the police were willing to share. Luckily, the third result down was an incredibly helpful public information site which listed not only all of the police actions within the past twenty-four hours, but displayed them all on an interactive map, offering different icons for specific crimes committed.

God bless the Internet.

There were emoji fists for assaults, cross-hairs for shootings, an enigmatic stick figure which for some reason represented robberies, flames for arson, as well as many more. The one Donny figured he would need was a small blue circle with a question mark in it listed simply as "other."

There was only one such icon anywhere in Hackensack the night before, listed as "300 Block of Railroad Avenue and Stanley Place; Protective Custody." There were clusters of other icons all over Manhattan, which was also displayed on the map, everything from assault to armed robbery and burglary abounded in Manhattan, but in the corresponding square mileage of the Garden State, the only other crime listed last night was a shooting just outside Jersey City. Donny felt an absurd burst of pride for his home state. Compared to New York, Jersey looked like an absolute paradise.

"If you have a truck, Gregori," Donny said, as he turned away from the booby-trapped computer, "And, of course, the three million dollars, I think we can get you your cocaine in about an hour, give or take."

From behind Fedin, the office door swung open, and Sokolov joined them once more.

"Alexi, we have some wonderful news," Fedin informed him. "Donny is confident the missing cocaine will, after a short detour to help rid our streets of some criminal *negry*, soon be in the capable hands of the Drug Enforcement Agency. Isn't that good news?"

"Yes, indeed," Sokolov agreed. "Couldn't come soon enough, actually, as I have unfortunately just lost my prisoner."

Donny felt his muscles instantaneously and painfully tense.

"What?" Donny asked, trying to keep his tone neutral.

"Yes," Sokolov nodded. "We were just forced off the road on the way down here. A group of African American thugs in ski masks forced us off the road, held me at gunpoint, and forcibly removed you from the rear of the vehicle."

"What the hell . . .why?" Donny asked.

"The devil is in the details, Donovan," Sokolov explained. "After the coke is in the hands of the men in question, my report will make everything fit together very nicely."

"But, it makes me look guilty!" Donny snapped.

"Maybe yes," Fedin said, suddenly sounding less friendly than before. "Maybe, no. It does depend a lot on the story the *negry* tell when they are arrested. Maybe, Alexi here can make sure some of them don't get arrested, so long as they tell the correct version of the events. The version which indicates that the *other* guard in the armored car was the one who stole the cocaine. The same man who arranged to sell the cocaine to the damned *negry* and talked them into kidnapping and framing his young and innocent partner for the crime."

"Think of it as a little insurance," Sokolov explained. "All good friendships are mutually beneficial, Donovan. You can help us, and we can help you. We all have reasons to stay good friends, right?"

"We are friends now, right Donny?" Fedin asked, his voice returning to its previous melodious pitch of friendship and camaraderie.

"Of course," Donny forced a smile, and tried to will the muscles in his neck and shoulders to release. He picked up his still mostly full cup of rum from where he had left it on the desk, and drained what remained in a single go.

It helped a little.

Chapter 30

THEY PARTED ways at the diner, after Not had paid the check of course. Karkus said he had a pile of other cases which needed his attention as well, but Not should expect a daily call for updates and just to check in.

"Get me your new cell number as soon as it's active," Karkus had insisted as they stood outside the diner, readying to head in opposite directions. He pressed a business card into Not's hand, and then with a small nod, turned and headed back to his car.

Not walked the short distance to Alto's All Tow feeling a curious mix of trepidation and hope. After such a long period of unemployment, and the accompanying descent from frustration, to anxiety, to fear, to desperation, Not found even a second round of false accusations of major felonies could not shake the joy he felt from going to work again. The cold wind stung his face, and his entire body ached from both the unaccustomed physical exertion of the day before as well as the largely sleepless night, but overall he still felt good.

Topher's junkheap coke mule had been moved, likely to the back lot or perhaps it had already been hauled away for scrap, in order to clear the doors for the mechanic's bays. No one would have known it had recently been a key component in a major crime. It certainly hadn't given off a coke-fortune vibe of any kind. Hell, by now it could have already been crushed, cubed, and melted down, along with any evidence it may have contained.

Not felt a passing pang of guilt.

If he had told Karkus everything Topher had told him in the cell, Not may have stopped the old truck from being hauled away. At this very moment, jumpsuit clad police investigators could be scouring dirt and rust flakes from the rusted bed which could contain clues to point to Not's innocence.

Or, to implicate him further.

Either way, what was done was done, and the truck was gone.

Good riddance.

One garage door stood open, but the others had been closed against the wind and the cold. Through the windows Not could see the armored car had also been removed. Likely to a Federal crime lab being vacuumed clean for potential evidence or clues.

As Not strode through the front door, bypassing the coffee station on his way to the employee only section, he noted from the large clock on the wall it was only ten minutes to four.

Sitting in two of the thrift shop chairs were two of the mechanics Not had met yesterday. They were sipping coffee and watching television. On screen, two young men were celebrating by screaming and posturing, with a couple of high fives thrown in for good measure. Not had no idea what was being said, because the only words other than "yeah!" and "I told you!" were being bleeped out by the censors. However, the banner at the bottom of the screen scrolled the message "You are *not* the father!" in large white lettering, so Not had a pretty good idea of what had happened up to this point.

"Have either of you guys seen Josue or Mr. Alto?" Not asked of the two men, whose names he couldn't remember, and whose name badges he was unable to read from his place in the doorway.

"Alto is still out, but Josue and Helen are in Alto's office," said one man, who Not suddenly recognized as Francis Xavier, better known as "Bob."

"He'll kick your ass, he hears you call 'em that," said the other man, whose name Not was still unable to recall.

"All the more reason to take advantage while the door is closed," reasoned Bob.

"Is it okay to knock, do you think?" Not inquired.

"*Knock* yourself out," offered Bob.

"Jesus, man, that was terrible," the other man opined.

Not smiled politely at the pun, but internally agreed it had in fact been awful. He crossed the room, cheered on by the studio audience on television, bleeped at by some sad and angry woman who still could not say for sure just whom exactly had fathered her child.

"Who is it?" Josue called, in response to Not's knock.

"It's Not," he answered.

"Not what?" called Bob from behind him.

"Definitely not the first time he's heard that joke," opined Bob's companion.

The door opened quickly, and Josue looked both surprised and concerned.

"Holy shit," he managed, "You're here. I didn't think you would be here tonight. I was ready to take the evening shift."

"But, um," Not stammered, wondering if he had just been fired. "Karkus told me he called to let you know I was released. I wasn't charged."

"No, I mean, yeah," Josue contradicted himself. "He called to say you were out, but I figured after a double-shift and a shit day like this you would take the night off."

"So, I still have a job, then?" Not confirmed.

"God damn, man!" Josue laughed. "Of course you do!"

Not felt a weight lift from his chest, but could think of nothing he could say. Josue seemed to study Not for a few moments, on the verge of asking a question, the topic of which Not could certainly take a guess, but then Josue seemed to think better of it.

"We done, then?" Troy said from behind Josue.

"What? Oh, yeah," Josue said, as if suddenly remembering he had been in the middle of a conversation. "So, we're good, right?"

"As good as can be hoped," Troy confirmed. "Given the circumstances."

"Alright, then," Josue nodded.

Troy pushed his way past the other two men and headed out the way Not had just come in.

"So what . . ." Josue paused, and then seemed to reconsider. "How much of it can you talk about?"

"Well, my lawyer says not much," Not admitted.

"Okay, so let me put it this way," Josue tried, and motioned for Not to come into Alto's office. "Not to sound too much like a dick, but do we need to start looking for a driver?"

Alto's spartan office was now filled with banker's boxes, each filled with hanging file folders. Some of the boxes looked nearly new, and others had the scuffed and dusty appearance of having been stacked somewhere in long term storage. Each box was marked with a month and a year, going back, as far as Not could tell, for about three years. They lined the wall, and were stacked on the black leather porn couch.

"The feds went through all our paperwork, and interviewed all the employees who were here today," Josue stated with a bit of regret, and then motioned for Not to have a seat in one of the thrift shop chairs from the break room brought in for the sake of the interviews he supposed. "Which is to say, you now have a bit of a reputation here, whether you earned it or not."

"Shit," Not said for the sake of something to say, but he had pretty much assumed it would happen.

"Which, to be perfectly honest," Josue shrugged, "is not necessarily a bad thing. As far as I can tell, you may have just become a legend after one day on the job. Just don't get too mad if you're called Scarface from time to time."

"They told you what got taken?" Not said, more of a statement than a question.

"They were concerned that if we were to come across it, we might want to open it to see what was inside, and they didn't want to see a grease monkey overdosed on the evening news. You know, because we're all so stupid that if we found a barrel full of liquid blow, we'd all dive in head first, right?"

"I didn't have anything to do with it, Josue," Not said, hoping it sounded like conviction and not desperation.

"I was supposed to be on the late shift, kid," Josue reminded him. "And, honestly, I can't say I would have done anything different from you, and I told them as much. We've had police cruisers hauled in here after a wreck, and ambulances too. If we can have those vehicles, why not an armored truck? Bottom line, it's a privately owned vehicle brought here at the request of the driver. You did nothing wrong, and like I said, I probably would have done the same. It could have just as easily have been me in the cell last night, but you were just in the wrong place at the wrong time."

"Thank you, Josue," Not said with real gratitude. "Does Mr. Alto feel the same?"

"Christ, Paul thinks this is divine retribution against him for breaking a commandment," Josue said and rolled his eyes. "He will probably ask you for forgiveness when he sees you."

"Seriously?" Not asked, amazed.

"Seriously," Josue confirmed. "He may ask if he can make it up to you in some way, an act of atonement, right?"

"But, it wasn't his fault, it. . ."

"Doesn't matter," Josue interjected. "If he feels guilty, then he'll want to do something to make it up to you. It's usually money, or something like it, take it or don't, but if he offers to give you something, then he wants you to take it. It's not just, you know, like, a gesture. To him money is to make amends, and to have it accepted makes him feel better."

"Did . . ." was as far as Not got, before his brain kicked in and he thought better of the question he had been about to ask.

"Yes, he did, and no I didn't," Josue answered for him anyway. "I don't want the prick to feel better."

Josue glanced at his watch, and then stood from where he was seated behind the desk. Not stood as well, grateful for the chance to end this awkward conversation and just get to work.

"Did you get a phone?" Josue asked, indicating the as yet unopened package Not was holding.

"Yeah, but it needs a few hours to charge before I can use it," Not confirmed.

They headed back out to the break room toward the repair bays.

"There should be a USB adapter for the cigarette lighter in the glove box, otherwise you can pick one up at any gas station. As soon as you activate it, text me and I'll save you to my contacts, then forward you on to everybody here. You'll get a bunch back with just the sender's name as the text. Save 'em all in your contacts, so everybody can get a hold of each other. Sick policy is if you can't make your shift, you have to find someone else who can."

"Got it," Not said.

"We can't make this an official policy, but unofficially, if you *can* take a shift, you *do* take the shift. Don't cancel a date for it or anything, but if I've got somebody running a truck with a fever because you wanted to sit at home and watch reruns, then unofficially I'm gonna be pissed."

"Got it," Not said again.

They continued on as they talked, walking through the now mostly empty mechanics bays, and then out the door in the back which led to the vehicle storage yard. The Peterbilt stood idling just outside the gate, and on the back was the Shit Heap Topher had apparently used to smuggle the barrel full of cocaine all the way back down to almost exactly where it started. Alto stood beside the passenger side of the cab, speaking to Troy.

"Wait," Not said, "Isn't that . . ."

Evidence.

He had almost asked if they were removing evidence, but stopped himself just in time. They didn't know it was evidence, because the only person besides himself and Topher who knew this truck was used in the theft was Donny.

Apparently, it hadn't been crushed yet after all.

It wasn't too late to call Karkus. Not considered the thought, but once again rejected it. Still too much of an unknown to warrant the risk. It couldn't hurt him if it were gone.

"Yeah, it's the piece of shit you left on our doorstep, thank you so much for *that* by the way, it was a bitch to move," Josue agreed. "We dragged it around the corner this morning to the lot, and Troy, hillbilly that he is, just fell in love with the fucking thing."

"But," Not stammered, wondering what he could say without getting himself in deeper. "What about the owner?"

"We ran the plate and the VIN and found it was registered to some shitkicker in Pennsylvania. Didn't even know it was gone, can you believe it?" Josue laughed. "Apparently, the guy has a whole yard of showpieces like this one, and had to go out and check to make sure it wasn't still there. Troy offered the guy hundred bucks for it, and now he's the proud owner of this particular piece of shit."

Not knew he should say something, but for the life of him could not figure out what he should say or how. He didn't know why either. Topher had admitted to removing the barrel from the back and stashing it in a house about a block away, but then someone else had ripped it off. There probably wasn't anything in the truck now which could get Troy in trouble, and there wasn't anything about it which could help them find the missing coke.

Still, Not had felt better when he thought the truck would just disappear in a scrap heap somewhere, destined for recycling. If Not ever saw it again, he would prefer it to be in the form of paperclips, or soda cans ten years from now.

"So, drop it off at Troy's place and then hit the turnpike and listen for the radio, okay?"

"Wait, *I'm* driving this to Troy's?"

"See you at midnight, okay?"

TROY LED the way in a beat up old truck, superior only to the one he had just purchased with the slight advantage that it could still move under its own power. Not would have figured maybe Troy had bought the Shit Heap for parts, except any part harvested from the Shit Heap would probably do more harm than good to the health of a running vehicle.

Not followed as Troy led him north to an even more run down and industrial part of Hackensack than the one from which they had started out, and was only mildly surprised to see him head toward a single-wide trailer parked at the narrowing end of an empty lot belonging to the Bergen County Public Works. Slightly more surprising was how easily he found himself buying into the stereotype. Old guy with mutton chops, probably a white-trash redneck who lives in a trailer. In this case, it all seemed to be accurate and true, but his generation had been raised to believe all stereotypes are wrong and you were a bad person if you believed in them. Now, when confronted with the very type of people for whom those stereotypes exist, he somehow felt embarrassed.

Was it still bigotry to call a person a redneck or white trash, when he fully and completely lived up to the stereotype, perhaps even took pride in said stereotype? Could he use the word redneck? Was it like black guys and the N-word? If so, he should be able to; he was white after all.

It didn't feel right, though.

About fifty yards distant was the closest out building, which appeared to be a warehouse whose use by the Public Works administrators ended sometime in the previous century. The trailer sat at the crust side of a pie-shaped wedge of scrub land between where Kenderkamack Road and the train tracks came together as they ran below State Route 4. It had been there long enough for the tires to crack and rot off and for a full forest of weeds to have grown up from the cracked concrete below, which acted as natural fencing to keep the snow drifts from reaching under the trailer, so Not guessed the Public Works folks either rarely used this facility, or had taken note of Troy's presence and had, in the long standing tradition of New Jersey bureaucracy when presented with a problem which was not explicitly their own, shrugged it off.

Not pulled up next to the trailer, slowing the rig and preparing to stop, but then noticed Troy was not stopping at the trailer. Instead, he continued on in his truck to the abandoned warehouse a short distance away. The warehouse was vaguely barn shaped, but most of the front of the building was taken up by an enormous doorway.

It was not yet five o'clock, but the winter sun was dropping below the horizon, so the interior of the warehouse was dim. Not could make out several vehicle shapes inside. As his headlights swept across the entrance, Not was able to see the shapes of other beatdown old trucks, as well as a couple of vintage muscle cars covered in rust and primer. Apparently, Troy was a bit of a collector of worn-out American rolling iron.

Not pulled up perpendicular to the entrance, and then past it, so he could back the flatbed inside and drop the old truck wherever Troy wanted what was likely to be its final resting place to be. Troy drove directly into the warehouse, parked, and got out to guide Not in.

Following Troy's directions, Not backed in at an angle which would drop the Shit Heap just inside the doorway closest to the street. When Troy signaled him to stop, Not put the truck in neutral, set the parking brake, and began to tilt the bed. When it was in position, Not began to climb out of the cab to lower the truck off the bed, but Troy waved him away and lowered the truck himself. When the back bumper of the Shit Heap touched the ground, Troy waved for Not to pull forward. So, Not popped the parking brake, put the big truck in gear, and idled forward slowly, riding the clutch. The Shit Heap scraped and squealed as it clung to the bed, but eventually slid free like a pancake from a spatula to a plate. Not watched from the warm comfort of the cab as Troy detached the chains from the old truck, and re-secured them on the bed.

Troy gave him a thumbs up and a scowl, and waved again in a way which could only mean "good-bye." Not returned the wave, and got the tow rolling once more. Unsure if the far side of the lot had an exit, Not circled the truck around to go out the way he came in. As he cranked the big wheel clockwise with his left hand, he reached for the radio mic with his right.

"This is Alto's in the big truck," Not said, keying the microphone. As he swung the truck around, the headlights swept once more through the entrance to the warehouse, and Not reversed direction on the steering wheel to correct his direction left toward the exit. However, when the lights briefly brightened the interior of the warehouse, Not had a momentary view, like a camera flash, of Troy at the rear of the Shit Heap, the camper top open and the tailgate down. The bottom of a blue barrel on a handcart was clearly visible.

"Son of a bitch," Not finished.

"Alto, 10-9, say again, Alto, 10-9"

"Sorry," Not realized he had said the last part into the microphone as well. "Alto's big truck at Kenderkamack and State Route 4, I am 10-8"

"10-4 Alto, we have no 10-43 calls at this time."

"10-4 Dispatch," Not replaced the microphone on the dash, and popped open the glove box to find the USB adapter for his phone, splitting his attention between his search and the road, which he hated to do, but didn't want to give any outward sign he had noticed anything out of the ordinary.

Topher was a lying son of a bitch, and there was no way in hell Not was going to get left holding the bag again.

"You'll be hearing from my lawyer," Not said to no one in particular.

Chapter 31

THREE MILLION dollars was much less impressive but far heavier than Donny had imagined it would be.

Fedin led Donny further down the short hallway to another anonymous office just after Sokolov's departure to both complete his detailed report on the unexpected and rattling ordeal of being accosted by persons unknown and relieved of his prisoner, and then on to ensure his report would be verified by known associates of the perpetrators when they were apprehended, which would be whenever Sokolov got the all clear call from Fedin to confirm the cocaine was securely, and beyond a reasonable doubt, in the possession of these menaces to society. Inside the office was no furniture, but rather large boxes with shipping labels from every pharmaceutical company Donny had ever heard of and several he had not.

"Jesus," Donny mused. "You just keep this stuff in an empty office with no security?"

"Oh, no, not at all, Donny," Fedin smiled. "So, don't go getting any ideas. We are in a vault right now, walls are reinforced concrete, covered in drywall so if I need it to appear as an office again, a quick coat of paint will be all that is required. The door has a steel core, and I will caution you not to touch any of the boxes, as a few of them are security decoys set up in a similar fashion to my computer screen."

"Gotcha," Donny said, putting his hands in his pockets. "I'll just stand over here at the door."

"Don't go far," Fedin asked, as he scanned the boxes, pausing now and again to read a label. "I will need your help lifting some of these in a minute, my back, you understand."

"Yeah, sure," said Donny, surprising even himself at how agreeable he had become at the promise of the imminent delivery of three million dollars cash into his hands.

He watched as Fedin worked his way around the room, reading the labels and pausing once in a while apparently to consider something before moving on and continuing his search. Donny found he wasn't even curious as to what the fat Russian was doing, but rather was feeling uncharacteristically trusting and relaxed. Perhaps it was the fatigue, or all the unexpected turns the past two days had taken. Christ, was that all it had been, two days? No wonder he felt so tired.

He had been a busy, busy boy.

The drink hadn't helped either. He had never been a good daytime drinker. For some reason, he could drink all he wanted to after the sun went down, but whenever he had a drink during the day, he always felt ready for a nap. He tried to stifle a yawn, but it did no good. He practically felt his jaw creak when it opened wide.

"Little sleepy, Donny?" Fedin asked without turning from his search.

"To be honest, yeah, I am," Donny confirmed. "I was just thinking how I was never much of a daytime drinker. I don't feel buzzed or anything, just kind of relaxed and a little sleepy."

"That is probably the Rohypnal," Fedin said matter-of-factly.

"Yeah, right," Donny said with a small laugh, and then ran the words through his head once more. "Wait, you roofied me?"

"Just a little," Fedin confirmed, his back still to Donny. "But you are in no danger, Donny. It is just a little extra protection on my behalf. I am not a young man anymore, and, if I am being truthful, not in the best shape either. So, Alexi added a little Rohypnol to your drink, just a little you understand, to make sure I would be okay when he left us alone."

"Makes sense," Donny agreed, surprised to find he was not even mad.

"I thought so," said Fedin, and then indicated a box on top of one of the stacks. "We will need this one first, I think. Would you be so kind?"

"Sure," Donny agreed once more. He joined Fedin at the stack of boxes, and lifted the top one to the floor. Fedin then moved to a previous stack he had examined, and pointed to a smaller box, third from the top.

"This one next, please," he requested.

Donny complied without comment. Fedin moved back through the stacks he had checked and indicated three more boxes, each one smaller than the last. When Donny had all five boxes on the floor, Fedin nodded in satisfaction. He pulled a box cutter from his pocket, and handed it to Donny.

"Please," Fedin cautioned, "be sure you do not cut deeply. Just enough pressure to split the tape, you understand."

Donny nodded, and split the tape on the box closest to him, the smallest box had been the last one to come down from the stacks. Using the box cutter, Donny gently parted the clear packing tape with which, from the wear and tear on the cardboard and the remnants of previous layers of tape beneath, the box had been obviously sealed and resealed several times. Inside were several balls of crumpled up newspaper, and three stacks of one hundred dollar bills in heat-sealed clear plastic wrap. The bank's paper band around each stack indicated ten thousand dollars.

Donny set the three stacks to the side and opened the next box. It too contained crumpled-up newspaper and wrapped stacks of money. Eight stacks in the second box. Donny added these stacks to the first three, and the pile next to him grew to one hundred and ten thousand.

The next box was bigger than the first two combined, and Donny remembered it as being far heavier than the last two, but lighter than the first two. There was no paper padding in the third box, instead it was packed from bottom to top with sealed stacks of hundreds. Fifty in all.

Donny added them to the pile, and the value grew by five hundred thousand dollars.

The fourth box contained one hundred and ten similar stacks, and the final box one hundred and thirty.

Donny had stacked them up like poker chips, ten bundles high and three rows deep, with one odd bundle left over on top.

Three million and ten thousand dollars.

"I did not have the exact amounts pre-sorted, I'm afraid," Fedin acknowledged. "But I would always rather lose a little more out of my pocket, than have you feel I did not keep my word. Call the extra ten thousand an apology for the Rohypnol, a cowardly -- but I feel necessary -- betrayal of trust. Do you forgive me, Donny? Are we still friends?"

"Yeah," Donny said, his eyes never leaving the money. "We're still friends. No harm, no foul, right?"

"I am very glad to hear you say that," Fedin genuinely sounded relieved his breach of etiquette had been forgiven. "Now, you are certain where the cocaine is located?"

"Yeah," said Donny again, his eyes still on the money, but his brow suddenly drawn down in worry. "What bothers me is I don't know why it's there. It wasn't what we had agreed to. None of this is really what I had in mind when we started out."

"Yes," Fedin sympathized, and continued in a passable Scottish accent, "'But, Mousie, thou art no thy lane, in proving foresight may be vain: The best laid schemes o' mice an' men gang aft a-gley, an' lea'e us nought but grief an' pain, for promised joy.'"

"What?" Donny asked, unable to make out many of the words.

"A poem, just a stanza of it really, titled 'To a Mouse' by the Scottish poet Robert Burns, after he accidentally ploughed into a mouse's burrow. The more modern translation is 'the best laid plans of mice and men often go awry, and leave us nothing but grief and pain instead of promised joy.' I am paraphrasing, of course, but I find it interesting though most people have heard the phrase of 'The best laid plans of mice and men . . . '"

Donny nodded when he realized Fedin had paused to see if Donny had in fact heard the common phrase before, which of course he had, just never in the original wording as spoken by a fat Russian doing a Scottish accent.

Fedin continued after noting Donny's nod. "Nearly everyone I have asked was unaware of the next line Burns had penned all those years ago."

Donny shrugged to show he should also be included in Fedin's list of the great unwashed masses whose education did not include the complete works of Robert Burns or other similarly useless information.

"'Still thou art blest,'" Fedin said, once again with a thick Scottish tongue.

Donny, still feeling a bit sleepy and a lot dopey from his rum and roofie, decided to simply nod in what he hoped would be taken for understanding.

"So, now, repack all this money into a single container," Fedin continued, which Donny felt blessed to hear was his original voice, rather than the forced tones of Mike Myers' famous ogre. "Then, we shall take one of my delivery trucks, and go and retrieve my cocaine."

"*Your* cocaine?"

"That is your money," Fedin reasoned. "Or rather, it will be upon delivery of my cocaine, which shortly thereafter will become the *negry's* cocaine, and then ultimately the DEA's cocaine, you understand."

"My money," Donny mused, happily staring at the stacks upon stacks of cash.

"Yes," Fedin confirmed. "So, let's go get my cocaine."

Fedin bounced off quickly into another anonymous office door and retrieved a large rolling cooler, like a family might take to the shore, or use to tailgate at a ball game. One side had two large wheels built in and the other had a retractable handle, like a suitcase, so the whole thing could be easily moved despite the weight of large amounts of ice and water and beer.

It had a latch like an old-fashioned steamer trunk, though formed out of white plastic rather than brass. Donny unlatched the lid, and swung it open. The interior was scuffed but clean, although the cooler was not completely empty. At the bottom, secured with what appeared to be large amounts of clear aquarium caulk and epoxy, was a cheap cell phone in a waterproof case.

"I have had the foam rubber insulation of the cooler removed and replaced with the magnesium powder found in common road flares," Fedin stated proudly.

"There is something wrong with you, dude," said Donny, before he thought better of it.

"It is a hobby," said Fedin dismissively. "An unusual one, you understand, but a useful one. In this case, it is important to keep in mind that cash seized by the federal government can be used as evidence against you, and, if you are in prison, then the cash is no good to you anyway."

"So, I have to haul my money around in a rolling bomb?" Donny nearly whined.

"Not a bomb," Fedin corrected. "This is more of an immolation device. This will not explode, but rather will burn extremely hot from the inside out, hopefully destroying everything inside of itself in the process."

"Hopefully?" Donny said in disbelief.

"It is true," Fedin conceded, misunderstanding Donny's point, "I have never tried it with this much money inside before, so it may not be as effective. But, given the fact you cannot put out a magnesium fire with water, and anyone wanting to get inside this container prior to the magnesium burning itself out will have a very difficult time of it, I think there is a good chance it will still work fine."

Though his mind was slightly addled, Donny was able to understand what Fedin was really trying to get across. If Donny tried to double-cross Fedin and rip off the money, Fedin would see to it they both ended up with nothing. In addition, Donny had now officially been taken from federal custody by persons unknown, which, as he had not yet been charged with a crime, was a questionable offense at best, but it all but guaranteed he would be charged. And, since he actually did do what he would be charged with doing, getting out from under it would be a challenge to say the least.

Donny filled the cooler with the stacks of bills, closed the lid and latched it.

"Alright," he said, "Let's go get your cocaine."

"I THINK we must face the facts, Donny," Fedin said, his voice heavy with regret. "The barrel is simply not here."

Donny had nodded off on the ride over and had awoken with a head both slightly clearer but also painfully throbbing.

"Yeah, I can see that," replied Donny through clenched teeth. "But, look at the tracks. It *was* here."

They stood in the laundry room of the boarded up house, Fedin's box truck sitting proudly in the driveway, looking like it had every right in the world to be there, perhaps to start hauling away some of the ruined furniture. At least, it is what they would claim if anyone asked about their presence. Donny stared at the tire tracks in the dust and grime on the floor of the laundry room. They were definitely the same as the tracks left by the handcarts they used at work. The barrel had been here, and Topher had been arrested here, but for public drunkenness rather than for being in possession of a ridiculously large amount of cocaine.

Topher had brought the barrel here, but the cops didn't find it.

Had Topher already sold it?

Could it be possible? Topher hadn't even known he would be helping Donny rob the truck until the day they did it, let alone know they would be stealing cocaine, which Donny hadn't even known. There was no way he could have set up a deal so quickly.

Then again, Donny thought, hadn't he?

Maybe another Sokolov got to him, not a DEA agent, but another crooked cop of some kind? Maybe the cop found him there, saw what he had, and ran him in for public intoxication while he ran the other way with the cocaine. Topher was just dumb enough to fall for it too, Donny fumed. Why the hell had he come here in the first place? There was no reason for it that Donny could tell. It wasn't in a neighborhood Topher would go to or even have reason to know about.

He tried Topher's phone again, but with as little success as all of his previous attempts.

It just didn't make any sense.

Which meant, Donny knew and agonized over the knowledge of, he must be missing something.

"I think then, my friend," said Fedin from the doorway behind him, "this is where we will part ways. I will keep my money, and it is like you said earlier: no harm, no foul."

"Hold on," Donny said, rounding angrily on Fedin. "That's not true. They think I escaped from federal custody because of you and your pet Fed. What the hell am I supposed to do now?"

"You overlook a very large benefit," Fedin reasoned as he walked out of the ruined house which, apparently, for a very short time had an unreasonably large boost to its overall value. "You are no longer in federal custody. You would likely have been charged anyway, Donny. My advice: now you should run."

Donny was about to raise another objection, try to get Fedin to toss in some of the cash from the cooler, at least the ten grand he had thrown in for slipping him a roofie, when he followed Fedin out the door, the words fell dead in his mouth.

Through the backyard of the neighboring house and across the train tracks, Donny spotted the truck he had provided for Topher being loaded onto a flatbed tow truck. Sparks were visible even from this distance as it was dragged along the blacktop and up onto the truck bed.

Donny found the missing piece of what had happened.

They had overloaded the old truck and collapsed the suspension. Topher had been towed and caught a ride here, and then hid in the house, probably to hide the barrel from curious eyes, and then put it back in the truck . . .

Before he came back here to get arrested?

It didn't make any sense.

At least, Donny thought so until he saw who was driving the truck.

Goddamn.

What were the fucking odds?

Donny watched as good ol' Harry Johnson climbed in behind the wheel, and, once again, it all clicked into place. Topher must have seen the armored car here and knew sooner or later the Feds would be coming for it. So, he moved the barrel out of sight until they came and went, then put the barrel back, for lack of a better place to stash it around here.

He would have stuck out, standing around outside a crime scene. He must have come back to the house while he waited to hear if Donny had gone to jail or not, and to try to get hold of that freakshow pimp.

Dammit! Maybe he *had*, and that was where the barrel was going right now. After all, the truck had obviously sat here all day, while the Feds came and went, and Topher sat in a cell somewhere. Topher had definitely been out of jail long enough to have made a few calls, and arranged to have the truck taken somewhere for the sale.

It made sense.

At least, it made enough sense to sell it to Fedin. Maybe it would provide a chance to liberate the cash from its plastic prison.

"Greg," Donny said, and Fedin turned to face him. "I know where the barrel is, in fact I am looking at it right now."

"Where. . ." Fedin began.

"No time," Donny said, and started running for Fedin's truck in the driveway. "They're leaving."

Fedin took one look at Donny's face, and then jiggled to keep pace.

They quickly got into the truck, Fedin behind the wheel at his insistence and Donny riding helplessly in the passenger seat. The box truck had an eight cylinder engine, but it was geared for torque rather than speed, so it wound slowly up through several small gears, and had to slow significantly at any corner to keep from tipping. Fortunately for them, the tow truck accelerated just as slowly, and Not was unaware he had any reason to hurry. They were able to catch up within a minute, and then hung back by a block or more, so as not to be too easily noticed. A bit of a challenge, of course, as they were driving a large white box truck, but it couldn't be helped at this point.

"The truck on the bed is the one Topher used to haul the barrel back down from where we stopped for dinner," Donny explained, and told Fedin what he had seen when the truck had been loaded onto the tow bed. "I think the barrel was too much weight for it, and the suspension gave out."

"So, he had it towed," said Fedin, understanding what had happened. "But, then why take it out of the broken truck only to put it back into the broken truck?"

Donny outlined the scenario as he thought it may have happened, emphasizing the importance of the fact the guy driving the truck ahead of them was also the guy who picked up the armored car when it "broke down," even providing the air quotes in his narration, and then hating himself for it.

"I see," said Fedin, though his tone implied he was not sure if he believed it. "And, who is this Mr. Creepy?"

"A drug dealing pimp Topher met while bouncing at a club," Donny shrugged.

"And this is his actual name?" Fedin asked.

"No," Donny shook his head. "No, I can't remember his real name, but it was what we all called him."

"And, he will be armed, we can assume?" Fedin asked.

"I don't know," Donny admitted. "I would assume he will be."

"And, will he have people with him?" Fedin asked.

"People?" Donny asked, and then he understood Fedin's meaning. "I only ever saw him with his hookers, some boys as well as girls, but still, you know, just hookers."

"Then," Fedin smiled. "This should not be a problem."

They followed the tow northward to what appeared to be the backlot of a public works storage yard which had been long in disuse. Fedin pulled into the parking lot of a coin operated laundry on the opposite side of the street, and backed the truck in so they could see where they stopped before approaching on foot. The sun was setting behind them, so they could easily see across the street, but would not be easily seen from that vantage.

"Could you recognize your friend from this distance?" Fedin asked.

"Yeah, no problem," Donny confirmed, and hoped he was right.

An old truck, not too dissimilar from the one on the tow bed, had driven into what looked like an abandoned warehouse. Donny had briefly wondered why the hell Topher had gone out and gotten a second truck so similar to the first one which had apparently failed to be able to do the job. The answer was obvious when the old man with long white sideburns stepped out of the oversized door to the derelict building.

Topher wasn't here.

He must have . . . Maybe he . . . Donny was at a loss. Any answer he tried to provide at this point would be shooting blindly. Maybe he already sold the barrel to this guy, or maybe the barrel wasn't in the back of the truck at all. Maybe it had been ripped off by a dirty cop, like he had thought before he had spotted the truck. Maybe sideburns over there just liked shitty old trucks.

Maybe . . . maybe . . . maybe.

"Donovan," Fedin said from the seat beside him. The use of his full name, just as it had when he was a kid, got his full and complete attention. "I would like to propose an approach, but you may take objection to it."

"Why?" Donny asked, readying himself to leap from the truck as soon as a gun appeared.

"It means using some of the money from the cooler," Fedin said in a tone of regret.

"Um, --"

"Before you object," Fedin pushed on. "Allow me to offer my guarantee to replace any lost cash if we are successful."

"Well. . ."

"I know it is not our agreement," Fedin continued. "But hear me out. You will take ten thousand from the cooler and walk over there. I will follow, but will approach from beneath the overpass, so I will not be easily seen. No money has changed hands yet, I am almost certain. Why else come out here?"

"Well. . ."

"You will tell him the barrel already has a buyer," Fedin bullied on. "You will offer him the ten thousand for his trouble. If he accepts, then everything will be back to the

265

original agreement. If he does not, I will come out of the shadow from the rear of the building with this."

Fedin produced an ugly looking blocky gun from a holster on his ankle. Donny was not familiar with guns, but the hole at the dangerous end looked big enough for Fedin to stick his pinky finger all the way inside, and he had fat fingers.

"One way or another," Fedin assured him. "The barrel will be coming with us. I have no love for pimps. It is a dirty business, and they do nothing but facilitate the spread of disease."

Donny realized that Fedin had mistaken the man with the sideburns for Mr. Creepy. Donny had only seen the pimp a couple of times at the club, once Topher had described the situation to him, coming to see the sideshow had been a nightly pastime for the better part of a month. It was like watching a live soap opera. Mr. Creepy had been a monster when it came to his employees, but had been immaculate in his appearance and exuded a chilling confidence which had been pretty sexy, actually. If Donny had just randomly met him in a bar, he probably would have bought the man a drink.

However, he had never described his the pimp's appearance to Fedin, and he had logically assumed the man driving the truck was who Donny had previously claimed. There was no apparent benefit to Donny from correcting the assumption at this point.

This might even be easier.

"You'll be covering me the whole time, right?" Donny asked, mostly just so he didn't appear too eager to agree. This was a chance to get some cash in his pocket. If the whole thing went sideways, he would at least have some running money.

If Fedin thought he was going to stop at taking just one bundle, though, he was sorely mistaken.

"Of course," Fedin managed to sound a little wounded at the implication.

"Okay," Donny went for it. "You head on first to get in position, I don't want to be left out there with just my dick in my hand and have you still half a block away. I'll get the cash and get there by the time you arrive."

"Agreed," Fedin nodded, and then paused. "Of course, if I see you walking the other way rolling the cooler down the street, I only need to make a call to trigger the conflagration, you understand."

"Of course," Donny mimicked Fedin's earlier wounded tone.

Fedin nodded and re-secured his pistol in his ankle holster. He did not slip so much as roll out the door, pausing only to close it behind him before he headed with relative swiftness up the block toward the overpass for State Route 4.

Donny popped the door open and jumped down with the practiced grace of any person who has repeated the same action over and over again for years. He walked quickly down the passenger side of the truck, keeping the truck between himself and the direct line of sight of the door of the warehouse.

He raised the rear door of the box truck a few feet, just enough to access the cooler and allow a little light to come in from the laundromat behind him, which was blessedly empty at this time. Donny flipped open the lid of the cooler and started pulling the plastic wrapped stacks of hundreds and stuffing them down the waistband of his pants. He was able to line eight stacks total around his body. He considered adding a second row, but opted not to as they would be more likely to lose traction and slip down his pants leg while he walked. Even more so if he had to run. Instead he added an additional stack to each of his pants pockets and one more in each of the inside jacket pockets of his heavy winter coat, unable to use the exterior pocket because of where he had pushed through the stitching with the can of aerosol coolant what felt like years ago, but was in fact just the previous day. It had become such ancient history in his mind that he was surprised to find he still had the pack of cigarettes and the cheap lighter in his other pocket.

Without really thinking, simply allowing his hands to move as they wanted, Donny pulled a cigarette from the pack and lit it.

He took a deep drag, and pushed his exhale out through his teeth, what a high school friend had called a "fog machine," as the teeth caused the exhaled cloud to diffuse into more of a haze. He had, in total, $100,000 secured around his person. He would have liked to run a couple of loops of duct tape around the bundles at his waist, but settled for tightening his belt a notch.

Well, he thought, if he had to run at least he had some start-up cash for when he got to wherever the hell he ended up.

With that comforting thought in mind, Donny closed and secured the door to the box truck. He hated the idea of leaving 2.9 million dollars in a cooler in the back of an unlocked box truck in a shit part of town, and then nearly laughed out loud at the irony.

"Can't be helped," Donny said to no one in particular. If Fedin didn't see him crossing the street pretty soon, he might get nervous and decide to trigger the firebomb, and then all the money would be lost anyway.

Donny started back up the side of the truck, but stopped quickly and turned away from the street as Not came back out in the freshly unloaded tow truck. The truck turned onto the street. going back the way it had come, accelerating without pause, so Donny was pretty sure he had gone unnoticed.

Puffing steadily on his cigarette, Donny strode confidently across the street, walking straight on toward the gaping entrance to the weathered old warehouse, from behind which he hoped Fedin was currently approaching in a far more stealthy manner. Donny figured if could keep the old guy watching his brazen approach, then it would increase Fedin's chances of getting in without detection.

When he was about twenty yards out, Donny stopped. An engine had just rumbled to life inside the building. Donny had just enough time to wonder how the old guy had switched the heavy ass barrel from one truck to another so quickly, when a second engine roared, followed by a third and a fourth. All sounded like big block V8's without a single decent muffler among them.

Donny wondered if he should try to wave the old guy down, buy time for Fedin to get to him, or if he should hide so they could try to follow him. He looked back at the distance to the mattress truck, about sixty or seventy yards for him, but over one hundred yards for Fedin. The old guy with the sideburns would have at least a mile or two head start before they both made it back and started rolling, which meant he would essentially be gone unless they got extremely lucky.

The engines in the hanger revved up and began to move inside the building.

Donny could make it back first, though, and the mattress truck was unlocked. He could dump the cash from the cooler, and probably hotwire the truck before Fedin could make it back.

If Fedin didn't simply trigger the cooler when he saw Donny running for the truck.

If Fedin didn't rig some sort of testicle shredding landmine under the driver's seat for anyone who tried to steal his truck.

Neither option sounded good, but both sounded exactly like something Fedin would do.

The throaty V8's were closer now, close enough for Donny to hear the angry dolphin squeal of power steering which was low on fluid.

Only option left was standing his ground and hoping he could bluff it.

Donny put the cigarette in the corner of his mouth, planted his feet firmly about two feet apart, and stuffed his hands into his jacket pockets, keeping his elbows out. In his mind, he looked like Clint Eastwood awaiting a showdown.

He kind of wished he had the hat.

The significance of the other engines only sank in now that it was far too late to run and hide.

Four engines running meant four vehicles, which would mean there were at least four more people in there, not just the old guy. He and Fedin were outnumbered, not the other way around.

"Shit," exhaled Donny, around the cigarette. "Too late now."

The engines revved louder and Donny saw headlights brighten the entrance, but then four sets of worn out brakes squealed and screeched as all four vehicles came to a stop, but continued to idle.

Donny stood in his badass pose for a few more seconds, figuring they stopped when they saw him, and were trying to decide why he was there. Likely, one of the four would come out to investigate. Donny tried to guess which one it would be.

When he heard doors opening and banging shut, he guessed they were discussing what to do next, and perhaps one or all of them would walk out to talk to him.

He maintained his badass pose, and watched the silhouetted figures move in the headlights. Donny watched and waited, burning his cigarette down to the filter, and feeling his cheeks grow hot and then numb in the cold.

They weren't leaving.

269

"I guess we stick with Plan A," Donny mumbled, and lit another cigarette from the tip of the old one before he flicked it out into the increasing darkness. He heard it sizzle out in the snow as he started forward once more.

He crossed the remaining distant quickly, making no attempt to keep his footsteps quiet in the snow.

Confidence, he knew, was key. If he walked in like his big brass balls made him bulletproof, then they too would assume he was.

"Why the hell did I have to bump my ass all the way here in this piece of shit, Troy?" Donny heard as he was getting closer.

"I know, right?" called another. "Why couldn't I bring the Caddy?"

Donny stepped into the doorway and re-assumed his badass pose.

"Image, mostly," said the old guy with the sideburns. "Think of it as a negotiating tactic."

Five men stood in a small group around the blue barrel, which now sat upright, still strapped to the handcart, in the center of a circle of light created by the headlights of three pickup trucks, a Mustang, and one of those big blocky muscle cars from the late '60s which Donny could never tell apart, maybe a Roadrunner. None of the vehicles looked like they post-dated the Carter administration, and Carter had held up much better.

None of the men looked particularly menacing, despite the fact they were all wearing hunting camouflage and rifles were visible on gun racks in two of the trucks . They were all at least in their later fifties, mostly with receding hairlines and beer and burger guts. They would have looked more at home on a community golf course, or maybe a bowling alley.

One of them, completely bald on top but with a thick ring of hair around the sides and back, shook a small vial and examined it closely. The liquid inside appeared black at first, but when baldy turned to show it to his friends, the vial crossed directly in front of one of the headlights, and Donny could see it was actually a dark brown, like black coffee.

"It's cocaine," the bald man confirmed. "Very pure, too."

"How pure?" Asked one of the other men, but Donny could not tell which one had spoken.

"Can't be exact with this test," the bald man shrugged. "Coloring this dark indicates at least 90% pure or better, but that's the best I can do right now."

"Holy shit," said another of the men.

"What did I say, right?" asked Sideburns. "Way too good to pass up, right?"

"But, holy shit, Troy," one of the men nearly whined to the man with the sideburns. "We can't handle this, this is way too big, I mean. . ."

"We don't even handle coke, man," said the man to the left of Troy. The man was the tallest of the five, but looked like he couldn't weigh more than one hundred and twenty pounds, tops. "I only have to cook up two to three batches a year to keep our stock up, and that's selling to meth heads, man! They are not exactly the picture of restraint, you know? If they could buy more, they would."

"We'll figure it out," Troy nearly growled. "We cannot let this slip by! If we have to sit on it for twenty years and parcel it out a gram at a time, then so be it. It's not like the shit goes bad or whatever, right?"

The last question was directed to the bald man holding the testing vial, who was so surprised he nearly dropped it into the still open barrel.

"Well," he said as he attempted to recover his cool. "All pharmaceuticals will lose potency over time, but if stored properly, not in any way a user would notice. They'd probably just assume it's been cut a little more."

"See?" Troy demanded of the men.

"A bit of a moot point, really," said Donny from the doorway, letting his presence be known since they seemed to be completely oblivious. "Since the barrel is already spoken for."

All five men jumped as if they had been unexpectedly pinched in the nut sack. The bald guy started to turn to run for one of the vehicles idling nearby, but Troy steadied him with a hand to his shoulder. The others took their lead from Troy, and straightened up and tried to look tough.

"Who the hell are you?" Troy asked.

"The rightful owner of that barrel," Donny affirmed. "And, like I said, it is already spoken for."

"The fuck it is, you little. . ."

Troy took a step toward Donny, and the other men straightened as well. They seemed to take their cues from Troy, but were likely also emboldened by the realization that Donny was just one man and they were five. They might be older and out of shape, but five against one can make just about anybody brave.

They were all brought up short -- in both actions and speech -- by the appearance of a stack of cash from Donny's pocket.

"For your time," Donny tossed the stack of bills to Troy's feet. "No hard feelings, right?"

Troy stooped and picked up the cash, read the amount from the band inside, and then turned to show it to his friends.

"So, just so I'm clear," Troy said slowly. "You say this barrel is yours?"

"That's right," Donny nodded.

"And," Troy continued. "You're going to give me. . ."

"Us," said the tall man to his left.

"Us," corrected Troy. "You're going to give us this money as sort of a finder's fee?"

"Sure," Donny shrugged. "Call it what you like."

"And, we'll go on our way, and you take the barrel," Troy finished working it all out. "Is that what I'm hearing?"

"Yep," Donny confirmed. "Or, my friends outside can shoot you, and we'll take the money and the barrel, if you would prefer?"

"No!" the bald man exclaimed, earning a withering look from Troy.

"He ain't got friends outside," Troy chided the bald man.

"But we don't need to find out one way or another, do we?" demanded one of the other fat middle-aged men, who had remained silent until this point. "This is just easier, right?"

"We don't need trouble, Troy," the tall skinny man added.

Troy seemed to consider for a second, and then smiled.

Donny felt his stomach begin to sink and twist, hoping it didn't show on his face. The one with the sideburns, Troy, was going to try to pull something. His voice and face made no secret of it at all. Donny tensed for the shot he was pretty sure was about to come his way.

"Yeah," Troy shrugged. "I guess you guys are right."

Troy dropped the stack of cash into a pocket of his jacket.

"Come one, boys," he called as he turned toward his old truck. "Let's leave the man to his barrel."

Donny watched with a mixed sense of relief and unease as the men in the camouflage hunting gear turned and hurried to their various shitkickermobiles, dropped them into gear one by one, and then proceeded to drive out like they all had different places to be.

Troy even offered a friendly wave as he passed by.

Something was not right.

Donny ran to the barrel and nearly knocked it over. Peering into the small round opening set into the top, still uncapped, he was able to see all the way to the bottom.

It was empty.

Only a small sludge of residue slopped around at the bottom of the barrel.

Just enough, he supposed, to test.

Chapter 32

NOT WATCHED the odometer until it rolled over two miles from where he had dropped Troy, and then pulled down a mostly empty side street. He had intentionally driven away from all the major roads and highways, his most logical route to take, so if Troy decided to head back to the shop, he wouldn't come stumbling across Not.

Once stopped, he was able to root around through the glove box and find the battered adapter plug Josue had mentioned, and then struggled with the clamshell packaging in which the convenience store cell phone had been imprisoned. Not spent a joyless few minutes tearing through unreasonably tough plastic, untwisting tie wires, unsheathing the tightly bound charging cable from its plastic choker, and taking the USB wall adapter out of its small cardboard box.

Not plugged in the phone to charge, and then perused the activation instructions. He flipped through the small instruction booklet, and discovered it could be activated through the phone itself, via the phone's internet browser, if the phone was connected to a Wi-Fi signal.

Not powered up the phone, ignoring the direction to allow the phone to charge for eight hours before turning it on. By-passing all of the startup screen tutorials, he found the screen for the phone's settings, located the Wi-Fi icon, and instructed the phone to search for open networks.

A moment later, his small phone screen was filled with Wi-Fi network names ranging from the factory default name of the router and a number, to cute or clever names like the somewhat dated "Pretty fly for a Wi-Fi," or the philosophical "Wi-Fi Not?" Most of the signals icons also included a small icon for a padlock, indicating Not would need a password to get access. However, he spotted one which had three of the five signal bars filled in and the generous offer to "Take my Wi-Fi, please!" The name along with the fact there was no padlock icon was all the invitation Not needed.

The screen offered a small spinning icon to show it was working, and then proudly announced it had established a connection with the network. Not spent a few tedious minutes entering the activation information into the required fields on the webpage. Aware that he was on an open network, Not did not provide any of his own actual information.

He listed his name as "Nunya Bisneaz," with a random address and email generated by a website created for the specific purpose of providing useable false information on forms.

When he purchased the phone, he had also purchased a prepaid card for minutes and data, which he fished out of his pocket and ripped free from the cardboard and plastic packaging. He added the information provided to the quickly dwindling number of open fields on his activation page, then entered his old cell phone number to see if it was still available after he had cancelled his previous service.

He was happy when the field turned green, indicating the number was still available. Not submitted all of the form information, and a message popped up on the screen indicating all actions had been successful and his phone activation would take place within the next twenty-four hours.

Well . . . shit, Not thought.

He had spent nearly twenty minutes trying to get the damn thing active, and he still couldn't make a call.

Not put the truck in gear, intending to go and find a phone he could use to call Karkus, when the phone pinged and indicated he had a new text message. Not dropped the stick back into neutral, and retrieved the phone from the seat beside him. The text message stated his phone was now active, and gave a status of how many texts he could send and receive, minutes he could speak, and gigs of data he could use before the purchase of another card would be required.

Not pulled out Karkus' business card from his wallet and keyed in the number.

"Steven Karkus," he answered on the third ring.

"Hey, it's Not Johnson," he said, trying to avoid the oft heard joke of "it's not what?"

"Hang on," Karkus responded immediately, and then Not could only hear some shuffling and other noises of something moving near the microphone. "Okay, I have you in my contacts at this number."

"Thanks," Not said, unsure of what else to say. "Listen, I need to give you some information. Can we talk about it over the phone, or should we speak face to face?"

"Is it time sensitive?" Karkus asked.

Not considered the question.

"Yeah," he decided. "I think it is."

"Then you better tell me now," Karkus said. "Listen, I'm in my office and I am alone, so I'm going to put you on speaker. I need to have my hands free to take notes, okay?"

"Yeah, sure," Not agreed.

Not heard the thump of the phone hitting the desk, and then the sound of a drawer opening and closing as Karkus retrieved paper or pen or whatever else he needed to get his notes.

"Okay, go," Karkus called, his voice more distant now.

Not gave a complete recounting of everything he had been told by Topher while they were in the holding cell together, and then everything which had happened since his return to work this evening, right up to the point where he was now sitting in a tow truck on a side street, and wondering what he should do next. Not was pretty sure he heard Karkus slap his own forehead in frustration a couple of times, but to his credit he had not interrupted.

"How long ago did you drop off the truck?" Karkus asked.

Not glanced at the clock on his new phone, "I think about thirty minutes now."

"Why did you wait so long to call me?" Karkus seethed.

"I had to set up my phone," Not felt like an idiot.

"Okay," Karkus said and then said nothing for a few moments. "Okay, do you have an invoice, or GPS data, or anything else which might implicate you in the removal of the truck with the barrel in it?"

"No," Not explained. "Troy also works for Alto, so it was just a favor. He bought the truck from the actual owner today. He. . ."

Not fell silent as a thought occurred he had not considered before.

"He may not even have known the barrel was there!" Not almost shouted. "He just likes old trucks, you know? Maybe he. . ."

"He knows, Not," Karkus interrupted. "From what you told me, the police and the feds have been at your shop all day. *Everyone* at your work knows about the cocaine and the blue barrel. He's probably the one who took it from your friend Topher, saw him from the shop when he was moving the barrel, or something. Then hid it back in the same truck and moved it far enough away so it couldn't be included in the DEA's warrant to search the shop."

"No, Troy doesn't work nights," Not corrected. "Last night it was . . .shit."

"Who?" Karkus asked.

"It was Josue or Alto," Not admitted. "It had to have been one of them. I dropped the old truck on the street, and then picked them up. They dropped me at home, but said they were on their way to the shop."

One day.

One goddamn day of work after nearly a year, and his short respite from unemployment was over. Even if he was able to get out from under the DEA, he couldn't go on working at Alto's after this.

A person was either dirty or clean, Not figured. If they were willing to get dirty once, then they would again, and they could not or would not help but to sling the filth on all of those around them.

"Josue just sent you to drop off the truck," Karkus stated, letting the implication hang there.

Karkus was right.

Not had already been dragged into the mud pit. He needed to find the edge and get himself out before he was sucked under entirely.

"What do I do?" Not asked, surrendering to the inevitable. "Quit?"

Rather than the immediate affirmation Not had been expecting, Karkus paused in silence which dragged on for nearly a minute.

"I am at a bit of an ethical fork in the road, I'm afraid," Karkus spoke up finally. "I should advise you, given the information you have now provided me, that your chances of getting out of this without some jail time are slim to none."

"But, I. . ."

"Didn't do anything wrong," Karkus finished for him. "I know you've *said* that, but the fact is you have. You transported stolen goods, stolen narcotics no less, and aided and abetted in the committing of multiple felonies. You *state* you had no knowledge of this, but your history with those involved and the fact that you continue in aiding and abetting, will not be overlooked. Even if everyone else involved swears up and down you didn't know what you were doing, you will still likely be arrested and charged."

Not had no idea when he had started crying, and he only realized he had started doing so when the first sob escaped from his chest. He set the phone down on the seat beside him, among packaging cast-offs which had so recently held the phone, and wiped at both eyes with his hands.

It wasn't fair.

If felt childish and pathetic to be sitting here and crying because the other kids hadn't played fair, but it was sure enough what he was doing. He had played by the rules. He had worked hard, he had been a good person, so why was this all happening to him? Again. And by the same person, no less?

It just wasn't fair.

Not picked up the phone once more, his eyes still welling up some tears, but the hitching sobs back under control.

"So, what do I do," Not asked again.

"With the current evidence against you, your options are limited," Karkus flatly stated. "First, you could try to run. I don't advise it, but I bring it up just in case you've been thinking of it. Running will only work against you, and you don't have enough money to be able to run very far or very long. It's a bad option, so don't try it."

"Hadn't even crossed my mind," Not lied.

"Second option," Karkus continued. "Has an A, B, and C to it. Option two-A is you immediately turn yourself in and give all the information you have to help try to catch those you know to be involved. It is not a very good option, as it only implicates you further and merely provides hearsay against the others."

"Okay, next?" Not asked.

"Option two-B, I contact the DEA with the information you have provided me, and try to negotiate a plea deal on your behalf. Again, not a great option because it only provides allowable evidence against you."

"Fuck, man," Not groaned. "If they're shitty options, then why are you telling them to me?"

"I want you to have all the information, so you can make your best informed decision, okay?" Karkus reasoned. "Option two-C, I will anonymously tip just the most recent location of the barrel to the police, and leave out all the rest. There is a slim chance, if the barrel is recovered in full, the District Attorney will just go for the easy win and simply charge those in possession of it."

"Really?" Not was not convinced.

"Well, like I said," Karkus cautioned. "It is a slim chance. Remember, the cocaine was legally produced and transported by a New Jersey company. If they bring the theft and all the rest to trial, then they have to go into where it came from. If they simply go for possession, it will be a slam dunk case which keeps the source out of the papers."

"I'm not sure. . ."

"Option three," Karkus powered forward, "means getting more evidence. Preferably, getting any of those involved in an audio or, better yet, video recording saying anything which points to their guilt and your innocence."

"So, you think I should. . ."

"I cannot ethically advise you to take any such course of action," Karkus powered over him once more. "I am simply outlining the options which help you. If such evidence were to come to light, then we would be able to secure their arrests without also implicating you."

"But how would I. . ."

"Most phones have audio and video recording capabilities," Karkus reminded him. "You should get familiar with your new phone."

Not reached for the small owner's manual sitting in the midst of the rest of the phone trash on the seat.

"Option four," Karkus continued. "The last option I can think of right now is to do nothing and hope they get away with it."

"What?"

"The only case against you right now is you helped two armored car guards to offload their cargo to a non-sanctioned transport vehicle." Karkus reasoned. "They both gave statements that all of your actions were done at their request, which was done at the request of their superiors. Somewhere between here and Hobart, one of the barrels was taken. *We* know who took it, and where it went, but *they* don't. If we do nothing, and they get rid of the remaining evidence. Well . . ."

Not could almost see the shrug Karkus was making on the other end of the phone.

They might get away with it.

The idea was both relieving and nauseating to Not. On one hand, he was fairly certain if anyone could come out of a steaming load of shit smelling like lilacs, it was probably Donny. On the other hand, it would mean the little motherfucker was going to get away with it again, and this time Not would have to choose whether to knowingly allow him to do so.

Sadly, it seemed like the best choice.

"If it helps you decide," Karkus said. "The likelihood of the barrel still being where you dropped it off is extremely small. The location you described practically screams drug deal. By now, they would have already made the deal and the barrel would be out of your life forever."

Before Not could respond, the radio erupted from below the dashboard.

"This is Alto Shop. Not, do you copy? Say again, this is Alto shop calling the big rig. If you hear me, copy back. This is Alto--"

"This is Not," he cut in. "What's up? Over."

"Let me know what you decide," Karkus said, and then ended the call.

Not pushed end call on his phone and set it on the seat beside him.

"Hey Not, it's Bob," the voice from the radio came again. "I was on my way out when the phone rang. Box truck broke down, State Route 4 near the Grand Avenue ramp."

"Loaded?" Not asked.

"Yeah," Bob confirmed. "Mattress truck packed top to bottom."

"Just mattresses?" Not returned. "A standard should be able to handle it."

"They asked for a flatbed, and tonight you're it."

Not thought again about the barrel, and Karkus' appraisal of the whole situation. By now, the coke was probably out of his life forever.

"I'm on it," Not confirmed. "Over and out."

He the big truck rolling and carefully negotiated the tight conditions of the narrow back streets, until he was able to get back out to a major thoroughfare.

Could he live with himself if he did nothing? Could he come back to work knowing his supervisor, or his boss, or both, conspired with one of his co-workers to sell a barrel full of cocaine?

Sadly, the answer seemed to be yes.

More to the point, he couldn't quit. He couldn't face his father and tell him he quit the only job he'd been able to land in nearly a year. He couldn't face another year of searching.

Not listened to the comforting rumble of the big diesel engine, and adjusted the slide for the temperature inside the cab. For the first time in a long time he had felt useful again. He had felt proud of the work he had done, and had felt appreciated rather than pitied.

It would be just as hard to stay.

To have to look at Josue, at Troy, at Alto and know what they had done, but be powerless to do or say anything about it. On top of everything, everyone else there now thinks he is some sort of master criminal now. Would he ever be invited to a poker game or backyard barbeque? It did not seem likely.

Most folks didn't invite known criminals into their lives.

Then again, this *was* New Jersey.

NOT STEERED the large truck up the on ramp and he immediately spotted the road flares. The sun had finished setting a short while ago, and the road was bathed in the sick orange-pink light of the big sodium-vapor street lamps. The road flares stood out like bright red pimples on the face of a giant. A large white box truck sat hulking on the shoulder. Not pulled the big truck past, turning on the rotating yellow hazard lights on it's roof, and then backing up the shoulder to position the bed in front of the breakdown.

In the rearview mirror, he could see two men were in the cab, but they didn't have any interior lights on, maybe it was a battery problem, so they were mere silhouettes behind the glass.

Not pulled on his gloves, and stepped down from the truck. He pulled his clipboard, with a fresh invoice ready to go, from beneath his seat, and the large four-cell flashlight clipped on the door for easy access.

As he approached, both of the doors on the cab of the box truck opened at once. The passenger slipped out and went down the side toward the back of the truck, maybe to check on the flares, and the driver, a fairly round man, approached Not.

"Good evening!" The fat man called. "The engine just cut out on me as soon as I got on to the road."

"We should check the battery," Not called. "Would you mind popping the hood?"

When the man got closer, Not noticed the gun in his hand.

Chapter 33

"YOU DID very well, Donny," Fedin's voice called from the darkness, and Donny could hear his footsteps echoing through the now very empty space, now that the collection of rolling rust had moved along to fall apart somewhere else.

"Not really," Donny fumed.

Fedin's ample shape came into focus as he drew closer to the large open bay door. The street lights were distant, but the unobstructed space of the vacant public works lot allowed some of the light to come in.

"It's empty," Donny stated flatly, and then rocked the barrel back and forth once for emphasis. Fedin's smile fell from his face, and was replaced with stoic complacency, as if he had really expected no better.

"Your pimp is more clever than I gave him credit," Fedin said with just a touch of admiration. "Though I must admit, I was expecting someone appearing a bit different."

"He wasn't Mr. Creepy," Donny came clean. "And, Topher wasn't any of the guys over here, so I don't think he set this up."

"Damn," Fedin said, but without enthusiasm. "They have probably split it up into several smaller containers, one for each of those trucks, and are now heading off in five different directions. We could try to catch at least one of them, I suppose."

Fedin completed the last sentence with a shrug, both palms held out flat in an "if you want to try, I guess we could" sort of gesture, though his eyes held the truth of how pointless he thought it to be.

"No," Donny shook his head. "They brought it in like this. They were testing it when I walked in. I think this was a kind of, like a, well, like an investor's meeting. Troy, the guy

283

with the sideburns, was trying to get the other guys to pitch in to buy the stuff."

"And the barrel was what?" Fedin asked. "Brought for authenticity?"

"Something like that," Donny agreed. "Part of the sales pitch, I guess. To show them just how much there was, and, yeah, I suppose to show the, what do you call it, you know, where it came from?"

"Provenance, I think is the word you're looking for," Fedin said quietly, in a tone which suggested pondering. "So, you believe the men in the trucks will be going to purchase the cocaine now?"

"Yeah, maybe," Donny shrugged. "They didn't seem to be a hundred percent on board with this. I got the idea Troy was the point man, and he called in his buddies because he didn't have the cash to do the deal himself. Did you see the plates?"

"Too dark," said Fedin.

"They were all from Pennsylvania," Donny explained. "Except for Troy, his plates were Jersey. They were complaining too, about having to drive all this way in these shitty old trucks, which apparently Troy asked them to do. Said it was for image, a negotiating tactic."

"They are trying to lowball the price," Fedin said knowingly. "I have played the ignorant immigrant myself many times to try to get a better position on my opponent, you understand. Stereotypes can often be useful."

"So, they're playing the hayseed card to try to get a discount," Donny mused. "First time I've heard of that one."

"If the seller is motivated, any plausible excuse to lower the price will work," Fedin said knowingly. "It just depends on what you think they will believe."

Donny considered the situation and his options. If he were to walk away right now, he still had ninety thousand in cash, but would be wanted for god knows how many charges. He didn't know what the statute of limitations was on robbing an armored car, or for narcotics trafficking, but he knew the statute of limitations for auto theft in New Jersey was at least five years, so he had to imagine this would be significantly longer.

He didn't even know if there was a statute of limitations for federal crimes.

So, his best case scenario was that he would have to be running for at least five years, and worst case he would be a wanted man for the rest of his life.

Ninety grand wouldn't last a lifetime.

It would still be in his best interests, Donny decided, if Fedin got what he wanted and got Sokolov to clean up the mess. If things didn't work out, he could still bail with the cash and he would be no worse off.

Unless, of course, he got arrested.

Or shot.

But . . . three million dollars . . .

"We need the invoice," Donny said. "Troy had the truck towed here, so his name and contact information will be on the invoice in the cab of the tow."

"Surely, it will be false --"

"He needs to provide a valid photo ID," Donny shook his head. "Unless he has a really good fake handy at all times, he hasn't had time to get one made."

And, Not is too much of a Boy Scout to break the rules, Donny finished in his head.

"Ah, I see," Fedin smiled. "If we can find Troy, we can get the cocaine even if they have already made the purchase. Even if it is on it's way back to Pennsylvania . . ."

"He can take us to it," Donny finished.

"I must say, Donny," Fedin said with what sounded like genuine affection. "You are far more resourceful than I initially gave you credit. So, how do we find the tow truck?"

"That," Donny smiled. "Is actually the easy part."

THE TWO men moved with as much haste as Fedin could manage back to the box truck. As Fedin could not manage a pace much faster than a slightly fast walk, Donny took the time to enjoy another cigarette, even offered one to Fedin which earned him a disappointed look.

"What?" Donny asked, ready to refute any anti-smoking argument Fedin could lob at him.

"How I was raised, you understand," Fedin explained through puffs of cold-clouded breaths, "not even the women smoked filters."

For some reason, Donny actually felt embarrassed. He was so unaccustomed to the emotion that he nearly dropped the half-smoked butt to fizzle out in the snow. However, before he could do so, his pride took back over and he flauntingly took another drag.

Fuck the Russian, and fuck his attempt to impugn Donny's masculinity.

Donny smoked the cigarette to the filter, and then lit another simply out of spite.

"When we get to the truck," Fedin said, digging the keys from his pocket. "We need to return to fetch the barrel."

"Why?"

"Well, for one, Donny," Fedin explained as if to a child. "It is evidence in a crime, and I am certain we left shoe prints, and other physical evidence which could help to build a case against us if the barrel is found any time soon."

"True," said Donny, not allowing his tone of voice to betray his annoyance at being condescended to. "Why not just torch the truck then? Shove the barrel in the back, and destroy the all evidence?"

"It will only guarantee the truck is found sooner rather than later, and there are certain to be traces of the plastic from the barrel still in the truck, even if it does burn completely," Fedin said, continuing to speak as if Donny were suddenly feeble minded. "Secondly, as I said, it is a piece of evidence for a crime. It would be much better if it *were* found, but found where and when we would like it to be found, you understand, and in the possession of those with whom we would like it to be associated. Even in its current state, it has value."

Donny said nothing, but simply nodded in agreement as they reached the truck. He was both impressed and cautioned by Fedin's ability to think through the long game. It was a great asset to have, provided Fedin and Donny remained on the same team. Donny was wary of what might happen to him if Fedin decided he no longer needed Donny in the game.

They quickly retrieved the barrel from the warehouse, Donny was able to lift its hollow weight into the back of the truck without assistance, and as soon as he rejoined Fedin in the warmth of the truck cab, he began to give directions.

"Get us to the closest highway, pull to the side, and kill the engine," Donny directed.

They drove back out to Kinderkamack and passed beneath the closest highway, State Route 4, on their way to find an on-ramp. Fedin kept the highway in sight as he followed along on surface streets until he reached the Grand Avenue entrance.

Without even attempting to merge, Fedin powered straight to the shoulder and killed the engine, and then looked expectantly to Donny.

"Pop the hood," Donny said, and then climbed out of the truck.

He had fished a few road flares from the breakdown box under the passenger seat. He was surprised to find any Fedin had not somehow managed to cobble together into some form of booby-trap.

After setting them to burn at a safe distance from their back bumper, Donny trotted quickly to the front of the truck and raised the hood. He located the fuse box in the sickly melon-tinted light of the sodium vapor lamps the lined the highway, and started pulling all the fuses. He wiggled each one free from the pressure clamps at the bottom of the fuse box which held each one in place, but then left them in place, loosely, so they could easily be pushed back in if they needed to start rolling under their own power again.

After re-securing the lid to the fuse box, Donny rejoined Fedin in the cab of the truck, which was still warm, but would cool quickly.

"Try the engine," Donny suggested.

Fedin did and the key turned with a dull click.

"In case anyone comes along before our tow gets here," Donny explained. "They can try to jump start us, but it won't do any good."

"What did you do?" Fedin asked.

"Don't worry," Donny affected a tone as if comforting a frightened child. "I can fix it easily."

"Ah, the fuses," Fedin nodded. "Good idea. Not obvious at a glance, but quick to reset."

Donny said nothing, and had to try very hard not to pout.

"What now?" Fedin asked.

"Now," Donny smiled, happy to once more have the conversational advantage. "We call for a tow."

He was not prone to regret, but Donny did take a moment to think through how much easier this whole thing would have been if it had just been gold scraps in the truck.

Sure, he would still have been brought in for questioning, but most of these headaches would never have occurred. He had a hard time believing a Russo-American gangster and his pet federal agent would have kidnapped him for a bunch of gold scrap. He doubted there would be a bunch of competing interests for a bunch of gold scrap.

He wondered, why not? It was maybe not quite as valuable, but it would have still been worth a shitload of money. Even the cops and the feds took this one so much more seriously. Joe had been ripped off before. He had told Donny all about it one time over lunch. He had not shut the door at the back of the truck completely. It had closed, but not latched. Some guy had seen an opportunity, and grabbed one of the deposit bags and ran.

The whole thing was caught on camera, both from the interior of the truck, and from the security cameras of the grocery store in front of which Joe and his driver at the time had been stopped, picking up the deposits for the day. The video came out great, Joe said. The back of the truck was almost center screen, and it showed Joe getting out of the truck, closing -- well, almost closing -- the door, and then heading into the store.

A few seconds later, along comes some guy, blue jeans and t-shirt, wearing sunglasses but just because he happened to have them on, not in any real attempt to disguise himself. According to Joe, you could see him do a double take at the door, and then cautiously approach and try the handle.

When it swung open, he jumped back a step, then grabbed the first bag he saw and started running. The door stood open for another minute, completely unguarded, except for the apparently useless driver, but no one else came by.

Joe came back into the shot, and was seen immediately securing the door and getting on the radio.

The guy got away with just over seventy thousand in mixed bills, and they never caught him.

Joe of course was questioned by the police, he had left the door open after all, but had been let go after just a couple of hours of questioning.

Why couldn't have this just gone like that had?

Fedin had concluded his phone call and they sat in silence until they heard the slow approach of a large rumbling diesel.

"Here we go," Donny said.

Fedin simply nodded his agreement.

"When he pulls up," Donny continued, "you talk to the driver, the invoice book will be in the truck. I'll hide around the side of the truck, and then sneak into the cab while you keep him busy, okay?"

The big truck in front backed up to a stop, the yellow lights pulsing across the highway to caution other drivers to give them some space. Donny slipped out the passenger side door, and heard Fedin open the driver's side door, but did not turn to watch his progress but rather focused on his own.

The section of the highway they were on was at ground level for the entrance ramp, and a small shoulder dropped down from the pavement. It was not steep enough to conceal him completely, but there was a bank of filthy plowed snow which lined the demarcation between the concrete and the soil. If he crouched and scooted by quickly, he would probably be able to get by unnoticed if Fedin was able to keep Not distracted while he passed.

Donny carefully found his footing over the packed and ice-crusted snowbank and down the other side to the shoulder.

He discovered he could likely get by unseen, but not unheard. Each step in the packed icy snow produced a muffled creaking crunch, like tearing into thick Styrofoam, which could easily be heard between the bursts of traffic roaring past.

He waited until he heard cars approaching, and then jogged forward a few crunching feet, pausing when he heard their engines begin to fade away to wait for the next round of cars.

The space between the bursts of traffic dragged out, and Donny could hear Fedin and Not speaking, but was too far to discern the individual words.

Another few cars roared by, and Donny was able to progress by a few awkward leaps, but was still short of the passenger door by a long arm-length.

He could hear more cars approaching, and prepared to take the final short leap to the door handle. Just before the cars reached them, Donny heard Fedin's voice, much closer than before, call his name from just the other side of the snow bank.

The noise of the traffic made everything after his name unintelligible, so he held fast where he was, still hidden by the large pile of frozen filth and snow sloughed from the lanes.

Fedin, his tone slightly exasperated, tried again.

"You may come on out, Donny," he called. "Our friend, has told me there is no invoice for Troy's earlier service."

Chapter 34

"DO YOU have an invoice in the cab of your truck for a man named Troy?"

Not was so sure this was a robbery, the words "driver's don't carry cash" still almost spilled out of his mouth. He had heard of being held up for cash, for the car you were towing, and for the truck itself, but never for an invoice. However, after his thoughts had a chance to catch up to the shift of the nature of this hold up, he understood.

The blue barrel.

His life had come to revolve around that goddamn blue barrel.

"I don't have an invoice for Troy," Not said grudgingly.

"Is it not standard practice to invoice every job?" Asked the gunman.

"Well, yeah," Not admitted. "But this was sort of a favor. Employee benefit, you might say."

"He works with you? Troy?" the gunman clarified.

"Yeah, he drives the day shift."

"I see," the gunman seemed to mull over the taste of this new morsel of information. After a moment of reflection, he seemed to accept it was not shit and swallowed it.

The next question nearly knocked the wind out of Not.

"Tell me what you know about our friend Donovan."

Of course.

Blue Barrel.

Donny.

Maybe the fat man was a cop and would go for the hat trick and just take Not right back to jail.

Maybe the fat man would just shoot him.

Not found he wasn't totally against the idea.

"Is he here?" Not asked.

"Skulking around somewhere nearby, yes," the man answered.

Not wondered if it were true, or if this were maybe some elaborate ploy by the police to get him to incriminate himself. He had thought the same thing about Topher while they were locked up together in the drunk tank, but that had proved to just be run-of-the-mill paranoia, justifiable as it might have been.

Fuck it.

"He is an asshole and a liar who, for some reason, seems to keeps trying to set me up," Not had answered eventually. "If he has the chance, he will set you up too. Just for the fun of it."

Not expected to hear some bravado next, no one like Donny would be able to get one past someone like me, that sort of thing. Instead, the heavy set older man just nodded thoughtfully for a moment, turning his head slightly as if listening to distant music and trying to place the song.

"If you will excuse the rudeness of asking," the heavy man said. "You appear to have been crying?"

"Yeah," Not surprised himself by laughing. He surprised himself again by blurting out the truth. "Yeah, I was crying. I just got off the phone with my lawyer because Donny got me arrested, again, for some shit I somehow managed to help with even though I didn't know I was, and now I seem to be truly and royally fucked. Again."

"He has done this before?"

"Oh yeah. We used to work together at a different shop," Not said, giving the Cliff's Notes version. "He had me stealing cars, telling me they were repos. I got busted, but not Donny. The shop closed, and everyone got fucked, but not Donny. I've been out of work about a year -- until I got this job, just started yesterday, actually -- and as soon as I'm getting my life back on track . . . Bam! *Here comes fucking Donny* with an armored car full of cocaine to screw me over again."

Not paused, stunned to hear himself dump his whole purse out for this stranger. A stranger with a gun no less. This must be how it feels, he decided, to just not give a shit.

It was actually kind of liberating.

He counted himself lucky, actually. If he had broken down earlier, say in front of the Feds, then he would probably be looking at twenty years to life, or some such shit. As it now stood, a quick bullet on the side of the highway seemed almost merciful.

He found himself wondering when the man was going to shoot him, and nearly willing it to happen. Maybe, the thought occurred to Not, a small silver lining, he'd shoot Donny too.

"Wow," he said, mainly to stop his train of thought from rolling any further. "It sounds pretty ape shit crazy when I say it out loud."

"Yes," the man with the gun agreed. "It certainly does. However, after having spent some time with our mutual friend, I am inclined to believe you. Let's go get him, shall we?"

The man waved the gun toward the shoulder of the road, and Not led the way, followed closely by his captor.

"You may come on out, Donny," he called. "Our friend, Not, has told me there is no invoice for Troy's earlier service."

Not stared at the dirty snowbank, crusted with black and brown, small pockets of white peeking out from the noxious shell, it always reminded him of a marshmallow which had fallen in the fire.

The man with the gun repeated his invitation, but with a little more edge to his voice.

After a pause long enough for him to wonder if the man holding a gun on him was actually delusional, a voice unmistakably Donny called out from the other side.

"Bullshit! He's lying. There is always an invoice."

Snow crunched from the far side of the bank, and Not could see a pair of hands frantically clawing at the top.

"Not if it is done as a favor," the gunman called back. "From one employee to another."

"Troy *works* there?"

Donny's head poked up from the other side of the snowbank, but he paused when he spotted the gun in the other man's hand. Not could almost hear the gears turning in his head as he calculated his best outcomes for various possible next moves.

The gunman seemed to register this as well.

"Just a precaution, you understand," the gunman assured Donny. "Our friend here thinks I should perhaps not trust you so easily."

"Don't listen to this fucking liar. . ."

"I'm the liar?!" Not turned to launch himself at Donny. His hands pulled tight into fists, ready to deliver the full and bloody beating the comment merited, and which Donny so richly deserved.

He was brought up short when the gun first swung his way, and then toward Donny, who also decided to clam up.

"Gentlemen," the gunman's voice was on the verge of laughter. "We are all liars at one point or another. What matters at the moment is the location of Mr. Troy . . . I'm sorry, but I don't even know his last name."

"Josue told me yesterday," Not admitted. "But I forget. I just know not to call him Helen."

"That," the gunman said with a short, snorting laugh. "Sounds like there is an interesting story there."

He waved the gun to indicate the box truck, the tow truck, and the passing traffic.

"Perhaps you can tell me all about it after you secure my truck on the back of yours."

Donny climbed the rest of the way over the snowbank, and they all walked back to the two trucks. At first, Donny watched, near but not with the man with the gun, as Not tilted back the bed of the truck and began to play out the chain from the hoist to haul it into position.

"Donovan," the gunman called, "Please give him a hand. I would very much like to be out of the cold as soon as possible, you understand."

The use of his full name was apparently not lost on Donny, as he stepped up to help, uncharacteristically, without a single complaint or sharp remark. Together, they had the box truck secured on the back of the tow in what felt to Not like record time.

The three of them, Not and Donny leading and the man with the gun following a step or two behind, moved quickly toward the promised warmth of the cab of the truck. They paused just below the passenger door.

"I believe our driver will need to go up first," the gunman said, and nodded toward Not. "You understand, of course, if I hear you trying to use the radio or get out on the other side, I will have no other recourse but to shoot you, have Donovan stow your corpse into the back of the truck you have just so skillfully loaded, and then make Donovan my new driver?"

"Yeah, sure," Not hastily agreed. "No funny business."

"Very good!" the gunman appeared pleased.

Not stepped up and opened the passenger door, and slid himself across to the driver's seat, swiping all of the plastic detritus to the floor as he went. He placed both hands on the steering wheel, keeping them easily in sight, and then waited. The flushed and fleshy face of the man with the gun popped suddenly into view, and he struggled and rocked his generous frame into the seat. Standing, the man was obviously large, but seated he was almost comically rotund.

"Donny, my friend," he called down. "I am afraid you will not be able to fit in the cab with us. I am not a small man, you understand. Here are the keys to the box truck, you can ride in there and run the engine for heat."

"Bad idea," Donny called up. "Cars cannot be running on a flatbed, and passengers are not allowed to ride in the vehicle once the driver connects it to the rig. Either one will get noticed and get us stopped."

"Ah, I see," the gunman ruminated for a moment. "Then, unfortunately, you will have to ride in the box."

Donny said something below which Not was unable to hear clearly, but the tone of voice and the gunman's response were enough for Not to assume Donny was not thrilled at the prospect of riding in the unheated box of a disabled truck.

"I do sympathize," the gunman offered. "But it would look strange if we were to arrive without our friend Not visibly behind the wheel. It might put Troy, or his partners, on alert. Our best strategy right now is one of surprise, you understand."

There was a short pause in which Not assumed Donny was again speaking, but so quietly this time Not was unable to hear anything but the passing traffic.

"Of course. I will ask," the gunman said with a touch of sympathy. "The flashlight you carried when you first approached me, may I borrow it?"

Not had hoped the gunman had forgotten about the flashlight and had tucked it next to him in the hope he could use it as a club to knock the gun from the man's hand at some point.

"Sure," Not agreed easily enough, and handed over the large and heavy metal tube.

"There you are," the gunman took the flashlight from Not and passed it over to Donny in one fluid motion. After handing the long-barrel flashlight down, the large man slammed the door shut and then watched Donny's progress to the rear of the truck in the side-view mirror.

"How do you --" Not began to ask, but was silenced by the gunman holding up a hand for quiet.

"Do you have a lock or other manner of securing the rolling door of my truck?" the man asked without taking his eyes from the mirror.

"The latch should hold fine if he shuts the door hard," Not offered.

"Answer the question, please," the gunman said, his words were civil but not kind.

"Um," Not did a quick inventory of what he knew to be in the various compartments of the truck. "I think I have some cable-ties and some carabiners to connect the hoist chains."

"The latter, I think," the gunman said, sounding pleased. "In a moment, we will both climb down and walk to the back of the truck. Do not close the door and try to make as little noise as possible. Along the way, retrieve a carabiner as quietly as you can, and then proceed to the rear of the truck. If you try to run, I will shoot you."

"What if Donny isn't in the back?"

"Then I will shoot him instead," the gunman shrugged. "If you have no other questions, then let us get moving, please."

Not opened the door and climbed down being careful not to slam the door shut, as he was in the habit of doing. He walked down the traffic side of the truck, while the gunman paced him on the opposite. When Not paused at one of the chain bins to retrieve a carabiner, the gunman paused as well, though he seemed to keep his eyes focused on the rear of the truck the entire time. Not guessed the man with the gun trusted Donny about as much as Not did himself.

Not held the carabiner up to show the gunman, and the large man nodded and signaled for Not to proceed to the back of the truck.

The rolling door to the box truck was open about an inch, and the light from the flashlight could be seen a few feet from the door. Not assumed Donny was holding the flashlight, but then the beam rolled to the side a bit when it was kicked, Not assumed accidentally, with the side of Donny's foot.

"God-fucking-damn it," Donny cursed angrily from inside.

The gunman raised a warning finger to his lips, and then motioned for Not to open the rolling door. Not climbed up on the back of the tow while the man with the gun remained on the ground. He moved to the center of the door, where he would be able to most easily roll it open, and the fat gunman moved a few steps back to have a full range of sight with his pistol.

Not was so worried about being caught in the crossfire when he threw the door up, he leapt laterally and almost inadvertently fell off the side of the tow and in front of a passing delivery van. The van passed by close enough for the wind to whip at Not's jacket, and to startle the driver badly enough for him or her to feel justified in leaning on the horn for at least ten seconds.

As Not stepped away from the possibility of death by vehicle collision, he realized he had instead stepped closer to death by gunshot.

"Stop!" The fat man with the gun commanded, raising the pistol towards Donny.

Not took another two steps away from the road, briefly between the barrel of the gun, and the intended target, Donny, and prayed he didn't inadvertently save the asshole's life by taking a bullet for him.

Donny had dumped out the contents of a large picnic cooler, and had apparently been scraping at the bottom of the cooler with the truck keys the gunman had tossed to him. Not could see there was something dark on the bottom of the cooler which seemed to be the object of Donny's efforts, but Not lost interest in what Donny was doing when he realized the large pile of shallow plastic bricks next to Donny was actually comprised of shrink wrapped bundles of money.

"Stop!" the gunman repeated, but this time added. "You'll set it off!"

Not brought his focus back to the cooler quickly. The only time he had ever heard anyone say anything remotely close to that was in the movies when dealing with a bomb. The words seemed to have the same effect on Donny, as he dropped the keys and quickly backed away. Now he had a clear view and Not could see an old cell phone had been somehow glued and molded into the bottom of the cooler.

"Holy shit," Not muttered. It *was* a bomb. He had loaded a truck with a bomb onto the back of his tow, and now Donny was fucking with it and was going to set it off.

There seemed to be no limit to how much worse the situation could get when it involved Donny. You think you've hit rock bottom, but then the evil motherfucker just starts *digging*.

Not was surprised to find he was still able to be surprised by the man.

"Give me the keys, Donovan," the gun moved up to be vaguely threatening.

Donny clenched the keys tightly for a moment, then, in what was a perfectly Donny act of spite, he tossed the keys to Not instead. The gunman simply nodded.

"It seems," the gunman called up to Donny, "Not was right to warn me."

"I just. . ."

"Until I get what I am paying for, then the money is not yet yours, Donovan,"

"I don't want to be locked in with a firebomb is all," Donny whined.

"Here," the gunman reached into his jacket pocket and pulled out a phone. It was a flip-phone, the bottom of the line from the same pay-as-you-go company from which Not had also purchased his phone.

"There is only one contact saved," the gunman stated. "You would do well not to call or text it."

"Why?"

"Donovan," the gunman said as if to a child. "If you have the phone, then you know you will be safe, you understand?"

"Yeah, I guess, but. . ."

"No, Donovan," the gunman cut him off once more. "We do not have time, and I am too cold to argue."

The gunman looked at Not and waved to the door. Not climbed up onto the bumper of the box truck, so he could reach the pull strap to close and secure the rolling door. Donny stared coldly at him but made no move to try to interfere.

"Sorry, Donny," Not said.

"No, you're not," Donny snapped.

Not smiled, and pulled the door downward.

"Not in the least."

Not slammed the door down hard enough for the latch to engage, and then secured it in place with the carabiner. Still aware the gun was pointed vaguely in his direction, Not climbed down on the side away from traffic and then took the lead as they proceeded back to the cab of the truck.

"Now," the gunman said, when they were once more secure in their seats. "I would like to continue our previous conversation, as we drive to your shop. First, may we have a proper introduction? My name is Gregori Fedin."

"Harris Johnson," said Not, offering his hand. "But, everybody calls me. . ."

"Not," finished Fedin. "Yes, I gathered as much. While we drive, allow me to share with you the information I have at my disposal, in regards to this current situation in which we find ourselves, and I will ask you to also be as forthcoming, and of course please do feel free to correct any information which our friend Donovan may have gotten wrong."

"Listen, whatever Donny told you about me, I really am not involved in any of this," Not protested.

"I believe you," Fedin assured him. "But, I do think perhaps we could help each other."

"How?" Not asked, though he knew it was likely a bad idea.

"Listen first," Fedin cautioned. "Tell me what you can. If nothing else, I can offer you a man who has escaped from Federal custody, along with an empty barrel which has recently held large quantities of cocaine. They are both currently locked in the box truck behind us. Without the cocaine, neither is of any use to me, but perhaps may come in handy for you."

Not said nothing, but could not help but hope there was a bit of light beginning to shine at the end of this particular tunnel.

Taking Not's silence for consent, Fedin began to speak. Not listened.

Chapter 35

DONNY SAT in the cone of light provided by the flashlight, and blew smoke into the darkness which surrounded him.

The cargo area of the box truck was not insulated and without the engine running was not in any way heated, but wrapped in his winter jacket -- without the wind chill to whip the body heat away from him -- the conditions were at least tolerable.

His first apartment was colder than this most winters, and just about as small.

Cleaner too. New mattresses came wrapped in plastic, and, given Fedin's vivid description of the used mattresses, they must either wrap them up before they transport them, or haul them away in a different, far less sanitary, truck

It was too bad there weren't any, new or used, in here now, as there was no seating provided. Donny laid the handcart flat at the furthest most point away from the rolling door, against which he had slid the incendiary cooler, still relieved of all of its cash, just in case Fedin decided to borrow Not's cell phone and dial in a double-cross. Donny used the empty barrel as a seat, with the stacks of heat sealed cash piled loosely beside him.

The roll up door had no release catch on the inside; the cargo hold of a truck like this was never intended to carry passengers, thus there was no need for there to be a way to open the door from this side of it. It was a bit of a moot point, anyway, as Donny was pretty sure he had heard a lock clack into place as soon as Not had secured the latch.

He could tell they were rolling once again, but had no idea the speed or the direction. The raised position of the heavy duty truck suspension resting on top of another heavy duty truck suspension absorbed most of the bounce from the road.

However, the combined high center of gravity of both trucks made the box truck sway constantly, so Donny could not clearly tell if they were turning, or merely going around a curve.

Not that it mattered.

He knew where they were going, and approximately how far away it was from their current position. They had driven from there not too long ago in the very truck in which he was now imprisoned. It shouldn't take long to get there, a mere fifteen minutes or so.

Short enough, Donny knew he needed to work quickly.

Moments after he had felt the initial jolt of motion as they started to roll forward onto State Route 4, Donny had stripped off his heavy coat, and then the thin polyester and rayon blend uniform shirt his company made them all wear. He had complained many times about the complete and total lack of natural materials in the uniform, but praised the heavens now for his criminally cheap overseers at, what had to be by now, his former employer.

As soon as he was free of the shirt, he quickly redressed in his heavy coat and retrieved his cigarettes and the cheap disposable lighter he had almost not bought in favor of a free book of matches from the store. He congratulated himself on his forethought and the expenditure of an extra dollar.

Polyester was flammable.

Donny had learned that little tidbit in a fire safety portion of the first aid course he had been required to take -- along with the sexual harassment training, and bloodborne pathogens training which had been required for some odd reason -- before being allowed to drive an armored truck. Polyester was in fact very flammable. It was also not recommended to be worn by anyone in an industry where one might be exposed to fire, because when it did burn, it did not turn to ash, like natural fibers, but rather into a gooey, sticky, molten mess which would bond with the skin.

After the training when Donny had asked why they had to wear these hazardous shirts, his direct supervisor said they were only hazardous if exposed to flame, and it hardly ever happened. Then why did they have to be trained on what to do if it did happen? Well, *hardly ever* was not the same as *never*.

Fastening the bottom two buttons, he lined up the bottom edge from the front and rear of the shirt, creating a straight fold up both sides . Pinching together and inch of fabric from the front and back of the shirt, Donny applied the flame from his lighter until the fabric from the shirt caught fire. He let the flame grow for a count of three, and then blew it out. The fabrics from the front and back of the shirt had melted together to form one rounded, glassy black worm of goo. Donny blew on it until it hardened and then gave it a tug. To Donny's amazement and appreciation, the melted seam held.

He lit a cigarette and then pinched together the next inch from the front and the back, lined them up, and applied the flame.

It only took about five minutes to seal up the bottom of the shirt.

He considered trying the same with the neck hole, but didn't think the rounded edges would match up well enough. He would just have to be careful.

Laying the shirt back flat on the floor, Donny began to line up the stacks of bills inside, making a rectangle wider than the base of the cooler, but would not need to be as tall. He was able to fit all of the cash within the shirt, though it strained against the buttons as he sealed it all up inside.

Donny connected the sleeves by buttoning each cuff to its opposite, and in just a few minutes he had fashioned a kind of lumpy messenger bag.

It likely wouldn't last long, if he had to run, but it could not be set on fire by a phone call either, which Donny thought weighed heavily into the pro column.

The truck rumbled on, and Donny was not sure what else he could do.

He wanted to try the cell phone Fedin had given him, but he wasn't sure if it was booby trapped in some way. If he tried to make a phone call, would the phone explode in his ear? Or perhaps release a vial of some toxin or acid? Maybe Fedin had filled it with poisonous spiders just for the hell of it.

The truck slowed, rocking Donny on the barrel toward the cab of the truck, then came to a full stop. He tried to listen for the sound of approaching footsteps, but sounds were either muffled by the walls of the box, or hidden beneath the thrumming idle of the diesel, which Donny felt in his feet more than heard.

Donny flipped open the phone and hit contacts. True to his word, Fedin had only one number saved. Holding his thumb over the send button, Donny trained the flashlight onto the cooler he had positioned front and center, pressed against the rolling door. When the door went up, if he didn't like the look of the situation, Donny would fire up the cooler, grab the cash, and try to jump past them in the confusion.

Donny finished his cigarette, crushed it under the toe of his boot, and then lit another. He sat on the barrel and smoked, the flashlight held steadily on the cooler and the door, which still did not open, no matter how much he willed it to do so.

He heard and felt the engine idle higher, but the truck did not begin to roll again. The deep rumble rose in both pitch and volume, echoing around the empty space of the cargo hold, and effectively blanking out all exterior noises.

Because of his position, he was unable to plant both feet firmly when he realized the increased idle was because the bed of the rollback was being raised and the floor had begun to tilt. Unable to grab anything for purchase, he stumble-ran-fell all the way to smash into the roll up door which he had been so patiently waiting for to open. The palms of his hands stung as they slapped against the door, which boomed and rattled from the impact. Donny was able to mostly break his fall, but worried he might have broken both wrists in the process. The concern for his wrists was fleeting, as he was unable to stop from delivering himself a jolting knock to the forehead.

He heard, rather than saw, the handcart and barrel sliding to join him, as he had dropped the flashlight when he hit the door, and now it only illuminated a few square inches of corner space. The empty barrel did not bring much force, but the steel handcart to which it was strapped hit the rolling door hard enough to rattle Donny's teeth, which were pressed against it at the time of impact. He hoped it had not hit and or ruptured the cooler, more so he hoped it would not ignite, as he had very few ways to avoid getting burned if it did.

He checked the phone in his hand, and thankfully saw he had not hit the send button during his fall.

Small favors, he thought.

There was a momentary roller coaster feeling in his stomach as his box truck prison was released from the pinnacle of the ramp to roll down to the street below.

Donny understood Not was going through the motions as roughly as possible, completely aware Donny was being pinballed around in the back.

Appraising the situation honestly, if their places had been reversed, Donny admitted he would not have done it any differently.

Once more at a level position, Donny snatched up the flashlight and located his shirt-satchel with the money. He scanned the floor for any stacks of cash which might have tumbled out during the bumpy dismount, but was pleased to see they had all apparently stayed wedged inside. Allowing himself a short moment of pride in his craftsmanship, he then refocused on the business at hand.

The barrel and handcart lay across the doorway, taking up more than half the distance across, and the cooler filled much of the remaining space. The sudden tilt and roll had actually manufactured a better barricade than Donny had devised on his own.

Donny moved back toward the front of the truck once more, giving himself some running room if he still needed to leap over whoever opened the door in order to gain his freedom. He had been dragging the shirt-satchel of cash along by the sleeve-strap, but realized he might need both of his hands, should he actually have to fight his way free.

Quickly removing his coat, Donny draped the bundle of cash around his neck and shoulder, so the bulk of the money lay against his left side. With his jacket back on and re-zipped, the money was heavy, but manageable. It certainly felt more secure.

Donny waited and listened, as best as he was able given the limits of the truck, and heard the rumbling diesel grow louder to one side of the truck, and then the rumble cut to silence. He tensed in the darkness, readying to sprint through the open door while simultaneously thumbing the send button of the pitifully cheap and old-fashioned flip phone to ignite the Russian's cooler.

In his mind, it was a summer blockbuster, slow-mo action shot of coolness.

The door did not open.

Donny waited until his tensed legs began to ache, and he realized that if he didn't relax soon he would get a charley-horse when he tried to run, likely right as he tried to leap the burning cooler, which would end in more of a tragic viral video than an awesome action movie escape.

Instead, he lit another cigarette and thought.

He no longer had any confidence Fedin would, or perhaps ever could, do anything to help clear his name. More likely, he would just be served up as a sacrifice to the justice system as an appeasement for the missing cocaine. The loss of the actual drugs would be less of an embarrassment provided they were able to march the perpetrator in front of the news cameras at the courthouse and assuage the public's need to feel safe from all the bad people in the world.

All the evidence needed for a conviction was right here in the back of this truck: the stolen barrel, now empty, the driver of the armored car from which the barrel was stolen, and a large pile of cash.

The district attorney wouldn't even need to show up for this one, just list those three things as exhibits A, B, and C, and the jury would draw the obvious conclusion. The fact that the obvious conclusion was also the correct conclusion did not make Donny feel any better about his situation.

He pulled a drag off his cigarette and considered his options.

He had no tools or other means of escape, other than setting the cooler ablaze and hoping he did not burn or die from smoke inhalation in the enclosed space before it burned a hole large enough for him to slip through. He was not being watched at the moment, certainly a plus, but he had no idea how long or what they were planning right now without him.

He might be able to use the cell phone to call for help, but of course it might also accidentally incinerate his improvised prison with him inside of it. An additional drawback was the question of who he could call.

It wasn't like he could call the police.

Jennifer was great in the courtroom, but he didn't think she would be on board with a hands-on hostage rescue. He could try Topher again, but he hadn't had much luck there before. It crossed Donny's mind to wonder if he should wonder if Topher was okay, but the thought was fleeting.

He had himself to worry about, after all.

He also had the handcart.

The walls of the box truck were fairly thin particle board. If he used the handcart as a battering ram, aiming it a seam, a weak point in the side, he could likely break a hole open in the side and leap down from there. It wouldn't be quick, though, and it would certainly make a lot of noise.

305

He could not break free without being noticed, if there was anyone around him.

Was there anyone around?

Donny placed his ear to the wall to his left and listened, but heard only silence. He repeated the action on the right side and was greeted by silence there as well.

"He who hesitates is lost," he muttered to himself, remembering the famous quote but had no idea to whom he should attribute it, and quickly moved to right the handcart. Flipping the outdated phone closed and dropping casually into his pants pocket, he considered removing the barrel, but decided it would take more time and make little difference to the functionality of the handcart in its repurposed role as a battering ram.

Holding the cart by the two handle grips, he tried a couple of test runs from various angles around the limited space. The strongest point, and the one which would make the most noise, was the rolling door at the back. Unlike the walls, the door was quarter-inch plywood panels lined with metal on the exterior.

The smaller size of the panels actually would make them more difficult to break, versus the half-inch thick panels of the sides. The sides, though thicker, were made of flimsier material, lined only with a thin laminate sheet on the exterior to keep the weather out, and the larger single panels made it easier to break through.

Still, he was unlikely to be able to get it in just one go, so he wanted to make each hit do the most damage. Once he selected his spot and launched his first attack, he would alert everyone in the general vicinity to what he was doing, provided there was anyone out there to hear him.

He finally decided the best way to go was to retreat to the farthest corner, his back to the cab of the truck, and to run at top speed diagonally across the truck, aiming for the opposite corner close to the door. This would allow him to gain as much momentum as possible, as well as let him hit the wall with the pointed corner of the bottom of the handcart, which would hopefully act as a wedge to split through the wood.

He lay the flashlight in the other corner near the cab, lying flat on the floor against the wall, so as to focus the beam on his target but leave his hands free to push and grip the cart.

So focused was he on effecting his escape, Donny nearly didn't hear the flip phone ringing. When he did, he almost did not recognize it for what it was. Finally, on the fourth or fifth ring, Donny fumbled the phone out of his pocket and flipped it open.

"Hello?" he said cautiously.

"Donovan," Fedin spoke quietly. "I need you to listen carefully."

"Um, okay," Donny agreed, because there was really nothing else which could be said when someone asked you to listen carefully.

"I was just on the phone with Alexi and let him know we will not be able to bring the product to our clients, you understand?"

"Um, no, not really," Donny said truthfully. "You want me to. . ."

"Correct. Troy was not truthful with us, it seems," Fedin continued. "He was trying to middle the middle-man, as it were."

"What the fuck are. . ."

"Yes, correct, I am here now with the *actual owner* of the product, you understand. Do not worry my friend, the deal remains the same, and at the agreed upon price."

"So, if Alexi gets over here with those black gangbangers, he can still clear. . ."

"Yes, so you just sit tight, and hold down the fort, you understand," Fedin said brightly, still ignoring Donny's half of the conversation. "But be ready to roll if I call you"

Fedin disconnected, and Donny sat, no longer poised to make a Captain Nemo-esque attack run at the interior of a mattress truck, and tried to puzzle out what the hell just happened.

Fedin had called Sokolov and Sokolov was bringing the black guys Fedin wanted to be busted. Which meant the actual cocaine was here. Whoever the "actual owner" was, Fedin had talked them into selling the cocaine to him, effectively cutting out Troy, not that Donny cared one way or another. The real question was why had Fedin called him at all?

He glanced down at the weaponized moving equipment he was holding and understood that the whole conversation had been window dressing for the one simple message:

The deal was still on, so stay put.

Which, of course, was easy for Fedin to say. He was not the one currently locked in the back of a truck with a cop's wet dream worth of evidence against him.

Fedin had inadvertently told Donny something else as well. It seemed the flip phone could be used without setting off the contents of the cooler.

Donny lit another cigarette and decided to put the knowledge to good use.

Chapter 36

THE WINDOWS on the mechanics bays were all dark, as was the light in the small reception area. Alto's office door was closed, and the break room was empty. The television was still on, though the baby-daddy talk show had given way to the local evening news. A fresh layer of snow was expected before midnight, and the weather man jokingly asked why the danged groundhog had to see his shadow again this year. Not registered the words, but paid it no mind as he continued directly through into the mechanic's bays.

On the wall near the door, a large bank of switches turned on the various lights throughout all five of the bays. Still unfamiliar with the small mundane secrets of this new workplace, like which switch did what, Not opted just to flip them all rather than dick around for a minute or two which it would take to go through the trial and error method.

Three bays, the three closest to the Not, were occupied with standard size rigs, the oversized pickup trucks with the tow arm.

The fourth and fifth held the mid-size rollbacks.

Not walked quickly to the sixth bay with its raised ceiling and oversized door which allowed the big flatbed rig to enter. His footsteps slapped echoes off of the smooth concrete to bounce around the tall and mostly empty room.

Not freed the chain pull from the anchor hook on the wall and quickly ran up the door. He trotted back over to bay five and repeated the processes. Checking the cab of the truck currently in bay five, Not found the keys to be absent from the ignition -- not a surprise, as it would have been extremely careless to leave them in the cab -- but was able to retrieve them quickly from a peg board near the break room door. Not made short work of moving the truck outside to free up the space.

The urge to simply keep going as he moved the other truck to the street, to just floor it and not look back, had been nearly overwhelming. Run, run, run, RUN, RUN, RUN, had been chanting in his mind.

Without his phone, though, running now would only prolong the inevitable.

Unlike the old semi-rig he had been driving, the mid-sized tow, much newer and nicer, was equipped with the interactive screen Josue had included as part of his try-out run to Teaneck. As before, the Help button was pristine from lack of use.

Not pushed it.

THE SWEET victory this job had been just the day before had quickly soured in the last twenty-four hours.

He and Fedin had shared notes during the short journey back to the garage. Fedin, good to his word, had described how he had become involved, and what he intended to do with the cocaine.

Not found himself cringing a bit at the language the Russian used to describe the rival drug dealers, but allowed it was a foreign word and may not be nearly as racist as he assumed it to be.

Although Fedin's plan wasn't strictly legal either, it did have the benefit of making sure the cocaine ended up back in the hands of the DEA, rather than up the noses of half the student body of Hackensack.

Holding up his side of the bargain, Not told Fedin everything he knew about the whole fiasco, including the information Topher had given him while they shared a cell.

It was oddly liberating to be able to speak so openly and candidly. He had finally found an ally who could see through Donny's bullshit, and who was actively taking action to stop him.

Best yet, he had been able to record the whole conversation.

When they had first started rolling, the new phone had binged to indicate a message.

"Do you mind if I . . ." Fedin had picked up the phone to see what the message was. "Your phone is telling you there are open Wi-Fi networks around you."

"Sorry," Not had said, holding his hand out for the phone. "I can turn the notifications off."

Fedin handed the phone over to Not, who looked at the lock screen and tried to remember if he had to swipe up or down or left or right to get to the start screen. Then he saw the Wi-Fi icon was available, and illuminated, on the lock screen, so he simply tapped it to turn it off. However, Not also noticed the camera icon was available on the lock screen.

He swiped the icon to the right, and the phone's camera activated.

A small virtual slide button at the bottom took it from still photos to video. He hit record, and then put the phone, screen-side down, on the seat between them, hoping Fedin would take the gesture as proof he had nothing to hide, and would not call his bluff but ready to feign ignorance if he did.

"Sorry," Not had said again. "It's a new phone, and I haven't got all of my settings done yet."

"Yes, I can see," Fedin had nodded toward the shared footwell littered with all of the phone's packaging. "Small world. The phone I gave to Donovan is the same brand."

"Do you like them?" Not had asked, hoping it sounded like a natural conversation, and not strained or forced, though that was how it had felt.

"It hasn't let me down yet," Fedin had allowed. "Donovan on the other hand . . ."

Fedin had returned to the subject at hand and had rattled off, quickly but with lots of detail, all that Donny had told him so far, and what their plan had been.

Not had filled in with some missing information supplied by Topher, but for the most part, Fedin had done the talking.

"So, what is it you want from me?" Not had asked.

"Simply what you are doing," Fedin had assured him. "Take us back to your employer, and then take me to his office. I am sure he will have our friend Troy's address in one of his files. After, I will ask you to sit quietly in the room until my business is done, and we will part ways as friends. You understand, I don't really have any use for you once we are at our destination, but neither do I wish you any harm."

Fedin had waggled the gun once more. Not had taken it as the fairly straightforward gesture it seemed to be. Don't cause any trouble, and Fedin wouldn't shoot him. Not hoped the

311

gesture could be seen on the camera, but for all he knew he was just taking a video of the upholstery on the roof of the cab. He didn't even know if their voices were coming through clearly.

Not had been unsure the whole ride back if the camera had in fact even been recording the whole time, and could conceive of no way of how he could check it without tipping his hand to Fedin.

However, just before they had arrived, the phone had made a new noise, a kind of building crescendo of the electric hum of an overworked transformer, and Fedin picked up the phone once more. Not tried to keep his face neutral while preparing to act surprised when Fedin found the camera screen was open and recording. He readied a what he hoped would sound like a heartfelt apology and shock that the phone was recording, completely on accident of course, but it was a new phone after all, and he wasn't used to all the functions.

If Fedin didn't buy it, then Not could tell him he wouldn't need to bother with finding Troy to get the cocaine.

He hadn't wanted to say so when Fedin had told him about what had happened in the old warehouse where Not had dropped Topher's old truck because he didn't want to risk it being recorded, and it would be his only card to play if Fedin caught him recording their conversation.

"Your battery is full," Fedin had said, and held the phone up for Not to see. A large green cartoon of a dry cell battery filled the black screen with an illuminated 100%! in bold and happy white lettering below it, like he had done well on a test, rather than simply plugged in a device and left it alone.

At the bottom corner had been a small red blinking dot, which he hoped like hell meant it was still recording.

"Thank you," Not had said, surprising himself at how calm and normal he was speaking, and then surprised himself further when held his hand out for the phone. "I need to hang on to it though in case my boss calls."

"Of course," Fedin had said, and unplugged the phone for Not and started to hand it over, but instead placed it on the seat between them once more. "You understand, I will be quite upset if I see you making any calls, texts, or if you say anything foolish to anyone who calls you?"

"Yeah, man," Not had said with more bravado than he felt. "You're the guy with the gun, I get it."

"Very good," Fedin had said, and the subject was closed.

When they had reached Alto's All Tow, he opened the door but paused before getting down.

"I need to go inside to open the bay door," he had said. "But I need you to stay here."

"Why?" Fedin asked, more curious than suspicious.

"I want to leave it running," Not had said simply, and truthfully.

"Of course," Fedin had easily agreed. "When you enter the door, I will begin counting. If I reach thirty before seeing you again . . ."

Again, he waggled the gun for effect.

"I'm just going to roll up the doors," Not had assured him.

"Very good," Fedin had nodded. "I am happy to stay here where it is warm."

BREAKING ONE of the cardinal rules for the second time that night, Not left the keys in the ignition to the mid-size flatbed, and trotted back to rejoin Fedin in the cab of the old rig. Proceeding to break a second cardinal rule, Not moved as quickly as he could to drop the truck into the bay without any consideration in regards to the safety and wellbeing of the cargo in the back of the truck.

Donny was likely getting bumped around in there a bit, but unfortunately unlikely in any permanently disfiguring way, despite Not's best efforts.

Of course, one could always hope.

With Fedin's truck deposited in bay four, Not quickly but professionally set the bed down right, and backed it into the fifth bay, making it ready to roll for the next driver, though Not was fairly sure it would not be him.

He knew by now, one way or another, he would never head out on a run for Alto's again.

Fedin now climbed down from the passenger side as Not lowered the bay door, the chain pull rattling too loudly to allow either man to speak and hope to be understood or even heard. When the second door was also secured, Not turned to Fedin, intending to ask him if they should let Donny out of the back of the truck, but was stopped by another voice calling out through the garage.

"You're back early, Not," Josue called from the door which lead to the breakroom. He must have been in Alto's office when Not had come through a few minutes ago. "Is everything okay?"

"Well, um . . . ," Not trailed off as Fedin came around the front of the truck with the gun in full view.

"Shit," Josue said. "No, I guess not."

"What's going on?" Alto now asked, appearing in the doorway behind Josue. "Not, why'd you park. . ."

Alto's voice trailed off as he came further into the room and was able to see the gun in Fedin's hand. Not would have felt bad for them if he hadn't been sure that one or both of them had somehow found the barrel Topher had hidden. Instead of doing the right thing, they had let Not get arrested, let the DEA think Not had somehow helped to hide or sell the cocaine, let Not, once again, take the fall.

With that in mind, bringing Fedin here was, in terms of the backstabbing going on, no worse than a shaving nick.

"This is Gregori Fedin," Not said, making the introductions. "He would like to buy the cocaine."

Fedin offered Not a slightly puzzled look, but said nothing.

"What are you. . . ," Josue started to protest, but Not just wanted it to all be over.

"The cocaine you took from the burned out house," Not clarified for them. "The cocaine in the big blue barrel which you have since emptied out into something else, probably another old drum you've got around here, so you could send the barrel in the back of the old truck along with Troy to be tested. You know, the cocaine you let me get arrested for taking? *That* cocaine?"

"Now, Not, that is just. . . ," Alto began to protest.

"It must have been close," Not continued. "Did you see Topher moving the barrel? Is that how you found it? Were you able to empty it before the cops got here, or did you stash it somewhere and wait until they had gone?"

"Okay, let's cut the shit," Josue said, a hint of exasperation in his voice. "Is this a robbery or a business proposition, Mr. Fedin?"

Fedin followed Josue's gaze to the gun in his own hand, and seemed almost as if he had forgotten it was there.

"Forgive me," Fedin said, and stowed the gun back in his pocket. "I must admit I am caught a little off guard as well. I was under the impression a man named Troy was in possession of the cocaine. Am I to understand that it is actually the two of you with whom I will need to negotiate?"

"Troy's. . ."

"Troy was the first to make an offer," Alto said, sounding happy to be the one to interrupt Josue this time and to regain control of the conversation. "However, no money has yet to change hands, so I would say we are still at the table, right Josue?"

"Yeah," Josue grudgingly agreed. "I think that's fair to say. What are you offering?"

"Three million," Fedin said, his tone betraying his knowledge that this was a very low price. "But it is three million in cash, tonight. Also, I can promise you the cocaine will never reach the streets. It will instead be delivered into the hands of the DEA."

"Are you some kind of millionaire good Samaritan, or something?" Josue asked with obvious disbelief. "Don't get me wrong, I'm not a fan of the shit either."

"But you'll sell it, right?" Not asked.

"But," Josue continued, still addressing Fedin and ignoring Not's interruption, "what's in it for you?"

"Well, I do pride myself in trying to help my community," Fedin said, his voice dripping with false modesty. "But, no, I will also see a profit from this, a small one you understand, less than what you will make tonight. I intend to resell the cocaine at only a slightly higher price to a horrible street gang . . . I hesitate to even dignify them as people. They are animals, terrible creatures who do terrible things to good people, and as such deserve to be caged. I will see to it *they* are in possession of the cocaine when it is discovered by the DEA."

"And how will you do that?" Alto sneered. "Do you have the DEA in your pocket?"

"Yes," Fedin said simply, and left Alto without a retort.

An awkward silence ensued which lasted nearly a minute. Alto and Josue exchanged cryptic glances, and both looked towards Not and Fedin repeatedly studying their faces, but for what Not had no idea. They probably were trying to decide if they believed the story and how they wanted to handle this rather sudden but possibly fortunate turn of events.

Not had to admit that Fedin's pitch did sound fairly appealing.

Get rich while getting some criminals -- well, other criminals, *real* criminals they were sure to be thinking -- off the streets. Being able to sell a shitload of drugs guilt free and at nearly no risk was a pretty seductive siren song.

"We would like to take a moment to discuss your proposal in private," Alto said, and Josue nodded in agreement.

The two men retreated into the break room, and closed the door behind them. Not was unable to hear what they were saying, but he could take a pretty good guess the whole conversation was going to boil down to whether or not they believed it, and even if they didn't did they really have much of a choice.

Fedin, after all, did have a gun.

If they ran out the front door of the shop, they couldn't take all the cocaine with them, and Fedin would simply take it for free. If they called the cops, denied what Fedin or Not would tell them, they would still run the risk of the police finding the cocaine and arresting them.

"Not, may I borrow your phone, please?" Fedin asked.

"Sure," Not said, as he could think of no good reason to say no and not raise suspicion. They were, for all intents and purposes, still on the same side. Then he remembered, "Oh, it's still in the truck."

Before Fedin could say anything, Not ran to the cab of the truck and retrieved the phone. Tapping the screen to wake the phone, Not quickly closed the camera app, and swiped back to the home screen as he trotted back to where Fedin still stood, and held it out as casually as possible.

Taking the proffered phone, Fedin dialed a number from memory and then spoke quickly and quietly in Russian for about thirty seconds. He listened, and then spoke again. Not could not follow what was being said, but the tone sounded like he confirmed whatever had been asked by the person on the other end of the phone.

Fedin hit the end button, and then immediately dialed again from memory. As he hit the send button, the door to the break room reopened, and Josue and Alto walked back in.

"Donovan," Fedin spoke quietly. "I need you to listen carefully."

Fedin raised his voice a little, and looked toward Alto and Josue as they approached.

"I was just on the phone with Alexi and let him know we will not be able to bring the product to our clients, you understand?" Fedin said brightly into the phone.

"Correct. Troy was not truthful with us, it seems," Fedin continued. "He was trying to middle the middle-man, as it were. Yes, correct, I am here now with the actual owner of the product, you understand. Do not worry my friend, the deal remains the same, and at the agreed upon price."

Not watched as Josue and Alto exchanged an angry glance and realized they had been about to counter-offer for a higher amount, but Fedin had just swept the option out from under them. They were still unable to go anywhere without leaving the cocaine, and here was Fedin already on the phone with reinforcements.

"Yes, so you just sit tight, and hold down the fort, you understand," Fedin said brightly. "But be ready to roll if I call you."

The implication of people on standby, ready to back up Fedin at a moment's notice was obviously not lost on either of what Not now thought of as his former bosses. Josue gave a slight shrug, a what-are-you-gonna-do-about-it kind of shrug, and then let Alto step forward to speak.

"Now, Mr. . . . Fedin was it?" Alto waited for Fedin to nod in affirmation before proceeding. "Mr. Fedin, we have not agreed to sell you anything. We have not, for that matter, even acknowledged our possession of anything that you would like to purchase."

"Are we back to playing coy, gentlemen?" Fedin sounded amused. "I thought, after Not's very astute deductions and your own partner's urging for you to 'cut the shit,' that we would simply lay our cards on the table. I have laid mine down. It is too late, I am afraid, to try to bluff."

Josue mumbled something to Alto which Not was too far away to hear clearly, but which he thought was "just take it." Alto opened his mouth as if to speak, but then closed it again without a word. He looked to Josue for help, but Josue simply crossed his arms and looked at the floor.

"We, well, ah, that is, um" Alto started and stopped several times, before he got his verbal feet under him again. "What I am *trying* to say is that we don't actually have the cocaine here. We moved it to a safe location after we sent the barrel with Troy to be tested. Now, I do appreciate that your offer is in cash and could be in our hands tonight, but the value we calculated from the weight on hand was far, far . . . more."

Alto trailed off as Fedin turned and started walking back to the box truck parked in bay four. He tossed Not his phone as he walked, and pulled the gun from his pocket as soon as his hand was free.

"Not, run up the door in front of my truck," Fedin commanded, but he headed for the back of the truck rather than the driver's door. Not did not bother to watch where Fedin went, as he had a pretty good idea of what he was after. Instead, he did as he was requested and rolled up the garage door and allowed Fedin's truck access to the street beyond. It also allowed the cold wind access the garage, and a flurry of snow blew in around him.

Not wondered if he should run.

He now had the phone and the opportunity. If he sprinted, he could be around the corner before Fedin could jiggle his roly-poly self out to the street to see which way he went. He could be free and clear and on the phone to Karkus, or to the police, or even to his Dad to get a ride home. He could just walk away.

But, help was coming.

If he left now, there would be no one to ensure Donny also got what was coming to him, and Not was not too proud to admit that he wanted some payback.

Not turned away from the open door and walked to the back of the truck, and almost immediately realized he had made the wrong decision.

"Where did you hide the money, Donovan?"

The door to the truck stood open and Fedin was pointing the gun at Donny, who was still inside. The old picnic cooler which was somehow also a bomb was once more laying open, and like before it was empty, but now the pile of money that had lay beside it was nowhere to be seen.

"It's my money," Donny sounded like a child about to throw a tantrum.

"Give it to me, Donny," Fedin said, his tone softer this time.

"No! You said--"

In the movies it would have been in the shoulder or the leg. Blood would spurt in great gushing splashes, but Donny would clamp a hand over the wound, and would be okay in the end.

On television, it would have been a warning shot into the ceiling, or gut shot that was never even seen, just implied by the red wet shirt under Donny's hand.

Fedin shot Donovan in the head.

A wet meat explosion slapped against the wall behind him and it was over.

The quickness of the brutality somehow made it worse.

Not watched Donny's body fall, not all slow motion like in the movies, but crashing down upon itself, legs bending and twisting in ways which would have been horribly painful, if Donny could still feel pain, and the sound of his head hitting the floor of the truck brought back an immediate sense memory, likely heightened by the smell of burnt gunpowder in the air, of the fourth of July he dropped a whole watermelon on the kitchen floor.

"Go in and find the money," Fedin turned the gun on Not.

Feeling more numb than scared, Not climbed into the truck and looked around for a large pile of cash. Aside from the cooler, the barrel and handcart, and the pile of Donny, the cargo space was empty.

"It is probably on him," Fedin prompted. "Hidden somewhere on his body."

Not approached the body slowly, conditioned to expect a jump scare from the newly dead, but Donny's jumping days were over. He had landed, his legs folded clumsily beneath him, mostly on his back. One eye was slightly open, and blood was pooling around the back of his head. For some reason, Donny appeared to have aged thirty years in the instance of his death. Not felt his stomach turn as he realized the reason for this transformation.

Donny's hair and scalp was gone. His exposed skull, in the dim light of the truck, gave the appearance of baldness and added an unlived lifetime onto his appearance.

He also seemed to have developed a beer gut in the last half-hour.

Donny's body was much larger and out of proportion than he had remembered, so he unzipped Donny's jacket.

Underneath was a crude sort of sling Donny had apparently fashioned out of his work shirt, and inside of which Not could see the rectangular shapes of the stacks of cash. He slid the sleeves, which Donny had fastened as a strap around his neck, out from under Donny's broken head, coating the sleeves with blood and bits of hair and flesh.

He turned and half carried, half dragged the surprisingly heavy lump of cash to the open door, and the waiting Fedin.

Fedin was standing on the bumper and had pulled the door down about a quarter of the way. He was still pointing the gun at Not, but turning every few seconds to keep an eye on Josue and Alto, who had crept up behind Fedin. Not saw that Alto had pulled a short barrel revolver from wherever he had been hiding it, but was not pointing it at anything in particular.

"Toss the money out, Not," Fedin instructed. "And gentlemen, the opportunity for negotiation is over. You may take my offered payment, and when the heavily armed animals of whom I spoke of earlier arrive shortly, I will deal with them. Or, you may shoot me, and they will kill you both, take everything worth taking, and then most likely burn this building to its foundation just to tidy up."

Alto looked to Josue, but lowered the gun.

Not would have loved to think that his safety had something to do with the decision, but more likely it was the large bloody bundle of cash which was promised to soon be theirs. The threat of imminent violence probably didn't hurt either.

"Not," Fedin looked turned his attention back to the truck, raising the gun once more. "The money please."

Not complied, and tossed the shirt-satchel of money out to Fedin, who simply allowed it to thump heavily on the floor beside him. Without looking, and without taking the gun away from Not, he called out his commands to Alto.

"Come here and place the gun in my hand," Fedin's tone implied that no argument would be tolerated. Alto quickly complied, but only allowed his eyes to stray from the money for seconds at a time. He placed the revolver, what Not had always heard called a snub-nose, into Fedin's outstretched palm.

"Thank you, Paul," Fedin returned to his pleasant, we're just good pals, voice. "You pick up the money, but don't go anywhere with it yet. I think you were bluffing before, you understand? When you said the cocaine was not here?"

Alto began to nod, but when he saw that Fedin was not looking at him, he did manage to work up a feeble, "Yes."

"Very good," Fedin praised him like a puppy. "I will finish my business here with Not, and then you will take me to the cocaine, you understand?"

"Yes," Alto said, but with more power returning to his voice.

Fedin slipped the revolver into his coat pocket, but his short and boxy automatic never wavered from Not's chest. Still too much in shock to do much else, Not braced himself for the shot which he was sure would come next.

"Not, I will need to borrow your phone again, please."

Without comment, but with a sinking in his stomach at the loss of the conversation saved in the video, Not tossed his phone out to Fedin, who immediately slipped it in his pocket, next to Alto's gun.

Now, would come the bullet.

Fedin instead pulled the clip from the gun and tossed one bullet onto the floor behind Donny's body. He popped the rest of the bullets from the clip like coins from a roll, and dropped the small pile of them into his jacket pocket along with the revolver. The clip then sailed past Not to clatter to the floor near where the bullet fell.

"My advice, Not, my friend," Fedin said, reaching up for the strap dangling from the bottom of the door. "Is to fire the round into his chest, or, if that is too much for you, then into the floor where it will not be noticed. When the police arrive, explain how you wrestled the gun away from him and shot him in self-defense after you were locked in here by persons unknown."

Fedin tossed the gun back beyond the body as well, but stuck the clip in his pocket.

"Don't worry about my prints on there," Fedin assured him, as if this were the sticking point to his plan, and held up his gloved hands. "I have never handled that gun without gloves on. You still have all you need to demonstrate Donovan's guilt, and he certainly won't be contradicting you."

Fedin jumped down, holding onto the strap handle, and brought the door down with him in a resounding boom. It plunged Not into near total darkness, but his flashlight from the rollback was still shining brightly in the corner. At least in the darkness, Donny's blood was not as noticeable. Seconds later, Not heard the carabiner clicking back into place, and effectively locking him in, just as he had done to Donny.

"Good luck!" Fedin shouted through the door.

"Should have walked away," he said to no one, since Donny was no longer listening.

Chapter 37

"WHAT CAN you give me in cash?" Topher asked with a patient resignation that he had been forced to develop in the last few hours. "For everything in my apartment."

Of course, some places had not needed negotiating. The bank had been simple enough. He had closed out his checking and savings account and pocketed the eight one hundred dollar bills, and the seven singles. His boss at the club he had been bouncing hadn't yet cut the checks for the week, but Topher was able to get him to pay him out half of his check early -- an advance to pay for emergency dental work, supposedly -- by promising to work every holiday for the rest of the year.

A promise Topher had no problem making because he had no intention of keeping it.

That had fattened his stack of bills by another seven hundred dollars.

The best idea he had come up with, at least the one which had been the most profitable so far, was the car title loan. He had gladly handed over the pink slip for his old wheels and in return got a cashier's check for eighteen hundred dollars, half the blue book value of the car, though he had been hoping for more. Then, he had had to cough up about forty bucks to get the check cashed, but it put his traveling money total at over $3200, and he even got to keep the car.

If they wanted to come down to Florida to collect it, they were more than welcome to do so.

Unfortunately, after the car, he had run out of any big ticket items. He owned no valuable jewelry to pawn, and his art collection consisted of posters neatly taped to the wall.

After the check cashing place, Topher had returned home and tossed all of his clean clothes into the hamper, and

323

stuffed it in the trunk of his car. Walking back up the long driveway to take one more look around for anything which might have some value, Topher noticed the kitchen light was on in the main house. On impulse, he knocked to see if anyone there wanted to buy any of the stuff he was about to leave behind.

"Everything in there, for whatever cash you've got on hand," Topher tried again, and pointed from the doorstep to the loft above the garage.

The guy who had opened the door, a fourth year community college student who was delaying the onset of adulthood for as long as he possibly could, and whose name always failed to come to Topher's mind because there was just not much worth remembering about the man, stared blankly at Topher for another few moments before speaking.

"Why would I want any of your stuff?" he asked, likely not intending to sound snotty, but succeeding in doing so nonetheless.

"How about this?" Topher tried a different tact, no longer needing to remain on good terms with his neighbors. "After I walk away from this door, if I return to my loft it will be to set fire to everything inside of there. You might be able to get your car out in time, you might be burned alive if you try. Of course, if none of the stuff in there is mine, then it wouldn't be mine to burn. Either way, after tonight, you will not see me again."

The kid started to laugh it off, Topher could almost read the words "yeah, right" die from his lips as he saw that Topher was not kidding.

"I, uh, I don't know how much I've got, man," the kid stammered.

"Why don't you ask the other two," Topher suggested. "Maybe you could all go in on it together."

"They went out."

"Oh, so yours is the only car in there?" Topher asked with mock pity.

"No," the kid shook his head for emphasis. "They got picked . . .oh shit."

"So, maybe you could get your car out, but not theirs, huh?" Topher reasoned. "Maybe you should just go check their rooms. Bring whatever cash you can find. I bet they'll thank you for it later."

The kid turned and ran through the kitchen, leaving Topher in the open doorway. For a second, Topher wondered if he should follow to make sure the kid wasn't calling the police, but then discovered he could follow the kid's progress through the house by the booming of his footsteps on the old wood floors, and the crashes and thumps of various items tossed around the rooms he was ransacking.

Less than a minute later, the footsteps came banging back down the stairs and back down the hall to the kitchen. In his hands was a crumpled pile of loose bills, but in his arms was an enormous glass pickle jar filled with change.

"This is all the cash I could find," the kid said, and with a touch of panic both endearing and a bit shaming for Topher, he added, "I'm sorry about the change, but it's all I've got."

"This'll do," Topher plucked the bills from the kid's hands, and stuffed them in his pocket without even counting it. He now felt like an absolute shit, and just wanted to be gone. He pulled the key to his apartment from his keyring and tossed it to the kid. "It's all yours."

He turned and hurried down the driveway to his car without looking back, and hoped the kid's curiosity about what was in the garage would win out over his shock and embarrassment from being bullied by Topher. If it did, maybe he would go out to see what all the fuss was about rather than call the police.

Either way, though, Topher was done and gone. He was going to point his car south and drive until he needed to sleep.

As he climbed in behind the wheel and started the engine, he wondered if he could make it to Florida in one shot, with stops for gas and food of course.

He thought, maybe, he could.

His phone began to ring and he pulled it out to scan the number on the screen. It wasn't a number he recognized, so he swiped to ignore the call, and dropped the phone on the seat beside him. Seconds later, it began to ring again. Topher picked the phone back up and checked the screen.

Same number.

Again, he swiped his thumb across the icon to 'ignore' and dropped the phone back onto the seat beside him.

It started to ring again.

325

"Hello?" Topher answered, figuring that telling the person off would be the fastest way to get them to stop calling, as they were obviously not getting the hint.

"Topher don't hang up!" Donny hissed into his ear through the phone.

Topher hit end and dropped the phone again on the seat beside him.

After a few seconds, about the time it would take to hit redial and for the cell phone company to route the call, the phone started ringing again.

Topher let it ring, and put the car into gear.

He was done with Donny.

He was going to Florida.

After a few seconds, on the eighth ring, it stopped ringing, gone to voicemail Topher assumed. Maybe he would listen to it later. Maybe when he was on the beach. Maybe he would just toss the thing into the ocean, skipping it across the water like in a beer commercial.

The phone started ringing again. This time it got to seven rings and then stopped for a few seconds, then started ringing again. Again, a count of seven, and then stop, and then a few seconds later it started ringing again.

Topher knew Donny would eventually tire of this, but it would take a very long time. Perhaps as long as an hour or more. Then he would take a break, fume about it for a while, and then call him again and the whole process would start over.

What could Topher say to him, though? Sorry, I lost the cocaine? I know you got arrested and all, but I hid the shit in a burned out house, went to warm up a little, and when I got back it was gone? See you when you get out of prison? By the way, you kept my name out if it, right?

Then again, Topher considered the situation, if Donny was able to call him over and over again, he couldn't be in custody anymore, right? Unless of course, he was calling Topher to try and get him to say something incriminating over the phone so Donny could earn a reduced sentence. All the more reason not to pick up the phone.

His phone pinged to alert him to a text message.

Knowing who it would be, Topher still found himself unable to resist the Pavlovian response built up around hearing a text message come in. He lifted the phone and read:

gt 3 mil csh
nd hlp
cl lwyr

In an instant, Topher was transported back to his sophomore year in high school, when Donny, who was a freshman at the time, would text him in class. He had gotten hundreds of messages like these, maybe even thousands.

Some text speech was universal. Phrases like LOL and OMG had actually become part of commonplace conversations, even after the need to shorten the messages had become obsolete. He hadn't even seen a shorthand text in years, and for some reason it made him worry for Donny more than the content of the message ever could.

Got three million cash, Topher translated in his head. Need Help. Call lawyer.

It had to be 'got' rather than 'get,' in the first line because Donny would have used 'nd' again if he needed three million dollars in cash, not that Topher had even the remotest chance of getting his hands on such a sum of money. It had taken him the whole afternoon just to liquidate all his worldly possessions for three thousand dollars.

The last line had to mean that Donny wanted him to call the lawyer who had contacted him last night, to pass along the idea of calling Mr. Creepy under the guise of taking care of Donny's fictional cat. Her number would still be saved in his under his received calls in his phone.

He knew he shouldn't call, that he should just chuck the phone out the window and keep heading south, but the text, the desperation laced with nostalgia in of the shorthand message made Topher pull to the side of the road, and retrieved the lawyer's number from his calls received list.

"Topher?" she answered on the first ring.

"Yeah, I just. . ."

"I'm going to put you on speaker," she interrupted.

Topher could hear the clunk and shuffle of the phone being moved around in her hands, the echoey sound of the space heard when a phone is away from the head of the person on the other end of the line. Topher listened to a clunk and scrape as the phone found a new resting place on the desk.

"Topher?" Donny's voice, but sounding distant, and hollow. Topher realized he was hearing Donny's voice from a second phone set to speaker and then placed next to what he could only think of as "his" phone, though both of the phones no doubt belonged to the lady lawyer.

"Yeah, I'm here," Topher said, a bit reluctantly.

"I've got no time to go into details, okay?" Donny began. "So, just listen. I'm locked in the back of a truck, but I got three million bucks, okay?"

"I'm gonna need a little more detail than that, D," Topher said gently, the fear in Donny's voice obvious beneath his usual bluff and bluster.

"The tow shop," Donny hissed. "They had the Shit Heap here, see. I followed them, we did, the Russian Nazi guy who had the DEA kidnap me, he and I, we followed them, they were taking the Shit Heap away, right? So, we. . ."

"Whoa, D," Topher broke in. "I think you went into too much detail, there. You are at the tow shop where the truck is?"

"Was," Donny corrected. "Some old hillbilly with sideburns took it."

"Are you high, Donny?"

"Roofied, just a little, earlier, but I'm over it. Pretty sure."

"I can't tell if I should be taking you seriously or not," Topher rubbed his temples.

"Just come get me!" Donny begged. "I'm locked in the back of a big white box truck, and I'm at the tow place, I think, and, shit, man . . ."

Topher was pretty sure Donny was trying not to cry.

"I'm going to call the police," the lawyer's voice suddenly broke in. Topher had forgotten she was there, listening to the whole conversation as it was projected throughout her office.

"No!" Donny croaked. "If they see cops, they'll bail and I'll be busted. This guy has a pet DEA agent, Jen!"

"Donny, I'm a lawyer," Jennifer said, stretching the last word into three syllables. "I am required to report any knowledge of a crime that has been or is going to be committed."

"What about client confidentiality? Huh? What about that? What about . . . shit."

"What?" Topher and Jennifer both said at once.

"Hang on," Donny said, and Topher again could hear the open whoosh of the phone passing through empty air, and then the thunk of it being set on a hard surface. From what sounded to be a great distance, but was more likely mere feet away, Topher could hear the loud rattle and clunk of a door being rolled up.

Topher could hear another voice, quiet and calm, but just a little too far from the phone to be heard clearly.

"It's my money," Donny responded to whatever the other had said. Topher knew from that tone of voice, coming from Donny, whoever the other person was had better be prepared to block if Donny could line up a clear foot to the other man's nuts.

The other voice spoke again, even quieter than before.

"No! You said. . ."

The sound of the gunshot boomed so loudly in Topher's ear he nearly dropped the phone. The nerve rattling explosion was followed by a dull but heavy thump directly into the microphone, which was the sound, Topher was fairly sure, of Donny collapsing and landing directly on top of the phone.

Topher listened carefully for movement, or breathing, or moaning, or any sign that Donny was still alive, but could hear nothing.

Dead.

It was the conclusion his mind wanted to make, and Topher felt an immediate relief followed by nauseous guilt at that sense of relief.

If Donny was dead, it meant there was nothing that Topher could do, and he was off the hook. He could simply hang up the phone, and keep heading south until he hit sand.

If Donny was dead, then Topher was free and clear.

He would have gone to help Donny, already going through the motions of reframing the situation to make it acceptable to a degree where he could live with himself. The only thing he could accomplish, now that Donny was dead, was to either get himself killed or get arrested, neither of which would bring Donny back to life.

It had nothing to do with the likelihood that the three million dollars, if it had ever existed at all, was now gone, taken by whoever it was who had shot Donny, not that Topher had only been going to go rescue Donny for the money, but now there was no one to rescue, and no money, so the only thing to do was to hang up the phone, put the car in gear, and hit the road.

"Are you still there?" the lawyer spoke up so quietly, so close to him, that Topher had to stifle a very un-masculine shriek.

Topher considered hitting the end button. If she called back he could just ignore it. Hell, he could toss the phone out the window, or pull the battery, or . . .

"Yeah," he answered. "I'm still here, but I don't think we can do any . . ."

"Listen," she snapped. "He's moving."

Topher listened, but heard nothing. Just the noisy silence of an open phone line. She was likely trying to convince herself there was something she could do, that it was not over, much in the same manner Topher was trying to reinforce the opposite conclusion. She wanted Donny to still be alive so she could still save him. She was a lawyer, a defense lawyer, and there had to be at least a small part of her that went into the profession out of a desire to help people, to save them, to be the hero.

Topher had saved people before, broke up fights, pulled abusive boyfriends off of the men or women they claimed to love, while still slapping the shit out of them, but after a while he noticed he was breaking up the same fights with the same people week after week. The same girl was getting slapped by a new guy again and again. Some people, he had decided, either could not or would not be saved, and he had come to accept the idea that there was a good reason why we have recognized the concept of a lost cause.

This line of thought, though, was knocked aside as Topher unmistakably heard the sound of something being moved over the phone's speaker. The soft shushing shuffle of material being slid across the mouthpiece followed by the dull meaty thump of something heavy landing on the phone once more.

"He's hurt," the lawyer said. "Tell me where they are, so I can call the cops."

"Some repair shop," Topher closed his eyes and tried to remember the name of the place, he had seen the sign but hadn't really cared about it at the time, but it wouldn't come into focus. "I can't remember the name. It was something cute, and had 'tow' in the title."

"*Where*?" she shouted.

"Railroad and Passaic!" Topher shouted back. "Listen, you stay on the line with him and talk to him if he comes around. I'll call the cops."

Topher disconnected the call on his end before she could argue, or remind him again she was a lawyer, both of which she was very likely to do. He quickly tapped 911 on the touchscreen keypad, but did not yet swipe his thumb across the little green phone icon. Instead, he put the car into gear and started toward Railroad Avenue as far above the limit as he could safely push it; the sun had set a while ago, and the melted snow of the day was quickly freezing into layers of invisible ice across the roadways.

With Donny in jail, he could have gone on to Florida.

With Donny dead, he could have gone on to Florida.

Hell, with Donny just mysteriously gone, assumed to have somehow screwed him over again, he could have gone on to Florida.

Knowing Donny was shot, but still alive, locked in the back of a truck and likely left to bleed to death, was just not something Topher had within himself to ignore.

True, he had stopped feeling like a hero when he had interrupted the same fights week after week, and night after night, but he still had done it.

He supposed, he was his own lost cause.

He swung right onto Railroad, barely slowing at the stop sign, and headed North towards Passaic. The garage would be on his right as he approached, so he planned to drive past and get a good look at the situation. If no one was around, he would stop right in front, run in and carry Donny out. If that wasn't possible, he would pull around the corner, and complete his 911 call, and then play it by ear.

WITH AMAZING swiftness, it all went to shit.

As he approached the shop, though, he found neither of his planned options would be possible. In front of the shop, parked end to end opposite all of the mechanics bays but on the southbound side of Railroad Avenue, were a couple of rusted out old muscle cars and three shitty pickup trucks like the one he had so recently been driving. Standing in the road, using the trucks for cover, were four or five middle aged guys, dressed in hunting gear, and aiming deer rifles across the hoods.

As Topher braked hard, but without locking up the wheels or risking loss of control on the slick winter roads, two men came out of the front door of the garage. Both men were older, the white guy had a head full of grey hair, while the Hispanic guy was salt and pepper with still more pepper than salt. They both wore heavy winter coats over identical work pants, and the grey-haired man had a kind of lumpy purse or something slung over his shoulder.

They both looked at Topher as he stopped just a few feet from them, rather than at the row of rifles aimed at them from across the street. However, once they saw he was not a threat, the line of trucks and cars, with the men and guns, did not go unnoticed for long.

The older man put on what Topher always thought of as a gameshow smile, and appeared to be raising his hand to wave to the men across the street, when the door behind him swung open once more.

One shot rang out.

Topher saw the flame burst of the gunshot come out from the open shop door, before it began to swing closed again, but it was all it took to start a barrage of bullets from the opposite side of the road. He saw both of the men on the sidewalk take several hits each before a stray bullet or a ricochet smashed his passenger window, and Topher ducked down and covered his head with his hands.

He stayed down until the firing stopped. He heard the door to the shop swing open once more.

Cautiously, Topher raised his head to survey the damage.

The men in hunting gear were hustling across the railroad tracks, keeping their heads and shoulders hunched down, trying to make smaller targets of themselves.

Both of the old men lay on the sidewalk, but neither one was moving.

The door to the garage was slowly swinging closed for a second time. Topher checked the bodies again and discovered he was right.

The lumpy purse was gone.

Chapter 38

THE FIRST thing was to get the flashlight. Then, to track down the bullet, the magazine, and the gun. He wasn't going to use them in the manner Fedin had suggested, but a gun with one bullet would be better than none if he needed to hold out until the police arrived.

When he had hit the "help" button, Not had hoped for a more immediate response. Instead, he had listened to the repeated beep of the holding noise until an operator came on the line.

"I'm in trouble," Not had said without further explanation. "Send the police right now!"

Unable to wait for the response, Not had killed the engine, but he was certain he had been heard. The GPS on the truck would work whether the engine was running or not. It would provide the location.

He just had to hold out until the cops got here.

The gun was quick enough to find, as was the magazine, they stood out against the pale wood floorboards of the truck, but the bullet took a little more searching. Not scanned the interior of the truck, walking slowly toward the back sweeping the flashlight from left to right, and inspecting every inch of the floor.

He was certain Fedin had thrown the shell past Donny, but he didn't think the throw had been hard enough for the bullet to have bounced back toward the rear door. He was rewarded for his patient approach a moment later when the flashlight glinted off of a bright brass casing, caught in a shallow trench which ran along the edge between the floorboards and the back of the truck's cab.

It was a fat, squat bullet, reminding Not of a robin's egg. He flipped it to check the base of the bullet and stamped into the casing around the firing pin was .45 Cal.

Jesus. No wonder Donny dropped so fast.

Not was very happy he had been able to get the money off of Donny without having to flip his body; the bullet had probably taken most of the back of Donny's head off when it had come out the other side.

For the same reason, Not was also happy that he, so far, had kept his flashlight trained at the floor of the truck, rather than the ceiling or walls, where the remainders of Donny were now dispersed and drying.

He tried not to think of it, and tried to breathe through his mouth, thankful it was February and not July.

Holding the flashlight under his left arm, Not pushed the single bullet down against the spring in the magazine until it clicked in, then slid the magazine into the grip of the gun until he felt another click. Before sliding the top to cock it, Not checked the side of the gun, near the trigger guard, to make sure it had a safety he could engage so he would not accidentally shoot off his dick when he put the gun in his pocket.

He spotted a small sliding switch near his thumb, and pushed it forward. The magazine popped back out of the handle of the gun. Not clicked it back into place, and checked both sides of the gun.

The magazine release was the only switch he could find.

Maybe this model didn't have a safety.

He debated quickly about the pro's and con's of leaving the gun uncocked, and decided he would likely be able to hear anyone opening the latch before they came in, so on balance with his earlier concern of accidental dick removal he concluded he would rather leave the gun, and not himself, uncocked.

Carefully, almost gingerly, Not put the gun into his pants pocket, and tried to decide what he should do next. He scanned the flashlight around himself, knowing he would see some unpleasant gore, and he was not disappointed. From about chest level up to the ceiling, the entire rear of the truck cab was a masterpiece from Jackson Pollock's worst nightmares.

Donny lay in the middle of the floor, but toward the rear of the truck, directly in front of the door, was the large blue barrel on a dolly, and the picnic cooler bomb.

Not recalled there was a phone or something in the cooler, but when Donny had tried to access it, Fedin had warned him it would set it off.

Then Fedin had given Donny his phone.

Not put the flashlight back on Donny. He didn't much relish the idea of looting a corpse, but neither did he like the idea of waiting to be shot, or blown up by the cooler thing, or maybe just arrested and charged with murder, along with grand theft, drug trafficking, and god knows what else.

Not knelt down beside the man who had caused so many problems in his life, including the current circumstances, but couldn't help feeling some pity for him.

Gently, Not patted down Donny's pockets and pulled out items when he found them. From the inside pockets of his jacket, Not found cigarettes and a lighter and ten thousand dollars in cash wrapped in plastic.

He set them both aside with little interest, as he did not smoke and the money would do him no good unless he got out of this situation alive and free.

The pants pockets were empty, but Not found a strange lump at Donny's middle. After untucking his shirt, Not discovered Donny had stashed more bundles of cash around his waist. It was too bad for Donny that Fedin hadn't shot him in the gut, as the cash would have likely absorbed the worst of the damage.

Ironically, he was also fairly certain Donny would have been aghast at the idea, as it would have meant the money would be ruined.

Not pulled the other stacks of cash out and laid them down with the first he had discovered. As he moved around to the side, Not noticed the cash girdle continued around the back as well and he would have to flip Donny to get them all.

Bracing himself both for the difficulty of having to move dead weight, and for the as of yet unseen horror, Not heaved on Donny's shoulder and hip and flipped him, a little more roughly than intended, onto his stomach. Not was able to rationalize his actions by taking comfort in the fact that at least Donny's legs were able to flip out to a less painful looking position.

On the floor, where Donny had been laying, was the phone.

"Donny?" A woman's voice called out from the phone. "I heard you move. Talk to me you son of a bitch, tell me you're not dead!"

Not picked up the phone, but just held it for a moment and felt his stomach sink. Was it his mother? Did he have to tell Donny's mother her boy was dead? Dear God, had he called his mother to say goodbye, and got shot while he was on the phone with her?

"Donny, you fucking cock-choking little shit, you answer me!"

Unsure whether it was the profanity or the tone of voice which made him move, Not knew there was nothing he could say which would be worse than what the silence was doing to whoever was on the other end of the phone.

"Um, hello?" Not tried.

"Who is this?" the voice swung from desperate to suspicious with a smoothness more intimidating than the tone itself.

"I'd rather not say," Not said cautiously, but added, "for now."

"Listen up, asshole," the voice grew more assertive. "I am a lawyer and I demand to speak to my client, Donovan Allen, right now or I will be on the phone with the police in ten seconds. Nine, eight, seven, six. . ."

"Donny's dead," Not blurted. "But calling the police sounds pretty awesome, actually. Could you do that for me, please? I tried earlier, but they're not here yet."

The phone hissed dead air for a moment that seemed to stretch on longer than the mere seconds that ticked by on the phone's display.

"He's dead?" she sounded close to tears. "Are you sure?"

"I'm locked in a box truck with his corpse, okay?" Not could hear in his voice that he was losing it, but in a way it felt so good to do so. "I just had to search his body to find this fucking phone, okay? The back of his head is gone, okay?"

"Shhhhh, alright? Shush," the lady said, sounding calm and composed once again. "I've got 911 on the other line, you're at the towing garage, right?"

"Yeah," Not felt relief at the mention of 911. "Alto's All-Tow on Railroad Avenue. I'm locked in a box truck, in garage bay number four. There are at least three other guys here, and I know one of them is armed. He said a bunch more are on the way."

"Shit," she sounded both scared and impressed. "Hold on, and I'll pass all that along."

Not waited for the woman, the lawyer, to come back on the line. From outside, he heard what sounded like gunfire, and wondered if Fedin had decided to simply shoot Josue and Alto the way he had Donny. The whip-crack pops continued on for over a minute though, way more than the revolver could have held, and the sounds were coming from the street, not the shop. For a hopeful moment, Not considered the possibility that the shots came from the police. Then he realized that if he could hear the shots, he would have heard the police identify themselves first and give them a chance to surrender.

Maybe Fedin's back up either turned on him or ran into trouble themselves.

Maybe Josue or Alto had another gun stashed somewhere.

He wondered if either one of those possibilities would increase his chances of coming out of this alive.

"Still there?" the lawyer had returned.

"Yeah, and hey," Not spoke hurriedly. "If the cops are still on the line, tell them the cocaine from the armored car is either here, or was sold by Paul Alto and Josue Viejo. A guy named Troy was also involved, but I don't think he matters anymore. The man who shot Donny is named Gregori Fedin, and he told me he has a DEA agent in his pocket, but, I don't know, that might be bullshit."

"Uh huh," said the lawyer, sounding like she was taking notes, which she probably was for all Not knew.

"Are you still on the line with the cops?"

"Sure am, hon," she said.

He had gone from "son of a bitch" to "hon" in about a minute.

"In the truck with me is Donny's body, the stolen barrel from the armored car, and a picnic cooler which is also some kind of bomb."

"Hon?"

"Yeah?" Not asked, trying to order the thoughts of what information he should share next.

"Can you tell me your name now?" the lawyer asked sweetly. "And, what is your role in all this?"

337

"Yeah," Not sighed. "My name is Harris Johnson, but I go by Not, and I had the bad luck to be driving the tow truck last night when Donny decided to rip off his own armored car."

"Okay, hold on," the lawyer said, and then Not could hear her relaying information to the police through another phone.

He sat and leaned back against the wall, and began stacking and restacking the bundles of cash with his free hand, simply because they were there. Each bundle was ten thousand dollars, and he had pulled one from Donny's pocket, and four more from his waistband. The value of the blocks had little draw for him over their use as a way to focus his attention on one small space in front of him, and let all the rest fade into the periphery.

He wondered if he was in shock.

He didn't feel particularly shocked, but more emotionally exhausted. Like, he wanted to be scared, or angry, or something, but he just didn't feel it.

Instead, he just sat in the dark and played with some blocks.

He stacked them up in a tower, then knocked it over. Then he tried to set them up like dominoes, but the edging of the plastic wrap wouldn't let the stack balance on the thin end. Not was trying to figure out if he could make a house of cards with just one hand, or if he would need to set the phone down, when the lawyer came back on the line.

"Are you there, Not?" she asked.

"Yep," Not said, holding two blocks of cash, pinched by their edges with one hand and he tried to get them to balance against each other to make a triangular arch.

"Okay, help is on the way," she assured him. "They already had a car on route, but now they are sending everything. They know where you are, and they are coming to get you, okay?"

"Okay," Not agreed.

"Is Donny really dead?" she asked after a pause.

"*Really* dead," Not affirmed.

"Shit," she said.

They didn't really have anything to say to each other after that, though neither one hung up the phone. They both just sat, listening to the other one breathing, and waiting for the sound of the police making themselves known.

"Did you check for a pulse?" the lawyer asked suddenly.

"No," Not admitted. "Fedin blew the top of his head off. I saw his skull."

The silence and waiting resumed. Not picked up a block of cash once more, but then set it back down.

"Skull or brain?"

"What?" Not asked.

"You could see his *skull*, or you could see his *brain*?" the lady lawyer pressed.

"His skull," Not shuddered a little at having to visualize it again.

"Check for a pulse!" the shout coming through so loud the phone speaker crackled.

"But-"

"Check for a pulse!" she insisted.

"Fine," Not gave in.

Using his free hand for balance, Not scooted his butt across the floor until he was next to Donny's body. He laid his hand on Donny's chest, but felt no heartbeat or breath. Knowing she would ask, Not gingerly slid his hand up Donny's chest until his palm rested on Donny's throat. He pressed two fingers against the still warm neck, just under the jaw.

"Holy shit."

Chapter 39

"COME ON out of there, son."

Topher sat back up in his seat and turned to look out of the driver's side window. One of the men in hunting gear, taller than the rest but skinnier too, held a rifle casually and comfortably, aiming it at Topher from the hip. Topher had no doubt, especially at the minimal distance between them, that the man would be able to shoot him easily.

Three of the others had already gone inside, and the fifth man had set his rifle against the front of the garage, and was dragging one of the two bodies inside.

"Come on out," the man repeated. "I'm not going to hurt you, but I can't have you running off to get the cops until our business is done here, alright?"

Topher cautiously raised his hands, and then slowly reached for the door handle.

"Listen, son, I get it, wrong place wrong time, all that, but I need you to put a little hustle on it, okay?" The man let the rifle go with one hand, and allowed the barrel to drop toward the ground. He pulled the car handle for Topher, and held the door open. "Get on inside and sit quietly in the corner, okay?"

Topher got out of the car, and considered trying for the gun. The tall guy was skinnier than Topher was, but he had at least a few inches of extra reach on him, and as Topher stepped out of the car, the tall man had turned his body away, holding the rifle at the furthest distance from Topher. There would be no way to make a grab for it without first broadcasting his intentions to do so through his body language, so Topher decided to just play it meek and compliant for now. He held his hands up, and allowed himself to be marched inside the waiting area of the garage.

The fifth man had dragged both bodies into the waiting area but had just left them in the middle of the floor. He had retrieved his rifle, and was standing off to the side and was pouring himself a cup of coffee from the waiting room guest station.

"You want a cup?" he called over his shoulder, Topher assumed to the tall guy.

"Nah, be up all night, if I start now," the tall man explained.

Topher could hear other voices talking from the room beyond. The conversation sounded fairly civil, though several of the voices talked over each other. It was like they hadn't just killed two people in cold blood just a minute or two before.

Maybe they did this kind of thing all the time, though Topher got the impression these guys were hobbyists at best. The hunting gear and rifles were just not practical for criminals in urban New Jersey. Also, when they spoke, they sounded country.

Not southern, just rural.

Still though, they killed those two guys pretty easily, and then got a cup of coffee. Topher decided he would do well to remember that.

"You wanna watch the door, or should I?" The tall man asked.

"I got it," the other man said. "Take him on in and see what the hell is going on, okay?"

"Can do," the tall man said, and then waved the rifle toward the door at the back of the room, indicating Topher should go through it.

The next room was larger, and better lit. It appeared to be a break room for the mechanics and tow truck drivers. There were tables and chairs, a refrigerator and a microwave, and a television which was on but muted. The far wall was lined with ten of the large five gallon gas cans, what Topher's dad used to call jerry cans.

Two men were seated at one of the tables: a man in camouflage like the others and sporting a serious set of mutton chop sideburns, and a heavyset older man in an expensive looking overcoat. The man with the sideburns had a rifle laid across the table, and the well-dressed fat man had a pistol on the table in front of him pointed at the man with the sideburns.

The two other men were standing against the wall, and divided their attention between the conversation at the table and the television on the wall. It was one of those game shows where contestants try to complete a ridiculously difficult obstacle course, so the lack of volume didn't really take away from their understanding of the program.

"Really, this is just wasting time we don't have," the man with the sideburns reasoned. "The cops are probably on their way--"

"And, whose fault is that?" the fat man inquired pointedly.

"Yours, you smug fat fucker," snapped the man with the sideburns. "We had a deal with those two outside, and you tried to cut in on our dance."

"I could say the same thing," he held his hands out palms up and moved them like a balance scale, as if to say who is to say who is right?

"Listen," Sideburns began again, with an easier tone. "I know I was Alto's first call, 'cause I'm always his first call. He lost ten grand at the casino, needs a loan tonight he tells me, and I say no problem. I know a guy. Needs a gun that can't come back on him? No, problem. I know a guy."

Sideburns paused for effect, then continued, "So, when he stumbles ass-backward over a fortune of coke and doesn't have a clue what to do with it? Hey, I say, no problem. I know some guys."

"Your point?" Fedin asked.

"We got dibs," Sideburns reasons.

Fedin dismissed this argument with a shrug.

So, again, Sideburns changed his tactics.

"Okay, so he tried to screw one of us, or both of us, or fuck it who cares? They're dead," he reasoned. "So, let's take care of us. We'll take the cash, you take the coke, and we all win, right?"

"No, not really," countered the fat man. "The police will be coming here soon. Someone will have heard those gunshots and reported them. With the police arriving, I will no longer be able to move the cocaine, as I had wished, so no thank you. You are welcome to take the cocaine, if you want it, and I will keep my money."

"If the cops get here, you won't get to keep it," the man with the sideburns said, trying a new strategy.

"Maybe yes, maybe no," the fat man reasoned. "But, I will not be going to jail. I am simply here as a customer. My truck is in the garage, after all. I just had the bad luck to walk into this whole mess."

"You always take a gun to pick up your truck?"

"This belonged to the late Mr. Alto," the fat man said smugly, lifting the pistol just a little. "I simply picked it up from where he dropped it, to defend myself, you understand, after he was gunned down in front of his own store. By a disgruntled employee, if I am not mistaken?"

"Shit, Troy," said the tall man behind Topher. "Let's just get the coke and get out of here. That was the original plan, right?"

"And it will take twenty years to sell it all, gram at a time out back behind your bowling alley, that's what you said, right John?"

"No, that's what *you* said, Troy," one of the men watching television groused. "*I* said we can't handle this, that it was way too big--"

"Johnny, shut the fuck up," Troy snapped. "You *never* had any balls."

The tall man behind Topher laughed, and all eyes turned toward him. He shifted uncomfortably for a minute before speaking.

"Cause he's got a bowling alley, see?" He looked around for understanding. "He's got a bowling alley, but never had any balls. It's funny 'cause it's ironic, you know?"

The man called Troy, he of the amazing sideburns, stared coldly at the tall man behind Topher for a moment, and then continued.

"Anyway, where were we?" he asked nobody in particular. "Oh right, yeah I do work here, which is why I'm not too worried about the cops. I don't think most of the folks in this neighborhood give much of a shit about anything, but the chance of them calling the cops is maybe fifty-fifty. So, yeah, they might be coming and if they do show up, well, my old friends and I were just heading out on a camping trip when we stumbled across my boss breaking the law. We tried to make a citizen's arrest, but he shot at us. We were able to hold the other guy though. Five words against one. Even better though, of course, would be if none of us were here when the cops showed up."

"One man's word can be enough if it is heard by the right people," the fat man shrugged.

Troy seemed to consider what the other man might mean by his fortune cookie response, but then seemed to shrug it off.

"Alright," Troy sounded as if he were about to give up. "I'll try one more time, tell me where the money is or one of my boys will put a round in you."

"Like I said, when we first sat down, I will shoot you before they can get a shot off," the fat man countered. "The cocaine is in the gas cans behind me. Take them and be gone."

Troy took in a deep breath and let it slowly out.

"Okay, John, Tim, you two start searching the place," Troy started to bark out commands, but was drowned out by the groans of the other men.

"Come on, Troy!"

"Let's just get the shit and go!"

"Yeah, man," said the tall man behind Topher. "I think we need to get moving. We're gonna get what we can and go. You can come with us if you want."

The two men seated at the second table seemed to take this last idea as a directive. They stood, shouldered their rifles, and then both walked over to the line of gas cans and each grabbed one can in each hand.

"Christ," groaned one. "I'm going to get a hernia."

"Don't be a pussy," huffed the other, though his face also showed the strain.

"I believe I have a handcart in the back of my truck," the fat man offered, smiling at Troy in smug victory. "The white box truck in the garage."

"I'll get it!" the tall man behind Topher volunteered, sounding eager to avoid lifting the cans unaided. Topher was not surprised. He doubted the man had enough muscle mass to even slide one of those cans, let alone lift it from the ground.

"Come on," he tapped Topher on the shoulder. Topher went along willingly. He figured he had a much better chance of getting the weapon away from the tall and skinny man if they were alone, and he definitely had a much better chance of not getting shot if he was away from all the other guys with guns.

Topher led the way into the garage, and spotted the large white box truck several stalls down, and backed into the garage. He felt his stomach jump into his throat.

That must be the truck Donny was in.

For fucks sake, he had forgotten all about Donny. In all the shooting and listening to all these people argue over the cocaine, which he had stolen in the first place, Topher had lost sight of why he had come back here in the first place.

Donny was locked in the back of the truck.

He had been shot.

He had also said he had three million dollars.

Topher felt a greasy wave of guilt spread over him at the last thought, but he could not deny it had been there.

The men in the break room were still looking for the money, and Topher guessed it was the three million that Donny had claimed to have. On the other hand, the fat guy in the nice coat had also said this was his truck, and if it was, and he was trying to hide the cash there, then why would he send them to get the handcart out of it?

Was Donny still in there?

On the phone, Topher had heard Donny tell someone it was his, and Topher had assumed the "it" was the money. Maybe it had been the coke? Had Donny been trying to get the money and keep the coke too? It sounded like something Donny would do, but it just didn't make sense.

None of this made sense.

Who the hell were these guys who dressed like weekend warriors? Who was the fat guy who seemed to have them all cowed, despite being outnumbered and outgunned?

The door in front of the truck was still rolled up. He wondered if he ran right now, would he be able to make it out before the man with the rifle could line up a shot? If he did, what about Donny?

Topher recognized that he was in way over his head on this, but he didn't think he could live with himself if he didn't at least try.

As he approached the back of the box truck, he decided he needed to focus on keeping the main thing the main thing. He would open the back of the truck. If Donny was in there, Topher would try to help him. If he wasn't, or if he was dead, Topher would try to make it out the door.

They stopped at the back of the truck. Topher saw the latch was held closed with a spring clip carabiner, the kind he had used as a keychain when he was in high school. He unclipped the carabiner and set it aside on the bumper, and then reached for the latch release.

"Hold up," the tall guy said behind him. "Take a couple steps off to the side there, okay? Here's what we'll do. I'm going to roll the door up and check out what's inside. If everything is cool, you're going to climb in and pass me down the handcart. Then, I'm going to close you up inside there. You got a cell phone?"

Topher nodded.

"Good. Once I close the door, you count to 100 and then call the cops to come get you, okay? I'll put a shot in the ceiling and tell them I dropped you and put you in the truck."

"Thank you," Topher said, genuinely touched this guy was trying to help him.

"Not your fault you're here, you know?" The tall guy said, as if it explained everything.

He rolled up the door, and Topher screamed as the man's chest exploded.

Chapter 40

"I HEAR somebody," Not whispered excitedly into the phone. "I think maybe the cops are here."

"Hold on," the lawyer stated, and then added, "don't do anything yet."

The hollow silence returned to Not's ear as the lawyer put the phone down once more to return to the other line. Not realized she still must have the 911 operator on the phone.

It made sense, he supposed, as the police would want to have updates from the inside, if possible, before entering the building.

It dawned on him that there were two complete strangers sitting on the phone, coordinating an effort to save his life. A strong wave of gratitude washed over him and he hoped he would have a chance to say thank you to the woman on the other end of the line.

"Hide," she said when she returned, her voice straining for calm. "The police are still in transit. They are not in the building."

"Shit," Not mumbled, and fumbled the gun from his pocket. "What do I do about Donny?"

"Check his pulse again," she said after a pause. "Is he steady?"

Not put the gun on the floor beside him and pressed his fingers once more to Donny's neck. The beat he felt before was still there, and still steady.

Blood still oozed from the edges of his remaining scalp, and the bullet had left a crease in his skull when it had liberated most of Donny's skin and hair from the top of his head as it went, but Donny was, and seemingly continued to be, alive and stable.

"Same as before," Not reported.

"Then they'll probably still think he's dead," she said, and then repeated, "hide."

Not picked up the gun again and moved away from Donny.

There was really nowhere to hide except for behind the barrel, which lay on its side, strapped to the dolly, directly in front of the rolling door. Not lay himself across the floor on his right side, the barrel against his belly, and extended both of his arms across the bottom of the barrel, holding the gun just inches from the middle of the door. The latch was in the bottom center, so whoever opened it would be standing right there, maybe a foot beyond.

He pulled back the slide, as he had seen so many action heroes do in the movies, and once more readied his only shot.

He had never fired a gun before, but he knew enough to know it would kick back when he fired, so he would have to brace himself. He also knew a .45 was one of the largest handgun bullets out there, so he should be ready for the gun to nearly tear his arm off.

Even if the gun kicked like hell, Not would still be likely to hit the person, as he would be firing nearly point blank.

He had no idea what he would do about whoever the person had been talking to, maybe throw the gun at him and run. It was the best idea he could come up with, and there was no time to think of another. The latch rattled as it was undone, and Not focused at the few feet of space where the man would be when the door opened.

The next moment happened faster than Not could follow, just flashes of information registered before he fired.

The door flew up, and he was flooded in brightness.

There was a man he had never seen before.

He had a gun.

Not swung his arms up just a little, bringing the pistol in line with the man's chest, and then he pulled the trigger.

There was an eruption of red.

And then Not was on his feet and leaping over the barrel.

He landed on the body of the man he had just shot and lost his footing, landing in a sprawl next to the body. Looking up, he saw the other man was standing directly in front of him.

Not tried to throw the gun at him, but from his knees he could only manage to fling it forward from across his body, so it ended up being more of a half-hearted toss, which the other man caught easily.

Pushing himself backwards, Not scuttled like a crawdad across the body, and then pushed himself to his feet and ran directly away from the other man.

This was panic.

Not's senses seemed to have gone haywire. He could feel his heart pounding in his chest, physically thudding against his sternum so hard it hurt, but could not feel himself breathing.

He was suddenly very aware that his ears were hot, but the muscles of his thighs felt rubbery and weak. He stumble-ran away from the second man, what his mind could register as an immediate threat, but he could not focus on where he should go.

He started towards the door which lead to the break room, then remembered he had left the garage door open so he should run there instead.

He turned to go back.

He took two steps back the way he had just come and saw the second man standing there, holding the gun. Forgetting it was the same empty gun he had just thrown at him, Not turned back to run toward the break room once more.

He burst through the door of the break room, saw there were two men sitting at the table, and one of them had a pistol on the table in front of him. One of the men was half-risen, Not recognized him as Troy, and the other seated man, who Not now recognized as Fedin, merely smiled and watched him as he bolted past.

Without breaking stride, he turned and made it to the door to the waiting area. Wrenching the door open, Not ran toward the outer door, the door to the street, the door to freedom, before tripping over the two bodies sprawled across the floor and collapsed on top of them both.

"Now, who the fuck is this?"

Not lifted his head, pulling his face from the legs of yet another dead man.

The street door to the shop had been opened by two more men, both dressed in camouflage, and both had hunting rifles slung over their shoulders.

"Isn't that the kid who dropped the truck off earlier today?"

"Oh, for fuck's . . . has he been here the whole time?"

"How the hell should I know?" the shorter bald man whined. "Troy said the place was empty after five."

"This is just an absolute cluster fuck," said man who had spoken first. "We should just cut bait now with what we have."

"What about Hank and Troy?"

They both seemed to consider for a moment, and then their faces seemed to fall with the understanding that it wouldn't be right to leave without their friends. A third man, also in camouflage and complete with rifle, trotted up behind them from the street.

"What's going on?" He asked.

"I called the cops," Not said, although unsure why he was saying it. "They'll be here any second."

The three men shared a look and then turned back toward the street. The most recent to arrive called back over his shoulder.

"Cops are on the way, Troy!" he bellowed. "Grab Hank and the shit and go! We're gonna get gone!"

"We'll meet you later!" the bald man called as the door to the street swung shut.

Not was unable to right himself without pushing against the body directly below him. As he gained his feet, he realized he had been lying on top of the corpses of Alto and Josue.

He felt a pang at their deaths, despite the fact that they had been willing to let him go to jail so they could try to get rich. An opportunity had fallen into their laps. Maybe on any other night, they would have done the right thing, but maybe they saw this as a way to set things right between them for good. From what Josue had told him, Alto almost certainly saw it that way.

Money atoned.

For their faults, they had been decent guys. He had liked them both. He certainly didn't think they had deserved to die.

Likely, neither had the man he had just shot.

The weight of what he had just done a few minutes before now came crashing down on him. The man in the garage, he hadn't deserved to die either, but Not had just killed him.

He had killed a man.

His stomach and bowels seemed to liquefy, his knees went wobbly, and for a moment Not was pretty sure he was about to collapse into a pile of his own vomit while, in an amazing feat, simultaneously shitting himself.

"Where the hell were you hiding?" Troy's voice spoke up from behind him.

"Box truck," Not croaked, still trying to hold the contents of his stomach down while also willing his ass to remain clenched, he had no further focus to spare for either a lie or a witty retort.

"Why?" Troy sounded genuinely curious.

"Fedin locked me in after he shot Donny."

"Who's Donny?"

"He and Topher stole the cocaine from the armored car," Not said, and then dry heaved.

"Who's Topher?"

Not avoided answering by vomiting all over the corpse of his former employer.

While he struggled through the pinching grip of his stomach spasms, the face of the other man outside the box truck clicked into focus.

It had been Topher.

How and when Topher had gotten here, Not had no idea, nor did he have the inclination to think about it at this time, as his battle to keep himself closed at both ends came close to losing on both fronts.

"Jesus, kid," Troy said with undisguised disgust. "Get back in here. Get yourself together for Christ's sake."

Troy shouldered the rifle, and grabbed Not under his arm and helped him to his feet. As soon as Not was stable, Troy brought the rifle back down and made it clear that Not did not have a choice in the matter.

Back in the break room, the revolver remained on the table, but Fedin was gone. Not's phone had been put on the table next to the pistol.

Troy turned slowly from the doorway and carefully scanned the room, keeping the rifle pointed in front of him and ready to fire, but Fedin was not anywhere to be seen in the room.

Troy waved Not to the empty table, where Not gratefully collapsed into one of the chairs.

Crossing the room quietly, Troy glanced back at Not to make sure he was seated away from both the phone and the gun, then he pushed open the door to the late Mr. Alto's office, and checked for Fedin there.

Satisfied that Fedin was not trying to ambush them, Troy turned back to Not.

"Did you call the cops?"

Not, not trusting to open his mouth for fear the vomit would begin to flow anew, simply nodded.

"How long since you called?"

Not held up five fingers, then wobbled his hand in a more or less gesture.

"About five minutes?" Troy sounded a little relieved. "Alright, I still have time then."

He shouldered the rifle once more and walked over to the wall where four of the big five-gallon metal gas cans stood against the wall. He grabbed a handle in each hand, and turned back toward Not.

"I sent a guy in there to get a handcart from the truck you were in," Troy said quietly. "Was that the shot I heard? Is he dead?"

Not met Troy's eyes, and then nodded.

Troy studied Not's face for a moment, and then nodded as well.

"Figured as much when I saw you coming through like a spooked deer," Troy confided. "Too bad. He and I go way back."

Not said nothing, but he did not look away.

"Just sit there and wait for the cops, got it?" Troy asked. "If you try to follow me out with the peashooter on the other table, and I will put you down, you hear me?"

Not just nodded. He felt sick and numb.

"That fat prick is around here somewhere, so if you want to use it on somebody . . ."

Troy offered a small shrug, his intent clear in his gesture, though his arms were weighed down with the gas cans.

Troy disappeared through the door to the waiting area, and a moment later Not heard the door to the street open and slam closed.

Not put his head on the table, and enjoyed the coolness of the tabletop against his cheek and forehead. The police would be here soon, he reassured himself. He had no idea what would happen after they arrived, but he was alive and the police would be here soon. For now, it was enough for him to be able to rest for a moment.

A phone began to ring.

Not raised his head and looked at his phone on the other table, next to the shiny silver revolver. The screen of the phone was lit up, and an old fashioned icon of the phone receiver waggled back and forth to indicate a call was incoming.

Not tried to will himself to ignore it, but found the need to answer a ringing phone overpowered even extreme nausea and exhaustion.

Heaving himself out of the chair, he stumbled the few feet between the two tables and collapsed again with great relief into the new chair. Not swept a finger across the screen to answer, but didn't bother to pick up the phone. Instead, he tapped his thumb against the speaker icon, and laid his forehead back against the gloriously cool table top.

"Are you in position?" A voice called from the phone.

"Huh," Not's response was muffled by the proximity of his mouth to the table surface.

"We are arriving on-scene now, no lights or sirens. Locals will be ready to breach in thirty. Are you in position?"

"Um, who is this?" Not asked, sitting up in the chair and staring at the screen.

"Shit."

The phone went silent, and a message appeared on screen reading "Caller has Disconnected."

Not heard the door to the street slam open, and seconds later, Police in riot gear burst into the room. Not watched the door in amazement as they just kept coming in, one after another. All of them were shouting as they ran to fill the room:

"Police!"

"Don't Move!"

"Get to the truck."

"Don't Move!"

"Hostage is in the truck!"

"Police! Don't move!"

The fifth or sixth man through the door was not dressed in riot gear, but had a bullet proof vest over his dress shirt and slacks. Large gold lettering on the front of the vest read DEA.

He headed directly towards Not, and raised a shotgun.

"Gun!" he shouted.

Not saw the flames burst from the end of the gun as he felt his chest implode.

Chapter 41

HIS HEAD hurt.

There had been a loud noise.

Donny opened his eyes, registered that the light was bright enough to hurt, so he closed them again.

He was pretty sure, from the feel of the floor against his back, that he was still in the back of the truck but now the flashlight was gone.

Fedin had shot him.

He moved his arms slowly, mostly to see if he could, and discovered they responded just as he hoped they would. Gingerly, he felt along his chest and groin, and everywhere else he could touch without moving his aching head.

Everything appeared to still be attached and was free of bullet holes.

With apprehension, he let his right hand carefully move up to head. He slid his finger up his forehead, gritting his teeth against the increasing pain until it suddenly stopped at his hairline.

Or, rather, where his hairline used to be.

Now, all his finger felt was a hard, smooth but slightly textured surface, like a wet slate tile.

He continued to explore with his finger, finding the edges of the pain that continued around his forehead, each ending with the hard, smooth, and numb area of his head.

It slowly dawned on him that he was touching his own skull.

He let his arms collapse to his sides once more.

THE TRUCK was bouncing. Donny could hear voices but not register what they were saying.

Topher?

It had sounded like Topher, but now it sounded more like Fedin.

Donny opened his eyes slightly, squinting against the bright light from the open door of the truck. The round shape in front of him, near the entrance almost certainly had to be Fedin.

He was talking to someone outside of the truck.

Something was handed up to him, long, like a cane but fatter.

The truck bounced as Fedin moved around. He laid the fat cane down next to Donny, and moved further into the truck where he retrieved something from the floor.

Donny's head nearly split in half from the clatter of the door being rolled down once more.

He let his hand creep over to where the fat cane had been lain, and gently slid his palm over the object.

He found a trigger.

Not a cane.

A rifle.

There was noise coming from outside of the truck now.

Crashing and shouting.

Gunshots.

From inside the truck, Donny heard Fedin hitting buttons on the phone, each giving a slightly different electronic shriek which seemed to somehow push shards of glass into his brain.

Fedin's footsteps slowly rocked the truck once more as he approached the rolling door, his phone call now apparently complete.

He was near Donny's feet.

On the same side as the rifle.

Donny closed his eyes in the darkness and focused all his energy and effort on his arm.

He gripped the rifle tight, and used the shoulder brace as a fulcrum to lever the rifle barrel upward.

He wanted the head, and tried to estimate what the proper angle would be to kill Fedin.

His arm began to tremble from the exertion.

The veins at his temples throbbed and he could feel fresh trickles of blood begin to flow down around and over the tops of his ears.

The barrel of the rifle pushed against something.

Something soft.

"Good enough," Donny mumbled.

The sound of the shot, in the enclosed space, slammed into Donny, an invisible tidal wave, and the pain erupted once more through his head washing Donny again into the blackness.

Chapter 42

TOPHER LOOKED again into his rearview mirror.

Thirty seconds later, he would have been surrounded by police.

He made the turn onto Passaic, but it was a large and busy street, and his passenger window was still shattered. He felt conspicuous, so he turned left at the first chance he got. He pulled into the parking lot of a restaurant, and pulled around to the back where he hoped he would not be noticed.

Leaving the engine running, he reached down and pulled the trunk release. He would use the tire iron from his trunk to knock out the rest of the shattered glass, and scrape as much of it as he could from the car seat. It might be unusual to drive with the windows down in the middle of winter, but it wasn't illegal. It would also attract less attention, or so he hoped, than would a shattered window which contained what could only be a bullet hole in its center.

Walking quickly to the trunk, Topher glanced into the backseat and the cooler there. He felt the loose stacks of bills in his pockets, and reminded himself to add those in with the rest. It would be a good idea to ditch the bloody shirt that still held them as well.

He shook his head in disbelief at what had just happened.

First, the guy from the holding cell, Not, had come bursting out of the truck, tossed him a gun, and had taken off with all the composure of a kid who had just broken his neighbor's window.

Topher had watched him go for a second or so, then returned to the truck to check on Donny.

He hadn't had much hope when he had seen the far wall of the truck, but he had gone in to investigate anyway. Donny's body lay off to the side toward the back, from where the blood had pooled, Topher could tell that the body had been moved for some reason, but it didn't change the fact that Donny looked very dead.

He had tried to prepare himself for this outcome on the drive over, but how do you prepare for the fact that a man with whom you had once shared every intimacy now lay dead in front of you.

Sure, Donny could be an absolute son of a bitch, but he had also been sweet, and funny, and loving.

Topher had felt tears beginning to well, and had looked away.

Then he had spotted the bundles of cash stacked next to the body, and Topher had let his instincts take over.

He grabbed the cash, five bundles in all, and stuffed it into the deep pockets of his winter coat. He stood and had meant to say something, a goodbye of some kind, to Donny when the man had spoken up behind him.

"Are you Topher?"

He turned to find a fat and well-dressed man standing on the ground at the rear of the truck, looking up at him with a grim expression of pity. Topher cocked the gun and held it where it could be seen, though he knew from its appearance when he caught it that it held no more bullets.

"This is the rest of the money," the man had held up a bundle which appeared to have been fashioned out of Donny's work shirt. Part of it was soaked in blood. "I believe he intended to split it with you."

Topher had moved to take the shirt from him, but the man instead took a step to the side to where a large cooler rested at the rear of the truck. He opened the lid and stuffed the bundle inside.

"This will make it easier to carry," he explained. Then he struggled to get up into the truck. Topher almost wanted to offer a hand, but he was too afraid to let his guard down.

Instead, he had continued to brandish the empty gun unwilling to call his own bluff.

"Would you please hand me the rifle from the ground there?"

Topher looked at the dead hunter and slowly shook his head.

"Please," the man asked. "You have the money. I merely want to be able to defend myself, you understand. Should they return before the police get here."

"Hold it by the barrel and lay it on the floor," Topher conceded.

"Agreed."

Topher knelt down next to the dead hunter, squatting so as not to take his eyes off the man in the truck. He lifted the gun and offered it barrel first, and the man immediately lay it down on the floor of the truck as he had promised.

"Take the money, now, and go," the heavy older man said, once he had regained his feet. "Our business is done. I have friends coming for me soon, you understand. I will wait here. It will be safest, I think."

Topher had nodded as if he understood, but in reality he had not a clue what had been happening. He had, however, understood that the cooler was full of money, and that Donny had been telling the truth and was going to split it with him. He had felt a horrible twist of guilt at every terrible thought he had ever had about the sweet, stupid, sometimes shitty, sometimes sexy, little fucker had to go and get himself killed.

"Did you happen to find a phone when you were in here?" the man had asked.

Topher had scanned the floor, the other man doing the same, and had spotted an old flip phone wedged under the edge of the blue barrel.

"There," Topher had said, and pointed with his free hand.

"Ah, yes," the man had said but made no move to retrieve it.

"Would you close the door for me?" the man had called from behind the barrel. "I think the others have gone, but better safe than sorry, you understand."

Topher did not understand in the slightest, but this man had just given him an entire cooler full of money, payment for the cocaine he had helped to steal to be sure, but also as compensation for the death of his friend, or so he could not help but feel.

Closing the door behind himself had seemed the least he could do.

The truck door had rattled down and closed with a bang. The latch had swung around and clasped into place, and

Topher had considered unlatching it again, so the man could get out if he wanted to, but had reasoned that if he had friends to the way, they could let him out just as easily. In the meantime, Topher wouldn't have to worry about some kind of double-cross coming from behind.

Trailing the cooler behind him like a redneck carry-on, Topher had crept up the side of the truck to the open garage door, and leaned his head just a little outside. Three men in camouflage were running away from the front door, headed to the other side of the railroad tracks where the line of old trucks and muscle cars sat waiting. Foggy exhaust floated up from two of the trucks and the older of the two muscle cars.

They had not looked back toward the building, so Topher had felt safe in creeping out of the door and trotting down the front of the building to where his car still sat. A trot was all he could manage, with the weight of the cooler tugging at his balance.

He had reached his car as the trucks and cars across the street rumbled and farted their way into motion. A mixed set of headlights, illuminated the southbound side of Railroad Avenue, and by the time Topher had the cooler secured in the back seat of his car, three had been gone.

Climbing into the driver's seat, he had jammed the key into the ignition and had been about to turn it when the door to garage had swung open once more, and the guy with the sideburns had hustled out carrying two more gas cans.

Topher held his breath, holding his hand on the ignition but not turning, and waited to see if he would be spotted.

Sideburns had hardly glanced in his direction, though, but had instead simply followed his friends tracks through the snow, across the railroad tracks which Topher had crossed himself the night before, hauling the incredibly heavy barrel, not even yet knowing what it had contained, but simply knowing it had been a lot of trouble to steal so it had to be worth it.

After all, Donny had said so.

Topher glanced in the rearview mirror at the cooler in his backseat, and decided Donny had not been wrong.

When the old guy in the camo was safely on the other side of the tracks, Topher cranked the engine to life, and hit the gas. The guy may be old, but he still had a rifle, and Topher had witnessed first-hand what the old guy and his friends could do with them.

The first police car had turned the corner behind him when he was approaching Passaic. Topher hadn't been able to see if the old guy had gotten away too, and in all honesty he really hoped he hadn't.

Whatever beef the men in camouflage had had with the two men who had come out of the building, those two men had been unarmed.

The guys with the rifles had just cut them down where they stood.

Maybe they had done the same to Donny, or maybe it had been the guys who had been shot down in front of his car. If so, good riddance to all of them.

May they all rot in jail or in hell.

Or maybe first one and then the other.

Whatever, Topher thought, dealer's choice.

He was on his way to Florida.

Topher retrieved the lug wrench from his trunk and opened the passenger door. He knocked the broken glass from the frame, and then used the wrench and the sleeve of his jacket to sweep what little glass remained on the seat to join the rest of the glittering pile on the ground.

He tossed the wrench on the seat, and slammed the passenger door shut.

Returning quickly to the driver's side, Topher got in and cranked the heat to maximum. It would still be a cold ride, but he needed to put some miles between himself and the debacle back at the garage.

Shit, he realized he forgot to put the loose stacks of money in the cooler.

He'd need gas soon enough. He could do it then.

He found his way to the turnpike and headed south.

Turning on the radio, Topher punched through all of his presets, settled on a station, and listened for about ten seconds before switching the radio back off.

He wasn't in the mood for music.

Keeping a close eye on his speed, Topher made sure to keep to a middle lane, and not go noticeably faster or slower than the rest of the traffic around him. He considered just heading for the airport, dumping the car in long-term parking, and buying a ticket for Miami. However, he would have a hard time explaining why his only carry on was filled with money.

A lot of money.

Certain to send up some red flags.

Topher heard the electronic chirp of a cell phone ringing, but it wasn't a ringtone he recognized.

He scanned around the footwell on the passenger side, and tried to remember the last time he had given someone a ride, or any other reason why he would have a stranger's cell phone in his car.

He felt the heat before he smelled the smoke.

From the rearview mirror he discovered the cooler had somehow caught fire.

Not just on fire, but a burning block of bright red flame. The redness of the fire was exemplified by the yellow orange flames which surrounded it when the upholstery of the back seat ignited around it.

Topher swerved towards the side of the road, but the lane was blocked by another car. Topher hit the brakes, to try to swerve in behind it, but the car behind him bumped into his rear end, when they were unable to slow as quickly as he did.

He felt as his car began to fishtail, and he fought to regain control, which was an extra difficult task as he was fighting to keep control of himself at the same time.

He could feel the heat through the back of the driver's seat, and he was pretty sure it too had now begun to burn.

If he wasn't careful, the backend would swing too far out and the car would roll, and then the cooler, the burning block of brimstone that it had become, would pinball around through the car and any chance he had at survival would be gone.

Of course, the fire was burning right above the gas tank as well, so if he didn't get out of the car soon, the heat would reach the tank and . . .

Topher felt the rear end start to swing again toward the shoulder of the road, so he turned the wheel into the skid. Miraculously, he felt the car come back under control, and he quickly guided it toward the side and the biggest snowbank he could see.

His back was definitely burning now, though he could not tell if his clothes or hair were actually on fire, or if he heat was burning him through his clothes.

He gripped the wheel tightly and leaned forward as far as he could while maintaining control.

He smelled his hair burning.

The heat surrounded him, and the skin of his back from the crack of his ass to the nape of his neck screamed in agony.

He reached the side of the turnpike, other cars had slowed or stopped entirely, though no one was approaching the inferno. Topher clawed at the release of his seat belt with one hand, and the door handle with the other.

From a distance, he could hear sirens approaching.

Topher blindly felt the door handle with the tips of his fingers on his left hand, his eyes forced shut by the burning glare and toxic air around him, while his right still frantically flopped around in search of the seat belt release.

His left hand found the handle.

The door beside him swung open, which brought both a blessedly fresh and cold burst of air, which washed over him and filled his lungs with clean and revitalizing air.

Unfortunately, the fire in the back seat needed the oxygen with the same desperation he did, and it roared higher and hotter after its first deep breath.

The seatbelt still held him firm across the lap as the fire sucked the cold air in.

His thumb found the seat belt release catch.

The fire, glutted on oxygen, flared up. The whole interior of the car was now a writhing mass of flames.

The gas tank ruptured, and the entire car ceased to be.

Chapter 43

IT HURT to breathe.

It also hurt to shift, to reach, to talk, or even to sit still and simply to continue to exist.

Mostly, though, it hurt to breathe.

Among his list of injuries the doctor rattled off at him when he was conscious and cogent enough to attempt a dialogue, were: a cracked sternum, separation of two of the ribs from the sternum -- which had required emergency surgery to reattach, lest the ribs shift downward and puncture the lungs and or heart -- myocardial contusion -- which was translated for him to mean that his heart was bruised -- and one of his lungs had partially collapsed and had needed to be re-inflated.

The bean bag round, though considered technically non-lethal, when taken directly to the chest in close quarters, had come extremely close to killing him. In fact, as he had flatlined for about ten seconds in the ambulance, it *had* killed him, if only briefly.

His father had been in the room when he had first woken up, though Not had been unable to speak with him then, as a ventilator tube had still been down his throat. He had only been conscious for a few minutes, long enough to see his dad smile and cry, before he had sunk back into blackness.

Dad had returned every day, and Not had been able to speak with him, sort of, the next time he had woken. They had removed the ventilator while he slept.

He had memories of others coming as well, though he couldn't say when of for how long, or if the memories were even real.

Mrs. Alto had stopped by, with flowers, and told Not how sorry she was this had happened. Paul was dead, she had informed him, so now she owned Alto's.

365

"I'll be honest, though," Mrs. Alto confided. "I can't drive. A car, of course, but despite being around these trucks for years, I can't drive or operate them."

She had paused to watch his reaction, or lack thereof, and seemed to take his non-response for encouragement.

"And, I am not going to learn," she declared. "I got American Eagle to finish out our week, so we've got just over a month until our next rotation."

Not had wanted to say thank you, but he thought it was time to consider a change of careers. This one just didn't seem to agree with him.

However, all he had been able to manage at the time was a raspy croak.

"I'm going to make you a proposal," she again seemed to take his silence for consent. "Keeping the Peterbilt running around the clock is wasteful, both on gas and man hours. Most of the drags from the turnpike can be handled by a standard truck, but when we need the big one then we really need it. So, my proposal is this: during the municipal contract week, you stay on site at the office. On call, like a firefighter or a doctor, and you be ready to roll when the call comes in. You'll work the midnight to eight shift, but you'll stay on the clock for the other two. I'll pay you cash for the shift you work, and equity for the other two."

Not managed another raspy croak.

"I've run the numbers," she pressed on. "With the two on call shifts as overtime, you'll be fifty percent owner, a full partner, in just over six years. You'll own the shop entirely, assuming regular pay raises, in just over ten."

Even if he could have spoken, Not did not know what to say.

"Then, I'll either retire, or, if I'm not ready yet," she smiled, "I can stay on in the same capacity, but as an employee."

Not managed a raspy grunt. Mrs. Alto seemed to interpret it as "why?"

"Well, because I need you to run the big guy, as I said," she answered. She paused and seemed to gather the words to explain something that she was not too sure of herself.

"Because Josue seemed to trust you. Because Paul seemed to trust you. Because you had every reason to run like hell over the last two days, but you stuck it out. Because it seems like the right thing to do."

She stood to leave.

"I've had the paperwork drawn up, and I left it with your lawyer. She's looking it over now. I've also spoken with your doctor and he thinks you'll be cleared to return to work just in time for our next turn in the barrel."

She ran the last few words again through her head and winced at the poorly timed idiom.

"Anyway," she pushed on. "Get better soon, partner."

KARKUS HAD been in almost as often as his father, who came daily for hours at a time, whether Not was awake or not.

Not had wanted to tell them both there was no point in sitting over him sleeping.

When he tried, he just gurgled and gasped.

His father sat and squeezed his hand.

Karkus sat and texted.

Eventually, his dad seemed to figure out the times he was most often awake, and would try to time his visits for then. Karkus, Not noted, did the same, as there was rarely a time he was awake which one or both of them were not there.

Every time he woke, Dad would smile.

Karkus always had news.

"The police are calling him a rogue agent," Karkus had informed him one afternoon. The bright pure white of the winter sun on snow poured in through the window and caused him to squint as he spoke. "The DEA are saying nothing, pending the outcome of their own investigation. However, it appears from several reports that Agent Sokolov immediately targeted you and tried to play it off as a righteous shooting."

As it turned out, almost dying from a beanbag round had actually been very lucky. According to police statements after the fact, Sokolov had shown up just moments before the police entered the building, already wearing his body armor, and had grabbed the shotgun from the trunk of a local PD cruiser, left open as a local cop had been retrieving his own gear.

The cop had not been intending to bring the shotgun, as he knew it was loaded with beanbag rounds, but had not been able to alert Sokolov, as the agent had simply grabbed the gun and ran for the door as the others had been breeching.

The officer instead alerted the commander in charge on-scene of what had happened, and Sokolov had been tackled by other officers moments after firing the round.

"DEA isn't saying much," Karkus shrugged as if this was to be expected. "Yet, anyway. The feel I'm getting from this is they're testing the water. They're trying out the angle that, since the whole matter began as a DEA investigation, Sokolov had acted within the boundaries of his authority."

"He tried to assassinate him!" Not's dad had spat the word in disgust.

"That is one way to see it," Karkus demurred, using his best lawyer voice. "And, it is the view with which I happen to agree, but on their side is some evidence which can cloud things for a jury. Not was in close proximity to a gun, alone in a room, several dead bodies strewn about, and completely unguarded despite having reported he was being held as a captive . . ."

Not fell back asleep as they talked.

THE NEXT day, they both returned, and the conversation continued.

Karkus opined that the whole thing stunk of being swept under a rug.

"Why can't we sue?" Not's father had demanded, and not for the first time.

"I didn't say 'can't,'" corrected Karkus. "I said 'shouldn't.' At least, not yet. If you push hard now, they will have to push back. They are making no noise at all about trying to bring charges against Not in all this-"

"Because he didn't *do* anything," his father snapped.

"Didn't do it and found not guilty are vastly different things," Karkus snapped back. "And, for the record, yes, your son *did* do it. He transported cocaine, he participated in a conspiracy to sell cocaine, and, oh yeah, he may have *shot a guy*!"

They all sat silently for a moment.

Despite it all, Not felt drowsy.

"Anyway," Karkus said at last, "I said not yet. Let them build their house of cards before we start huffing and puffing about damages."

With that, Not dozed off once more.

GREGORI FEDIN, who had turned out to be a mattress salesman of all things, had been rescued by the police after he had been found locked in the back of the box truck, and had been transported immediately to the same hospital as Not.

He had been shot in the ass, which apparently wasn't as funny as it sounded.

The bullet had been from a larger caliber hunting rifle, and had shattered the left side of Fedin's pelvis. He was arrested as soon as he was out of surgery, as Troy and his confederates had been found at a truck stop just over the Pennsylvania state line.

The cocaine was discovered in gas cans distributed throughout their vehicles.

Troy had been quick to throw Fedin under the bus, and, Karkus had been extremely pleased to point out, had not included Not in any role in the buying or selling of the cocaine.

"However," Karkus had also been quick to point out, "you are still yet to be free and clear. Neither Fedin nor Troy are taking the blame for any of the bodies in the garage, but both sides were very quick to blame the other for *all* of the dead."

Not raised his eyebrows and tried to point to himself.

"Initial reports," Karkus informed him, "seemed to conclude that both sides are full of shit."

Fedin's clothing had tested positive for gunpowder residue, including a considerable amount on his glove, indicating he had likely fired a gun, rather than just have been in the vicinity of one being fired.

The bullets recovered from the bodies of Josue and Alto appeared to match those of the hunting rifles of Troy and his confederates, though the police were still testing the ballistics to make sure.

The bullet which came out of Fedin's ass appeared to have come from the rifle found lying next to Donny, who appears to have shot Fedin.

Donny, who also occupied a bed somewhere in the same hospital, had yet to regain consciousness. Comatose, Karkus had explained, but not a vegetative state. The doctors were confident that Donny would recover.

Not was still amazed Donny was alive.

Fedin's bullet, Not had been told, appeared to have ricocheted off of Donny's thick skull, but had taken nearly all of his scalp along with it. When Donny had been rushed to the hospital, no one had taken the time to locate his scalp, so by the time is was found by Crime Scene Investigation the next day it was no longer able to be reattached.

Apparently, though, the skin grafts had been going well.

Not had been in emergency surgery to reattach his ribs when all of this had been happening, was washed and sterilized in the process, so the police had not bothered to check him for gunpowder, despite the fact that Troy claimed Not had shot his friend. Since Troy had previously claimed Fedin had killed everyone there, he had lost some credibility in his accusations.

Karkus said, "the current view is the rednecks killed Alto and Viejo and the Russian killed the redneck and attempted to kill your friend in the truck."

Not had tried, and failed, to say Donny was not his friend.

Karkus advised Not, "you should be disinclined to correct that point of view."

The discovery of Not's cell phone in the breakroom was the biggest blessing for which Not could have hoped. The recording he had made of the conversation between himself and Fedin had actually come out remarkably well, and Fedin had actually been visible a couple of times on the video.

In it he had given the police an excellent narrative of the crime.

Fedin's lawyer was claiming the recording was taken without his client's knowledge, and was therefore inadmissible in court, which Karkus said may or may not be true.

"It will depend a lot on the judge and how the media reacts to the trial when it starts," Karkus explained.

However, the recording had been enough for a judge to grant a search warrant for Fedin's business, which had revealed a number of other issues for Fedin, not the least of which was the injury of a police officer who had tried to access Fedin's computer, which had apparently exploded. This prompted the police to bring in the bomb squad to sweep the building, and several more explosive devices were found.

Along with a staggering amount of money and illegal pharmaceuticals.

Currently, Fedin was beginning to drop hints that he would trade his testimony against an unnamed corrupt DEA agent, whom everyone was assuming to be Sokolov, in return for a reduced sentence.

"They have the drugs, and they have plenty of bad guys to lay the blame on," Karkus had said. "You are still listed as a person of interest, but to be honest, I don't think they can figure out your role in any of it. If they had the money too, it would be a done deal, but . . ."

"What about Topher?" Not had croaked.

"Christopher Mason's car burned, just a few miles from the garage, on the 17 South," Karkus stated. "The fire department emptied a whole tanker on it, and they couldn't put out the blaze. They just had to let it burn down to nothing. They found that a large amount of magnesium had been placed in the car, right above the gas tank. No money, or body, was found, but I spoke to one of the firemen who had been on scene, and he said the car was like a doorway to hell. It burned white hot at its core for a while."

Not did not want to speak again, and it was too painful to shrug, so he just stared at Karkus until the lawyer continued.

"It's possible, at least the fireman says it's possible, that the money and his body could have just been cremated in the blaze," Karkus concluded.

He did not look convinced.

"But," Not had whispered, trying to use extreme economy on his words.

"There were a lot of witnesses," Karkus shrugged. "Who said they saw the driver of the car make it out and take off over the embankment. Though, they all agree he wasn't carrying anything."

"So," Not whispered, wishing Karkus would just get to the point.

"So, if I were trying to get away with millions of dollars," Karkus said, as if pointing out the obvious, "I might try to fake my own death as well. If I were partnering with someone who got away with millions of dollars, I might just sit there to calmly be a distraction while the police came bursting through the door, keeping them occupied as my partner made off with said millions . . ."

"No," was all Not could muster.

"Gotta admit, though," Karkus pressed, "it's one of the only motivators that I can think of to stick around after escaping."

Not just shook his head.

He didn't feel like trying again to explain.

He had barely been conscious for the last several days, and while he had been laying in the hospital bed, trying not to move for fear of dying once again, everyone else involved had been piecing the story together around him. He was impressed by how much they had gotten right, of course much of the story had been given to them from the recording on his phone, so in a way he had been able to tell them what had happened.

Karkus stared at him for a few more moments, waiting for Not to offer some kind of reply. Not was just coming to the conclusion that Karkus would not accept silence this time, and was selecting the fewest words possible for his reply when the door swung open.

Bursting into the room in a fury of teased hair and floral print clothing, Not was saved from speech by this explosion of noise and color.

"Excuse me," she said with obvious contempt for Karkus as she took in the scene, "My name is Jennifer Jones, I am a lawyer, and how dare you speak with my client without me present?"

"Your client?" Karkus snorted. "Mr. Johnson is my client. I'm Stephen Karkus with the Public Defender's Office, and. . ."

"PD?" Jennifer seemed taken aback. "Oh no, Not, hon, you don't need to slum it. I'll take this one pro-bono if I have to."

"Excuse me," Karkus snapped. "Mr. Johnson is *my* client. I have been representing him since his initial questioning, and. . ."

He turned accusingly to Not.

"Who the hell *is* this woman?"

Not just feebly moved his head.

"I am the woman who called the police for Not when he was trapped in the back of that truck," she answered for him. "I am the one who provided counsel for him when he was in peril, and I. . ."

"Got him shot," Karkus finished for her.

"I did no such thing," Jennifer gasped.

"If you were the one on the phone with the police, then you provided faulty intelligence. They thought he was in the truck, and he was not. You got him shot."

"He *was* in the truck," she snapped. "I had no indication that anything had changed. I told him to hide, and had no evidence that he had done anything other than to comply with that advice."

"Stop," Not managed, and they both fell silent.

Karkus and Jennifer Jones both turned to look at the client that they seemed to have forgotten was in the room.

"Why . . . you . . . here?" he croaked.

"Oh, right," Jennifer rummaged around in a satchel which appeared to serve as both briefcase and purse. "I have the contract your employer left with me. It looks good overall. I made a couple of changes to the language, closed a few loopholes, and added in a no-penalty early buyout clause, in case you just want to buy her out after the lawsuit."

For a moment, no one said anything and all eyes turned to Not. Karkus was the first to break the silence.

"What the hell is she talking about?"

Not struggled and gurgled for a few seconds.

"Miss-us . . . Alto . . . came . . ."

"Oh, for the love of God," Jennifer interrupted. She dug around through her satchel once more and came out with a tablet computer. "Type it."

Not tapped at the screen for a few minutes and summed up his conversation with Mrs. Alto. He paused and considered for a moment, and then added an answer to Karkus' previous question. He had panicked, tried to run, and been caught by Troy who threatened to shoot him if he tried to leave the building.

He handed the tablet to Karkus, who read through it, nodded, and passed it to Not's father, who read it and nodded, and then returned the tablet to Jennifer.

Not held out his hand, and Jennifer handed the tablet back.

Not typed, "Should I sign the contract?"

Jennifer took the tablet back, and showed it the two men as well.

"It's up to you, hon," she shrugged. "The contract is a good one, I can say that much. It's well-written and fair. Pretty good deal, too, if you ask me."

"I haven't read it," cautioned Karkus. "But, from what you wrote, I agree with Ms. Jones. Being employed, and at the same location, looks good for the case too. Guilty people run, and trustworthy people work."

His dad simply shrugged, knowing Not would do what he thought was best.

Not didn't really know Jennifer well, really had only ever talked to her one time over the phone, and she had also been Donny's lawyer which didn't stack up in her pro column. Still, she had done a lot to try to ensure Not made it out alive, when she had no motive at all to help him.

Maybe he just wanted there to be some kind of happy ending in all this.

Not held out his hand again to request the tablet.

"Can I hire you both?" he typed.

They exchanged glances as they considered his request.

Not was pretty confident this was what a zebra between two lions felt like.

It finally dawned on him just how much of a high profile case this might turn out to be. It would mean a lot of media exposure, which is what Not was fairly sure they were both after.

And money.

Not his, of course, he didn't have any. Money would come from this though, for the lawyers, at any rate. Media exposure, promotions for Karkus, new clients for Jennifer . . .

Or, maybe they were both just good people and wanted to do their best to help him.

Maybe this was a balance.

Maybe he had two good people fighting to help him as a kind of *mea culpa* from the universe.

At least, it was nice to think so.

"Team up?" Jennifer asked.

"I remain as lead counsel on all documents," Karkus demanded.

"Co-counsel, split the media," Jennifer countered.

"Can't," Karkus explained. "PD's office will pull me if he obtains other counsel."

"You take Lead on criminal, I'll take civil," Jennifer decided. "We'll flip flop the second banana spot."

"PD doesn't do civil. However, we just went over this, and it's-"

"Too soon to sue the DEA," Jennifer agreed. "But, it won't be forever. They're looking dirty on this, and Uncle Sam's got deep pockets."

"They might indict him just so they don't have to pay," Karkus warned.

"We'll wait to file until all the dust settles," Jennifer rolled her eyes. "We have time."

Karkus kept raising objections, and Jennifer kept supplying answers which worked to her favor. The tone began to change, still lightly hostile on the surface, but there was no real venom in either voice any longer. It sounded more academic, nearly playful, like a long forgotten exercise from law school, a game at which they had both excelled.

Not realized his presence in the room was no longer really necessary.

If it were in his ability, he would have gone out to get a cup of coffee, and let the two experts work out the details. What he wanted didn't seem to matter much, anyway to hear them talk.

"Contract?" he croaked.

Both lawyers looked a little startled by the reminder that he was listening.

"Of course, hon," Jennifer smiled at him. "Karkus was just about to invite me to lunch to work out the details."

"Was I?" Karkus asked sardonically, though he did not correct her.

Jennifer handed Not the contract and a pen. She flipped the pages for him, pointing to where he needed to initial, and where he needed to sign and date. When it was complete, she returned the contract and pen to her satchel and readied herself to leave.

"Shall we?" Jennifer asked, looking at Karkus. She blew a kiss to Not, and walked out of the room. Karkus shrugged toward Not, and followed.

He paused at the door and looked back.

"So long as no large deposits show up in your bank account," he cautioned, "I should be able to keep you clear when they run the indictments. You focus on getting better, okay?"

Not wanted to protest that no money would be coming to him, but he just couldn't bring himself to put up the effort. Karkus likely wouldn't believe him anyway.

His dad squeezed his hand, "I'm gonna get a cup of coffee, okay? Be right back."

Not tried to nod but instead just closed his eyes and escaped into sleep.

Epilogue

IT WASN'T the long sleeve shirt with the popped collar that made Sam look over the bartender with a more than cursory inspection. Though it was a little out of place for a beach-side bartender, particularly at the kind of bar which tended to hire a man more for his ability to fill out his shorts in just the right way than his ability to mix a good drink.

This time of year, it was mostly pouring shots and pulling drafts from the tap. Wait a couple more weeks until Spring Break, and every coed from around the country would be packing the place and ordering every complicated concoction she could remember, so long as it came with an umbrella and someone else who was willing to pay for it.

No, it wasn't the shirt, nor was it the obviously bottle blond hair and the from-the-can tan, because neither of those things tended to flip his skirt. Sure, he used a bit of product himself from time to time, but he hated sharing a shower in the morning and discovering an entirely new person.

It was his smile.

A man can change many things about his appearance, but a smile was more than skin deep. A smile was a non-verbal conversation. A smile is a flash of a person's temperament, a person's humor, a person's kindness. It was a glimpse at who the person truly was, and it could not be changed as easily as clothes, hair color, or even skin tone.

This man's smile was kind and full of joy.

Though the joy was a little strained. He moved as if he were, well, not in pain, so to speak, but definitely in some discomfort. His movements were stiff. His posture too erect.

He had hurt his back somehow, Sam intuited.

"Banana Sling, please," Sam ordered as he took a seat at the bar.

377

The bartender came even more erect as much at the sound of Sam's voice as he did at the order.

"You'll have to remind me what goes into that one," the bartender said.

"Dark rum, light rum, coconut rum, curacao, vanilla vodka, ice, and heavy cream," Sam rattled off from memory. "Don't ask me the measurements, because I always pour by touch. Then blend the shit out of it and pour it in your biggest glass."

"Coming right up," the bartender busied himself gathering the bottles, awkwardly pausing often to pull a bottle, check the label, and then put it back.

"The dark rum is usually in a dark brown bottle, Topher," Sam smiled sweetly. "If that helps."

"Bill," the bartender corrected, a little more forcefully than perhaps would be normal, and he tapped the name badge on his shirt. "The name's Bill."

"Terrible name," Sam opined. "You look much more like a Christopher."

"Bill," the bartender repeated again, staring Sam in the eye for a moment before returning to his search for the rudimentary components of a Banana Sling.

"What brings you to Miami?" he called over his shoulder to Sam, as he dug around in a cabinet for a blender.

"I've got a timeshare, Coconut Grove," Sam announced. "I come down here twice a year for a week or so."

"Really?" Bill sounded genuinely surprised.

"Yep," Sam said brightly. "I would have been happy to bring you sometime, if I didn't think you'd run out halfway through dinner."

Bill the bartender pointedly pressed the button on the blender, and put a momentary end to the conversation with a whiney roar of ice being chopped and booze being sloshed about.

Truth be told, he left it running a bit longer than necessary.

Sam nodded to him that his point had been made.

"So, are you a local boy then?" Sam asked, deciding to play along just to keep the conversation going.

"Sort of," Bill said, avoiding an outright lie. "I've got a little place off Tornado, about a block from Gibson Park. It's nice enough, I suppose."

"Overtown?" Sam nearly choked on his drink, which he had to admit wasn't bad. "Damn, son, are you trying to get shot? Is that why you sprayed yourself like an Oompa Loompa? Trying to get dark enough to make your lily white ass blend in?"

This earned him a couple of nasty looks from the other patrons in the bar. Although no one would accuse the state of Florida of being overly progressive in its racist attitudes, to openly discuss the racial tensions in certain parts of the city was considered *tres gauche*.

"Quiet down, Sam!" Bill hissed, forgetting for the moment that he wasn't supposed to know this particular hometown boy. "The boss'll make me kick you out of here if you start offending the guests."

The bar, though directly on the sand of the public beach, was technically part of the hotel beyond, and thus was private property. However, if Sam took three steps backward, he would be back on the public beach once more, so the threat was hollow and they both knew it.

"Tell me why you're hiding in Miami, *Bill*," Sam hissed back, "and I'll behave. I promise."

"Let me take my lunch," Bill sighed. "And we'll take a walk, okay?"

"Fine," Sam sighed. "But, you're buying my drink. Makes us even."

"Already done," said Bill, and smiled that smile which was all Topher.

It only took him a minute to clock out and slip his name badge into his pocket. Then the two men strolled down to where the surf had flattened out the sand and packed it down wet.

They left postcard worthy tracks down the mostly empty beach.

"Christopher Mason died in a car fire on the 17 South about five weeks ago," Bill said with no preamble at all. "William Swindon was born about a week or so after, or was reborn I should say. All his personal documents went missing just before he got checked into a Tallahassee hospice with Stage 4 pancreatic cancer. John Doe died not long after, but William Swindon made a full recovery."

Sam said nothing, knowing now that Topher was talking, the best thing he could do would be to let it come pouring out.

"It didn't seem right, for some reason, to try to take over his real name. Bad luck, maybe, I don't know. So, Bill it was. Bill has an apartment, a W-2, and is waiting for his Florida driver's license to come in the mail. They made me take the test again, believe it or not, since I didn't have a current license to switch over. It took me two tries on the written, but I nailed the road test in one.

"Bill Swindon has a secondhand car with Florida plates, and about forty grand in cash. Blood money left over from the death of Topher Mason."

Bill Swindon stopped and stared at his old friend.

"I still can't sleep on my back because I'm still healing," Bill confided.

"Burned?" Sam asked, wincing at the memory of his awkward movements around the bar, and a sudden wash of guilt for making him gather all the shit to make him a fancy drink.

"Car fire," Bill nodded. "I'm healing here. It's easy, and my boss, the guests, they all like me. I'd hate to have to run again, I could do it, but . . ."

Sam gave his new friend Bill a look of exasperated shock, and held his hand to his chest to feign a gasp of surprise. He held the look and waited until he was rewarded with the smile which he knew would be soon in coming.

"I'm sure I don't have the first clue as to what you mean, Mr. Swindon," said Sam in a passable southern belle. "Though, it simply will not do for you to spend one more night in Overtown. Tonight, you will stay with me in Coconut Grove, in the guest room I should stipulate, before you start getting any ideas of absconding with my honor, and tomorrow we will gather up whatever you need to keep from your, ugh, *home*. You will let me take you on a tour of some neighborhoods which won't keep me up nights thinking of you asleep there."

Bill had rolled his eyes at the idea that Sam had any honor left with which to abscond, but the smile stayed.

"You don't have to do that," he demurred. "I'm okay. I've stayed in worse neighborhoods."

"I'm sure you have, dear boy," Sam continued. "But you are falling victim to the movie ideal that a wanted man should stay in a bad neighborhood so as to not be noticed. No, no, no. *Everything* is noticed in a bad neighborhood. The police watch it closely, and the criminals watch even closer. Someone there will sell you out in a second, if they see any advantage in it for them."

The smile faded from Bill's face, and though Sam was sorry to see it go, it was important that he understand.

"Even if they don't, it's only a matter of time before someone around there will get shot, even if it isn't you," Sam continued. "That means police asking witnesses, taking down information, feeding it into the system. The more often it happens, the more likely it will be that someone finds out a dead man is renting an apartment."

Bill opened his mouth to argue, but then closed it again before saying a word and simply nodded at the logic being presented.

"You want to be forgotten and ignored?" Sam asked with sudden gaiety. "Then look no further than the 'burbs' of Middle America. Better yet, have you ever been on a boat?"

"Sure, the ferry going to Manhattan," Bill stated as if it were obvious.

"You could probably get a decent cabin cruiser for under twenty grand," Sam suggested. "Pay your slip fee in cash, and you are effectively off the grid."

Bill was silent and turned his gaze to look out over the water.

"Why are you doing this, Sam?" he asked. "Why do you want to help me?"

Now it was Sam's turn to fumble for words and look out at the water.

"Shit, kiddo," he grasped for the words, and dropped all pretense and went with the truth. "I've had a crush on you since I first laid eyes on you. Maybe it was the sweet smile, or the way you played tough guy at the door, but always helped people into a cab instead of just tossing 'em in the street . . ."

Sam trailed off and then turned to look Topher/Bill in the eyes.

"Why does anybody do anything?" he shrugged. "I like you, and you look like you could use some help. If I can give it, then it will make me feel good, okay?"

Bill considered the answer for a moment, and then slowly nodded. He tried to put an arm around Sam's shoulder for a hug, but it obviously pained him to lift his arm that high. He settled instead for taking Sam's hand. They started walking back toward the bar, where Bill would still need to finish his shift. Sam had already decided that he could think of worse ways to spend an afternoon than sitting in a bar sipping drinks, and watching the scenery walk by.

"If you were serious about staying with you tonight," Bill said suddenly, "I'd like to take you up on it."

"The offer was sincere, my dear," Sam lilted sweetly.

"I'll buy dinner," Bill offered, then cast a sidelong glance at Sam. "But, you get the tip."

Sam laughed loud and strong, startling a group of seagulls near the surf.

"Oh, you tease," he said, mock offended.

Bill squeezed his hand.

Sam squeezed back.

45818685R00233

Made in the USA
Lexington, KY
19 July 2019